HELL FAE KING

USA TODAY BESTSELLING AUTHORS
LEXI C. FOSS   **J.R. THORN**

Editing by: Outthink Editing, LLC

Proofreading by: Jean Bachen & Katie Schmahl

Cover Design: Covers by Juan

Cover Photography: Wander Aguiar

Cover Models: Sophie, Alex, Philippe, Forrest, & Camden

Hell Fae Realm Illustration: Tomasz Madej

Map Illustration: Nathan Hansen

Chapter Header Art: Ricky Gunawan

Chapter Character Art: Luminescence Covers

Published by: Ninja Newt Publishing

Digital Edition

ISBN: 978-1-68530-381-5

Paperback Edition

ISBN: 978-1-68530-382-2

AI Disclaimer: This book does not contain any elements of AI content. All art was designed by real artists, and all the words were written by the authors.

To the good girls who secretly crave a hard Dom degrading you while a soft Dom praises you...
As they share you.
Yeah.
This book is for you.

ABOUT HELL FAE KING

The board has been set.
The players have been chosen.

Vivaxia tried to make Camillia a pawn in our eternal game
—when she's wrong about her.

She's not meant to be a pawn. She's our queen.

The Hell Fae Realm is in dire need of one, especially when
rogue Virtuous Fae magic strikes.
Who is an enemy? Who is being controlled?

The last thing I want to do is punish the innocent, but
that's all part of Vivaxia's game. She wants to hurt me, and
deeply. That means dismantling everything I've built,
finding ways to make all of the kingdoms turn on me.

Had she planned for every outcome, she might have won.
But I know something a creature like Vivaxia will never

know, no matter how much she observes, schemes, or plans.

My realm is not built on fear. My subjects are loyal because of what I represent. I am everything the Virtuous Fae were not.

I don't control them. I let them exist exactly as they are—I let them fulfill their destiny how they see fit.

Destiny isn't designed by those with power.
It is forged with love and grief, and most of all…
With *Hellfire*.

Authors' Note: *Hell Fae King* is a dark romantasy with four tormented mates and no choosing required. If you like your antiheroes dominant and sexy, you've come to the right realm—the Hell Fae Realm, where the romance is hot and no forgiveness is required. This is the final book in the Hell Fae series.

HELL FAE KING

A NOTE FROM LEXI & JEN

Thank you for picking up *Hell Fae King*! We hope you enjoy this dark world as much as we do.

For those new to the series, we strongly recommend reading these books in order, as it is a continued story.

Just a note of caution: This series contains strong sexual undertones, violent scenes, and themes of dubious consent. There are also several strong male-on-male relationships in this world, and these men absolutely love to fuck each other.

That said, Cami is the heart of their relationship.

Or she will be...

Once the king finally fucking falls.

Their journey hasn't been easy. But it's about to get so much hotter.

We hope you enjoy the conclusion to the Hell Fae world.

Because it's time for the Hell Fae King to kneel for the Hell Fae Queen...

INTRODUCTION

Extraordinary power requires sacrifice.
However, what happens when that sacrifice becomes too
significant?
A good king will give everything he has to save everyone
except himself.
But a great king knows how to accept help.
And an even greater king knows when it's time to *bow*…
—Typhos

HELL FAE REALM

A REVEALED PAGE FROM LUCIFER'S BOOK, VITA

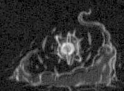

Once upon a time, an angel Fell. His feathers were stripped, his light was extinguished, and he landed in the fires of a broken land.

But this was no ordinary angel.

He knew his world was about to end before the ultimate betrayal arose, and inside him, he hid the source of his light. His true power. His ultimate revenge.

From that fiery ember of energy, he created a new world—the Hell Fae Realm. And within it, he accepted all the creatures every other fae realm rejected.

Nightmare Fae. Abominations. *Monsters*.

As his new court grew, various kingdoms were established. Each one is ruled by a protective Mythos Fae, and beneath them, various Fae Kings.

This entry is considered to be an index of those kingdoms and known species within. It changes and grows daily, but I am Vita, Lucifer's prized book. I know all. I document all. And now, I'll share that knowledge with you, dear reader…

Barren Lands: Desertlike dry areas with rocky landscapes and little to no water sources. Centaurs, Manticores, Minotaur, Air Dragons, Griffins, and Boggarts make these lands their home. It has also recently been used to house the Hell Fae Bridal Candidates within a unique paradigm.

Hell Fae Kingdom: A centralized kingdom that Typhos Lucifer calls home. All non–Nightmare Fae creatures reside here, as do Lucifer's infamous Hellhounds.

Marsh Lands: Murky waters and swampy plant life make this an ideal home for Nagas and Unseelie.

Morpheus Kingdom: This is the land of dreams, where Nightmare Fae feed on terror and fear. Ghouls and Strigoi call this place home, but one of Lucifer's personal creations lives here, too—the Kuntilanak Fae.

Netherworld Kingdom: Darkness and wisps of dull moonlight haunt the graveyards of this kingdom, making it an optimal home for Corpse Fae and Death Fae.

Underwater Kingdom: Vast oceans and coral-like castles paint this kingdom in a sea of unique colors. Kelpies and Water Dragons call this kingdom home, but some of Lucifer's personal creations, like Sirens, reside here, too.

Hell Fae Realm

Marsh Lands

Hell Fae Kingdom

Morpheus Kingdom

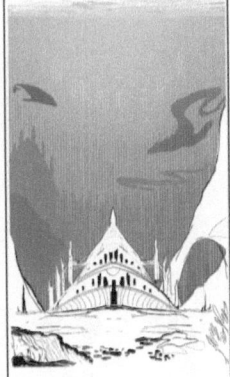

Underwater Kingdom

Barren Lands

Netherworld Kingdom

PROLOGUE
A NOTE FROM TYPHOS

Once upon a time, a woman betrayed me. A woman who pretended to be a mentor and a friend. A woman who provided guidance in dark affairs and enjoyed crafting illicit deals.

I knew better than to trust her.

But I indulged in her tricks, tried to beat her at her own game.

And *fell*.

Our souls weren't compatible, a fact I understood when I engaged in her twisted offer. I just didn't realize there would be a price for that lack of compatibility.

Oh, but she knew. She used that clause as a way to punish my soul for rejecting hers.

Only, that version of punishment ended up being my greatest gift of all. For my fall created the Hell Fae Realm. A place where Nightmare Fae thrive. A land protected by my source of power. My heart. *My spirit*.

But my world—*my creation*—is being threatened.

I thought the culprit was Camillia De la Croix, the

sensual vixen who has ensnared the attention of all those I hold dear.

My Prince.

My Commander.

My Warden.

For months, I've convinced myself that she's my enemy. A villain sent to destroy my Hell Fae Source.

And it turns out, I wasn't entirely wrong. She's absolutely a being of immense power with the ability to demolish everything I've built.

But she's not my enemy. Not really.

She's a weapon. A siphon created by my true rival—*Vivaxia*—to absorb my power and dismantle my realm.

Only there's something Vivaxia failed to take into account when she sent Camillia my way, something Vivaxia has always failed to understand.

All creations have souls.

And Camillia's soul is unlike any I've ever met.

She's stubborn. She's vengeful. She's intelligent. She's creative. She's *strong*.

Vivaxia may think she has the upper hand, that she may be able to wield Camillia in any way she desires, but I see the truth more clearly than before.

Camillia was never meant to bow; she was destined to rule.

She just needs someone to guide her.

Someone to show her how to siphon energy for her own use.

A king who can make her a queen.

It's time for me to accept fate. To stop questioning the yearnings of my inner circle and start admiring the diamond they've all claimed.

No more fighting.

No more accusations.

No more deals.

The truth is clear.

Our path is intended.

It's Vivaxia's turn to fall.

And I'm going to ensure that happens by teaching Camillia De la Croix how to *fly*.

CHAPTER 1

CAMI

Hot red sunlight streamed in through the gauzy curtains, the air holding a note of fire and brimstone, one I never thought I'd want to smell again.

But underneath was a current I adored, one doused in decadence and sin.

Melek, I thought, breathing him in as I rolled toward him on the giant four-poster bed.

Only, another scent lingered here, too. *Cinnamon*, I realized, inhaling deeply. *Burning cinnamon*. The aroma mingled with Melek's richness, making me dizzy with want.

I grabbed his bare thigh, then inched higher to his hips. He hummed in appreciation, his fingers going to my hair as I slid on top of him, ready to wake us both up properly.

My Virtuous Fae mate made me feel bold. Alive. *Ready for anything*.

"Mmm, I think I like you lust-drunk, Cami," he murmured, nipping at my bottom lip. "Had I known you would be this insatiable, I would have claimed you at a more opportune time."

I wasn't sure what he meant by that, nor did I care. I just wanted to kiss him. To *fuck* him. Or rather, for him to fuck me.

Again.

And again.

Because wow, Melek was... everything. His taste. His touch. His *tongue*.

I practically melted against him as he kissed me, his wicked mouth undoing every part of me and flooding me with need. I couldn't hear anything over the roaring in my ears, the sensation of being underwater overwhelming every inch of my being.

Melek smiled, his lips a taunting curve against my own. "Good morning, my king," he murmured.

My brow furrowed. *King?*

"Little prince," a deep voice replied, the warm tone sending ice through my veins.

Ice because it belonged to Typhos Lucifer. The Hell Fae King.

Oh, shit...

That was the source of cinnamon lingering in the air. I was in *his* bed. Well, the one he shared with Melek. His mate. His *little prince*.

A prince I was currently straddling while naked.

I scrambled for the sheets, wanting to cover myself, and unceremoniously fell off of him and onto the mattress near where Lucifer was currently standing.

His dark eyebrow winged upward, his striking blue eyes holding mine.

I swallowed, then grabbed the blanket again in an attempt to wrap myself up in it. But naturally, it was twisted beneath me, making it impossible to complete the task.

Which left me vulnerable and exposed to his burning gaze.

"I do hope you're a little more graceful when lost in the throes of passion, Miss De la Croix." He glanced at Melek. "Or did you keep her tied up all night?"

"I conducted an introductory course," Melek informed him. "We're still working on trust."

"Hmm," the Hell Fae King hummed, his gaze returning to mine. "A concept I'm all too familiar with."

My heart skipped a beat, the meaning beneath his words ringing through loud and clear. He didn't trust me. I'd touched his Source. And he'd recently learned that I was literally created to steal his light.

Because I'm a siphon. Crafted and molded by his enemy—Vivaxia. A Virtuous Fae who also happens to be my grandmother.

Yeah, *trust* was nonexistent between me and Lucifer. In his mind, I'd be better off dead.

Oh, he'd claimed he wanted to train me to become a queen, not just a pawn. But part of him wanted to remove me from the board entirely.

And that part of him was studying me now, causing his irises to flicker with blue fire as they tracked down to my throat and lower.

He's probably picturing me covered in blood, I thought, shivering beneath his open perusal.

The heat in his eyes as they returned to mine confirmed his thoughts, his hunger one that could only be driven by his need to *kill*.

"Yes, trust is absolutely going to be a challenge," he murmured, then turned away from us with rigid movements.

I held my breath, waiting for him to return with a knife

or maybe a handful of Hellfire. But when he stepped back up to the bed, he was holding a robe instead.

When all I did was stare at it, he leaned in to drape the plush red fabric over my body.

"You are far too tempting in this state, Camillia. Naked, partially aroused, equally afraid." He inhaled deeply, his irises flickering with more of those hypnotic flames. "It's making me want to test your limits, something neither of us is ready to do. So put that on. Because we need to talk."

He rotated away before I could reply, his muscular shoulders encased in expensive-looking black fabric, his pressed suit fitting him to utter perfection.

I couldn't help but admire the way it framed his ass as he walked over to a nearby bar to pour himself a drink.

Nor could I stop my gaze from homing in on his impressive package as he rotated again, his groin in perfect view from my space on the bed.

"It's the mating high," Melek said, sounding amused. "I'm rather enjoying it."

"Yes, I've felt your enjoyment all night," Lucifer replied flatly. "I tried to give you space to indulge, but unfortunately, time is not on our side."

"You've discovered something." The words from Melek lacked his amusement from seconds ago, his serious tone somewhat registering through the fog in my mind.

"I remembered something," he corrected. Energy vibrated the air as he pulled up a translucent screen, his voice deepening as he said, "Breakfast for three. Bring a variety of everything available."

"Yes, Your Majesty," someone replied, the voice androgynous in nature and seeming to float throughout the room.

Lucifer shut off the monitor, then settled with his

drink at a nearby table. "Join me," he said. Two words, uttered with a conviction that definitely resembled an order.

Yet my limbs refused to move.

I... I was frozen beneath this robe. *In the Hell Fae King's bed.*

Warm lips brushed my temple, nearly causing me to leap out of my skin. Except I was paralyzed by fear. So my heart simply raced instead. "He's not going to bite you, little angel," Melek whispered against my ear. "Not unless you ask him nicely."

Lucifer grunted and took a long swallow of his drink without looking at us.

Melek rolled over me to land deftly on the floor. My eyes widened as he sauntered toward Lucifer, utterly naked and very much aroused.

The Hell Fae King glanced up at him with an arched brow, then his expression disappeared from my view as Melek leaned down to kiss him. "Play nice, my king," he said, before vanishing into thin air.

Melek, I hissed in my mind.

Nothing.

I closed my eyes. *Ajax?*

Cami, he replied. *Are you all right?*

I... I swallowed, opening my eyes to glance at the Hell Fae King again. He had pulled up a screen, his focus seeming to be on the words scrolling across it. *Is he reading a newspaper?*

What? Ajax asked.

I shook my head. *Sorry, Lucifer is... I think he's reading... Never mind. Where are you?*

At Zenaida's with Shade and Zakkai, he muttered, causing my brow to furrow.

Is everything okay?

I believe I asked you something like that first, he drawled. *But yes, everything's fine. Just… negotiating.*

I nearly asked what he was negotiating when Lucifer said, "Do you need help with that robe, Miss De la Croix?"

My eyes squinted closed again. "N-no," I told him, hating that I actually probably did need help since my body seemed to be incapable of moving.

I just slept with the Hell Fae King's mate. Oh, I'd done more than that. I'd *mated* Melek. Typhos Lucifer already hated me. And I'd just given him fuel to hate me more.

Which one? Ajax asked, causing me to frown. *Az or Melek? Actually, don't answer that. I'm pretty sure you meant Melek since Az is off meeting with Maliki.*

Maliki? I repeated. *Who's Maliki?*

His half brother.

Oh. Did I know that? Maybe. I couldn't—

"Miss De la Croix?" Lucifer's voice came from right over my head, causing me to stop breathing.

He must have stood up and walked over to the bed while I'd been mentally talking to Ajax. *What's going on?* my Midnight Fae mate asked, sounding concerned. *You feel… nervous.*

I squinted my eyes in frustration, not liking at all how he'd described me. Mostly because it was true. Nervous. Terrified. Still aroused. *I'm fine,* I gritted out.

You don't sound fine, he hedged. *Where are you?*

With Melek and Lucifer.

Well, I *was* with Melek and Lucifer, anyway. At least until Melek had disappeared.

Do you need me? Ajax asked.

Part of me wanted to say yes. But I didn't want to pull him away from whatever conversation he was having with Zenaida, Shade, and Zakkai. It was likely important;

otherwise, he wouldn't be there. *No, I'm… I'll be okay. I'm just, as you said, nervous.*

Which I hated.

But how was I supposed to—

A warm touch on my jaw had my eyes flying open. Lucifer stood over me, his brow furrowed and his lips curling down. "You're terrified of me."

"I am not terrified," I ground out, the lie bitter on my tongue. Because I'd literally just used that word to describe myself seconds ago.

Lucifer withdrew his touch. "I'm not going to harm you, Camillia."

Yeah, he'd said that yesterday, too. Pretty sure he'd also mentioned that while dancing as well. But that didn't mean I believed him. Not after all the previous threats lingering between us.

Sighing, Lucifer sat on the bed, his large form somehow managing to fit in the small space between me and the edge of the mattress.

One big hand cupped my jaw, his palm a brand against my skin. "You have every reason not to trust me," he said, his soft tone almost as surprising as his touch. "But we're connected now through Azazel and Melek. I couldn't harm you even if I wanted to."

I nearly snorted.

Because yeah, *that* didn't convince me to believe him.

"What are you thinking?" he asked, his sapphire eyes searching my features. "Tell me so we can discuss it. But please don't lie."

I stared up at him, not sure how to respond to that. He probably already knew my every thought, given the connection he'd just mentioned between me and his two mates. So maybe this was a test of sorts to see if I would be honest with him.

Knowing Lucifer, it was exactly that. A way to measure my loyalty, to determine if I was worthy of his mates, worthy of being kept alive.

"There are a lot of thoughts rolling through my head," I admitted.

"Give me one and we'll start there," he suggested.

"Okay. How about your previous threats? Do you hear those echoing via the bond?" I wondered aloud. "Or is it just my uncertainty you're picking up on? The fact that you're telling me you can't hurt me, therefore you won't, doesn't boost my confidence in this situation."

However, admitting all this out loud was making me feel less frozen, and a little warmer. To the point where I could actually somewhat move again.

Only, I wasn't sure where to go with Lucifer sitting so close to me.

"I don't hear anything," he told me, confusing me.

"What?"

"I suppose I could try to access your mind through Azazel's or Melek's thoughts," he went on, ignoring my question. "But that would be a severe intrusion into your privacy and theirs, and that's not who I am."

I blinked at him, surprised by the sadness in the latter part of his statement.

"It seems you and I have misunderstood one another from the beginning, which is primarily my doing." His thumb traced the hollow beneath my eye, his gaze on mine. "I'm not one for starting over, as I believe history creates important foundations, but perhaps you and I can strike a compromise of some kind."

My throat worked, my mouth suddenly dry. "What kind of compromise?" I asked slowly, not sure what to think of this bizarre twist in our dynamic.

"A tenuous truce, perhaps?" he offered. "One that we

can strengthen as we learn more about each other." He shrugged, his hand leaving my cheek. "Honestly, in my very long life, I've never been in a situation like this before. We need to trust each other. But it won't be easy."

He wasn't wrong about that last part—it absolutely would not be easy.

"However, nothing worth having has ever been easy," he went on, his dark gaze capturing mine once more before slowly lowering to my mouth. "You kissed me yesterday."

The jarring change in topic had my lips parting, my mind instantly rewinding to the incident he referred to. "I thought I was dreaming."

"So you dream of me kissing you?" he asked, still studying my mouth.

"I dream of a lot of strange things." The retort fell from my tongue before I could swallow it.

But rather than be offended at me calling our interaction *strange*, he chuckled.

He'd laughed yesterday, too.

A sound I'd never heard from him before. At least, not like this. So relaxed and amused, yet not in a dark way.

"I imagine you do. Still…" He caught my chin, his touch just as hot as before. "You coaxed me into kissing you back."

My eyes widened. "*Coaxed* seems like a strong word."

"Does it?" he asked, leaning toward me. "Perhaps you're right. Perhaps *seduced* is a better word."

"I didn't *seduce* you," I fired back, but the words lacked heat and came out in a breath instead.

A breath that touched his lips.

Because his mouth was only a hairsbreadth away from mine.

"You're naked and in my bed right now, Miss De la

Croix," he murmured. "Perhaps you didn't mean to seduce me, but you have and you are." His lips brushed mine. "Scenting your sweet ambrosia-like arousal isn't helping matters."

A tremble worked through me, not born of fear so much as interest.

Because I could smell him, too.

His cinnamon spice. Underlined with Melek's decadence and Az's simmering bonfire cologne.

"I want a truce, Camillia," Lucifer said, the words spoken against my mouth. "Not a deal. Not an agreement. Not even a promise or a vow. Simply… a truce. Give me a chance to show you who I really am. Please."

CHAPTER 2

TYPHOS

T he word *please* lingered on my tongue like a curse. I rarely used it. Rarely *meant* it. But with Camillia De la Croix, it seemed utterly appropriate.

She's terrified of me, I thought for the thousandth time since entering my bedroom.

The woman had frozen upon seeing me, making her visibly frightened. That, coupled with Melek's mental comments, confirmed the cause—*me.*

She thinks you're going to kill her for mating me, Melek had said, sounding somewhat annoyed. *You should fix this, Ty.*

Then he'd kissed me and disappeared without further comment, telling me his words were more of a command than a suggestion.

I'd sighed, thinking it could be fixed once we all sat down to eat and discussed what I'd remembered, but Camillia hadn't even been able to look at me, let alone move.

And something about that had hurt.

She was naked in my bed, still partially aroused from

Melek's ministrations, yet frozen and unable to do more than flinch because she feared what I might do to her.

I really fucked this up, I realized again when she didn't reply to my request for a truce. I couldn't blame her for hesitating; she had no reason to trust me.

Just as I'd had no reason to trust her initially. She was a threat to my Source, to *me*. That threat aspect hadn't changed. But I now knew her intentions weren't nefarious. She was a pawn. A weapon encased in a beautiful, feminine exterior.

Melek had understood her worth long before I'd been willing to consider it, my history having made me too biased to see the queen standing before me.

But I noticed her now.

Camillia De la Croix may just become my equal.

And much, much more...

I inhaled, reveling in her bouquet-like aroma. So innocent and alluring. Except beneath it was a subtle scent of death, one that reminded me of wilting flowers.

That scent belonged to Vivaxia.

It was reminiscent of the gift she'd left behind inside Camillia, a gift designed to extinguish my light.

"You're dangerous," I whispered, my lips barely touching hers. "So fucking dangerous."

My nearness now was a testament to that. I'd been drawn over here as a result of a raw emotion tugging at my heart. An emotion I didn't fully understand but thought might be guilt.

Then I'd sat on the bed because I'd needed to be closer to her. Which led to me leaning down to this point, leaving our mouths close enough to touch without actually kissing.

"Trusting you will be my greatest challenge," I told her. "You were created to destroy me and everything I hold dear."

My touch moved from her chin back to her cheek, my palm easily engulfing the side of her jaw.

"But I see you now, Camillia. I realize you don't want to hurt me. However, you won't have a choice in your current state; the power inside you will come to fruition and destroy us both. Which is why we need to work together. Because I can't kill you. I *won't* kill you. Not just because of our mates, but because I see potential in you."

"Potential for what?" she asked, her wariness pricking my chest. I might not be able to read her mind, but I suspected the direction of her thoughts. She assumed I meant to use her.

"Potential to be anyone and anything you desire," I told her honestly. "You're strong, and I don't just mean in terms of power. I mean *you*, Camillia. Your spirit is a beacon, one that caught my eye the moment I first saw you. It might have been Melek who courted you in the beginning, but I noticed you, too."

Fuck, I'd more than noticed her. She'd been the first female in thousands of years to tempt me, to give me pause and force me to evaluate her potential.

That was partly why I'd considered her to be a threat these last few months. I didn't like how much I was drawn to her. And I hadn't appreciated that my men were falling for her, too.

An enchantress, I thought, evaluating her now. *And so much more...*

Camillia shivered beneath my touch. "Why are you telling me all of this?"

I pulled away from her mouth, needing to see her storm-like eyes. "Because I need you to know that I have no intention of harming you. I want to help you. More than that, I want us to work together."

She studied me for a long moment. "Because we share mates."

I lifted one shoulder. "That's one reason among many."

"And you're… not mad?"

I frowned. "About you touching my Source?" I guessed, thinking of the last time I'd acted angry toward her.

"No, about Melek."

My frown deepened. "What about Melek?"

Have you been up to something, little prince? I immediately asked him via a thought.

Always, my king, he murmured back. *But she's talking about me mating her.*

Cami confirmed that in the next instant with her words, causing my frown to shift upward into a grin.

"No. I'm not mad." I chuckled at the thought. "Melek does what he wants, and in this case, it's you. I'd be a fool to punish him for following his desires."

Especially when I was beginning to understand the allure of said desires.

"I must be dreaming," she muttered.

I arched a brow. "Does that mean you're going to try to kiss me again?" Because I might not mind that, though I wouldn't admit it aloud.

She was a temptation I couldn't afford to taste. A sin meant to tip the scales and drown my light.

Wanting her was forbidden.

Which naturally made me want her even more.

Perhaps after we dealt with the threat lingering inside her, I could consider exploring her with my tongue.

Until then, I—*we*—needed to focus.

"Yes," she said, the single word making me wonder if she'd come to the same conclusion as I had regarding focusing. But then she grabbed the lapels of my suit jacket and pulled me downward.

Her lips met mine in the next instant, the touch so unanticipated that I froze.

The same thing had happened to me yesterday, the shock of her unexpected touch rendering me momentarily stunned.

But the electricity humming through my veins hit my heart faster this time, allowing me to react quicker than our previous embrace.

However, I still wasn't fast enough as she pulled back before I could properly grab her and deepen the kiss.

She fell away, her eyebrows drawn down. "Real."

"Very," I emphasized. Every bit of this was *real*. The threat. The desire. The unequivocal *need*. I blamed Melek for stoking my inner flame, his fantasies having more than primed this infatuation.

But it was also Camillia De la Croix.

She really does have a magic pussy, I mused.

A pussy that tastes like ambrosia, Melek replied, his voice a deep murmur. *She's fucking addicting, my king.*

Hmm, I hummed, not wanting to commit to that opinion. But one look into my mind would provide him with confirmation of how I felt.

Clearing my throat, I pushed away from the bed. "Can we talk now, Miss De la Croix?" I asked her.

"Are we back to using titles?" she countered, some of her trademark fire highlighting her voice. "*Your Majesty.*"

My lips twitched at the snark underlining those two words. I wrapped my palm around her throat and leaned back down to press my lips to hers. Hard. Purposefully. With barely restrained need.

She gasped, the sound cut off as I squeezed her

delicate neck and deepened the kiss, just like I'd wanted to mere seconds ago.

Her hand went to my wrist, the opposite going to my head. But rather than push me away, she held on while I devoured her, not caring at all that I'd restricted her airway.

By the time I finished, she looked dazed. "Breathe, Camillia," I told her as I released her pretty throat.

She did as I commanded, her pupils blown wide with a mixture of confusion and arousal.

"Now put on the robe and join me for breakfast," I added in the same tone. "And don't address me formally. You're naked in my bed. Formalities are not required."

"But you—"

"Miss De la Croix," I interjected. "You've been using my last name. I was simply returning the favor. If you'd prefer Camillia, then call me Typhos."

I actually didn't mind her referring to me as Lucifer. It was much better than formal greetings.

And yes, I saw the irony in my preferences, given the lecture I'd bestowed upon her mere weeks ago.

However, everything had changed. *I* had changed.

I wanted to hear my name on her tongue. Not my title or Lucifer. But *Typhos*. Just once. At least once. Probably more than once.

"Okay," she whispered, staring up at me with a strange gleam in her gaze, one I couldn't quite decipher.

"Okay," I echoed, straightening and leaving the bed.

I turned away as she sat up, my instinct to watch her too strong. I needed to tame this forbidden craving before I did something rash.

Like rip the robe from her, splay her on the bed, and turn her midnight fantasies into a reality.

Melek appeared in front of me, his beautiful wings

fluttering once before vanishing at his back. He'd abruptly departed the room a bit ago to give me a chance to speak with Camillia. Hopefully, his return meant he was satisfied by whatever progress I'd made with his mate.

Or, more likely, he'd overheard my mental musings and wanted to observe my reactions to his female's magic pussy.

Thirsty, my king? he asked, his mental voice innocent and confirming my suspicions regarding his timely arrival.

I grunted. *Stop teasing me.*

Never, he replied, holding out my glass. At some point he'd refilled it, his trademark garnish glittering along the glass's edge.

I accepted his offering and took a sip while holding his gaze. *You realize I'm going to take all this need out on you later, yes?*

I do. I'm looking forward to it, Your Majesty, he practically purred into my mind.

He uttered that title just like Camillia had, making it clear that I was now linked to not one but *two* bratty subs.

I sighed and set my glass down to rub my aching temple. Melek reached up to brush his lips against my jaw. "I love you, my king."

I grabbed his nape when he tried to pull away and crashed my mouth against his, responding to his words with my tongue rather than with my voice.

He groaned against me, his freshly pressed suit wrinkling beneath my assault. But I didn't give a damn. Between him and Camillia, I was fucking done.

Both of them smelled like sex. Hell, had I arrived a few minutes later, I would likely have witnessed them fucking in real time.

Not that I needed the visual; one was already firmly implanted in my mind, courtesy of the devious prince before me. He clutched my lapels, accepting my bruising embrace with an eagerness I felt to my very soul.

The aroma of blooming flowers taunted me, the scent reminding me of a rose garden warmed beneath the rising sun.

Camillia.

I nearly growled as I released Melek. He wiped at his bottom lip, the trace of blood on his fingertips showcasing how hard I'd kissed him. But all he did was smile.

Little masochist, I said to him via our bond.

Only for you, he returned.

My eyebrow winged upward. *You wouldn't let Camillia hurt you for pleasure?*

If she was a sadist? Absolutely. He cocked his head. *But you're the one who gets off on punishments and pain, my king. Not our little angel.*

I glanced at the female in question, noting her red cheeks and the silky knot around her waist. She'd tied her robe with force, the fabric cinched a little too tight. Yet she didn't seem to notice; she was too busy gaping at me and Melek.

"That wasn't a punishment," I told her. "Just me claiming my mate."

"But you said you weren't mad," she hedged slowly.

I smiled. "I'm not mad, Camillia. However, I am possessive."

She swallowed, her gaze leaving mine. "Oh."

Fuck. This female had me all wrong, which was entirely my doing. And now I had no idea how to fix it. "He's mine, Camillia. And now he's yours, too. But your little fuck fest has put me in a certain mood. Not one where I want to *punish* so much as *claim.* Do you understand?"

Her eyelashes lifted as she met my gaze again. "Do you need me to leave…?"

I pinched my nose again and nearly growled. This whole situation was fucking infuriating. "No, Camillia," I ground out. "I need to talk to you and Melek. Together. Please."

And there's that word again, I thought bitterly.

It sounds nice in your voice, Melek returned without hesitation. *I think our angel likes it, too.*

A chime rang through the room before I could reply, a Hellhound in human form appearing with a tray in one hand and an envelope in the other. "This just arrived for you," Payan said as he held out the latter to me, his gaze on the floor as a show of respect. I didn't necessarily require their submission, but they often gave it freely.

I eyed the male curiously. "Aren't you stationed in the Hell Fae bridal camp?"

The Hellhounds were part of my personal guard, but they also managed security throughout the realm.

And last I checked, General Garmr had assigned this particular Hellhound to not only guard the paradigm but also assist Ajax as needed with protecting the candidates. So he should be on general paradigm security watch, nightclub bouncer duties, or dorm surveillance.

Of course, a lot had changed over the last few weeks with Ajax being out of commission. Garmr had been playing double duty with managing his Hellhounds in the paradigm and coordinating the royal guard around my palace.

"General Garmr shifted me to the palace, Your Majesty," Payan replied, bowing lower while still holding his tray and envelope. "I hope this doesn't displease you, my king."

Displeased wasn't the right term. *Confused*, perhaps. "I see." Something must have prompted this change. I'd have to meet with Garmr later to determine the cause. "Thank you for bringing everything up."

"It's my pleasure, Your Majesty," he said before creeping forward to set the tray on the small en-suite dining table. There were only two chairs, something I'd have to fix. Not that Payan noticed; he was still looking at his boots.

So rather than issue a request for more seating, I simply accepted the envelope from him and let him leave without further conversation.

While Melek lifted the tray covering to reveal a buffet of magical items beneath, I focused on the enchanted item in my hand.

This was no ordinary letter. I ran my finger along the familiar parchment, my lips curling downward. *A deal*, I recognized as I unfolded the document. *An ancient deal.*

Words glittered up at me in gold ink, causing my gaze to narrow.

I, Typhos Lucifer, agree to engage in all three mating vows with Vivaxia Lilithu. In exchange for this mating, Vivaxia Lilithu agrees to the following terms:

Azazel of Black Phoenix Clan will be a free entity. "Free entity" is defined in Appendix A. All terms apply.

Melek Morningstar will be a free entity. "Free entity" is defined in Appendix A. All terms apply.

Should the end mating prove unfruitful, the terms of this contract are still valid. However, in the event that a soul rejects the other...

The ellipsis melted down the page, the drops resembling blood as the words shifted into something new. Something that didn't belong.

You remember what happened next, don't you, love?

My heart fucking stopped. I could practically hear Vivaxia purring in my ear. Her presence was all around me, her words still scrolling across the parchment.

Your soul rejected mine. And our terms were quite clear, darling.

My jaw clenched as the deal reappeared...

However, in the event that a soul rejects the other, a blood sacrifice will be paid.

Blood was power. Upon my soul rejecting Vivaxia, I'd offered her a vial, just as the terms had implied.

But she'd grinned, her cold eyes exuding an evil I'd felt in my very soul.

You fell, love, the words said in time with my memories. *But was that your choice or mine?*

I snorted. *What kind of question is that?*

However, as more enchanted ink appeared...

Was that the blood sacrifice my soul desired?

I started to realize how important that question about my fall truly was...

"Blood sacrifice" was never defined. I rejected your vial and you fell. But did you bleed the way I wanted, sweet Typhos? Or did you grow into a being with so much more to lose? To **sacrifice***?*

The bold text on that final word had my blood going cold.

So many bonds. So much heart. So much **blood***.*

"Ty?" Melek's voice barely reached me, the pounding in my ears making it difficult to hear anything beyond my own racing pulse.

"Don't eat the food," I managed to grit out. "Get rid of it."

The tray had come with this enchanted letter. Brought to me by an unexpected source.

Vivaxia's message was loud and clear—I can access your inner sanctum. I can reach you. You're not safe. *No one you love is safe.*

That was why she'd mentioned the bonds and my heart, her riddle rather straightforward.

But what did she mean about the blood sacrifice not being my fall?

Did I fall on purpose? I wondered for perhaps the first time in my existence.

Vivaxia's statements played through my mind as more gold text scrawled across the paper.

I'm ready to collect now, Typhos. And I'm going to start with the blood that sets your heart aflame…

My gaze instantly flew to Melek. He stood near Camillia, the table between them empty. "Did you eat anything?" I asked him, unable to mask the urgency in my tone.

"No. I magicked it all away, just like you requested." He glanced down at the note in my hand, his brow furrowing.

The paper went up in flames, indicating the end of whatever spell Vivaxia had cast on the item.

I swallowed, her final threat echoing in my thoughts. *I'm going to start with the blood that sets your heart aflame…*

Camillia's knees buckled on a gasp, her palm flying to her chest as she cried out in sudden pain.

Melek fell with her, but he wasn't hurt. He was concerned, his mouth saying her name as he grabbed her shoulders. "What is it? What's wrong? Where does it hurt?" he asked, his panic causing my gut to clench.

Does Camillia set my heart aflame?

That… that didn't… Maybe? She certainly made it beat fucking hard.

I stepped toward her, my mouth suddenly dry. This had to be whatever Vivaxia had put inside her. The dying scent lingering beneath her—

Fire shot through my heart, ceasing all my movements.

So intense. So unexpected. So *hot*.

"Az," Camillia breathed. "Az!"

An inferno built inside me, my mind and soul registering Camillia's claim just as my heart went cold. *Ice* cold.

Because the flame inside my heart had just... *died*.

CHAPTER 3

AZ

A Few Minutes Earlier

I sat across from my brother, his golden eyes flaring with power he couldn't conceal. I understood that problem—my Phoenix energy always hummed beneath my skin, the vitality threatening everyone around me.

Maliki possessed a different kind of aura, though. His was deadly in nature, his actions precise and his words as sharp as a blade.

"Why are you really here, Azazel?" he asked, his deep voice holding a lazy drawl to it that contradicted the violent air about him.

Many fae had fallen for his charm, only to end up on the wrong end of his blade. But I knew him well. And I could more than feel the dangerous intent defining his every move.

"I need a favor," I admitted as I settled into the black leather booth behind me. Death's Den, the place at which my brother opted to meet, was nothing like Typhos's club.

There were no eternal-fire pits or red velvet ornaments here. Just gothic architecture outlined in bones and skulls, the obsidian interior reminiscent of a crypt.

I supposed that was accurate given its location in the center of the Netherworld Kingdom.

"A favor?" Maliki echoed, sounding amused. "Interesting, that. I believe I could have used one of those recently while being held by your king."

"He's *our* king," I corrected him. "And our brotherly relation is what kept you alive. Many would consider that a favor in itself."

He snorted. "If that's the hand you want to play, so be it. What's the favor?"

"It's not a hand, Mal. It's the truth." I leaned forward on the rocklike table, careful to avoid the untouched pitcher of spider ale in front of us, and gave him a hard look. "Typhos wanted to kill you. He held back for me. I felt it in our bond."

"Then I'm thankful we're related," he deadpanned, clearly not at all grateful for said relation.

"Why the fuck did you open that portal?" I wondered out loud. "You didn't even venture off in search of a mate. Hell, last we chatted, you didn't want a bride."

"And neither did you, yet my nose tells me that's changed," he tossed back.

"Circumstances changed," I said through my teeth.

"Indeed."

I remained quiet for a beat as a Death Fae wandered by us in a flowing black robe. There were several others lingering around at the bone-laden bar, their attires similar in nature as they knocked back shots of translucent liquid. Some Corpse Fae were in another booth at the back, a set of cards sprawled out before them.

This was the Netherworld Village, the area of the

Netherworld Kingdom where both Death Fae and Corpse Fae came to mingle. And Death's Den was the heart of it all.

A quiet place filled with lethal secrets, like the one I was about to reveal to my brother.

"Actually, my new mate is why I'm here," I told him softly. "Vivaxia has done something to her."

Maliki's posture went rigid, the name one he knew well. Not from his personal history, but from mine.

He was fortunate to have been born in the Hell Fae Realm after Lucifer's fall, our sperm donor of a father having survived long enough to fuck another female— Maliki's mother.

Neither of us knew if our father was still alive, but we hadn't seen him in over two thousand years. Of course, with our father having a strong amount of Paradox Fae blood in him, it was very likely he had just lost himself while time-traveling.

Or perhaps he'd opted to live in another timeline entirely. I didn't fucking care. He'd never been a father to me. Which was one of the many reasons I often avoided the small amounts of Paradox Fae magic inside me. I much preferred to embrace my Phoenix Fae heritage over the mixed origin that had created my father.

But Maliki wasn't like me. He indulged in all aspects of his nature, particularly the dangerous parts. Which was why I'd come to him with this specific favor.

"You're going to need to give me more information," he told me as he grabbed the full pitcher between us to pour himself a drink. "Like how the fuck a Hell Fae Bride ran into Vivaxia."

I replicated his movements to take some spider ale for myself. It wasn't my favorite drink, the venomous bite of the liquid leaving a numbing effect behind, but I could use a stiff drink.

Settling back into the plush leather, I held my brother's golden-eyed gaze. "Hit the button."

He smiled. "Finally. All this small talk was giving me a headache."

I gave him my best unamused look. We both knew I would have asked him to put up the privacy screen when we first arrived, but he would've demanded a reason.

Hence the purpose of the five minutes of *small talk* he'd just referenced.

"Just put up the damn screen," I told him.

He smirked and reached for the skull icon etched into the tabletop, only to pause right as his finger met the metallic symbol.

"Can we help you?" he asked flatly, his glittering gaze on me while his words were meant for the trio of Death Fae who'd just approached our table.

I didn't look at them, just sipped my ale. They knew who I was; everyone in this fucking realm knew my name.

And I was certain they knew Maliki, too.

He might not have an official title, but his reputation as Hades's pet assassin was well known. Especially in this kingdom.

"This ain't about you, Ghost," the Death Fae drawled, using Maliki's infamous nickname.

In and out in a flash, leaving only ghosts behind. That was his trademark. Most of the time the murders couldn't even be connected to him.

But the fae knew.

And they feared him in kind.

Which again left me wondering why the fuck he'd opened that portal to Monsters Night. He'd claimed it'd been to help the Ghouls find mates.

Bullshit, I'd told Typhos.

Good deeds weren't Maliki's thing.

Violence was his first love, something he displayed now as he slowly looked at the trio of Death Fae. Only, he gave them an easygoing grin, one that belied the blackness of his aura.

"It *ain't* about me?" he parroted back at the Death Fae, applying emphasis to the word *ain't.* Knowing my brother, he hadn't appreciated the poor grammar associated with that contraction. "Then why are you standing within killing range of my favorite blade?"

Said blade was nowhere in sight. But it would appear in a flash if this Death Fae so much as blinked wrong.

"We need to have a word with the Commander," the male growled, surprising me a bit.

"Then have a word, but make it quick," I told him as I took another sip of my drink. I didn't bother to look at the fae. This wasn't how I accepted meetings. And I had no intention of indulging—

Pain shot through my chest, causing me to drop my glass. It tumbled to the rocky tabletop with a clatter that I barely heard over the sudden roar in my ears.

What. The. Fuck?

I looked down to find my torso on fucking fire.

I leapt up from the booth, my inner beast raging inside me. The flames went out in a whirl of power, my energy instantly absorbing the unexpected assault. However, another soon followed, the soot-like magic foreign and deadly.

Maliki shouted something, but I couldn't hear him, my essence swimming around me in a violent wave to counter the attack.

Only this time, the inky enchantment blended with my

fire, creating an inferno of heat that made it impossible to breathe.

Fuck.

I ashed out of the cloud.

Except... except it *followed.*

Or maybe my ashing failed.

I... I couldn't see. I was being suffocated by an impenetrable black smoke.

Az! Cami screamed into my mind.

Cami...

Ajax was there, too. His voice was a rumble of fury that I swore I heard right next to me. *Don't you dare fucking die on me, Commander,* he demanded.

I'll just come back, I muttered to him. Not that I wanted to go through the painful rebirth process. I'd much rather *fight.*

Which was the word echoing now in his thoughts, as well as in Cami's mind.

Fight. Fight. Fight.

I tried, but I couldn't fucking see, let alone breathe. The inky substance was all around me, encasing me in liquid *fire,* burning my skin, and searing me to my soul.

What the fuck is this magic? I marveled, dizzy.

Death, Typhos replied, fury in his tone. *It's fucking death magic.*

I blinked. Or I thought I did, anyway. Regardless, Typhos's claim didn't make any sense. Death Fae sucked out souls. Corpse Fae possessed deadly touches.

But this... this didn't feel like either of their brands of pleasure.

I coughed. Gagged. Fought to breathe. All while my lungs and insides *burned.*

My inner Phoenix growled, furious that fire was eating

us alive. Furious that his element of choice had betrayed him. Furious that we could no longer move.

Or hear.

Or see.

Barely even think.

Because the world… had gone utterly still.

The rebirth process was on the verge of a new beginning.

I recognized it well. It'd been ages since I'd last died.

My eyes fell closed, my soul resigned.

At least it was quick, I thought softly. *My memories will return just as fast. I hope.*

CHAPTER 4

CAMI

A Few Minutes Earlier

Chaos.
      Darkness.
      Pain.

I couldn't focus beyond Az's agony, my soul demanding I go to him. Find him. *Help him.*

I clutched my head, not able to hear a word Melek or Typhos were saying to each other. My world revolved around Az. His mind was incoherent, his inability to tell me what was happening all the more concerning.

Take me to him! I shouted at no one in particular. I didn't know how to ash or teleport or shadow or anything else. Whenever I'd done it in the past, it'd been without my consent.

Or by using Lucifer's power, I realized.

"Don't even think about it, Camillia," the male in question growled next to my ear.

But his words escaped me on a passing wind, my instincts already engaging with the notion of flying. His furious shout echoed behind me, the heat of it chasing me into the darkness and vanishing as I landed inside a crypt.

Or... or not a crypt. A bar?

I swallowed, glancing around at the gothic interior.

Then froze at the nightmarish ball of black energy swirling before me. Not a Source, but... but *fae*.

Their auras matched the obsidian floor, their angry growls causing the hairs along my arms to stand on end.

"Rude," someone muttered as a sword appeared, one that flickered with golden flames.

My lips parted as the weapon sliced through the air, gliding through the dark auras.

A trio of corpses fell to the ground, the energy swarm ceasing instantly and allowing me to see Az's sprawled form.

I gasped and ran for him, only for the sword wielder to step into my path. "Plink."

"What?" I breathed, not understanding that word.

"He's talking to me," a voice hissed from right behind me.

I whirled toward the newcomer, only to be halted with an arm around my waist. A broad chest met my back for a brief moment before I went spinning through the air.

"You're ruining all my fun, Ghost," the newcomer— *Plink?*—growled.

"And what fun is that?" the sword-wielding male replied, sounding bored. "Trying to kill the Hell Fae Commander? Or playing with his mate?"

"*Both*," Plink snarled, his protruding jaw turning black to resemble ash.

Zombie, I thought in the next breath, gasping as his humanoid form took on the picture of death.

I wasn't sure if it had been his hands on me or the one called Ghost. Right now, I hoped it was the latter.

Because it seemed Plink possessed dark magic, the kind that *killed*. Or that was how I interpreted the wisps of gray smoke swirling out from his blackened fingertips.

Ghost didn't appear to be all that concerned, though.

He sheathed his sword and pulled out a dagger instead. "All right, Plink. Let's dance."

I jumped backward as the two men blurred into a deadly fog, their energy a chilling presence that shot ice through my veins.

Another presence soon joined them, causing my jaw to clench. I couldn't see them so much as feel them, their auras riddled with malicious intent.

More are coming, my instincts told me. *So many more…*

A frigid breeze caressed my being, reminding me that all I wore was a short silky robe.

But a glance toward Az had me forgetting everything and focusing entirely on him.

He wasn't moving.

Why isn't he moving?

Maybe a minute or two had passed since my arrival, yet it felt like much longer.

He should be moving…

I skirted along the edge of the room, the obsidian booths to my left and the open floor to my right. Ghost's sword was out again, the power flashing through the air as he fought the incoming horde of black spirits.

There are too many of them, I thought, my heart in my throat.

And I had no idea who this *Ghost* truly was. *Friend or foe?*

With the way he was protecting Az, I guessed the former. But that wasn't a guarantee.

Hell Fae Rule #13: Nothing Is What It Seems.

Hell Fae Rule #4: Don't Trust Anyone.

Several other rules applied here, but I stopped reciting them as I reached Az's prone form.

His skin was ice cold.

Dead.

No. No, that wasn't possible. Az couldn't die. He... he... I shook my head. *No.*

The air shimmered around me, causing me to fall into a defensive position over Az. I didn't have a weapon to aid in said defense, but fuck if I cared. I'd fight until my last breath. Wield power. Pull on the Hell Fae Source if I had to. Whatever it took to—

Ajax appeared, a glowing rock in his hand. The color instantly shifted to black, the jagged edges somewhat familiar.

The death stone, I realized, recognizing it. He'd shown me that rock back in the prison when I'd been his captive. Something about it being used to help prepare me for the Netherworld Kingdom trial.

That felt like a lifetime ago.

We'd never actually prepared for that trial, Vita having pulled me into a strange time loop that had stolen thirty days of my life. Then I'd been held for questioning, and life had been chaotic ever since.

Actually, my life had always been chaotic.

My time in the Hell Fae Realm had just been even more tumultuous.

Regardless, I had no idea what that death stone could do, yet I caught it reflexively as Ajax tossed it to me. The icy texture nearly had me dropping it, but a blanket of darkness swooped over us in the next instant, making me freeze.

Ajax cursed, his wand out and flaring with purple magic tinged with golden flares. He cast a spell I couldn't hear, the roar of the incoming wind drowning out everything else.

Another portal? I wondered.

Cami! Melek shouted at me, his panic barely piercing the deadly quiet in my mind. I blinked, startled by his intrusion. It was like I'd been living underwater, the eerie calmness at odds with the insanity unfolding around me.

I... I'd been cut off from my mates.

How? I wondered, another blast of ice coating my insides.

Because it reminded me of being with my mother and Vivaxia. I hadn't been able to reach my mates then either.

Glacial power blasted through the bar, blackening everything in sight.

Ajax yelled something I couldn't hear, his words lost to the screaming void.

I covered my mouth, the sooty air making it hard to breathe. I couldn't see either. Hell, I could barely feel.

But the rock sat heavily in my palm, the rigid texture grounding me in reality. Because it was real while everything else felt like a dream.

An eerie, freezing cold dream...

I shivered and closed my eyes.

Think, Cami, I told myself. *Think.*

My parents had always dropped me in fiery situations, never blizzard-like tundras. But the extremes were similar in a way, the intensity teetering on life and death.

This is the Netherworld Kingdom. Their power is based on souls, darkness, and the afterlife.

I hadn't been here before, but I'd read up on it a little while learning about the Hell Fae Realm.

So what's the purpose of this rock? I wondered. *Ajax had given it to me for a reason.*

Before, it'd been about training.

Now, it was about surviving.

Energy engulfed me, a foreign spell clawing at my skin with icy sensations. I swatted at it, but that only sharpened the blades. I gasped, the pain unlike anything I'd ever felt as arctic liquid shot through my veins.

Literally, I realized. *Or... or it feels...*

My limbs seemed to freeze with icy precision, snuffing out my inner flame.

Just like Az, I thought. *They chilled his Phoenix. Smothered his fire. And now... now they're doing the same to me.*

But as the frigid energy reached my fingers, it dissipated and the stone heated in my hand. I focused on the conflicting power, noting the way it countered the chill with warmth.

Except... except it wasn't truly *warm*; it was... *absorbing*.

I blinked, confused by that revelation. Yet I could feel the death stone pulling in the air around me, stirring some sort of enchantment inside that devoured the glacial power around it.

Like me, I registered in a heartbeat, my lips parting. *The stone is a siphon.* Or it functioned like one, anyway.

So how do I use it?

My fingers flexed around the sharp edges, the juxtaposition of cold and hot making me shiver and sweat at the same time.

Think, Cami, I told myself. *It's absorbing the chill like a flame consumes oxygen. And infernos burn hotter under the right circumstances...*

Thus, with the right parameters, I should be able to intensify the stone's siphoning ability.

I need to give it more oxygen...

Because the material—the *energy*—was already there, ready to be devoured.

I closed my eyes to focus on the parameters in the

equation, trying to determine how to bolster the conditions and enhance the power.

Lucifer's Source instantly opened itself to me, the beacon of energy ready and willing at my fingertips. I'd evaluate later why it was so easy to reach now. Just as I'd apologize to its owner later, too.

Az was what mattered at the moment.

Surely Lucifer would understand that.

Or want to kill me again, I thought bitterly. *Well, fuck that.*

These zombielike fae needed to *burn*, their icy presence overwhelming and deadly. *And hurting Az.*

I could feel it now—the blizzard swirling inside him and killing his inner fire.

He was nearing death, his flame almost extinguished. He might be immortal and capable of rebirth, but something about this felt... *permanent.*

No! I mentally shouted as furious vitality swam through me, Lucifer's power a kiss to my senses that roared through my veins. I fell on top of Az, one hand still clutching the stone while my opposite palm went to his chest, right over his heart.

Then I used everything inside me to ignite the stone, forcing it to take more, to blaze hotter than before, to *consume.*

But I didn't let the rock keep everything. Instead, I pulled some of that fiery energy into myself and out through my palm into Az. It was such a natural response, one I wasn't even sure I could do, yet accomplished as easily as breathing.

A rerouting of power.

My body *siphoning* the vitality and redirecting it.

What I was created to do, I thought dizzily.

I'd been doing this for years without realizing what it

had meant or how it had worked. But I was beginning to understand it now.

I'd done this with the portals—siphoning Lucifer's Source and releasing it into the vortex. It'd been about fighting fire with fire then, but I'd absorbed the power and morphed it into what the situation had required.

Just like with the many infernos I put out over the years.

Rather than shove those memories away, I embraced them and used them as fuel for my current task—*reviving Az.*

Everything blurred around me, the fight no longer important. Our location a distant concern. All I cared about was channeling the warmth into my Commander. My *mate.*

Mmm, I like the possession I hear in your mind, little warrior, he replied, his voice a purr against my mind.

Az, I breathed.

What's wrong? he demanded in the next instant. *What's... happening?* That purr was gone, his flirtation melting into a wave of confusion that quickly morphed into anger. *Fires.*

His recollection of events ripped through his thoughts, fueling his fury. He'd been talking to Maliki, his half brother, about a favor when a trio of Death Fae had approached.

Then they'd attacked him.

Which had turned into a swarm of others piling on, the mixture of Death Fae and Corpse Fae powers creating a swarm of lethal energy.

They hadn't all been in the bar, but channeling something from afar.

And he had no idea why it had happened.

But the why didn't matter because he was pissed and regaining his strength with every second.

I could feel the vitality swirling around him, all of it bolstered by my own gift.

He had enough to thrive now, yet I couldn't seem to stop, the power swimming through me with the force of a catastrophic hurricane.

I tried to pull away, to redirect the power, but I... I couldn't. I was a slave to the energy connecting me and Az. A slave to the *death stone*.

I attempted to drop it. However, my fingers wouldn't let go.

Az said my name, but it was lost to the torrential winds whipping through my mind. No. Not my mind. *Against my ears.*

I'd created some sort of power vacuum, the electric current unstoppable and charged by Lucifer's Source.

He's here, I realized, Lucifer's ferocity hitting me like a freight train. Still, I couldn't stop. I couldn't pull away. I couldn't *move*.

My name echoed from four male voices, all of them ones I knew deep within my soul. All of them connected to me in different ways. All of them my *mates*.

Except no. That... that wasn't quite right.

I have three mates, not four, I thought dizzily. But I... I was enchanted by four souls.

Ajax.

Az.

Melek.

And Lucifer... *through his Source*. He had the strongest hold on me, his energy leashing me in a way that had me feeling wrapped up in a myriad of ropes.

Like Melek's ribbons, I mused idly, the correlation one that nearly made me laugh.

But this wasn't funny.

It was dangerous. Terrifying, even. I... I didn't know where to go. How to process. What to—

A mouth sealed over mine, air flooding my senses.

Another hand was at my throat, making it impossible to inhale.

"Let go," a voice seethed against my ear.

I agreed with that assessment. *Yes, let go.* Because I couldn't breathe. Everything was too dark. Too heavy. Too *hot.*

"*Camillia.*" The deep tone reverberated through my being, demanding my submission. "*Let. Go.*"

CHAPTER 5

CAMI

I... I didn't understand. Let go of the death stone? Let go of Az? I... I couldn't feel either of them. So how was I supposed to release them?

"Listen to me," that voice said right against my ear. "Imagine you're standing on the edge of a beautiful lagoon. The water is a stunning sea-green color, and it's so clear that you can see straight down to the bottom. Above you is a blinding sun, causing heat to blossom across your skin, almost to the point of discomfort."

I swallowed as his lips tasted my neck, his warmth all around me, similar to the sun he just described.

"It's making you so hot, Camillia. Do you feel it? The sun's intensity?"

I tried to nod, my mind lost to this masculine tone, his cinnamon-like scent at odds with the scene he just described. But the underlying spicy note certainly matched.

"The water below is the perfect temperature to cool your skin," he went on, his mouth against my throat while his heat wrapped around every inch of me.

I had no idea where we were, how I felt him in every aspect of my being, but I... I didn't want it to end. This was a nice dream.

Lucifer, I thought, recalling all our previous nightly encounters. *Lucifer is talking to me.*

Listen to him, Melek whispered back to me. *Listen to him and he'll reward you.*

Oh, I nearly moaned. *Yes, I would like that.*

I know, Melek replied. But his voice lacked his usual amusement. Actually, he sounded a bit worried.

Is something—

"Camillia," Lucifer said, interrupting my mental conversation with Melek. "Focus on the sun. It's blinding. It's hot. It's *burning* you alive."

I trembled at the vivid sensations his words evoked, my breath seeming to come in pants.

"Jump into the water, Camillia," he told me, his voice holding a demand in it that I longed to obey. "Go for a swim with me, and I'll give you anything you desire."

My throat worked, my heart skipping a beat.

Anything I desire.

I... I wanted that. *Right?*

Maybe.

I...

"Now, Camillia," he ordered, not allowing me any more time to debate. "*Jump.*"

I squinted my already closed eyes and took a deep breath and... and... let it out in a scream. Because I couldn't move. I was trapped in the sun, melting beneath its fiery rays.

Bands of intensity tightened around me. "I'm going with you," Lucifer said against my ear. "Fucking let go with me, Camillia. *Now.*"

I didn't understand what he meant, but I desperately

wanted to go with him. So I clung to the arms around my middle and fought to follow his command.

Air whooshed around us, the blazing inferno flashing white behind my closed eyes, and then we were falling... soaring... *flying*...

Until we were nothing at all.

Just lying... on the ground.

I frowned. Blinked. And frowned harder. "Where...?" I coughed, my throat dry like I'd been locked in a sauna for hours without access to water.

A face carved from ancient marble—the kind statues were crafted to honor long ago—suddenly overtook my view. And a pair of the most beautiful blue eyes I'd ever seen stared down at me.

Lucifer, I breathed, his angelic features etched into impossible lines of perfection.

Fae, this close it was hard to look at him. Especially when he gave me all of his focus like this. "Are you all right?" he asked me, his deep tone matching the one I'd heard against my ear as he'd told me to let go.

I swallowed and tried to nod, but everything felt stiff. "Y-yes."

He shuddered over me, only then making me realize that he had me pinned to the floor of the... the... I glanced around, my brow furrowing again. We were in some sort of cave. All black rock with lava lines trickling down the seams, allowing some flickering red and orange light through.

It created an eerie atmosphere that should have left me uneasy, yet all I felt was peace.

The chilling power was nowhere to be felt, and my hands were—

My eyebrows flew upward. "*Az.*"

I'm fine, the male in question instantly replied, likely having heard his name echo through my mind. *You saved me.*

I... I did? I glanced around. *Where...?*

"Camillia," Lucifer said, that dominant air about him immediately capturing my attention again. "Azazel is okay. But I need you to breathe and remain calm."

I stared up at him. "Okay."

"Good girl," he praised. "Now inhale for me."

I did.

"Exhale," he said, his voice softening a little.

I obeyed him once more.

He repeated himself, and I continued to do what he ordered me to do for several minutes, the air around us seeming to settle in the cave.

"Beautiful," he whispered, his forehead falling to mine. "Now just exist with me for a moment."

I shivered beneath him, his heat bleeding into my skin.

My... my bare skin, I realized half a beat later. *I'm naked.*

"Shh," he hushed me. "We're almost settled."

I had no idea what he meant by that. All I knew was I had a hot Hell Fae King on top of my *very naked* body.

"Camillia," he growled. "Don't make me teach you how to breathe again."

"What are we doing?" I asked, pleased that my voice seemed to be somewhat less hoarse than before. Yet it still came out breathy.

"Calming the Source," he replied through his teeth.

My eyebrows pulled downward as I repeated those words in my mind, only belatedly recalling the chaotic energy I'd experienced while pushing the warmth into Az.

The death stone.

Lucifer's Source.

My inability to stop the transfer of power…

I swallowed. *Oh.*

I'd… I'd fucked up again.

And now I seemed to be alone with the one who would no doubt punish me for it.

Except he didn't feel angry so much as exhausted.

"Sorry," I whispered, unsure of what else to say to him. *Please don't kill me* lingered on my tongue. But in the next instant, I realized I wasn't sorry or apologetic at all. "I saved Az." That was what mattered. "So no, wait, I'm not sorry."

"You shouldn't be sorry," he said, his mouth close to mine. "I'm the one who needs to apologize. You need training, something I should have realized weeks ago. But I was too fucking stubborn to trust you. And it almost cost me dearly."

My eyes widened. *What?*

"I'm going to fix this," he went on. "*We* are going to fix this."

Fix what? I wondered, bewildered.

"Just bear with me another moment." His lips nearly touched mine before skimming my cheek on the way to my ear. "Hold on to me, Camillia."

My body obeyed his command on impulse, my hands clutching his shoulders just as a wave of hot energy pulsed through him. I closed my eyes, the heat a welcome kiss to my senses. Unfortunately, it dissipated too soon, leaving me shivering beneath Lucifer's intense form.

After a beat of stillness, I snuck a peek up at him.

He'd moved onto his elbows, his muscular body caging mine. "I suppose it only seems appropriate to begin your training down here. But you're going to need food first." His eyes dipped down to my exposed breasts. "And clothes."

My jaw clenched. "I can't believe I'm naked again."

"You do seem quite fond of losing your clothes in my presence, Miss De la Croix." His lips curled with the words. "Not that I'm complaining, but I suspect the others won't approve of you returning to the Netherworld without something on."

"Returning...?" I glanced around for what felt like the thousandth time. "Where are we?" Because I'd assumed we were still in the Netherworld due to the soot-colored walls and lava flows.

"A cavern deep under my palace," he told me. "This is where I first fell, Camillia."

He shifted off of me and stood, his hand held out in a gesture that would have shocked me mere days ago and still sort of did now.

Lucifer is offering to help me. To train me. To... to...

Wait.

This... is where he fell?

He cleared his throat and arched a brow. "Do you want a tour before we go?"

I stared at him and accepted his hand. "You know what? I think I do."

His lips twitched. "All right." He helped me up, then shrugged out of his jacket. "But put this on, Camillia. Your tits are fucking distracting."

I looked at the material he held out before taking in my nude state. "You've seen them before in that chain dress."

"I'm never going to live that damn dress down, am I?"

"Probably not," I admitted.

He shook his head on a sigh, then wrapped his jacket around my shoulders. The fabric went all the way to my knees, showcasing our substantial height difference.

Rather than let me go, he grabbed the lapels and

yanked me into his chest. "I'll apologize every day until you forgive me," he told me.

Then pressed his mouth to mine in a kiss that left me gasping against him. A gasp he soon swallowed as he devoured me with his tongue.

I clutched his shoulders, terrified that I might fall. Or fly. Or fucking disintegrate.

Because *wow*.

Holy. Faeing. *Wow*.

I... I'd been kissed by him before, but not quite like this. His touch resembled sin, his mouth a benediction underlined in wicked intent. And his scent... *Fae*, his scent... all cinnamon and spice and intoxicating *immorality*.

Melek experienced this for millennia. Yet he'd sought me out as a mate. *Why?* I wondered dizzily. *Why would you ever stray when you had a man like this at your beck and call?*

Because I met the angel of my dreams, Melek whispered back at me, clearly having heard my shock and confusion. *An angel I can't wait to share with my Ty. An angel for us both to worship, to put between us, and turn into a queen.*

I shivered, my nipples beading to harsh points as I tried to pull Lucifer closer. Melek's words were impassioned and hypnotic, his intent warming my blood. All while Lucifer stoked my inner fire.

But before I could fall deeper into this erotic abyss, the being of my dark fantasies pulled his mouth from mine.

"Usually, I pen my vows in blood," he said softly. "However, with you, I rather like this method more." He released the lapels of his jacket and cupped my face. "I'm sorry, Camillia De la Croix. I have a lot to make up for, and I'm going to start by training you properly. Which means returning to the others in Death's Den."

He brushed his lips against mine.

"I know I said I would give you a tour, but I'd like Ajax

to join us. There's a lot for him to learn, too." He released me and took a step back, causing me to stumble after him. He caught my hip and righted me. "Take a moment. When you're ready, we'll fly."

Fly, I thought dizzily. *Fall... fly... fall... fly.*

Would I ever be ready?

Probably not.

Especially with a kiss like *that* lingering on my mouth.

The Hell Fae King just sealed a vow by devouring me.

Oh, little angel, you're only beginning to discover what our king's mouth can do, Melek murmured via our mental connection. *Wait until he wraps that wicked mouth of his around your clit.*

My eyes widened, my cheeks on fire. *Melek!*

His only reply was a sensual chuckle.

"Let me guess?" Lucifer murmured. "Melek is whispering indecent promises into your mind?"

I closed my eyes.

And nodded.

"Mmm, maybe later I'll also teach you how to punish him," Lucifer offered. "But after we focus on your control. Because it needs a lot of work, Miss De la Croix."

"My control?" I repeated, not sure what he meant. *Control in sex? Control in how I give pleasure? Control in—*

"Your control when harnessing and siphoning power," he said, a knowing note in his tone, one that had me meeting his gaze again. The sensuous male of moments ago had disappeared behind a regal mask. "You nearly killed over three dozen Netherworld Fae with that death stone, Camillia."

My lips parted. "I..." I had no idea what to say to that. "I was just trying to save Azazel."

"I know. But in doing so, you almost annihilated several innocent souls."

Innocent seemed like a stretch considering what they were doing to Az.

Lucifer must have read my opinion in my features because he softly added, "They were under Virtuous Fae influence. There's a lot for us to discuss." He held out an arm. "So. Shall we fly, darling siphon?"

CHAPTER 6

AJAX

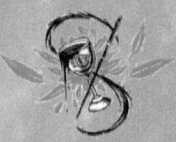

A Few Minutes Earlier

"Where the fuck did she get that?" Az's brother demanded, his finger pointing toward the black pebbles on the floor.

Pebbles that used to make up the death stone.

A death stone Cami had just used to bring a small army of Death Fae and Corpse Fae to their literal knees in agony.

My lips twisted, then I cleared my throat. "From me," I said. "But I had no idea it could do *that*."

"'No idea it could do that,' he says," Maliki mocked, shaking his head. "Un-fucking-believable."

"Where did you get it from?" Az asked me quietly, ignoring his joker of a brother. He sat beside me in a booth, the obsidian table cracked before us.

I ran my fingers through my tangled hair, then palmed the back of my neck, my body abnormally sore from everything that had happened here. I should be mostly healed by now, but those death fuckers did a number on my body and soul.

Az seemed to feel similarly, his actions slower than normal as he brought a glass up to his lips to down a shot of some sort of brown liquor. Bourbon, maybe?

Eh, probably not, given where we were. *Death's Den*. I'd never been in the skull-shaped bar before, only seen it from afar. Yet the death stone had led me right to Az's side with a softly worded incantation.

One Zenaida had told me to murmur.

Right after giving me the death stone that her grandson, Shade, had delivered to me months before.

"I think you misplaced this," she'd told me, setting it next to a plate of her famous cookies. "Too bad you never had a chance to show Camillia how to use it."

I'd frowned at the obsidian stone before meeting the prophetic woman's gaze. "Why do I suspect you're giving this to me for a reason?"

"Because you're a smart boy," she'd murmured, making me feel ten years old again. "Don't forget to give it to Camillia. It'll help."

"Help with what?" I'd asked her, hoping for more information. A hint. Anything to help guide my next moves.

"Training, of course," she'd replied. "She's going to need it. *A lot* of it."

Before I could press her for more details, I'd felt Az's pain.

Shade and Zakkai had both sat there with neutral expressions, saying nothing as I'd wheezed and coughed and reacted to my mate's agony.

Then Zenaida had tapped the table, right next to the rock.

I'd picked the stone up, then noted the scripted

enchantment on the parchment beneath it, and recited the words without thinking.

And landed next to Az.

Then I'd handed Cami the stone. Because fuck if I was going to ignore Zenaida's mysterious instructions.

Leaning my head back now, I explained all of this to Az while his brother listened.

"When Shade originally gave me that stone—on behalf of his grandmother—he'd told me it was for my date." He'd been cryptic as fuck, which was nothing new. "I'd assumed he was just trying to imply he knew about Cami. Apparently, his intentions went deeper."

It didn't surprise me at all. Shade had always worked seven steps ahead, and sometimes even five paces sideways.

"I don't understand why he gave it to you so long ago," Az said, a frown marring his features. "It's like he expected this to happen sooner."

"Or perhaps anticipated several different types of events," Maliki added. "He's part Fortune Fae, right? His mind is a web of potentials. All he knew was you'd need that stone eventually. I care more about *how* Zenaida acquired it."

"Likewise," Melek inserted, his tone and expression uncharacteristically serious. "Ajax, would you mind creating a protective barrier so we can speak freely?"

I stared at him for a beat, surprised by his request. Melek rarely asked me for anything. Hell, we barely spoke to one another until recently.

But the way he looked at me now made me feel seen.

I wasn't sure if I liked that change or not.

Rather than dwell on it, I glanced around to determine my enchantment options.

The club was vacant, the Corpse Fae and Death Fae—those who were awake and alive—having vanished in a cloud of icy mist. No one wanted to be here when Lucifer returned.

No one except the four of us, anyway.

However, that didn't mean there weren't any nosy fae lurking around outside.

With that thought in mind, I cast a fluid spell around the four of us, one that could not be seen or felt. But it basically silenced our voices for anyone outside our invisible bubble.

"You couldn't have done that the other day?" Az asked me. "Instead, you made a paradigm to show off?"

I arched a brow at him. "I don't need to *show off* for Cami," I told him, aware of the instance he was referring to. "Shade and I used to crack this enchantment all the time to listen in on conversations between my parents and a local tavern owner."

Anrika.

Recalling her name sent a jolt through my heart, her death one that still haunted me.

Just like the deaths of my parents and Emelyn.

All at Constantine's hand.

I braced for the wave of anger to assault my spirit, the fiery heat one I'd long embraced. But the usual fury didn't come, rather all I sensed was a hint of nostalgic amusement.

"I couldn't use this spell in the Midnight Fae Palace because I knew Shade would be instantly intrigued and fuck with my spell." Our elders had reprimanded us for spying on countless occasions, which only provoked us to perfect our technique. "We wouldn't have sensed him, but he would have been there." I was sure of it.

"Instead, Zakkai played the part of spy by breaking into your paradigm," Melek mused. "I do very much enjoy those Midnight Fae."

I frowned. "Zakkai did what?"

Melek gave me a look. "Come now, you can't be that surprised. You were talking about Virtuous Fae. Naturally, he wanted to listen." His focus went to Maliki. "A topic that brings us full circle to why I requested some privacy —-that stone is riddled with Virtuous Fae energy."

"I know," Maliki drawled. "That's why I asked how the Fortune Fae acquired it." He narrowed his gaze at Az. "Your little mate is quite a treat, dear brother. Care to explain how she knew what to do with that dangerous stone?"

"Cami is a gift," Melek murmured. "*Our* gift. Her talents are not for you to understand. So let's keep our focus on the origin of the stone and leave our mate out of this discussion."

Maliki grinned. "Possessive, hmm?" He glanced around the three of us, his golden irises twinkling with devilish intent. "That's fascinating."

"And entirely off topic," Az returned, his tone holding a bite to it. "What do you know about the stone, Melek?"

The Hell Fae Prince pursed his lips, his vibrant gaze falling on the pebbles once more. "It's a relic, one created by Vivaxia."

Az stiffened beside me.

"I saw her use it once to destroy one of her pets," Melek went on, seemingly oblivious to Az's reaction. "We need to find out how it came into Zenaida's possession." He blinked, glancing back at us all. "I'll talk to her."

"No, *we* will be talking to her," a deep voice interjected as Lucifer appeared with Cami beside him.

My brow furrowed, his sudden arrival dismantling my magic and reforming it in a blink. Almost as though he'd commanded it himself.

How the hell did he do that?

Cami made sense—she was my mate. My magic automatically wrapped around her, welcoming her into my space.

But Lucifer wasn't anything to me. Not my mate. Not even my friend. Hell, he wasn't even my king.

So how the fuck did he break through my spell without so much as a blink?

Was it his bond with Az?

"Are you all right?" Melek asked as he captured Cami's face between his hands.

His words and reaction had me blinking, my focus instantly returning to her and away from Lucifer's intensity. I'd figure him out later.

And determine a way to block him for good, I decided.

Oh, he might have offered a temporary alliance. But that didn't mean I trusted him. Not after everything he'd done and said.

"I'm..." Cami trailed off, then glanced at Lucifer before clearing her throat.

My eyes narrowed at that small detail. *Did he threaten you?* I demanded via our mental connection, my gaze tracking over her mostly naked form. All she was wearing was Lucifer's suit jacket—a look that would have been hot under any other circumstances. But not right now.

No. He... Her brow furrowed. *He helped me.*

My lips curled down to match her frown. Her response was unexpected. Especially considering Lucifer's previous reactions to her displays of power—a power she borrowed from his Source.

"Cami?" Melek whispered, his expression and tone reverent.

"I'm okay," she replied aloud to him, leaning into his touch. "A little startled, I guess. I'm just thinking about..." She looked at Lucifer again. "Tell them what you told me."

The Hell Fae King arched an arrogant brow. "Commanding me already, darling siphon?"

She gave him a look that said, *Yes. Yes, I am.*

Which would have previously earned her a growl from the powerful male fae, but now merely made him chuckle. "All right."

Surprise echoed in Az's mind, though he didn't outwardly show it.

Pretty sure my face wasn't nearly as neutral because all I could think was *What the fuck is happening?*

Typhos no longer sees Cami as a threat, but as an ally.

Yeah, that much I already knew from our conversation while walking through Lucifer's palace courtyard. *And you believe his intentions with her are good.* Not a question, but a statement. Because otherwise, Az would be jumping to Cami's defense. That much I trusted. That much I *knew.*

I believe his intentions where Cami is concerned are in a constant state of flexibility, Az admitted. *However, right now, his intentions are definitely good, yes.*

"The Death Fae and Corpse Fae were manipulated by magic. That's why they attacked you—they were being controlled by a Virtuous Fae."

Lucifer's words snapped Az's attention—and mine—up to the Hell Fae King. "You're certain?" Az demanded.

"Yes." The Hell Fae King shifted his focus to Melek. "You feel it, too, yes?"

The Hell Fae Prince nodded. "Yes."

"And you didn't think to lead with that?" Maliki interjected, his lazy sprawl across from me belying the dangerous glint flashing in his gaze. "Instead, you let me ramble on about the stone?"

Melek shrugged. "The death stone was just as relevant to our discussion."

"Hmm," the male hummed, his attention shifting to

Az. "And this favor you needed, does it involve the Virtuous Fae?"

Az drummed his fingers against the obsidian rock tabletop once, then pushed off the tattered booth behind us to lean toward Maliki. "I was going to ask you to take a trip through time and see if you could find out what Vivaxia did to my mate. But I'm rethinking that plan now."

"Because you see all this as a warning," Maliki replied. "A bit too coincidental that she would ensure a death stone ended up in your darling mate's hands just after siccing a bunch of Death Fae and Corpse Fae on you."

"Yes."

"Hmm," his brother hummed again. "That would be one hell of a favor, though."

"I think we've already covered the part about you owing me."

Maliki huffed a laugh. "I believe I rejected that claim rather soundly."

"You're alive, aren't you?"

"Am I?" Maliki asked, cocking his head to the side. "I suppose." His golden irises flickered with fire as his attention moved over Az's shoulder, his expression darkening in an instant.

A gentle stroke against my enchantment had me following his gaze, my own eyes widening at the dark figment standing in the shadows. *Who the fuck is that?* I wondered, causing Az to glance over his shoulder.

Hades, God of the Netherworld, he informed me with a mental sigh that told me how unenthused he was by this unexpected visit.

CHAPTER 7

AJAX

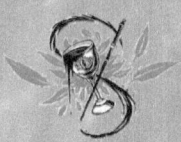

Why the hell is Hades here? I asked, both confused and shocked by his godly presence. Last I checked, the Mythos Fae—whom the Nightmare Fae often referred to as *Gods*—rarely visited their kingdoms.

Because my brother is his favorite pet, Az muttered, pushing out of the booth. "You might as well dismantle the barrier, Ajax. I suspect Hades has already penetrated it anyway."

"I have," a cultured tone deadpanned in reply. "But you can keep your barrier up. I have no interest in the Virtuous Fae. Only Maliki and a certain Goddess that he's supposed to be guarding."

"You mean babysitting," Maliki corrected him as he deftly climbed to his feet, his smooth motions reminding me of a predatory cat. "Your *Goddess* is asleep."

"And dreaming of another God," Hades bit off through his teeth. "Yes, I'm aware. *Very* aware."

Maliki's lips curled a little. "Jealous?"

"Hardly."

That denial only had Maliki's grin morphing into a

smile, one that seemed to be edged in cruelty. "Then you won't mind me embarking on a favor for my dear brother while Morpheus babysits the sleeping beauty for me?"

"You will not be playing with time," Hades said, his hard tone matching his stony features as he stepped out of the shadows and into the flickering lights of the bar.

Wow, Cami thought, her appraisal instantly grabbing my attention. *I can see why he's a God.*

Careful, little rebel, I murmured back to her. *I would hate to start a fight with a God out of jealousy.*

Her stormy eyes found mine. *I didn't say I want to fuck him.*

Yet you're admiring him like you'd enjoy seeing what he looks like without that suit, I returned. And considering the way both Az and Melek were looking at her right now, they'd noticed, too.

I don't think I could handle adding a fifth fae to my harem, she drawled, causing my eyebrow to inch upward.

A fifth? Who's the fourth?

Her cheeks pinkened in response, her eyes widening. *I... I meant fourth. Or fifth. I don't know. Lucifer is... well, he's... he's linked to Az and Melek and...*

I just continued to stare at her, not giving anything away with my mind or my expression.

I don't... She gritted her teeth. *I don't know, Ajax. I don't know what's going on. I don't know how to feel. I don't—*

I stepped forward and wrapped her up in my arms, the two of us ignoring the conversation flowing around us. All that mattered was demonstrating to Cami that I would be her ally no matter what she chose. No matter how she felt. No matter what she needed. *You're my mate,* I whispered into her mind. *I'll accept anyone you need me to accept.*

Although, the flex of power warming my back seemed to be testing my words before I could even finish them.

Except maybe Hades, I amended. But I was really only half joking. If Cami wanted him, I'd find a way to accept it.

I don't want Hades, she told me. *I was just... I mean, look at him, Ajax. He's* exactly *how I would picture the God of the Underworld.*

Netherworld, I corrected her.

Pretty sure my mythology professor would disagree with you, she muttered in response.

What?

Nothing. Never mind. I don't want him. I... I want you. Az. Melek.

And maybe Lucifer? I hedged.

I don't know, she admitted on a whisper into my mind. *I... I dream of him.* She uttered the words like she was confiding some big betrayal, one that appeared to be layered with guilt.

It's okay to dream of him, little rebel, I told her. *It's even okay to want him. But I still don't trust him.* And I wouldn't be able to trust him until I understood his intentions. Which, as Az had so eloquently stated, were in a constant state of flexibility.

Whatever the fuck that meant.

I don't trust him either, Cami returned. *Not yet.* Those last two words were underlined with hope, an emotion that had long died within my soul.

At least until Cami had come along and rekindled the fire inside me.

But that flame only burned for her now. And a little bit for Az, too.

Thinking of my other mate had me glancing at where he now stood shoulder to shoulder with Typhos, the pair of them seeming to be in some sort of standoff with the God of the Netherworld.

What did we miss? I asked, frowning at Az's back.

Lucifer asked Hades for his opinion on the Virtuous Fae magic used to manipulate the Death Fae and Corpse Fae, Az explained. *So now they're negotiating terms for an exchange of information.*

Because Hades won't just answer the question? I guessed.

Nope.

I couldn't help the smile taunting my lips. *And Lucifer has to bargain for it?*

Yep.

My amusement bloomed into a chuckle that had the Hell Fae King glancing back at me. "Is something humoring you, Warden?"

"Yes," I answered honestly.

"Care to share?" he drawled.

"Sure. I'm amused that you're being forced to play your favorite game—from the other side," I replied, not caring at all if my words pissed him off. Because fuck holding back. I'd bowed at his feet for over a decade. And he'd paid me back by threatening me and my mate, issuing ultimatums, and forcing me to partake in his fucked-up version of punishment.

Hell Fae King or not, I was done submitting to him.

His sapphire gaze held mine for a beat, his own lips curling at the edges. "Who says I'm on the other side?" he asked before returning his focus to Hades. "You seem rather keen on this portal, Hades. Perhaps I want more than information as payment for allowing it."

"Let's be clear, Typhos. If I want to open a portal, I will. This exchange of favors is purely for your benefit, not mine."

Lucifer folded his arms, the muscles seeming to flex beneath his dress shirt. "You mean you'll have Maliki open the portal on your behalf and test my mercy again."

Silence fell, the two dominant males squaring off once more.

Maliki opened that portal for Hades? I asked, my mental words for Az. *The one that went to the monsters' ball thing?*

Monsters Night, Az corrected me. *And apparently, yes. This is the first I'm hearing about it.*

I glanced at Az's muscular back since I couldn't meet his gaze. *Is that why he allowed your brother to leave his custody?*

Maybe, Az replied. *However, I think Maliki's release had more to do with whatever conversation Typhos had with Hades.*

I wonder what they talked about, I thought more to myself than to Az, but he heard the words anyway.

Me, too, he echoed.

"To understand the hows and the whys, you must first evaluate your realm and the satisfaction of your fae. What makes a former creation vulnerable to his creator? Displeasure, perhaps?" Hades's cultured tones echoed through Death's Den, the power underlining his voice causing the hairs to dance along my arms.

His ability to break through my privacy spell—one I hadn't bothered to disable even though Az had recommended it—wasn't surprising. I'd never met a Mythos Fae in the flesh, only heard rumors of their strong auras and obvious prowess.

Seeing Hades now, I believed those rumors.

"Your fae respect you," he went on. "You saved them. Cared for them. Created this realm for them. But doing so also isolated them. Until the trials. You knew they needed mates, yet turned it all into a test. I understand that. Admire it, even. However, your fae might not feel the same. And that hint of uncertainty…"

He trailed off.

But Lucifer finished for him by saying, "Creates a fracture that can be exploited."

"Yes." Hades took a step back. "Although, that fracture goes deeper than a fragile mental state, Typhos. One can turn a fae into a puppet with a mentally channeled spell. Controlling a few dozen fae at once, however, requires physical access."

"Meaning my walls have been breached."

"A fact I believe you already knew," Hades drawled as he looked at Cami. "A siphon's energy goes both ways." He shifted his dark eyes to Maliki. "Now you have no need to time-travel and can return to the task I gave you."

The lethal fae merely folded his arms and leaned against a nearby cracked wall. "We'll see."

Hades narrowed his eyes, clearly not pleased with Maliki's dismissive words.

But rather than comment on it, he looked at Lucifer again and said, "Might I suggest you handle the issues in Morpheus Kingdom? I suspect the building tensions there could be considered a weak spot in the realm. All those vulnerable minds…"

He trailed off once more.

This time Lucifer didn't finish the sentence, just nodded and replied, "I won't interfere with your hunt."

"Good."

"But keep me in the loop, at least until this *virtuous* problem is fixed," Lucifer added, his emphasis on the word *virtuous* clearly intentional.

"There won't be any 'loop' for a while. My quarry doesn't appear to be ready to run."

I frowned, wondering what Hades meant by that. *This guy talks in riddles just like Melek.*

Except Melek is playful, Az returned mentally. *Hades is just deadly.*

"Then I'll expect your kingdom to remain portal-free

for now," Lucifer said, drawing me back to the conversation between him and the intended Mythos Fae.

"For now," Hades echoed.

"Let me know when that changes."

"Sure," Hades agreed. Although, it didn't sound quite like an agreement so much as a placated statement. "Maliki?" He didn't wait for the male to respond, simply disappeared into a cloud of smoke and left a sole black feather in his wake.

Maliki sighed loudly in response, shoving away from the wall to retrieve the plume as it drifted through the air. "Duty calls," he deadpanned. "Next time, try not to start a bar fight, yeah?" That last part seemed to be directed at Az.

"Like you didn't enjoy it," the Commander drawled.

Maliki's mouth curled into a sinister grin. "I didn't enjoy it. I fucking loved it." With that, he vanished. No smoke. No feathers. Just... disappeared.

His nickname—Ghost—really was fitting.

Lucifer turned to face me and Cami, then glanced at Melek and looked over him like he was searching for something. I followed his actions and took in the Hell Fae Prince's suit-clad form, his pressed pants and crisp shirt as flawless as ever.

"Are you all right?" Lucifer asked, his voice soft.

"I'll be fine," Melek replied, the edge in his tone capturing my attention. "Ajax's barrier is helping."

"My barrier?" I echoed, flexing the protective spell around us. "You mean the one Hades and Lucifer both penetrated without so much as a blink?" I couldn't hide the annoyance in my tone. Powerful beings or not, it wounded my ego that they'd so easily infiltrated my spell.

It'd taken years for Shade and me to perfect our

abilities to slip through enchantments, yet those two had done it in a matter of seconds.

"Your magic invited me in," Lucifer told me. "And as for Hades, his abilities reside on a different plane of existence. Don't take it personally." He moved forward to look over Melek, his expression exuding a concern I'd failed to notice before. "You're sure?"

"Yes. As I said, the barrier is helping."

"Helping what?" I demanded, not liking this cryptic conversation. I'd assumed Melek had wanted me to create a privacy bubble to mask our conversation, but it seemed his intentions went deeper. "What haven't you told me?"

"A great many things," Melek replied with a wry smile. "But in this case, it's simply a weakness on my part that your magic is helping me mask."

"The Soul Yards in this kingdom drain his magic," Lucifer explained, surprising me. "Melek is all about life, while this place exudes death. It's why he never comes here."

My brow furrowed, a memory niggling. "You… you mentioned that once." What was it he'd said?

"Ty told me the next trial is in the Netherworld Kingdom. It's the one place I can't go. And I'm worried Cami won't survive it."

His words flowed through my head, causing me to glance at Cami in alarm. "Are you okay?"

She frowned back at me. "In general or right now?"

"Both."

"Then no, but yes," she replied.

I blinked at her. "Melek worried you wouldn't survive here…"

I returned my focus to the male in question, my instincts instantly tightening the barrier around us and bolstering the protective spell with another wave of power.

"Why did you tell me that?" I demanded. "Why were you worried about her survival in the Netherworld?"

"Because I knew she had Virtuous Fae gifts, but not what kind," Melek replied, his voice serious again. "My magic doesn't work here. I'm basically a human in this kingdom."

That had my eyebrow inching upward. "Really?" How ironic. My Midnight Fae soul was more than at home here in the Netherworld, the chilling energy calling to my Death Blood origin. Yet Melek was distinctly uncomfortable. Weakened. *Powerless*.

"Having murderous ideas?" Melek asked, sounding amused, yet there was a hint of exhaustion underlining those words.

"There's a lot I need to teach you," Lucifer interrupted before I could reply, his large form moving between me and Melek as though he thought I might actually embark on some of the *ideas* Melek had just mentioned. "Both you and Camillia, I mean. So we should go."

"I wasn't going to attack your prince," I told Lucifer honestly.

"I know." His blue eyes flickered with fire. "However, if today has proved anything to me, it's that you and Camillia are both woefully unprepared for your roles in my court. That's my fault. And I'm going to fix it." He held out his hand. "Starting now."

CHAPTER 8

TYPHOS

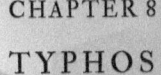

A jax eyed my hand with obvious distrust, the look one that wounded me more than I cared to admit. Did I deserve this reaction? Probably yes. But that didn't mean I liked it.

Hades's words circulated through my thoughts regarding weakened minds and how easily they could be manipulated. He didn't mean by any ordinary fae, but by Virtuous Fae. The creators of fae kind. Fae like Vivaxia.

Was Ajax's mind susceptible to her influence as well? Was his loyalty to me so far gone that she could squeeze through the cracks in his psyche and manipulate him into working against me?

Because that was what had happened in the Netherworld Kingdom tonight. Vivaxia had been able to control several dozen Death Fae and Corpse Fae, acting as a puppet master as she drove them to attack Az.

And she'd accomplished that because there were already seeds of distrust blooming in their minds.

Seeds that had been planted by me.

My punishments, I realized.

Hades hadn't mentioned that part, but he hadn't needed to. I'd understood what he was telling me—some of my fae were displeased with my leadership.

I'd known this for a while, hence the development of the bride trials. But it seemed that hadn't been enough.

Disquiet in the Netherworld made sense. I'd punished the fae here—as well as those in Morpheus Kingdom—for partaking in Monsters Night. But perhaps I'd been too harsh.

Or maybe my men didn't feel I'd done enough to sate their needs to take a mate.

Had I? I wondered. *Were the trials too much?*

I'd meant to test the brides, not my fae males. However, I supposed everyone had been tested along the way.

Including myself.

The Hell Fae Source had never approved of unmated female fae entering my realm because the Source was part of my heart. Part of me. And *I* harbored insecurities where females were concerned unless a powerful Hell Fae had vetted them. A leftover consequence of Vivaxia's betrayal.

I recognized that. Owned that. And had developed the trials as a way to force myself to see beyond my ingrained bias. To learn to trust. To embrace all fae, not just male fae.

Logically, I understood that males could be just as untrustworthy as females. Thus, the trials had been designed in a way that would force me to acknowledge that logic, to see that women could be just as trustworthy as men.

The heart of fae kind existed in the soul, hence the importance of distinguishing light and dark souls in the Hell Fae Realm. Intentions were important. Nightmare Fae were often misunderstood, and I'd wanted to ensure their intended mates could see through their monstrous masks and into the heart beneath.

Alas, looking at Ajax now and the distrust painting his features, I again realized how much I'd failed.

Here stood my Hell Fae Warden, the man I'd assigned to guard the infamous Nightmare Fae prisons, and not even he could see through the charades.

Because I'd never taught him how.

I'd never guided him.

I'd never *mentored* him.

That was about to change.

"Please," I pressed, still staring at Ajax. "We'll head back to the palace, have a meal, discuss a few things, and relax. Then you and Camillia will join me tomorrow for training."

"What kind of training?" Ajax asked, still refusing to accept my hand. Not that he actually needed it. He could easily shadow himself back to the palace. This was just meant as a gesture.

Or a deal, I supposed.

Only, I wasn't expecting anything other than his willingness in return for my tutelage.

Not that he seemed to believe me, if his suspicious expression was anything to go by.

I nearly sighed. It seemed our conversation in the courtyard yesterday did little in the way of mending the bridge I'd burned between us. That was fine. I could be patient.

Because in the end, I would prove myself to him and to Camillia.

And that process would begin by helping them understand me better.

"I've realized I never properly introduced you to my realm and the creatures inside it. I made some assumptions when I named you as my Warden, assumptions that have led to a severe fracture in our relationship. The training— or perhaps a better term would be *information sharing*—will hopefully help mend some of your misconceptions about me and my realm."

Of course, I would need to do more than lecture them on all the details. I would need to show them, too.

Or maybe it would be more worthwhile to skip to the *showing* part. That was always the best way to learn—by doing.

A plan began to form in my mind, an idea of sorts, one that should provide an exquisite introduction into light and dark souls.

It would also allow me to help Camillia hone her talents. She possessed the potential to become a queen, a true goddess, really. Technically, Melek already set her on that path as his mate. But her fate ran so much deeper than their bond.

She was powerful, as evidenced by her ability to wield the death stone and everything else she'd done while in my realm.

However, her display in the Netherworld Kingdom also indicated her lack of restraint. And she didn't appear to be able to see through the Nightmare Fae masks, her power having attacked almost everyone nearby as though each soul was an enemy when most were not.

That all was fine.

I would teach her.

An activity I very much looked forward to. Perhaps a bit too much.

There are so many things I could show her, I thought, glancing at her and finding her stormy irises locked on me in open evaluation. Almost as though she'd heard my musing aloud.

Or perhaps the hunger showed in my features.

Because I wanted to instruct her on a lot more than how to read and understand fae souls. I wanted to introduce her to various levels of control, and I wanted to demonstrate my power and train her to accept it. *In all ways...*

Fuck, I muttered to myself, forcing my gaze away from her. *She's far too tempting.*

Yes, Melek agreed with a whisper into my mind. However, his mental voice wasn't as playful as usual, reminding me of how much he was suffering in this kingdom.

I'd felt it the moment we first arrived, and that pain had only worsened the longer he'd remained here. Melek had expelled every ounce of his power to help Camillia, leaving him depleted and basically defenseless.

Ajax's barrier spell was all that kept my little prince standing, something the Warden didn't seem to fully comprehend. Fortunately, he hadn't taken the shield away after learning that Melek needed it. Instead, I swore I'd felt him strengthen it.

Or perhaps that was merely my hope coming through.

The five of us would be so much stronger if we worked together, not against each other. A fact I should have realized weeks ago. Hell, *months* ago.

I really have been blind, I marveled.

I prefer to think of it as otherwise consumed, my king, Melek murmured. *You care about your realm, Ty. Everyone knows that. Even Cami. You thought she was a threat and reacted accordingly. What matters is how you grovel now.*

Grovel? I echoed, shifting my gaze from Ajax to Melek and pinning him with a look. *I do not grovel.*

With her, you might, he replied, a twinkle in his alluring eyes.

Eyes that told me he was far worse off than he allowed anyone else to believe.

"Ajax, if you want to stay here, that's fine. But if you want answers, please join us in the palace," I said, my focus still on my prince. "Melek can't remain here any longer."

I stepped forward, wrapped my palm around my prince's nape, and pulled him to me. But before I could take us home, he reached out an arm for Camillia.

And she shocked me by stepping forward to join us.

My gaze slid to hers, a dozen questions peppering my thoughts, none of which I could voice.

"I'm hungry," she said by way of explanation. "We never ate breakfast."

Amusement touched my lips. "Indeed we didn't." *You know where we'll be, Azazel*, I told my other mate.

We'll be along shortly was his reply.

Wrapping my power around Melek and Camillia, I escorted them back to my quarters in the palace. The scent of food littered the air despite the tray having long since disappeared. "I need to ask Garmr about Payan." This had all started when he delivered the letter with our meal.

But before I could focus on that, I needed to ensure Melek healed properly.

Mere seconds in the palace and his color was already returning, his eyes flickering with life.

"Payan was one of the Hellhounds you sent after me in the beginning," Camillia muttered, causing my brow to furrow.

"In the beginning?" *When did I send a Hellhound after her? Or did she mean Ajax?* He'd been in charge of Hell Fae Bride recruitment.

"You know, when I became a Hell Fae Bride," she said, confirming my thoughts on what she'd meant. "I stabbed him in the balls."

Melek chuckled. "Why doesn't that surprise me?"

"That's why Ajax had to come kidnap me," she went on, shrugging. "Seems like a lifetime ago, but I recognized the Hellhound when he entered. I guess it's a good thing he didn't notice me. I doubt he likes me all that much."

Amusement rippled through my bond with Melek, causing my lips to twitch. After everything that had happened today—hell, over the last few months—Camillia still maintained an air of nonchalance. Like nothing had truly fazed her.

Because her commentary on Payan had been more of the musing variety, not a concerned statement. I suspect she would have happily stabbed Payan again had he reacted to her presence.

And something about that just intrigued me more.

She's fearless, I realized.

Except... she feared me. I'd seen that in her gaze earlier, felt the prickle of her terror against my subconscious.

Something I'd done, perhaps *everything* I'd done, had wounded her warrior heart and caused her to look upon me with dread.

That knowledge—that *realization*—wiped the smile from my lips.

"I'm going to prepare breakfast," I decided aloud, needing something to do. A way to show her favor. To start bridging this void between us.

Training required trust, something she clearly didn't feel for me. And it seemed Ajax didn't either.

Maybe I need to give them a few days to acclimate before we begin, I thought as I left the room. *Prove my intentions through actions. Leave them to get comfortable in the palace. Allow them to see the real me... in my palace.*

I also needed to figure out a way to fix the fractures in

my Hell Fae, determine how to regain their faith and make them less vulnerable to Virtuous Fae influence.

The Hell Fae Bride Trials had been put on hold as a result of the portals. Maybe I should take a few days to determine next steps, have some meetings with my lieutenants to discuss ideas and needs, and move from there.

That would allow me to be productive while Camillia and Ajax grew more comfortable.

Nodding to myself, I approved of my internal plan and set about making breakfast, a task I hadn't done in decades. Melek usually cooked, this part of our suite having been his realm more than mine. But I didn't trust anyone to handle our food right now, not after the letter incident.

Garmr would be first on my list for a meeting today.

After I finished taking care of my mates.

Or *mate*, I supposed.

My *mate* and Camillia.

Odd how mates *felt more natural*, I thought.

Then I squashed the idle musing and focused on the task.

It's just pancakes. Nothing more. Nothing less.

CHAPTER 9

TYPHOS

Feeling Azazel's return with Ajax, I paused my work at the stove and went back to increase the amount of pancake batter I'd whipped up.

Need any help, my king? Melek asked.

No. You're supposed to be relaxing.

I'm already healed, Ty.

I knew that, but it didn't change my answer. *I want to do this.* More so, I *needed* to do this. To properly take care of my circle. To prove that I was more than a tyrant king.

Melek seemed entertained by my adamance but didn't press further. Instead, he simply replied, *Camillia likes chocolate.*

Hearing that, I divided some of the batter into a separate dish and found some chocolate chips in our magically stocked pantry. The little cubby held everything we desired. Literally. All I had to do was think of an ingredient and it appeared. Very useful. Especially right now.

Humming, I got to work, the task of flipping pancakes

on a griddle coming to me with ease despite being out of practice.

Azazel entered as I started the chocolate chip batch, his irises swirling with a mixture of violet and black flames. "Melek said you were cooking. I had to see it for myself."

Ajax stood just behind him, his brow furrowing as he glanced around my Commander to take in the kitchen.

"You know I can cook," I told Azazel. "I've made you breakfast hundreds of times."

"Yes, but I haven't seen you flip a pancake in probably a century or more."

I shrugged. "The Hellhounds usually cook."

"But you don't trust them now because of Payan," he replied, likely having gathered that information from Melek. Or perhaps from my thoughts.

"I still have faith in them. But, as Hades pointed out, we have some weaknesses to see to. So until I've been able to properly evaluate everyone, I won't be trusting anyone outside of this suite."

Ajax grunted, drawing my focus to him.

"You have something to add, Warden?" I asked, my eyebrow inching upward.

He met and held my gaze without flinching. "You didn't trust me a week ago."

I cocked my head and set down my spatula to give him my full attention. "What makes you think that? I left you alone in the Midnight Fae Realm with a female I considered to be the ultimate threat to my realm. Was that not a show of trust?"

"That was about fae politics," he returned as Azazel stepped up to my side to take over my pancake project on the stove.

I moved out of his way but carefully ensured I slid sideways and not in Ajax's direction. His current mood reminded me of a temperamental Manticore; it was like he would charge me the moment he felt threatened by my presence.

And I really didn't want to have to retaliate.

So I simply folded my arms, leaned back against the counter, and held his gaze. "You've known me for over a decade, Ajax. When have I ever given a fuck about fae politics?"

His jaw clenched. "You've attended Interrealm Fae events."

"Begrudgingly, yes. And only because I intend to be there for those harmed when the efforts eventually fail," I informed him flatly.

His eyebrows came down. "Why would they fail? Do you have something planned?"

This time it was my turn to grunt.

Because *fuck*.

I'd worried before that Ajax's distrust might be a weakness Vivaxia could exploit. Now I knew for certain that it was.

I needed to fix this—*quickly*—or my entire circle could be at risk.

"History proves that these efforts often fail," Azazel interjected before I could comment. "Maybe this one will succeed. But we've seen so many failures over the millennia that we've perfected our abilities to help those harmed in the end. That's why Typhos has attended—to ensure he knows who may need him in the future."

"It also affords me an opportunity to be part of the movement should it actually succeed," I added. "This is definitely the best orchestrated effort I've witnessed, but fae like Constantine still exist in other realms. And you saw firsthand what he was capable of."

A cruel reminder, perhaps. But I needed Ajax to put

this into perspective, to realize that his ire toward me was somewhat misdirected.

Because I had no doubt his current sentiments were grounded in his previous experiences, his shields having been perfected over a lifetime of pain.

"There's a lot that I've done wrong here," I went on before he could reply. "A lot I have to atone for where you and Camillia are concerned. But if we're going to survive Vivaxia, we need to be a team. Which is why I want the opportunity to train you both, to prepare ourselves for the fight ahead."

It was the most straightforward and honest I had ever been with him. The most I'd ever given away.

Survive was a purposeful term.

Because that was exactly what we had to do, not just for us but for all of Hell Fae and Nightmare Fae kind.

If Vivaxia stole my light, this realm would burn.

And all the beings inside it would perish. Including us.

"But I can't teach you if you won't listen to me," I added, needing him to hear me. Needing him to *understand*. "You have your reasons for distrusting me, and I respect those reasons. However, if you continue to let them cloud your judgment, we'll never move forward."

A consideration that terrified me. I needed him to work with me, not against me. And not just because of his links to Azazel and Camillia, but because of his potential as a powerful ally. I'd made him my Warden for a reason. If only he could see that reason in himself.

"All I can do now is prove my intentions through actions, Ajax," I concluded. "So take the next few days to consider how you want to proceed. You'll either opt to learn with an open mind... or close me out entirely. That decision is yours and yours alone."

With that, I turned to grab two of the plates that were

stacked high with pancakes and teleported back to the bedroom in my suite.

Camillia glanced up from the table, her big eyes reminding me of turbulent storm clouds. The color was enhanced by her all-black outfit—one Melek must have found for her to put on in my absence. Or maybe he magicked it to life. Jeans and tank tops weren't exactly a popular fashion in the Hell Fae Kingdom. A corset and skirt would have been more fitting, to match the female hologram dancers at my nightclub.

An image of Camillia wearing just that flitted through my mind. A dangerous thought, one that quickly morphed into what she would look like tied to my bed with red ribbons around her wrists. Her ankles, too. Splayed. Helpless. Captive. *Mine to explore…*

She definitely wouldn't be wearing underwear under that skirt either, I decided. *Or I'd fucking burn it off.*

Mmm, I like where this is going, my king, Melek all but purred in response. *Do continue.*

I nearly growled in reply, the fantasy disappearing in a flash.

Camillia didn't trust me or like me enough to let me tie her up.

Let alone *burn* her clothes off.

Shaking my head to clear it, I focused on the food in my hand and set it on the table. "I'll be back with some syrup and drinks."

"Are those chocolate chips?" Camillia asked before I could vanish, her voice laced with an emotion I couldn't define.

Or maybe I didn't want to define it.

Fuck, I didn't even want to define this experience.

I'm cooking. For her. For Melek. For Azazel and Ajax.

Sure, I didn't trust anyone else to handle our food. But

I… I'd jumped into this without thought. Almost like I was trying to apologize with food rather than words. Or just care for them? I wasn't sure.

And it didn't matter.

We all needed to eat.

This was practical.

End of discussion.

Except Camillia had just asked me something. *Chocolate chips*, I recalled as she leaned down to examine her pancakes. I frowned at the action. "Melek mentioned you like chocolate, so I…" I trailed off and cleared my throat. "His plate has regular pancakes, if you prefer those. And I can make more."

Hellfire, I felt like I was an inept teenager. *What the fae is wrong with me?*

"No, I love chocolate chip pancakes, actually," she admitted, her cheeks taking on a pretty shade of red. "I… I was just surprised. Thank you." Her alluring eyes met mine, then shyly glanced away.

Another uncanny look from the warrior. But I much preferred this to her fear.

"Do you have a drink preference?" I asked, still feeling out of my element.

"Coffee," she answered instantly.

"Irish coffee," Ajax corrected as he walked in with Azazel, the pair of them carrying more pancakes. They could have shadowed and ashed in here, but the kitchen was connected by a door, so I supposed their method was nearly as fast as mine.

"Irish coffee," I echoed.

"I can make it for her," he said.

"Or you could show me how to make it," I suggested, genuinely curious.

He stared at me for a beat. "I was going to use magic."

"Oh." That was far less interesting.

"I can show you, my king," Melek interjected, pushing away from the table. "We have everything we need at the bar, just need to brew some coffee."

I glanced between them, not sure which offer to accept. I wanted to learn, but I also didn't want Ajax to feel rejected.

"And some whiskey, actually," Melek added, pausing beside Ajax. "Can you magic up some for me? Maybe some whipped cream, too?"

"It would be faster to just spell the drink," Ajax drawled, folding his arms.

"Yes, but it's not every day we get to teach Ty something," Melek replied with a grin. "Humor me, please?"

Ajax studied him for a beat, then glanced at Camillia before finally setting his gaze on me. "Fine. I'll teach you how to make one. But you're brewing the coffee."

I nodded and did my best to hide my amusement. *Thank you, little prince.*

For what? Melek murmured back, his mental tone the epitome of innocence.

However, he knew what he'd done.

Making an Irish coffee might be a small task, but it was monumental in this moment. Because Ajax was showing a subtle willingness to work with me rather than against me.

Assuming he didn't pour the pot of coffee on my head, anyway.

But it gave me a flicker of hope that I might be able to fix this after all.

A few days, I echoed in my mind. I'd originally stated that I wanted to start training tomorrow. However, I needed Ajax's acceptance, or my lessons would be worthless in the end. So I'd give him some time to make up his mind.

If this menial activity indicated a tentative alliance, I'd accept it.

And I'd do everything in my power to fortify it.

For Ajax. For Camillia. For Azazel and Melek. *For all of Hell Fae and Nightmare Fae kind…*

CHAPTER 10

CAMI

A Few Days Later

Pancakes had become a daily ritual. Chocolate chip. Doused in syrup. With a side of Irish coffee.

All courtesy of the Hell Fae King.

At least until yesterday when he'd disappeared after saying something about having a meeting with his lieutenants. I didn't know the details, but I also hadn't asked about it.

Then this morning I woke to a note warning me that training would begin today. Or perhaps he'd just meant it as a casual communication to let me know about his plans for us. But I'd translated it as a warning, one that both excited me and scared me at the same time.

It excited me because I wanted to learn more about Lucifer and his realm. I also really wanted to spend some alone time with him.

Which I shouldn't want at all.

Hence the reason it terrified me as well.

Although, I supposed I wouldn't really be alone with him. Because Ajax planned to come, too.

"I don't trust him," he'd said earlier after I'd shown him the note. I'd been in bed between him and Az, the fiery parchment having somehow landed on my pillow—without singeing it—while the three of us had slept.

Az hadn't commented or replied to Ajax's words, just rolled off the mattress and went to prepare some coffee for the three of us.

"I don't not trust him," I'd told Ajax softly. "A convoluted way of saying I want to see where this goes, I guess."

Ajax had studied me for a long moment before nodding. "Then I'm coming with you."

But first, he'd vanished with Az, likely to go spar or something, leaving me to my own devices for the morning.

Which was how I'd ended up in the Hell Fae Palace Courtyard.

Having a picnic.

With the Hell Fae Prince.

He'd substituted crêpes for pancakes, each fluffy pastry filled with melted cheese and smoky meat. A bit of a different fare than our usual morning sweets, but I wasn't complaining. Especially since he'd paired it all with caffeine.

Not Irish coffee this time, but cappuccinos. Somehow he'd created little hearts in the froth, a touch that I'd found both endearing and suspicious.

Because this whole *picnic* was a ruse.

Well, not a ruse, necessarily. But a way to butter me up before my training with Lucifer.

"I know what you're doing," I told Melek softly.

"Oh?" His eyes twinkled from the dual suns shining overhead, his pale skin a shade pinker thanks to the reddish glow all around us. My limbs resembled a similar hue, the ember-like atmosphere here in the palace courtyard seeming to represent all of the Hell Fae Realm. "And what am I doing, little angel?"

"Distracting me from thinking about Lucifer's training."

"Hmm," he hummed, taking a sip from his cup. "Or maybe I'm simply here to prepare you." He glanced around the courtyard, his irises lighting up from a nearby pillar of fire, one that was decorated with a variety of vibrant flowers.

I admired the colors for a moment, noting the way the vines trailed along the stone paths—paths that Hell Fae were openly walking while conversing softly amongst themselves.

"How is this preparing me for training?" I wondered aloud, watching as two Hellhounds sauntered up a path while tossing a flaming ball back and forth like a toy. When they took off at a sprint for a field of black grass, I winced, recalling the razor-like blades that had decorated the Midnight Fae Palace Courtyards.

Fortunately, this field didn't appear to be the same as they ran across it with ease while continuing to throw the fiery sphere to one another.

"Because this is where Ty plans to meet you," Melek said, snapping my attention back to him.

"What?" I glanced around the courtyard with renewed interest. Or maybe *fear* was the right word. "Here? Where everyone can see us?"

A shiver traversed my spine. The last time Lucifer presented me in front of his Hell Fae, I was dressed in chains.

Chains that barely covered my feminine assets.

I swallowed. *What is he planning?* I wondered, memories

of that infamous evening in his club assaulting me from all angles.

That was his version of a punishment, Cami, Melek answered into my mind. "He wants everyone to see how powerful you are," he added aloud. "That's why he chose this venue."

I glanced sideways at him. "How powerful I am?" I repeated aloud. "You mean he wants them all to see why he considers me a threat?"

Melek sighed and cut off a piece of the crêpe to bring it up to my mouth.

When I didn't accept his offering, he ate it himself. Then he leaned back on the blanket and propped himself up on his palms, his long legs stretching to cross at the ankles.

I stared at him, waiting for him to reply.

Instead, he tipped his head back to bathe his gorgeous face in the sunlight, his blondish-brown hair flowing back in a majestic wave.

"Your beauty isn't going to distract me, Melek," I told him.

"You think I'm a beauty?" he replied, his lips curling as his eyes closed. "I think you're stunning."

"He says without looking at me," I deadpanned.

"I don't need to see you to know what you look like," he murmured. "You exist in my mind. In all ways." He canted his head to peek at me through his thick, alluring lashes. "Although, I am a fan of your outfit choice."

I rolled my eyes. "I assumed training would require running or fighting or something athletic."

Ignoring me, he went on by saying, "Your legs look a mile long in those little black shorts. And that tight tank top exquisitely frames your breasts. It's too bad you're wearing a bra." His gaze turned devilish, his thoughts just as sinful. "Maybe I should fix that before Ty arrives?"

"Stop trying to derail the conversation."

"Would I do that?" he asked, the picture of innocence. His expression, tone, and general soft aura gave me no doubt as to his angelic heritage. But a sensual demon lurked beneath the saintly veneer.

A sensual demon that was currently considering ways he'd prefer to *derail the conversation* and ensuring I overheard every thought and detail.

"Do you do this to Lucifer?" I wondered aloud. "Fantasize openly about him?"

"Previously, yes," he admitted. "Lately, though, I've focused on you. And before you ask, yes, he's heard every word."

"I wasn't going to ask."

"Perhaps not out loud," he returned, grinning again as he tipped his head back once more into the suns' rays from above. "You can lie about your intrigue all you want, little angel. I know the truth. And it's a truth your mind has allowed me to learn."

I bit my lip, not wanting to touch that comment.

Was I interested in Lucifer? Yes. I'd have to be a fool to ignore his charm. Exquisite looks. Athletic physique. *Addictive kisses.*

I shook my head, forcibly clearing my thoughts. *Typhos Lucifer is not mine.*

Yet, Melek hummed into my mind, adding his own ending to my sentence. *But he could be.*

He hates me.

Does he, though? he asked softly. *Or were things just easier when you believed that?*

My jaw clenched. "Tell me about today's training," I

demanded out loud, refusing to indulge him in the topic of our mental conversation.

Because I didn't want to think about what I believed or what could be.

I wanted to focus on the now.

This courtyard.

The one littered with fluttering fireflies and blooming flowers that looked more venomous than harmless.

And the Hell Fae males dressed in black fatigues.

"Does he expect me to spar with a Hellhound?" I wondered, searching for the two that had been playing fetch with that flaming ball.

Melek huffed a laugh. "No, little angel. I think our king is well aware of your fighting abilities. Otherwise, he'd send you back to the camp to play with the other brides."

My brow furrowed, my gaze sliding to him. "What?"

He sat up, his eyes holding mine. "I suppose you wouldn't be aware of what they're currently doing, would you?"

Panic sent a bolt through my heart. *The Hell Fae Brides. The trials.* I'd been so removed from everything that I... I hadn't even thought of the others. "Are they okay?" I asked, a feeling of dread tightening my stomach. "What are they training for?" *Oh, fae.* "Is there another trial soon?"

Of course there was another fucking trial soon. Why did I even bother to ask?

And how could I have forgotten about the other Hell Fae Brides?

Fuck. I'd been blinded by Lucifer's beauty. His kisses. His... his *everything*. So much so that I'd forgotten the monster beneath his suits. The king who had taken me against my will.

Was it just the other day that I'd joked about Payan?

How I'd stabbed him in the balls when he'd tried to retrieve me?

I'd… I'd made light of my situation.

While forgetting that others are still suffering.

Hell Fae Rule #6: Only Look Out for Yourself—No One Else.

I'd really taken that one to heart, apparently. *I'm a selfish—*

"Cami," Melek said, the sharpness of his tone yanking my attention back to him. "The Hell Fae Brides are fine. The trials have been on hold since the last portal incident. Ty doesn't want to risk anyone's life—bride or otherwise—until we've handled the Virtuous issue."

I frowned at him. "Yet he has no problem sacrificing brides in the actual trials."

Melek's eyes narrowed, the expression uncharacteristically irritated. "He has no problem sacrificing dark souls. There's a difference."

I huffed at that. "So he plays God."

"Yes. He's the creator of this realm, Camillia. It's his duty to protect everyone and everything inside it."

"Then maybe he shouldn't have kidnapped and dragged a bunch of unwilling women here for the pleasure of his men," I snapped back.

Melek considered me for a moment, his cheekbones seeming to protrude against his skin as anger simmered in his gaze. "How much time did you spend getting to know the other brides and their motives?" he asked softly. Too softly. "How many of them were actually *kidnapped* and *dragged* here?"

When I didn't immediately reply, he arched a brow.

"Don't you remember what I told you after the first trial?" he pressed.

My brow furrowed. I hardly remembered the aftermath of that event. I'd barely been lucid.

Although, there were a few who had entered the trials willingly, their excitement having been both palpable and memorable during the trials I'd participated in.

But most of them had seemed nervous.

Only, I hadn't considered the cause of their nervousness. I'd just assumed they were in a situation similar to mine and displeased by being forced to participate in the Hell Fae Bride program.

Was I wrong? Did I make assumptions on behalf of the brides?

"Yes, but no one can fault you for it," Melek replied, obviously hearing my thoughts and choosing to answer aloud. His palm came up to cradle my cheek. "To understand the trials, you must first truly understand the purpose."

"To provide the Hell Fae with mates," I told him, aware of that part already from previous discussions.

Yet Melek shook his head. "Not quite. That's what Ty says, but his desire to satisfy the Hell Fae and Nightmare Fae runs much deeper than simply supplying mates for them. This is about his Source, his balance of power. Everything is at risk, which is something he'll never admit. But I see it. And I know that's the driving force behind every decision he's made, even if he's not aware of it himself."

Melek reached for my hand, his thumb gently caressing my skin.

You are the only one who can save him, he whispered softly into my mind. *That's what the Hell Fae Brides have been about from the very beginning—saving him from himself.*

I stared into his multicolored eyes. *I need you to elaborate, Melek. No more riddles,* I told him mentally, earning me a small smile from my Hell Fae Prince.

But rather than speak, he released me and wove his hands through the air. I squinted at him, not understanding his motions until a screen appeared before us.

One that displayed a gym.

And several women running around.

Bridal candidates, I realized after a beat, noting their numbers on the backs of their shirts. However, now their shirts reminded me more of jerseys. Maybe because they appeared to be playing some sort of game.

"They're training," he informed me as the screen panned to view the scene.

"For what?"

He shrugged. "Anything they desire, really."

"You're being cryptic again," I informed him flatly.

His lips twitched. "The trials are on hold, so many of them have opted to form alliances and play as teammates. It's an intriguing development, to be honest. One that demonstrates their compatibility for this realm. Because working together here is important. It's how we all survive."

"I see." Still a somewhat cryptic reply, but he'd provided a bit more context. *However...* "How is watching this going to help me understand the true purpose of the trials? And what does it have to do with today's training?"

Maybe I sounded impatient, but I was really tired of having to read between the lines. I wanted a straight answer. No more games. No more puzzles. Just a coherent response that helped me prepare for whatever Lucifer had in store for me today.

Because right now, I wasn't sure if I should be excited... *or run.*

CHAPTER 11

MELEK

You feel frustrated, Ty murmured into my mind before I could reply to Cami. *Are you all right, little prince?*

I'm fine, I answered a bit more curtly than intended. *Just preparing Cami for today's training.*

Hmm, and what have you shared?

Not enough, apparently, I muttered, more to myself than to him. But he heard every word, his confusion trickling through the bond. *I haven't given her any hints or tips,* I went on before he could comment. *I'll let you explain. I'm just trying to prepare her.*

This isn't a test, Melek.

I know, I replied. *But she doesn't understand that. She sees everything as a trial.*

Which brought me back to her comments and the screen before us.

I love you, Ty, but I need to concentrate on Cami. Forgive me, please. I didn't like to cut him off, but Cami needed me to focus right now.

Or rather, I needed *her* to focus. Not on the past and

what she thought she knew, but on the future and what it actually meant.

No forgiveness needed, little prince. You train her in your way, and I'll train her in mine. We'll be along in thirty minutes or so. Just waiting for Ajax to meet me in the dungeons.

Thank you, I replied, noting the timeline while studying Cami's impatient expression. "Ty will be here in thirty minutes," I told her. "He was just letting me know."

She winced. "Oh. Okay."

"That means we have thirty minutes to discuss the purpose and your training," I added as I shifted the screen to give her another angle of the gym. Not all the brides were engaged in the current game. Some were on the sidelines chatting and laughing with some lingering Hell Fae males.

Cami observed them for a moment, then glanced at a couple strolling along the sidewalk in black fatigues. "Did they just come from the, uh, gym?" she asked. "That is a gym, right?" Her eyes flew up to mine. "Where was the gym on the campus?"

I bit back the urge to chuckle at her rapid-fire questions. "It's an enchanted arena of sorts," I explained. "And it's new."

"Oh. So they're using this to train for more trials."

I didn't miss the subtle annoyance underlining that final word.

Cami's view of the Hell Fae Brides was skewed to her own experience, an experience that was deeply biased. And if I didn't help correct that viewpoint, it could impact her relationship with Ty.

While he should probably be the one to correct her misgivings, I felt compelled to try. Primarily because Cami was right—I'd been cryptic for too long. Her comments about my *riddles* were both amusing and frustrating.

I didn't mean to speak in riddles.

Or maybe I did.

Straightforward answers often eluded me. And where was the fun in spelling things out?

Alas, for her, I'd try. And we'd begin here.

"When the trials were suspended, the brides grew restless. Rather than send everyone back to their home realms, which could have dangerous consequences given their exposure to the Hell Fae Source, Ty decided to focus on community development. And part of that was by allowing the candidates to work with their suitors to create something."

"And they chose a gym?" she asked, sounding incredulous.

"No, they chose an arena filled with activities," I corrected her, panning the screen to show a pool, followed by a lounge, and then brought up an indoor ice-skating rink. "It's a place for them to relax and bond. A place for courtship without the harshness of the trials."

I returned to the lounge, then zoomed in on a table where several fae sat around, enjoying a meal.

Cami watched, her expression shifting between surprise and confusion. Her thoughts followed suit.

"They look almost normal," she whispered after a few moments of silence.

"You mean, like they weren't kidnapped and dragged here?" I drawled, using her previous terms purposefully.

She cut me a look. "You can't blame me for saying that. It's exactly what happened to me."

"I would never blame you for anything, little angel," I promised her. "I'm merely trying to show you that your experience is unique. Very few brides were unaware of the contract arrangements. Many even penned their own signatures in those contracts."

"Well, I didn't."

"A fact that isn't Ty's fault, but your father's," I told her gently.

"Lucifer still shouldn't have agreed to take my life without talking to me," Cami muttered.

"Maybe," I conceded. "But he had no way of knowing that your father wouldn't share the contract with you. As I said, most of the other brides were more than aware of their fates. And not only that, but they also embraced their candidacy with open eagerness."

I returned my focus to the screen and brought up an image of two females sparring on a mat. Cami frowned at it, her anxiety spiking as the fae spun around each other, their flare of magic blurring across the video feed.

When a glint of metal appeared, Cami winced, her mind telling me she expected the worst.

But then the girls went tumbling down in a fury of fire and ended up laughing on their backs, their daggers thrown carelessly to the side.

My lips twitched. "They're power-drunk." The longer the Hell Fae Brides remained in this realm, the closer they came to the Source.

Not in the same way as Cami, of course. She was literally able to *wield* Lucifer's power. However, all Hell Fae tapped into the realm's Source as a result of merely existing here. The candidates were no different.

I explained all that aloud while the two brides were replaced by a pair of male Hell Fae. Cami listened to me while observing them engage in a routine similar to that of the females, only they didn't land on their backs in a fit of laughter. Instead, the energy built until it exploded around them in a wave of spectacular fire.

Cami gasped as it almost instantly vanished, leaving embers behind that fluttered to the mat below.

"How did you do that?" one of the females asked, clearly as impressed as Cami beside me.

"I'll show you," the Hell Fae offered, inviting her onto the mat. "It's all about control."

"An excellent segue into our training discussion," I mused, closing the screen.

"Hey!" Cami reached for it like she wanted to bring it back up. "I wanted to see what happens next."

"He's going to do exactly what he promised—show her how to harness and manage the power humming through her soul from the Hell Fae Source."

My little angel blinked at that. "Because the brides are strengthened by Lucifer's power." Not a question, but a statement.

"Yes," I confirmed, even though she didn't need it. She'd been listening when I'd elaborated on how the beings in this realm benefited from the Hell Fae Source.

"So what they were just doing is basically what Lucifer plans to do with me."

I hummed, agreeing and not agreeing. This was a delicate discussion, one that required finesse and privacy.

While I could switch to a mental conversation, I opted to weave a quick incantation instead that masked our voices to anyone stupid enough to be eavesdropping. Almost all the fae who strolled by acted as though they didn't see us sitting here in the middle of the courtyard, but I wasn't naive. This area of the palace grounds typically saw maybe twenty Hell Fae throughout the day, most of them opting to enter through the main doors around front, not the back doors.

Yet several dozen had meandered by throughout the last hour, confirming word had spread that the Hell Fae Prince and his new mate were picnicking out here.

If they thought they were being clever with their sneak

peeks at us, they were wrong. I saw them. Each glance. Every tiny smile. Glimmers of intrigue. All of it.

However, I didn't mind.

This was all part of being a member of Ty's personal court, and it was something Cami needed to get used to.

Once the privacy barrier—not too dissimilar from the one Ajax had crafted the other day in the Netherworld Kingdom—settled into place, I magicked up another cappuccino for Cami, handed it to her, and set about finishing my crêpe.

Cami watched me. "That hum wasn't an answer, and your thoughts suggest Lucifer's training will be different."

"Because it will be different," I said before shoveling a bite into my mouth.

She stared at me. "So we're back to riddles?"

I studied her as I chewed, then swallowed. "No. I'm just hungry."

"And now you're stalling."

"Actually, I'm eating, something you should do, too," I replied as I gestured to her barely touched plate.

"If I eat, will you at least try to give me useful information?"

I arched a brow. "I believe I've already done that and more, little angel." I took another bite.

Meanwhile, she eyed her cup, her thoughts telling me she was debating throwing it in my face. But she quickly decided that would be a waste of perfectly good caffeine.

"Thank you," I murmured, acknowledging the result of her mental debate. "Hot coffee is quite unpleasant."

She huffed. "You'd deserve it."

"I wouldn't," I told her, tossing back my final bite before setting my plate aside. *I've been very forthcoming,* I added mentally. *And I made you come four times this morning on my tongue.*

Her cheeks reddened beautifully, the flush creeping down to her collarbone and disappearing beneath her tight tank top. A gorgeous sight, one that had me regretting her afternoon plans.

Fucking all day would be far more fun than what Ty had in store for her.

Alas, his training was important.

"I'm not trying to be vague or provide half-truths," I went on, returning to a verbal conversation. "I showed you what the Hell Fae Brides are up to because it's important to understand how they're changing and what it means."

"Okay," she conceded. "Tell me what it means."

I smiled at the hint of sass underscoring those words. If Ty were here, he'd arch a brow and likely start musing about various punishments for her demanding little mouth.

But I wasn't Ty.

And honestly, I probably deserved that command after all my perceived "crypticness."

"The Hell Fae Source is finally accepting females," I told her. "That's what it means. And you, my darling little angel, are the reason for that."

She frowned. "Because I keep touching the Source?"

I shook my head. "No. Because you're teaching our Hell Fae King how to trust again. His openness toward you, the fact that he's accepting you into his inner circle, is changing the very landscape of magic in this realm. And it's bringing a much-needed balance to the equation."

Rather than give her a chance to comment, I elaborated on how the Source was connected to Ty, how the beacon of energy was empowered by his essence, and how that connection created an ingrained bias.

"Because Vivaxia betrayed him," she said, her thoughts providing a glimpse into what she knew about the situation between Ty and Vivaxia. It wasn't much, something I needed to fix.

"It's so much deeper than a betrayal," I murmured. "Which is something Ty should explain, but I'm not sure he can."

He trusted Cami now; that wasn't the problem. It was more that Ty might struggle to recount the history in a fluent manner.

So many of his memories were kept in Vita, allowing his mind to thrive despite his ancient history. The unique outlet granted him a way to conceal past hurts and to heal.

And opening up that historical thread might bring back too much pain, a weakness he couldn't afford to embrace right now. Not in our current state of vulnerabilities.

"So that's why Vita stores his memories—to help open up his mind to new experiences. That's fascinating," Cami marveled aloud after I explained why he might not be able to tell her everything about Vivaxia's betrayal.

"Yes," I confirmed. Then I pushed forward and elaborated on the deal he'd made with Vivaxia—the one that had freed Azazel and essentially protected me—and explained how Ty thought he'd won. "She wanted him to be her mate, but he knew deep down that they weren't compatible. That his soul would reject her upon the final level."

Cami frowned. "He knew?"

I nodded. "Just like I knew my soul would eagerly mate yours. On some level, we all know. But knowing requires caring."

At her puzzled expression, I went on to tell her how Vivaxia had been too caught up in her own ego to even consider that her soul might be incompatible with Ty's soul.

Or maybe she knew all along, I thought to myself, thinking about her note from the other day. *Maybe she's been playing the long game.*

Ty had wondered something similar, his mind having puzzled out that perhaps she'd anticipated his rejection and had waited until he had something of true value to take from him.

"Their deal was crafted around his power, his *light*. That's why she wanted to mate him—to steal his gifts. And she layered that agreement to ensure she could. Only, his energy isn't something that can just be taken. Hence the cause of his fall."

I elaborated a bit more on those events, how the Virtuous Fae Source shattered as a result of Vivaxia's deal, and how the end result was him creating the Hell Fae Realm in what used to be considered Virtuous Fae wastelands.

Some of the details were ones she'd already heard, and some were new. But repeating this information mattered because I needed her to fully grasp the history to understand the present.

"His power has been growing ever since," I stressed. "And that growth has consequences, Cami."

She leaned forward, her food still forgotten on her plate.

I considered reminding her to eat. However, time was not on our side. And I wanted to finish this conversation before Ty arrived with Ajax.

So I continued by telling her my concerns out loud.

My concerns about the Source and how large it had become.

My concerns about the impact on Ty's soul.

My concerns about potential vulnerabilities throughout the realm.

And ended with my biggest concern of all. "Ty is at

risk of losing control." The words were so soft, spoken as a whisper between us. Because I'd never once admitted them out loud.

Oh, Ty had overheard the worries in my thoughts. But I'd never been so blunt before.

"He won't admit it. Or perhaps he simply can't. However, the truth is he's exerting too much energy, has taken on too much of a burden, and it's only a matter of time now before everything implodes." I paused to let all the information settle between us, my heart racing in my chest.

This was a lot to confide in her, and it was also a lot to lay on her shoulders. But she needed to know what she meant to me, to *us*.

"These Hell Fae Bride Trials were about finding mates for the Hell Fae, but they were also about finding a Hell Fae Queen," I added, voice still low. "Ty just hasn't realized that yet. However, he's beginning to. Because he's finally starting to see *you*. Now you just need to see it in yourself. And that, my sweet angel, is what today's training is about."

CHAPTER 12

TYPHOS

T*y just hasn't realized that yet…*
Those words reverberated through my mind, my connection to Melek allowing me to hear most of his current conversation with Camillia.

None of the reveals were new to me. I was very familiar with Melek's concerns, despite his attempt at hiding them from me. However, he was right about Camillia changing my outlook on everything.

That alluring little enchantress had achieved the impossible and had broken through each of my walls.

I'd fought her, thought I hated her, even. But now… now I saw her potential as an ally.

And so much more, a dark voice whispered in my head.

Ajax cleared his throat beside me, snaring my attention once more. Distrust swirled in his blue-black eyes, his expression exuding a lack of patience. Probably because I'd been in the middle of lecturing him about dark souls, only to freeze when Melek had started thinking about the true purpose of the Hell Fae Bride Trials.

He'd been focused on Camillia, but his thoughts had

been loud as he'd formulated what to say and how to voice it.

My little prince had been forthcoming, a trait I knew he struggled with deep down. He might not mean to be cryptic—another term floating through his mind on repeat —but he adored riddles and puzzles. Words were merely a tool to be used in a game.

However, he'd forced himself to be coherent and informative with Camillia. *You really love her,* I whispered to him.

He didn't reply, but I knew he'd heard me. And I felt his agreement pulse through our bond.

"Do you love Camillia?" I asked my Warden, causing the distrust to deepen in his expression.

"Why? What are you planning to do to her?"

"Make her a queen," I answered bluntly. "But that's not why I asked. I..." I frowned, not actually sure how to voice the reason for my question. "Melek loves her. I wondered if you do as well."

"She's my mate."

I waited for him to elaborate. When he didn't, I arched a brow at him. "That's not the same thing, Warden. Azazel is my mate, and I love him like a brother, not a lover."

"Cami is my lover."

"And that's still not the same as saying *you* love her."

"How I feel about Cami is none of your fucking business," he bit back. "And I don't see how it's relevant to what we're doing here."

I sighed. "It's not. I... I shouldn't have asked." Because he was right. At this point, his feelings weren't my business.

But I wanted them to be my business.

Which was a revelation in and of itself. One I wasn't ready to face yet. However, I wasn't sure I had a choice on that front.

Melek had thought about time being of the essence, mostly in terms of when I'd arrive for Camillia's training. Except deep down, he'd been thinking about the Source, too.

My imploding power.

My potential inability to hold this realm together.

My need for help. *From a queen.*

"Melek thinks Camillia can balance my power," I confided in Ajax, causing his brow to furrow. "If he's right, then your love for her will be imperative. Because she'll need you and Azazel for balance, too."

When he just stared at me, I decided to elaborate and shared everything Melek had just told Camillia. I wasn't sure what he already knew, so I didn't leave out a single detail.

And by the end, it seemed a little of that distrust had left his expression.

Or perhaps that was just wishful thinking.

Either way, I'd bared my soul in a way I'd never done before.

"Even if Melek is wrong about her potential as a queen, Camillia is at risk," I went on. "Because if I implode, Azazel and Melek will be impacted."

"Which Cami will feel and experience, too," he translated.

"As well as you," I pointed out. "So you can hate me all you want, Ajax, but you need me right now. And I need you."

His expression appeared to thaw just a tad bit more. "All right. And you think having Cami extinguish a dark soul is where her training should begin?"

I nodded. "Yes. The goal is to help her learn how to focus her power and master her control over it. This is also a simple task, one that she should be able to handle quickly. Which, if I'm right, will boost some of her confidence, something I think she needs."

He considered me for a moment before angling his chin in agreement. "All right. I see your logic."

"So you'll support my training exercise?"

"Support it how?" he countered.

"By being my Warden," I replied. "I'll be focused on Camillia's powers and ensuring they don't grow out of control. Which means I need you focused on the prisoner."

"I assume you have a certain prisoner in mind?" Ajax drawled, arching a brow.

My lips curled. "Indeed I do." The perfect one for Ajax to watch die. "You recall what I said about these dark souls? How I've trapped them in a nightmarish form as punishment?"

"And then had me supervise them under the guise that all Nightmare Fae had to be tamed?" Some of that distrust returned to his expression. "How could I forget?"

"I deserve that note of sarcasm," I admitted. "But at some point, you're going to need to take my apologies seriously."

"Oh, taking them seriously isn't the problem," he drawled. "It's believing them that's an issue."

"I don't think believing them is the issue," I countered. "I think *accepting* them is the problem." I folded my arms to mimic his defensive stance. "You're angry, and rightly so. I should have explained who you were guarding from the beginning. I didn't. I acknowledge that mistake. Now I'm going to make amends."

"By training me properly," he muttered. "Yeah, I got that."

My lips curled. "No. By giving you a dark soul whose extermination I think you'll very much enjoy."

That eyebrow of his arched even higher, reminding me a bit of myself.

Maybe that was what drew me to Ajax in the beginning—our kinship. I saw myself in his suffering. He was angry. I'd been angry, too.

Hell, I was still *angry*.

But I channeled it into power and protection, something I suspect he would do now that he had someone he cared about. *Someones*, actually. Because I had no doubt he would guard Azazel and Camillia with the same ferocity and passion.

"There's someone I've kept here, a soul that Zakkai and Shade wanted to be imprisoned and tortured in a very unique way. I'm not sure if they ever told anyone else. By your expression right now, I'm guessing not," I went on, noting Ajax's piqued curiosity. "Zakkai removed her life source from the Midnight Fae Source, and I tied her to the Hell Fae Source instead."

"Her?" Ajax repeated.

"Well, you have noticed some of the Nightmare Fae in your dungeon are females, yes?" I asked, causing the Warden to roll his eyes.

"Yes. The Sirens are notably irritating."

I smirked. "The Sirens are not the only ones. I've trapped dark souls in all sorts of forms."

I paused then and realized this also served as a teaching opportunity.

"Before the Hell Fae Bride Trials, the dark souls under your watch were some of the only females I allowed in my realm," I explained. "The other females in my realm are mates of high-ranking and well-trusted fae, and there are very few of them. But the dark souls kept here are actively being judged by the Source. And I masked many of them in nightmarish forms that rivaled their inner sins."

In this case, I'd chosen an Unseelie, as they were known for their trickery. They also valued beauty, which wasn't exactly a sin but could be if vain enough.

And this female—the one Zakkai and Shade had brought me—was notoriously vain.

A treasure hunter. A betrayer. A wannabe black widow without the power or prowess to properly slay.

Uttering all those facts out loud had Ajax staring at me. Hard. "Who did they give you?"

"A Midnight Fae named Dakota."

Ajax visibly stiffened. "She helped Constantine kill…" He trailed off, pain flashing in his eyes. He didn't need to finish his statement. I knew what he meant to say—*She helped Constantine kill my parents. She helped Constantine kill Emelyn.*

I might not have been there that dark day, but I knew all about the executions Constantine had carried out in the Midnight Fae village.

He'd encapsulated several fae with a spell, holding them captive while he'd killed loved ones after claiming the Midnight Fae Council had agreed to their fates.

"Dakota led several of the accused up to that podium," I said softly. "And that was after all of the manipulative acts she conducted on Constantine's behalf. Today is her judgment day."

"That bitch has been in my dungeon for ten fucking years?" Ajax snapped, seeming to come out of his morose state and diving headfirst into one fueled by fury.

I saw his fist coming before his arm even flinched.

Still, I let his knuckles meet my cheekbone, more than ready to accept his brutality. He had a right to be angry. Perhaps not at me, but I'd be that outlet for him if he needed it.

Typhos, Az whispered into my mind. *Why does Ajax suddenly want to kill you?*

It's fine.

That's not—

It's fine, Azazel, I replied as Ajax took out a wand.

"You put that treacherous bitch in an Unseelie form and let me *guard* her?" the Midnight Fae seethed. "I ought to—"

"Go grab her and deliver her for Camillia to destroy?" I interjected while voicing my words as more of a suggestion than a demand.

He narrowed his gaze. "I'm not letting that bitch anywhere near Camillia."

"In her current state, there's not much she can do. And you'll ensure she stays that way." I started walking down the corridor, not bothering to tell Ajax to follow because he was already right on my heels.

"You have no idea what that crazy fae has done."

"Oh, I'm very aware of *everything* she's done," I countered. "That's why I accepted her soul from Zakkai. She more than earned her fate here."

Which served as yet another lesson for Ajax.

For a decade, he thought his role was to simply guard the rogue Nightmare Fae. Little did he realize those rogues weren't really Nightmare Fae but fae of other origin whom I'd subjected to this prison to live out their worst fears.

Hence the reason so many of them were dangerous and angry.

The paradigm had become a courtyard of sorts while preparing for the Hell Fae Bride Trials, something that had served two purposes.

First, it'd allowed some of my dungeon dwellers to taste a bit of freedom and amplify hope—hope that they might escape. Only for that freedom and hope to be yanked away.

And secondly, it'd provided a training ground for the trials.

I'd let some of the dark souls roam free to see which candidates could see through their mirages, and also to test the goodness of the brides.

So many female fae wanted to join the Hell Fae Realm, as evidenced by all the agreements I'd penned that had allowed them to participate in the trials. Some of them were agreements between me and their parents, but most were between me and the fae themselves.

Naturally, I hadn't trusted any of their motives.

Which had led me to craft a purpose for all the dark souls lingering in my dungeons.

Some of Ajax's ire dissipated as I explained all that while we walked, his interest piqued once more.

"How do they live out their worst fears?" he asked, focused on that tidbit of information.

"In a myriad of ways. Each dark soul's imprisonment is personally crafted, like that cell you once put Camillia in with the enchanted furniture," I told him, recalling that event clearly. "The whole purpose had been to make her uncomfortable."

I might not have visited personally, but I knew what had been done.

Just as I'd known about my little prince trying to enhance her accommodations. *So many plays. So many games. All of it so much clearer now. Hmm.*

I hear you thinking about me, my king, the male in question murmured into my mind.

Always, I replied, layering that single word with affection and promise. Because I was suddenly in a punishing mood.

Which had me all the more excited for Camillia's training this afternoon.

Is she ready? I asked him.

As ready as she can be, I think.

Good, I replied, pausing outside of Dakota's cell door. *See you soon, little prince.*

"Camillia had only been a visitor in this dungeon, not a permanent ward," I said, facing Ajax. "You saw her accommodations as plainly as she did. But as you've learned, mirages are a powerful tool in this realm. And your dungeon is no different."

The more I confided to him, the more I realized how badly I'd fucked this up.

I'd put him in charge of a prison he hadn't fully understood, made him a Warden in name only while my power served as the grand master here. He'd basically been placed here to ensure no one entered or escaped. But I hadn't afforded him the opportunity to truly lead.

That would change.

Starting now.

With a single thought, I unwove the veil around us and let him see the prison for what it truly was—a dungeon of nightmares. Each one shaped for the captive in the cell.

For Dakota, it was a stage.

One I knew he would instantly recognize.

"The village," he whispered, taking a step back as the landscape etched into her walls came into view.

A sea of faces stared at the Unseelie standing in the center of the room. Some shouted spells. Others screamed. And one in particular cursed up a storm.

That female seized Ajax's attention, yanking him toward the door once more. *"Emelyn."*

CHAPTER 13

AZ

SEVERAL MINUTES EARLIER

"F*uck!*" I shook out my hand, then glared at my smirking half brother.

I'd still had some energy to work off after sparring with Ajax earlier, and I'd stupidly decided to seek out Maliki as a potential outlet.

Seems I wasn't the only one spoiling for a fight, I thought, narrowing my gaze.

"Where the hell did you learn that trick?" I demanded, taking in the magical barrier he'd created around his face.

A face I'd just attempted to punch, hence my now aching fist.

"I asked if you wanted limits, and you said no." He shrugged. "Your choice isn't my fault."

"And your response isn't an answer."

"There was a question?" he asked, feigning innocence.

I grunted. "Fine. Keep your secrets. I don't need them." But it was good to know how he wanted to play.

Black flames crawled up my fingertips and over my palms, causing his lips to curl in anticipation.

He crouched.

And I pounced.

Weapons formed in his hands upon impact, the deadly daggers twirling and slicing as I unleashed Phoenixfire all over him. His blades blocked my attacks, sending them back my way to be absorbed into my skin.

My eyes narrowed. It'd been a while since we'd last sparred. Ajax was my preferred partner now. However, recent events had made me a bit nostalgic for my brother. Or perhaps I was just intrigued after our last meeting.

Something was going on with Maliki. Something big. It might not be my place to learn more, but my curiosity was piqued. So I figured I'd drop by for some sparring and some potential answers.

But it seemed my brother only wanted to fight.

Fine by me.

Ajax had ramped me up with all his brooding and quiet fury. He didn't trust Typhos. While I might not feel the same way—because I could hear Typhos's current intentions—I understood Ajax's feelings.

And, unfortunately, it was up to Typhos to regain Ajax's faith.

Which he seemed to be doing a piss-poor job of right now because every time I checked on Ajax, all I heard was murderous thoughts.

Typhos had kept a lot from him.

I supposed I had as well, something Ajax and I would need to work out later. But the prison's wards and the magic within it weren't mine to reveal or to explain. Those cells and the souls inside of them belonged to Typhos.

Only, I couldn't help feeling a twinge of guilt for how

much I'd kept from Ajax over the last decade of friendship. It hadn't been intentional, just intrinsic.

Typhos was my mate. Therefore, I protected him and safeguarded his secrets.

But Ajax was mine now, too, and in a very different way from Typhos. I probably—

Pain lanced through my jaw as Maliki's fist connected squarely with my face.

No. Not his fist. His fucking *foot*.

"I thought we were sparring," he drawled. "But you're over there daydreaming."

I grunted and spit a mouthful of blood onto the ground. "You're an asshole."

He threw his arms wide, his lips curling into a cocky grin. "Never claimed to be a saint, big brother."

"All right." I called upon my sword, the enchanted blade appearing as easily as my Phoenix.

Maliki's golden irises swirled with similar power, his own weapon appearing, the magic flickering with golden specks while mine burned with violet flames.

"Rules?" he asked, giving me a chance to set the terms again.

"None," I replied, a growl underscoring the word. He might have adopted some new tricks, but so had I. *Because of Ajax and Cami.*

Crouching, I waited for Maliki to make his move.

That smirk died on his face as he disappeared into a shadowy mist, his essence all over the vacant Soul Yards we'd chosen to spar in. This was his playground, the cemetery-like field littered with eerie magic that flickered in the air.

But unlike the ghostly strands of old souls floating around, my brother's spirit was very much alive.

And connected to mine in a way no one else's was.

Because he was my flesh and blood. Which made it easier than it should be to focus on his ghostly form.

My sword shifted left only to swing back to the right and clash against his metallic blade, sending purple and gold sparks up into the air.

He disappeared again and we repeated the dance, causing another lightning bolt to shoot up from our position.

I didn't watch where that jolt ended, but heard it explode somewhere high in the sky.

We'd have an audience soon, the Death Fae no doubt seeing our light show from their nearby castle. *Let them come*, I thought. *Let them fear me.*

Some of those assholes had tried to kill me a few days ago. Manipulated or not, the hurt still remained.

Sure, I would have come back. *I think, anyway.*

But that wasn't the fucking point.

They'd attacked me and I was *not* pleased. They needed a reminder of my position as Hell Fae Commander. A reeducation on what the fuck that actually meant.

And Maliki was the perfect one to help me provide that lesson.

Our swords clanked again, drawing a maniacal laugh from my insane little brother. He craved lethality. Enjoyed the sensation that came with living on the edge, never knowing what may or may not be his last breath.

Some might even say he yearned for death.

Crazy bastard, I thought, matching him move for move as we parried across the Soul Yards. Maliki leapt over one of the deep rivets in the ground, his Corpse Fae energy kicking in as he ghosted through the souls streaming upward from the cavern below.

I made to follow, only my limbs locked in place as a shock of pain rippled through me.

Pain that came from the *inside*, not the outside.

My feet teetered on the edge of the steep cliff, a chilly spirit brushing within an inch of my nose.

Maliki was suddenly there and yanking me backward, concern etched into his features. "What is it?" he demanded, suggesting I'd released some sort of sound or an expression to indicate my sudden agony.

"Ajax," I whispered, locking in on my mate's dark suffering.

Words and images floated through his mind, all focused on his past. *Constantine. Dakota. Emelyn. Anrika.* When the names of his parents came next, I left Maliki behind in a cloud of ash and went straight for the dungeons.

All while cursing Typhos.

He'd let the wards fall, allowing Ajax to see the interior of Dakota's cell. It was her own personal hell, one framed by the screams of the lives she'd helped Constantine take.

Lives that meant something to Ajax.

Screams that would destroy his heart.

Force him back into a time he didn't want to live.

Make him relive that fated day…

Cami's voice echoed in my mind as she screamed Ajax's name, her energy latching on to mine as we both went straight to Ajax's side.

Typhos didn't react, almost as though he'd expected our arrival. A beat later, his mind confirmed it.

This was the training.

His fucked-up version of revealing the truth to Ajax while also providing Cami with a safe place to react and use her power.

My hands curled into fists. *Typhos.*

Give it a moment, he told me, his mental voice layered with command.

But Melek looked just as concerned as I did when he popped in a blink later, his glittering feathers disappearing in an instant. "I thought we were meeting in the palace courtyard."

"Change of plan," Typhos replied quietly.

"What the hell is this?" Cami demanded in the next breath. "What are you doing to him?"

"I'm showing him the truth," Typhos answered simply.

"And what truth is that?" she asked, her fury a whip against my senses. She was angry on Ajax's behalf. Angry that he was hurting. Angry that she couldn't fix it. Angry that she didn't fully understand it or what Typhos meant to do here. *"You're hurting him."*

Typhos frowned. "No, I'm not. His past pain has nothing to do with me. If anything, I've helped him."

"By what?" She flung her arms outward. "By putting him in charge of your little dungeon of horrors?"

Typhos pushed off the door frame, his crossed arms falling to his sides as he stared down at my fiery little mate. "Dungeon of horrors?" he echoed, his brow furrowing. "This sacred space has a very specific purpose, Camillia. One I was in the middle of demonstrating to Ajax. It's a place where bad souls are punished."

She scoffed at that. "You mean souls you tricked into accepting a deal—one designed in a manner that favored you, not them. And now you're punishing them for reneging or failing whatever terms you laid out."

His lips flattened into a straight line. "Not only is that summary inaccurate, but it's inadequate as well."

Cami stepped toward him, her gray eyes flickering with the power of an incoming thunderstorm. "I don't care if you feel it's accurate or not. Ajax is suffering. Fix it," she said through her teeth.

He studied her for a long moment, then went back to leaning against the door frame, his expression bored. "Why don't you fix it for me?" he suggested. "Use my Source. Siphon my power. And remove the cause of his suffering."

Typhos, I said into his mind.

Let me teach, Azazel, he returned.

This isn't teaching. It was pissing her off instead, a fact I was about to add, but he started speaking into my mind before I had the chance.

Just because this isn't the way you would teach her doesn't make it the wrong way. It's simply different. And different methods should be respected.

I sighed. *All right.* He wasn't wrong. But he wasn't exactly correct either.

Because Ajax was being ripped open by the display before him, the screams shattering his heart into a million pieces, all while he stood as frozen as Dakota did inside her cell.

Of course, Dakota wasn't recognizable in this form at all.

And, truthfully, I would have had no idea who the soul inside this creature was had I not been connected to Typhos's thoughts.

On the outside, she resembled a tattered Unseelie. Wings shredded to ribbons. Hair yanked out in some places, while dirty clumps hung from others. Eyes wild. Dried lips circled in a perpetual scream that couldn't be heard.

Probably because she no longer had a voice.

A decade in this dungeon was enough to render most fae mindless.

Typhos was excellent at many things; torture was chief among them.

He'd crafted this "reality" in a way that forced Dakota to face all her darkest sins over and over again. To hear the pleas and cries of those who had been killed while she'd helped a monster try to seize a realm. But what couldn't be seen were the sensations that went with the agonized shouts.

Typhos wasn't just forcing her to witness it all, but to experience each death as well. To feel their distress. Their fear. Their *hurt*.

Every cell in this dungeon was uniquely designed, and this was the personal nightmare he'd manifested for Dakota. One he'd spent ample time crafting because he'd wanted her to suffer more than most.

It was a nightmare he'd visited several times over the last ten years to perfect, something I heard in his mind now.

He'd ensured this soul paid for her sins tenfold. *For Ajax*, I realized.

And you, Typhos whispered back to me. *He's always meant a lot to you. Therefore, he means a lot to me.*

The words were a breath in my mind while his eyes were on Cami.

She looked ready to kill Typhos. Only a minute had passed since we'd arrived. Maybe two. But she'd amassed a hell of a lot of distrust over the last sixty or so seconds. "What game is this?" she demanded. "You force me to watch Ajax suffer while you offer me some sort of deal involving your power? Say you'll let me use it... but for a price?"

"We're not negotiating, Camillia De la Croix."

"Then what are we doing?" she asked through her teeth.

"Well, I'm observing," he drawled. "And you appear to be stalling while Ajax suffers."

Her lips parted.

Melek shook his head.

And I... I just sighed. Again. "Cami—"

"No," Typhos interjected, cutting me a look. "This is between me, Cami, and Ajax."

Melek moved to my side, his power seeming to hum beneath his skin. But he remained silent as he watched the Hell Fae King with our mate.

My teeth clenched. *She doesn't understand.*

I know, Typhos returned. *And that's my burden to take on, not yours.*

I shook my head. He was going to make this worse. But his words from earlier played back through my mind. While this might not be the way I would handle it, that didn't make his way wrong.

Fine.

I took a step back, hands up, and let him lead.

Two minutes, I told him. *Then I'm intervening.*

I won't need more than one, he promised me.

Yeah, we'd see about that.

Because at this rate, Cami was going to try to hit him before she listened to him. We both could hear Ajax's mind and the broken thoughts fluttering through it. He was standing right in front of us, but he wasn't *with* us.

He was back in the Midnight Fae Realm.

Standing on a podium.

Locked down under a spell.

And watching everyone he loved... *die.*

CHAPTER 14

AJAX

"Salayla and Tor of the Death Fae have knowingly aided and abetted abominations throughout the Midnight Fae Realm," Constantine Nacht announced, his voice carrying through the village square.

I could hear him.

Understand him.

See him.

Yet I… I couldn't feel his power. His energy. His sense of existence.

Because he's not real, I told myself. *He's not here.*

But his words… his words were *very* real.

"Salayla and Tor of the Death Fae have also declared their allegiance to the Quandary Bloods," he went on, causing the crowd to shout in fury.

Not at Constantine, but at Salayla and Tor.

My parents.

I blinked, trying to look away from them. But my focus was on the stage, on Constantine, on this farce of a trial.

Yet inside I wanted to *scream*. To *burn*. To annihilate every fucking traitor in this square.

This is wrong, I thought. *So fucking wrong.*

Why can't I move?

Constantine's spell...

Whispers of it hummed in my ear, his magic paralyzing and forcing me to watch my parents' executions. *And Emelyn's...*

How do I know that? I wondered.

Because I've lived this day before, I realized in the next beat. *None of this is real.*

Oh, it'd happened long, long ago.

That wand glittering with red magic. The words that came next that solidified my parents' fate. The spell that marbleized my parents' skin as they knelt and pleaded with the crowd to save them.

I shivered inside, the vivid execution playing out in my mind.

Yet Constantine was still talking before me. Still listing offenses from that damn scroll clutched in his hands.

"Based on the testimonies provided by their son, Ajax—"

I stopped listening, my eyes narrowing.

I hadn't provided any testimonies. It was all bullshit. A mental mindfuck meant to break me. To shatter my parents. To *hurt*.

And it had.

Oh, fuck, had it *hurt*.

Followed by Emelyn's...

I swallowed, my gaze sliding to her back. She stood still as stone several paces before me, trapped under the same spell.

They would unfreeze her soon, just like my parents, and then...

I closed my eyes, refusing to relive this scene.

It's not real.

It's an illusion.

Manufactured by… by Lucifer.

My brow furrowed, that last thought kick-starting my heart.

Lucifer.

We were in his dungeon. He was showing me Dakota's cell. Her personal prison. Her hellscape. Her *nightmare.*

He was forcing her to relive her sins, but it went deeper than that. I could… I could feel it through Cami.

Her face appeared in my mind, her beautiful, angelic features taking my breath away. *My Cami.*

I'm here, she told me. *I'm right here, Ajax.*

I opened my eyes, wanting to see her, and found myself staring into Emelyn's eyes instead. Dark orbs. Dark hair. A face painted in perpetual fear and torment.

My last memory of her, I realized, my chest aching. *That's not what I want to remember.*

I wanted to think about her secret smile. Her laugh that no one else ever heard. Her happiness that no one else ever saw.

My first love.

Except… that no longer felt right.

I'd cared about Emelyn. Valued her friendship. Enjoyed her company. Loved that I could provide her with joy in a dark time.

But as I observed her in this cruel montage, reliving her death all over again, my chest ached a little less. Because my heart belonged to another now.

Does that make me selfish? I wondered, staring at Emelyn. *Am I selfish to love another? To love someone… more?*

I couldn't ask her because she wasn't really here. Yet I suddenly knew what she would say. *You deserve to be loved, Ajax. You deserve so much more than this…*

They were words from long ago.

Words she'd said to me once during a walk through the woods.

She'd never proclaimed to be the one who would love me the way I deserved, and now... now I understood why.

Because our love was nothing like the feelings I possessed for Cami. It didn't touch how I felt about Az, either.

They were my mates. My reasons for life. My *heart*. I breathed for them. My soul was theirs in every way.

And Emelyn had started me down the path toward that fate.

Her loss meant more than I could ever have realized. Because without it, I wouldn't be here. I wouldn't have become Lucifer's Warden. I wouldn't have met Az. *I wouldn't have met Cami.*

I wasn't someone who indulged in thoughts of guardian angels or predestined paths; that was Shade's chessboard, not mine.

However, I understood it now. Saw the big picture. Realized that everything I'd been through had shaped me into the fae I needed to be for Cami and Az. To be their mate.

Emelyn blinked before me, her eyes falling closed as though for the last time.

Only that wasn't how it had happened that fated day— she'd looked right at me while she'd died. Held my gaze with her last breath.

But this simulation had her closing her eyes... *in peace.*

What was it that Lucifer had said? These cells were magicked for their inhabitants. Crafted to create nightmarish hellscapes to torture his prisoners.

So why is the visage changing? I wondered.

Because you're not a dark soul, Az whispered into my mind. *Typhos devised this room to punish Dakota... for you.*

I frowned, my limbs finally thawing as I turned to look at Lucifer. "Why?"

"Because I couldn't give you Constantine," he said quietly, somehow following my question. Maybe because of Azazel. Maybe because he anticipated my query. I didn't know. Nor did I care.

Typhos stepped closer to me, his sapphire eyes swirling with power as he held my gaze, making it impossible to look away.

"You were so riddled with pain and anger when we first met. I had to do something to avenge you. Something to make it right. When Zakkai and Shade brought her to me, I knew what I had to do. And now it's time for you to decide what's next. Do you want to end her suffering? Strengthen it? Leave her in this state for another decade?"

I stared up at him, at a loss for words.

When he'd told me to meet him in this dungeon, I'd assumed it would be some meager lesson about how to pick a creature for Cami to practice her magic on. While I'd somewhat begun to understand that dark souls were masked as Nightmare Fae, meaning none of the beings housed here were true Nightmare Fae, I had no idea how deep the magic went or how intricate everything was.

"You should have explained this place to me long ago," I told him now, both irritated and awed at the same time. "You basically made me a babysitter for your pet project."

"I did," he conceded. "And now I want to make you a true Warden, to give you my masterpiece and let you manage it however you want."

"Why?" I wondered out loud. "Why would you give this to me?"

"Because I've extended my powers too far. I need

help." He looked away from me and toward someone just behind me.

Cami, I realized, sensing her heat and scenting her flowery perfume. She'd said she was here. I'd known that. And yet, I'd been so consumed by Lucifer that I'd nearly forgotten.

"Melek told you I created the trials to find a mate. Or a queen, I believe." Typhos glanced at Melek and then back at Cami. "Maybe I did. Maybe I didn't. The point is moot. You're part of this circle now, regardless of your feelings for me." His focus shifted to me. "As are you. Which means it's up to all of us to find balance, to ensure this realm survives. Making you a true Warden is the obvious next step."

I studied him for a moment, thinking through everything he'd said to me over the last... *Fuck, was it only an hour or so?*

It felt like he'd imparted a lifetime of knowledge upon me in a day.

But something he'd said to me before reaching this cell played through my mind now, reminding me of what had brought us all here to begin with. *Cami's training.*

He'd wanted to select a dark soul for her to extinguish, to help her learn control while also offering me a gift of sorts.

Dakota's death.

She'd been the one to walk my parents up onto that stage. Emelyn, too.

I could still hear her taunting *laugh*.

Only, she wasn't laughing now. Actually, she appeared almost dead. "Is she even coherent anymore?" I asked.

"You tell me," Lucifer returned, clearly taking his role as teacher seriously.

Rather than press him, I focused on Dakota. But then I thought better of it. "Cami?"

"Yeah?"

I glanced back at her. "Can you sense anything? With Dakota, I mean?"

Cami frowned and moved to my side. "I…" She trailed off and swallowed. "I only sense darkness in her."

"What do you sense in Ajax?" Lucifer inquired softly.

Cami shot him a look, one that said she wasn't pleased with him. "Pain. Because of you."

Lucifer grunted. "Look deeper, Camillia."

"Why?" she fired back, her feisty energy causing my lips to quirk. Leave it to Camillia De la Croix to amuse me in an otherwise dark situation.

"Because he's trying to teach you," Melek interjected. "This might not be the venue Ty originally intended to use for today's lesson, but he's improvising."

Cami crossed her arms. "And I'm supposed to just accept that?"

"Are you intentionally being a brat?" Lucifer asked, arching a brow at her. "Because you should know that I have a penchant for putting brats in their places."

That only had Cami narrowing her eyes more. "I am *not* being a brat."

Melek coughed.

"I'm not!" She threw her hands out to the sides and spun to face me. "Lucifer hurt you, then told me to use his power to help end your suffering."

"He wanted you to kill Dakota," I translated, nodding. "That's the training exercise—extinguishing a dark soul."

Her lips parted, her arms falling at her sides. "He wants me to *kill* someone?" She turned on Lucifer in the next blink. "Why the hell would I want to *kill* someone?"

I winced.

When Lucifer and I had been discussing our plans, I hadn't quite considered *this* potential reaction. But seeing her fury now, I wasn't exactly surprised by it.

Cami wasn't a killer, let alone an executioner.

Fuck, I thought. *This is going to get bad...*

CHAPTER 15

AJAX

While my mind spun with potential ways to fix this, Lucifer pressed onward.

Because he clearly didn't grasp or sense Cami's mounting fury.

"You want a reason?" he asked, sounding bored. "Okay. That *someone* hurt your mate. You felt his pain. She was part of the cause. And if you look into her soul, you'll see just how dark and twisted it is, how there's no coming back from everything she's done. So technically speaking, she deserves to live in agony for eternity. But I'm offering you a chance to end her cruel existence, should you choose to."

"*Cruel* is a rather ironic term coming from you, given that you're the one who created this *cruel existence*," she told him.

"No, Dakota did that to herself," I said before Lucifer could explain. "All of the cells are crafted by the inhabitants' nightmares. Their memories and sins create the illusions; Lucifer's magic just fuels them to life."

She blinked at me. "Wait. Do you... do you *agree* with this lesson?"

"I agree that Dakota should die," I answered vehemently. "But if you don't want to kill her, I'll do it myself."

She blinked at me. Then she looked at the still-frozen Unseelie inside the room. She hadn't moved an inch despite her cell door being wide open. She literally couldn't. Because her nightmare had essentially turned her into a statue—just like Constantine's magic had done to me.

"Okay, so... so maybe she deserves it," Cami conceded after a long, thoughtful moment. "But what about the others? How many of these *dark souls* are here because of deals you tricked them into signing?" Those questions seemed to be for Lucifer because she looked at him, not at me. "We both know your deals are never fair."

"Do we?" he countered. "Or do you just assume you know everything about *my* deals?"

"Can you prove otherwise?" she challenged him.

"Yes," he answered without hesitation, causing her jaw to snap shut. She obviously wasn't expecting him to respond so quickly and adamantly in the affirmative. "In fact, I think that's where you and I will go once this is done. Because you clearly need a lesson on how I draft agreements."

She took a step away from him, only to realize that it put her nearly in Dakota's cell, so she paused mid-move. "I..." Her brow furrowed, and she returned to her spot beside me, only she fully focused on Lucifer. "You would show me your deals?"

"Yes." Uttering the word the second time had the same effect as before, causing Cami to blink at him.

He arched a brow, his expression challenging her now, just as she had with her previous tone.

She remained silent in response.

"Well?" he taunted. "What do you see in Dakota? Is she redeemable?"

Cami's jaw ticked, but rather than reply, she looked at the former Midnight Fae. It only took her a few seconds to say, "No. She's not."

"Why not?" Lucifer pressed. "Because of how Ajax feels about her?"

Cami slowly shook her head. "There's no light inside her."

"And what about Ajax? How much light is inside him?"

Cami looked at me, her gaze assessing. "He has some spots of gray, but his soul is good and his intentions are admirable."

"Now evaluate me," Lucifer dared her.

"No," she replied.

"Why not?"

"Because I'm not ready to see your soul yet," she whispered.

Lucifer stayed quiet for a moment, then conceded with a nod. "Can you sense any of the other dark souls here? In this dungeon?"

She didn't answer right away but eventually gave a small nod.

"How do they compare to Dakota?" he asked.

More silence as she considered his question, the answers seeming to float through her mind as she evaluated all the souls she could sense. It was fascinating to observe as her mate, her ability unique from my own.

I could sense darkness and the occasional intention, but she was almost *tasting* their auras.

Because she's a siphon, I realized, intrigued by how her gift worked.

She was taking a bit of each soul, evaluating their power and how it had been used in the past... and how it would be used if freed from this hell.

Too many of them were unapologetic, including Dakota. All she wanted was status, and she didn't care who she hurt to acquire it.

There was no compassion in her soul. No regard for others. Her only aspiration in life was to seek her own happiness.

Which would have been fine if her happiness weren't manifested by hurting those she considered to be beneath her.

She has no conscience, I heard Cami think. *None at all.*

There were a few others who gave off the same impression and a handful more who derived pleasure in harming others.

By the time Cami finished, she was shivering and shaking her head. "I don't want to stay here."

Melek stepped forward, but Lucifer held up a hand to stop him. "Camillia."

She looked at him, and whatever he saw in her expression silenced him. As I could hear her mind and feel her fear of what this place represented, I understood.

This was too much. She wasn't ready to kill anyone, even a dark soul. Not when she didn't fully understand how all these souls had become so evil.

Part of her still questioned Lucifer's deals, though deep down she seemed to be accepting that perhaps she'd misjudged some of this.

But until she knew for sure, she couldn't proceed.

"Please," she whispered.

Lucifer lifted his palm for her before anyone else could

respond. "Come. You and I will continue this lesson in my den," he said.

She started to lift her hand, then paused. "Just me and you?"

"Yes," he replied. "I want to show you how my agreements work, and the Warden has work to do here." He glanced at me knowingly. "The dungeon is officially his." His focus shifted to Azazel. "I think you should help him."

Az—who had been interestingly silent throughout this entire "lesson"—simply nodded. "There are things we should discuss."

I frowned at that. *What kinds of things?*

Things, he simply echoed in my mind.

"What about Melek?" Cami pressed, drawing my focus to her before I could question Az's vagueness. "No. Let me rephrase. I'll agree, but only if Melek comes with us."

Lucifer's lips curled. "You're negotiating with me? After just criticizing me for my deals?"

She stared at him. "Can he come or not?"

The Hell Fae King's smile grew. "Melek is welcome to go wherever he desires, little one. He's my prince for a reason."

"I'll only go into your den if Melek comes with us," she rephrased.

Lucifer eyed her with open curiosity. "Any other terms?"

"Melek *stays* with me. By my side. Until I say otherwise."

"Those are much better terms," Lucifer praised.

"Melek also takes me to wherever we're going, not you."

"You think I mean to take you somewhere nefarious?"

"*Den* is a vague term," she pointed out, causing Lucifer to fully smile now.

"Someone has been studying deals."

"Someone recently tried to take my mate," she informed him. "I was forced to learn."

Some of Lucifer's amusement died as he glanced at me, aware that she was talking about the mating agreement he'd tried to force on me. "Well, that someone was a fool. But unlike the souls in this prison, he seeks redemption." Completely sober now, he dropped his hand and looked at Melek. "You know where I'm going."

He didn't wait for Melek to confirm, just blinked out of existence and left a solitary burnt feather behind, one that changed form and melted into a golden key.

I stared at it, startled by the magic and what it represented.

He'd said the dungeon was officially mine.

And he'd meant it.

I could feel the magic settling all around me, looking to me as its new master. He hadn't removed his protections or his warped enchantments, just left it behind for me to wield and manage as though it were my own.

I could feel the power of it crawling over my skin, causing the hairs to lift along my arms.

It was… invigorating. Terrifying. *Fucking electrifying.*

"Ajax?" Cami asked, drawing my attention to her. "Are you going to be okay?"

I held her gaze for a beat, fully thinking through her question.

For years, I'd answered similar inquiries with sarcastic retorts or muttered affirmatives. I'd taught myself not to care, because deep down, I hadn't been okay at all. I'd been in pain. Destroyed from the inside out.

But then a little rebel changed everything.

In this very fucking dungeon.

She'd challenged me. Called to me. Made me see her. Fall in love with her.

And Az had been there as the backbone behind it all, coaxing us to play, seducing us in every way.

The two of them had stirred my soul, forced me to live again, and taught me how to heal. I wasn't all the way there yet, but I was on my way. Walking down a path toward a brighter future. One where I would be... okay.

More than okay.

Amazing, even.

Because I had them. I had a family. I had *this*.

I leaned down to pick up the key, aware that it meant so much more than what it resembled. Because this wasn't just about being Warden. It was about being a Hell Fae. About being part of Lucifer's inner circle. About being an extension of his power. About being mated... to the Hell Fae King.

Perhaps not romantically or intimately, but through my bonds with his mates. *Cami via Melek. Az directly.*

We were a circle now. United. Maybe not entirely or completely yet, but we were headed in the right direction.

And because of that... "Yeah," I said, finally answering Cami. "Yeah, I'm going to be okay."

I pulled her in for a kiss and let her hear my mind, feel my emotions, see into my soul.

Thank you, Cami, I whispered into her mind. *Thank you.*

I didn't do anything, she argued as my tongue slid into her mouth.

On the contrary, little rebel. You did everything and so much more. She just didn't understand it yet. *You made my heart beat again. Taught me what love really means. And I'm going to spend eternity ensuring you know just how thankful I am.*

But first, she had a lesson to attend. Just as I had a dungeon to explore.

When you're done playing with deals, let me know, I murmured via our connection. *I want to worship you with my tongue.*

She shivered. *We could just go do that now...*

I smiled against her mouth and shook my head. "I know you're a rebel, Camillia De la Croix. But even you can't renege on a deal with the devil. Now go continue your lesson."

"I didn't actually agree to anything," she pointed out.

"Nor did he force you to," I returned. "So have a little faith and see where it goes."

Her eyes rounded a bit. "You're telling me to trust him?"

"I'm suggesting you give him the benefit of the doubt and see what he wants to show you."

Her brow furrowed. "Did he drug you?"

The key warmed in my palm as my lips curled. "No. He just showed me the truth." I looked over her shoulder at the cell beyond—to Dakota's still form and the faces on her walls. "And now I'm ready to start healing."

Lucifer had punished Dakota for long enough.

It was time for her soul to move on.

And it was time for me to finally let go.

CHAPTER 16

CAMI

L eaving Ajax in the dungeon wasn't easy, but I heard in his mind what he needed to do. And I couldn't watch him execute Dakota.

Did she deserve it? Yes.

Did I want to witness her death? No.

It also wasn't my death to take. Ajax needed his vengeance to heal. Somehow it seemed Lucifer had known that. Or that was what I'd gathered from the thoughts of my mates.

Lucifer had created that nightmare for Dakota as a way to punish her for hurting Ajax.

Because he cared about Ajax. He had from the beginning.

And Lucifer took care of those he cared about.

Hell, it seemed Lucifer took care of *everyone*, not just those in his inner circle. But the entire realm.

Az, I thought as I wrapped my arms tighter around Melek.

It's okay, little warrior, my Phoenix Fae mate murmured into my mind. *I'll look after our Warden.*

Of course he knew that was what I wanted to say. He could hear all my concerns and likely feel my unease. Which meant Ajax could, too.

Thank you, I whispered back to him.

Don't thank me for something I would do naturally, Az returned. *He's my mate, too. And we have some things we need to work out between us.*

My blood warmed a bit at the sensual threat in his tone. *Maybe I should come back...*

His responding chuckle heated my veins even more. *You're always invited to join us, little warrior.*

I was thinking I'd like to watch, I admitted, fantasizing about the two of them together while they *worked out* their issues.

Hmm, he hummed. *That might be fun, too.*

"I don't know what you're saying to Azazel, but I think I like it," Melek said against my ear.

"You can tell I'm talking to Az?"

"I can feel it, yes," he murmured. "And it's obviously a conversation I would enjoy overhearing."

Because he could sense my reaction to Az's commentary. Right. *If I'm not careful, Melek might want to watch, too.*

Not sure Ajax would be keen on that, Az replied.

But you would be?

Today? No. At another point... maybe.

That... that was interesting. *I see.*

Surprised, little warrior?

Yes, I admitted.

I didn't say I want to fuck Melek. But if he wants to watch me master you and Ajax, I wouldn't be opposed.

Just not today? I replied.

Not today, he repeated. *Today... is for Ajax.*

Oh, I whispered back, suddenly understanding. *Because you have… things to work out.*

Yes.

I nodded. Not that he could see me. I was… I glanced around. Well, I was somewhere inside Melek's wings, his gold feathers wrapped around us both as he took us to meet with Lucifer.

His den, he'd said. Whatever the hell *that* meant.

I sighed, suddenly exhausted from everything Melek had shared today coupled with what had just happened in the dungeon. I wasn't sure I had it in me to join Lucifer in his *den,* or wherever the hell we were meeting him.

Goose bumps pebbled my arms, uncertainty settling in my gut. I couldn't handle anything else new right now, not after feeling all those *souls* from the overheated prison.

Fae, I'd forgotten how hot it burned down there.

How uncomfortable it felt to just walk in those corridors.

How horrible it had been my first time there…

Yet my cell had been nothing compared to Dakota's cell. She lived in true purgatory.

"Technically speaking, she deserves to live in agony for eternity. But I'm offering you a chance to end her cruel existence, should you choose to."

Lucifer's words echoed through my mind as the familiar walls of the palace appeared around me and Melek, the flowing lava a welcome sight. Because it meant we weren't going anywhere unique. Just home.

I stilled. *Home,* I repeated to myself. *Is this home?*

It… it felt comfortable. And the scents reminded me of my mates.

Mint.

Embers from a simmering bonfire.

Sin.

Underlined with burning cinnamon.

I inhaled, then frowned at that last bit. *Cinnamon.* That part was Lucifer. My eyes instantly scanned for him, but he was nowhere to be seen. However, I knew exactly where he was—behind the massive double doors ahead.

Doors I recognized.

The Contract Room.

Melek had shown me this before. Only, the chains were no longer crisscrossed and the skull-shaped fastener wasn't spewing flames like the last time I'd been here. The metal doors were also ajar, almost as if to invite us inside.

"He calls this his den?" I asked, raising a brow.

"It's somewhat attached to his den," Melek replied.

I looked at him. "Physically or metaphorically?"

"Both and neither," Lucifer called from behind the doors. "I consider it an extension of my den, and there's a door I can use that connects them. But it's not attached in a typical sense."

Yeah, because that wasn't ominous at all.

Rather than focus on what Lucifer had just said, I opted for another topic. One I used as a distraction from whatever was about to happen behind those heavy doors.

"Did you fly us here?" I asked Melek. "Because usually we travel a lot faster than that." And it felt like I'd been wrapped up in his feathers for several minutes, not seconds.

"I lingered," he replied, the cryptic comment one he left hanging between us like bait.

"Do I even want to ask what that means?"

"He was coating you in his scent," Lucifer answered, this time from the doorway as he poked his head out. "Trying to make you even more alluring than you already are." His sapphire gaze went to Melek. "The tiny shorts and tight white top weren't enough?"

Melek shrugged. "You didn't seem to notice the outfit choice, so I decided to make her skin glow."

Skin... glow? I dropped my gaze to my arms and cursed as gold glittered up at me. "Melek!" I was covered in his fucking golden jizz again. "Ugh!" Now I needed a bath. Or a shower. Or... or to be dunked in a damn ocean. "This stuff takes forever to wash off."

"Oh, I noticed," Lucifer said, ignoring my outbursts. "I *always* fucking notice." The edge in his voice stirred the hairs along my arms and had me glancing at him again.

I swallowed at the whirlpool swirling in his dark blue eyes, his intensity making him that much more beautiful.

Not the ocean I wanted to be dunked in, I thought, holding his gaze. *But I could absolutely lose myself in those oceanic irises.*

A long moment of silence passed, tension seeming to crackle in the air. Or maybe that was the fiery walls nearby. I couldn't say. I... I was hypnotized by that look on Lucifer's face.

Only, it vanished in a blink as he stepped backward into the contract room. "Come in, Camillia. There's something I want to show you."

He disappeared from view before I could ask for details. Not that he'd probably give any of them to me.

Sighing, I started forward, only to freeze outside the doors. Not because I was afraid, but because my distorted reflection in the metallic sheen reminded me that I resembled a damn disco ball again.

"You're going to scrub all this crap off of me," I told Melek. "And then you're apologizing by feeding me chocolate-covered strawberries in the bath."

"Mmm, it's a date," Melek replied as he hugged me into his side. "Maybe our king will join us."

Wait, what? I—

"Only if Camillia learns how to behave," Lucifer

replied from behind the door. "I don't reward brats. I punish them instead."

I blinked, his earlier commentary regarding my brattiness filtering through my mind and causing my eyes to narrow.

"I wasn't being a brat," I argued, resuming my walk toward his contract room. "Your lesson, or whatever you want to call that back there, was hurting Ajax. I reacted appro..." I trailed off in the middle of the word as I stepped through the threshold.

Because *wow*.

I couldn't say what I expected, but it wasn't this. "Holy fae," I breathed, my gaze traveling up the endless wall of files. It... it just kept going. There was no roof. Just a sky of swirling paper above.

And golden quills.

I jumped back as one sailed by my head, a memory clicking into place of the last time I saw one of those. It'd been during Melek's tour. He'd warned me to stay away from it. Something about it having unpredictable properties.

That's an understatement. The entire palace is riddled with unpredictable magic.

And Lucifer was the most unpredictable of all.

He stood in the center of the space near a single desk. There was no other furniture. Not even a chair. Just a simple wooden desk.

"You claim to know a lot about my deals," Lucifer said as the doors closed behind Melek. The rattle of chains that followed suggested we'd just been locked inside, too. "Enlighten me, Camillia. What do you think you know?"

"I know I didn't agree to be a bride," I told him. "That you made an arrangement with my father for my life without my consent." I folded my arms. "It's a fair deduction to assume there are others like me who tried to break free from one of your arrangements. And as you've said, you enjoy punishments. Ergo…"

I waved a hand, allowing the statement to fizzle and burn between us.

Lucifer considered me for a moment. "That's it? That's your grand summary?"

"You also tried to force Ajax to mate you," I added. "Should we talk about that again?"

He didn't immediately reply, just stared at me. "Your opinion of me is quite low."

That… wasn't true. I'd actually begun to respect him a bit. But I didn't feel the need to voice that out loud. So I just held his gaze and waited for him to say more.

"All right." He snapped his fingers, making me wince at the unexpected sound.

His lips curled down in response, his gaze narrowing a bit.

Then a paper appeared on the table before him, the lone document the only item on the dark wood.

A quill appeared next.

"We'll start from the beginning," he murmured, taking the feather between his fingers and scrawling across the page.

I frowned, not following. From this distance, I couldn't see what he was writing, so I crept forward.

My frown deepened when I realized what he'd conjured with that snap. "That's my contract."

"Technically, it's *my* contract," he returned. "One I had with your father. And now"—the edges of it began to burn —"it's no longer active."

I blinked. "No longer…" The parchment went up in flames, the flickering red ends glittering with magic.

I watched in awe as the paper melted away, my father's

inscription disappearing into a flare of bright embers that swirled in the air.

"I don't…" I lifted my gaze to Lucifer. "What does this mean? Will my father be punished for this?"

Only…

Only, my father couldn't be punished. Because he was dead. At least according to my mother.

Which meant the deal was already inactive.

And therefore this all meant nothing. It was just for show. "You're trying to trick me," I said before he could answer my previous questions. "Why? What lesson is this?"

His brow furrowed. "I am not trying to *trick* you, Miss De la Croix. I'm trying to start over by destroying the contract that binds you to my realm. And as for your father, he upheld his part of the bargain by having his daughter participate in the trials; thus, his soul is still free from my Source."

I snorted. "Yeah, because he's dead."

Lucifer looked from me to Melek. "Is this confirmed?"

"No, because it's the first I'm hearing about it." Melek stepped up to my side, his palm pressing to my lower back. "Why do you think he's dead, little angel?"

"My mom told me he's dead," I replied, a little startled that I'd failed to mention that to my mate.

Is it normal not to think much about a parent's death? To not really mourn the loss?

Maybe too much has happened for me to process what my mother had said. Or maybe… maybe I just wasn't normal.

"I see." Lucifer's voice seemed to deepen with those words. "I released him from my Source as part of our deal, so I can't easily confirm your mother's claim. But I'll look into it personally."

"You think she lied?" I asked, even more startled now.

"I think it's possible, yes," he replied. "It's also possible that he was her puppet all along, something I should have caught when he approached me with his offer."

"You had no way of even suspecting Virtuous Fae influence, Ty," Melek interjected. "Don't take that blame on yourself."

"He was my responsibility, and I failed him. It's as simple as that, little prince." Lucifer waved a hand through the air, causing a blank sheet of parchment paper to appear. "But we're not here to discuss my shortcomings. This is about training Camillia. And to do that, she needs to understand how I make deals." He focused on Melek. "So let's show her how it's done, little prince. Make me an offer, one I can't refuse."

CHAPTER 17

CAMI

I gaped at the Hell Fae King. Not only did he just suggest my father might have been under my mother's influence when he'd engaged in the deal regarding my fate, but he also seemed to think my mother might be lying about my father being dead.

And he intended to look into it—*personally*.

"Why?" I blurted out, cutting off whatever Melek had been about to say. "Why do you care?"

Only, he'd answered that already. *He was my responsibility, and I failed him*, Lucifer had said.

"Do you really think he was manipulated?" I added aloud before he could respond to my previous questions.

Because I already knew the answers.

I... I was just struggling to process them.

"Wouldn't that mean your deal with him was already null and void?" I went on. "Or... or would that not matter? Would you punish him anyway?" *Are there other innocents in his dungeon? Souls that were otherwise good?*

No, I thought in the next breath. I'd felt all the

creatures imprisoned in those cells. They weren't good souls.

"But why deal with them?" I muttered out loud, more to myself than to Lucifer. Except, I actually did want that answer. "If you knew they were bad, or if you knew they were manipulated by a Virtuous Fae, why…?" I trailed off, puzzling through all of the information I'd learned today.

I wasn't making sense. I knew that. But I… I was struggling to compare my father's situation to the dark souls in the dungeons.

"Why didn't I notice them before?" I wondered aloud. "I was in that dungeon a few months ago. I didn't feel them then."

Maybe because I hadn't been paying attention. I'd been a little caught up in my own captivity.

Because my father signed my life away to the Hell Fae Bride Trials.

"Wouldn't you have noticed my father's soul?" I asked, finally looking at Lucifer.

He stared back at me with a mixture of emotions I couldn't quite read. Amusement twinged with confusion, perhaps? I hadn't exactly been all that eloquent.

Lucifer didn't immediately reply, likely because he wanted to see if I had any other rambling questions to throw at him.

"I can see intentions—good and bad—in everyone around me," he finally said, his words measured. He probably expected me to cut him off. Or maybe he was attempting to ensure a fluent response.

Regardless, it didn't give me much.

So I held his gaze and waited for more.

"No one has a purely light soul," he went on. "They're mostly shades of gray. Some are just brighter than others."

"And my father's?" I prompted.

"Wasn't dark," he replied. "I wouldn't have allowed anyone with a dark soul to engage in a deal regarding the Hell Fae Bride Trials. Only those with good intentions were allowed to offer themselves or their daughters."

"Yet you designed your trials in a way to test the intentions of those brides," I said, recalling what Melek had said and what I'd mostly ascertained for myself.

"Yes. Because intentions can shift at any moment, and I did what I needed to do to protect the Hell Fae Realm." He canted his head to the side. "One thing you need to understand, Miss De la Croix, is that no deal is equal to another. Offers vary. Goals differ. And who I negotiate with changes daily."

I folded my arms. "But they always end the same, right? With the other person being in your debt in some way?"

"The deal itself is typically the debt," he returned flatly. "Someone comes to me with an offer, and I tell them the price. It's as simple as that."

"And if they renege on that price, they're turned into a Nightmare Fae and imprisoned as punishment."

His eyes narrowed. "No. Only dark souls earn that fate, something you already know because you felt their intentions in that dungeon."

My lips pursed. Because he was right—I had sensed the evil in that place. But what about the candidates like me? The ones who didn't want to participate in the trials? "Some of your deals involve innocents," I hedged. "Innocents like me."

His gaze ran over me in a hot wave of interest. "*Innocent* is not a term I would use to describe you, Camillia."

I wasn't sure if I should be insulted... or turned on. Because that glimmer in his smoldering gaze suggested he was considering a list of sensual terms, one I might like to hear. Preferably in a breath against my ear. While he...

I cleared my throat, not wanting to indulge that train of thought.

He's the devil. He hates me. And he has a prison full of literal nightmares.

"Many types of fae come to me with offers, but there are three who are more common than most," he told me softly, his gaze meeting mine once more. "There are those who are desperate and willing to do or give anything in exchange for something they need. Then there are those who partake in a deal for thrill-seeking purposes. And last but not least are those who engage me for their own selfish gain. In my experience, it's that last group who tends to fail the terms of our agreement."

I swallowed. "And what about my father? What group does he fall into?"

He considered that for a moment, his expression giving nothing away. "He exchanged your life for his own freedom, something I would typically consider to be selfish. But if your mother influenced him with her Virtuous Fae magic, then his situation was unique."

"Do you evaluate someone's soul before agreeing to a deal?" I wondered out loud, curious if he'd taken note of my father's intentions while engaging with him.

"I evaluate objectives more than souls," he replied and stepped around his desk to lean back against it. His long legs stretched out before him, one ankle resting over the other as he slid his hands into the pockets of his dark slacks. "Your father's objective was clear—he wanted to cut ties with my Source so he could be with your mother. I didn't think to dig further into that need; he wasn't the first or the last Hell Fae to make such a request."

"Did the fae before and after him offer you the lives of

their daughters, too?" I asked, unable to keep the snark from my voice.

His lips twitched. "No, Camillia. Yours was a unique case. Most of them offered a task or a service in exchange for me releasing them from the Hell Fae Source. But your father seemed to think I needed a better offer, something I'd found amusing at the time." He glanced away, his gaze turning thoughtful. "In hindsight, I should have wondered why he felt such a high price was required. It's not like my Hell Fae are prisoners."

I snorted. "We're not? Because it certainly felt that way during the trials."

"For you," he murmured, returning his attention to me. "Hell Fae Bridal Candidates were kept in the paradigm for observation and testing, so yes, you were a captive. But my Hell Fae—the ones with free rein through my realm—are not. Free will is something I very much value. I would never force someone to remain here who didn't want to be here."

"Unless they're a bridal candidate."

"A different situation entirely."

"In your mind," I pointed out. "But not in mine."

"Because you don't understand my world," he replied. "And thus far, you've been too closed-minded to try."

My eyebrows flew upward. "I'm standing right here, aren't I?"

"Yes, and throwing off an attitude that's making my palm twitch," he bit back. "Being here and being willing to learn are not the same concepts."

My jaw clenched. I had no idea what he meant by the *palm twitch* comment, and I didn't want to ponder that for too long. So I focused on the latter part of what he said.

"I want to learn," I told him. "I want to understand. But I can't ignore that a deal—one I had no say in—is why

I'm here. I also can't just forget what I felt in that dungeon or what I experienced as a bridal candidate. So if I'm giving you an *attitude*, it's because you deserve said *attitude*."

"Because I agreed to an offer that in the end has benefited you more than anyone else?" he asked, his eyebrow winging upward.

My teeth ground together even more as a retort taunted my tongue.

But he wasn't done speaking.

"You're mated to my Prince, my Commander, *and* my Warden." He pushed away from his table to come to his full height. "You've been given access to the deepest depths of *my* realm. You're now standing in a sacred place, surrounded by secret agreements. I even took you to my lair, a place *no one* has entered except for those inside my inner circle. Yet you want to harp on a deal I wasn't responsible for crafting. A deal I would have been a fool to refuse. A deal *your father* offered."

"Ty—"

"No," he bit off, his gaze still on me. "This is on me to fix. I accept that. But we can't move forward while these emotions simmer between us." He moved into my personal space, his hand suddenly on my nape. "You're angry with me? Fine. You want to punish me for your father's choices? Fine. But consider what it's doing to your mates, Camillia. What it's doing to *us*. Because I can't teach you if you're unwilling to learn."

I glared up at him. "I'm not unwilling." And I was really tired of him saying that. "Questioning you and your motives is a natural response to the situation, Typhos. I can't just trust you, not after everything we've been through."

"You mean *won't*, Camillia. You *won't* trust me. Faith is a choice, not an inherent feeling. I've wounded your faith in me. I understand that. But we can't change the past. We can only move into the future. Which means either you're going to *choose* to trust me, or you won't. That decision is yours, darling queen. Not mine."

Darling queen echoed in my head, overriding everything else he'd said. Because all I could hear was the word *queen* on his tongue. Not spoken as a noun so much as an endearment.

Why? I wondered. *Why would he call me that?*

Because he's starting to realize your potential, Melek whispered back, obviously listening to my thoughts. Or perhaps I'd broadcast them. *He respects you, little angel. You might not see it, but I do. This lesson proves it. He's being patient and taking responsibility for his faults, all while trying to answer your questions. Ty wants to fix this. But he's right—the success of this endeavor relies on your acceptance. Either you allow him to make amends, or you continue to hate him.*

I don't hate him, I replied via our mental connection.

Just as he doesn't hate you, he murmured, his voice a caress to my mind. *Look into his eyes. Really look. And you'll see that his feelings are anything but hatred.*

I swallowed, my attention returning to the male before me—the one standing far too close. His gaze held mine with a dominance that caused my heart to skip a beat.

"Most of my deals are crafted to benefit the Hell Fae Realm," he informed me, his voice seeming to soften with each word. "There's power in agreements, specifically the successful ones. You've experienced the darker side of my world, the offers devised for personal gain. Offers like your father's and offers like the one I gave to Ajax. But most agreements are benign and consensual."

He squeezed my nape once before releasing me and rotating toward the endless wall of shelves.

"These are my active offers," he went on. "Every scroll

is an ongoing deal, each agreement taking up residence in my mind, as I personally monitor every outcome. There are some I pay more attention to than others. Some that I'm anticipating will fail."

He waved his hand, causing several papers to appear out of thin air and float down to the desk.

"I make deals with dark souls for a single purpose—to have a hold over them. On very rare occasions, a dark soul can choose a path of redemption. Typically, however, the dark soul seeks to trick me into a bargain. Then he or she quickly learns that deception is a game I mastered long ago."

The documents on the wood magically organized themselves into a pile of ten or so pages.

Lucifer rested his palm on them, his eyes capturing mine once more. "These are the live contracts I hold with those I expect to fail. All the others in this room will succeed in some way or another, and the majority of those successes will be in favor of the offeror, not me."

He picked one up off the desk, his gaze skimming the words. Then he proceeded to read it aloud, the deal one between him and a female Lunar Fae.

It only took me a few seconds of hearing the words to realize why he'd chosen this one specifically—the woman had offered him her three sons in exchange for helping her find safe passage through the Human Realm.

"She's in Los Angeles," he added. "And she has no interest in actually leaving. She seeks fame and fortune, and she's willing to destroy everything and everyone in her path." He pulled up a mirror to reveal a familiar woman on the other side.

My eyebrows rose. "Isn't that...?" I trailed off, my mind failing to conjure the name I was looking for. I'd seen it in the media outlets dozens of times, but I rarely paid attention to famous humans.

Except she wasn't actually mortal, apparently. But a Lunar Fae.

"She's a singer," I went on. "But her name is escaping me."

Lucifer said it for me, then followed it with a scoff. "You have no idea how many mortals she's hurt in her pursuit. They're not usually my concern, but I find that how you treat a lesser being speaks volumes about your own sense of character."

I couldn't disagree with him there, so I simply nodded. "And her sons?"

"Are currently in my kingdom. They're half-breeds, their respective fathers having been various other types of fae." He set the paper down, the ink seeming to writhe across the page in response to his touch. "The real reason she bargained them away was to hide her previous affairs because she's a Lunar Fae Royal. If the pack discovered the truth of her illicit liaisons, she would be killed by her mate—the Alpha King."

"Oh." I blinked. "And you helped her escape…?"

"So she thinks," Lucifer replied, his lips curling slightly. "Her sons are abominations by Lunar Fae standards. They would have been killed had they been discovered. I accepted them as payment to save them, and I've been waiting for her to fail our terms so I can imprison her for her cruelty."

"But she gave you her sons. That's what she promised, right?"

"In exchange for passing through the Human Realm. However, she hasn't passed through. She's remained there. That nullifies our terms." He tapped the parchment, drawing me forward to read the text for myself.

"Does she realize that she's in breach of your agreement?" I wondered out loud as my eyes scanned the words written in his elegant penmanship.

"Of course not. She thinks she's won, and she's too caught up in her perceived success to consider an alternative." Lucifer removed his hand, causing the script to writhe once more. But the words didn't change. They simply wavered.

"When will you inform her?"

"When her sons are ready." He flicked a finger at the mirror, making it disappear. "They're currently devising her nightmare, something to do with a hole in the ground where she's fed nothing but scraps."

My eyebrows rose. "That's oddly specific."

"That's how they grew up—hidden away from the pack, treated as pet rats in a hole where she hid her sins." Something flickered in his gaze. An emotion underlined in darkness and fury. "They were feral pups when she dropped them at my door. One of my Hellhounds took them in. It's taken years to rehabilitate them, all while she's gallivanted around the Human Realm creating more havoc and pain."

I glanced from him to the paper and back to him. "So this agreement benefited your realm because you acquired more fae." I spoke the words slowly, trying to understand. "But really, you're helping them survive. And you'll be punishing a dark soul to appease them."

"I'll be punishing a dark soul because it gives me a reason to repurpose their vitality," he replied. "The fact that it'll avenge some of her wrongdoing is merely a benefit. The primary reward—the reason these agreements are so beneficial to *me*—is it gives me an excuse to exercise my abilities. I essentially siphon the energy from the dark soul and feed it into my Source, which in turn protects my realm."

"Siphon," I repeated, the term obviously striking a chord.

"Yes. I used to be a siphon like you. Only, I turned off that ability a long time ago." He frowned. "Well, *turned off* might not be the right term. After realizing there was power in deals, I restructured and redeveloped my skill to use my talent for protection rather than destruction."

"You're a siphon, too?" I asked, unable to hide my shock.

"Used to be," he repeated, a small smile flirting over his lips. "But technically, yes. My power has just evolved, like I said."

I blinked at him. "Oh." *Is that why he no longer considers me a threat? Because he understands my ability?*

It's why he wants to train you, Cami, Melek replied, hearing my thoughts. *And why he keeps thinking of you as a queen.*

I swallowed, not sure how to reply to that. Instead, I focused on everything he'd said about his deals and what he did with the souls—*energy*—he acquired from them.

It's how he powers the Hell Fae Realm, I realized.

Yes, Melek replied, even though I didn't need the confirmation.

Meeting Lucifer's gaze, I said, "So you've absorbed a lot of power over your lifetime, creating this vast universe of kingdoms where you protect your Nightmare Fae and Hell Fae, and the Source has now grown to a point of potential mismanagement."

I looked at Melek for confirmation, my assessment primarily derived from his various explanations, but he didn't respond. Instead, he stared at Lucifer, drawing my focus back to the Hell Fae King.

"That's my prince's assessment," Lucifer said after a

long, drawn-out moment of palpable tension. "And it's one... I'm beginning to accept."

Surprise flitted through Melek's expression.

"I owe you a boon, little prince," Lucifer went on. "Care to take advantage of that now? Or would you prefer to play later?"

Melek considered him for a long moment, his lips slowly curling up at the sides. "I always want to play, my king."

"I know."

"And you did tell me to make you an offer," Melek added.

"I did."

"Hmm." His multicolored irises flickered, his devious energy seeming to thrum to life in our bond. I couldn't hear his thoughts, but I could sense he was crafting something sensual.

Something dangerous.

Something involving me.

Melek, I warned.

Shh, he hushed, his attention still on Lucifer despite his mind clearly being focused on me. *I'm thinking, little angel.*

"This all began because of your deal with Pierre De la Croix," Melek went on out loud, his words causing my breath to stall in my lungs. "It seems only natural that we negotiate similar terms. For educational purposes, of course."

I gaped at him. "Similar terms?"

"Quiet, Camillia," Lucifer said. "This is between me and Melek."

"Yet it involves me." I couldn't hide the exasperation in my voice. "You can't be ser—"

Lucifer's mouth covered mine before I could finish, his

kiss demanding my silence. My submission. My... my *everything*.

Such a quick move, so utterly unexpected, and I... I succumbed.

I let him hold me. Kiss me. *Master me.*

Because he was a king.

A God among the fae.

Typhos Lucifer.

And I was a slave to the power unleashed from his lips to mine.

How....? I thought, breathless. *Why?*

One moment, I'd been ready to kill him. To hate him. To... to *scream* in protest. Yet now I felt utterly possessed.

By the time he released me, I could barely think. He hadn't even slid his tongue into my mouth. Just used his lips. His aura. His *power*.

"This is an exercise in trust, darling queen," he said, the endearment rendering me speechless once more. Not that I had enough oxygen in my lungs to formulate words. "Watch and learn. And most important of all, believe that your mate will protect you."

His lips ghosted across mine once more, then he released me with a suddenness that rivaled how quickly he'd grabbed me.

Only, a broad chest caught me before I could stumble backward, and strong arms encircled my waist. Then Melek's mouth brushed my ear. "I believe there was mention of a need for a bath or a shower," he murmured, his voice silk against my senses. "Let's start the negotiation there."

CHAPTER 18

AJAX

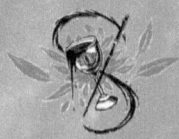

I folded my arms, my eyes glued to the pile of ash on the cell floor.

That pile used to be Dakota.

Or what was left of her, anyway.

I'd taken down Lucifer's glamour—a trick Az taught me shortly after the Hell Fae King had left—and had waited for Dakota's mind to resurface. Only, she hadn't moved. Hadn't spoken. Just stared at the wall with a vacant look, like she was still trapped in the past.

I could have uttered an enchantment to knock her out of it and forced her to come back to the present and face me. But seeing her in the flesh—her Unseelie disguise having vanished when I'd dismantled Lucifer's nightmarish enchantment—had done nothing for me.

"You seem disappointed," Az said, his tall form lounging against the wall beside me. He was the picture of casualness with one ankle resting against the other, his stance and expression indicating he was unbothered by the death spell I'd just performed in front of him.

"I guess I expected to feel more," I told him. "But I

don't feel much of anything at all, except for maybe relief." Which was strange.

Whenever faced with my past, I usually experienced pain. Sometimes sadness. And I always reacted with fury.

Yet… I felt oddly at peace right now. Like I'd just closed the cover on a finished book.

"Cami has changed everything for me," I whispered out loud, aware that she was the source of my contentment. Or perhaps my growth. I wasn't quite sure what label to put on it, but I recognized what she meant to me, how she'd helped me heal. "I don't think she meant to, but she did."

"She's changed everything for all of us," Az replied, sounding amused. "I've never seen Melek serious about anything, nor have I ever heard Typhos apologize. Yet both of those things have happened more than once in the last week alone. And as for me…" He trailed off, considering. "She makes me feel alive in a way I've never felt before."

I nodded, understanding what he meant. "She taught me what real love is," I said, then winced at how cheesy that sounded out loud.

But it was the truth.

Emelyn Jyn was my first love.

Camillia De la Croix was my true love.

The former taught me how to feel, how to care, how to open my heart and experience small doses of warmth in an otherwise cold world. Then her death encased my soul in a frigid tomb for ten very long years. Until Cami broke through with her rebellious energy and alluring persona.

She woke me the fuck up and yanked me headfirst into her fiery world. And I'd been trying to catch up ever since.

I stared at the pile of ashes once more, waiting for some profound experience to take over. Mere moments ago, those walls held a nightmare I relived often in my mind. Yet taking down the spell felt oddly relieving, like closure. As though I could finally move on with my life and reside in the present instead of the past.

Does that make me a bad Midnight Fae? I wondered, still focused on what remained of Dakota. *Or does it make me a good Hell Fae Warden?*

I contemplated the questions, let them roll through my mind, and decided that neither was truly correct. I wasn't a bad Midnight Fae for moving on, and I wasn't exactly a good Hell Fae Warden for it either. I was just me. Ajax. A Midnight Fae tied to the Hell Fae Realm.

Because of my Phoenix Fae mate and our gorgeous little rebel.

I closed my eyes, my mind instantly connecting to Cami's thoughts. She was lost in a sea of power, captivated by Lucifer's explanation of his deals. Various emotions flickered through our bond. Anger. Arousal. Fear. Intrigue.

I almost asked if she needed to be rescued, but I felt a bolt of determination ripple through our connection.

A determination to *trust*.

I wasn't sure what inspired her to feel that way, nor did I want to intrude any further.

So I pulled back and returned my attention to Dakota's lifeless cell. I had considered turning her into a statue—like Constantine had done to my parents and Emelyn. But I'd opted against it and used a simple exsanguination spell.

Anticlimactic and quick.

Very unlike what she probably deserved. However, I hadn't seen a reason to prolong it. Not when Dakota appeared to be mostly mindless anyway.

Twirling my wand in my hand, I considered the cell before me. It was minimalistic now that the glamour had vanished, leaving the room bare. Lucifer hadn't said anything about preparing it for another inmate, so I decided to just empty it entirely for now.

With a muttered spell under my breath, I drew a pattern with my wand and noted the gold flares dancing around my purple magic. "I don't know if I should thank you for the Phoenix Fae enhancements or punch you in the face for forcing them on me," I told Az.

His violet gaze flickered with black as his animal peeked out at me. "You could do both. Punch me in the face and then show your gratitude by sucking my cock."

I arched a brow. "I'm not that thankful."

Az pushed away from the wall, his Phoenix staring at me again through his gaze. "Are you sure about that?"

My eyes narrowed. "I'm very fucking sure."

He canted his head in that birdlike manner he often favored, his chest meeting mine.

But I held my ground and stared right back at him, our heights nearly even. "I won't submit to you, Az. Not right now. Perhaps never again." Because I still wasn't entirely okay with everything that had happened between us.

Oh, I understood it. And I even felt bad for enslaving him with Virtuous Fae magic. However, there were past hurts that had not yet healed.

Az searched my eyes, almost as though he was seeking answers from deep within my soul. He wouldn't have to search too far, our bond keeping my mind open to him in a way I could never reject—even if I wanted to.

Which… which I didn't.

Deep down I knew that.

Az was my friend. Maybe even my best friend. I loved Shade like a brother, recognized our history together, and knew he understood me better than most.

But Az had been with me during the darkest period of my life. He'd helped me heal in his own way. Gave me an outlet for the pain. Never poked or prodded, just remained a steadfast presence at my side.

He'd hurt me, yes. Badly. However, I could feel his remorse, as well as his reasoning. It was convoluted and fucked up. And it all led to one inevitable conclusion—forgiveness.

I just wasn't sure how to reach that end or when I would be ready for it.

Az pressed his palm to my cheek, the touch strangely gentle for him. And it was completely at odds with the fire brewing in his gaze.

"I'm sorry, Ajax," he said. "I'm sorry I imprisoned you with my power. I'm sorry I forced you to watch Cami suffer. I'm sorry I chose my allegiance to Typhos over my allegiance to you. And I'm sorry I failed you not just as a best friend but also as a mate. It felt wrong at the time, and I hadn't understood why. But I get it now. I deserve far worse than a punch to the face, which is why I accept the hits to my heart. It's what I earned through my actions."

I frowned at him. "Are you feeling all right?" Because I'd never heard him sound so apologetic, let alone emotional. *Hits to the heart?* What kind of poetic shit was that?

"You're the one who said Cami taught you how to love."

"I said she taught me what real love is."

"Same thing."

"Doesn't explain your rant," I retorted.

"Doesn't it, though?" he asked, his lips curling as his thumb traced my cheekbone in a gentle caress. "Maybe Cami has softened both of us."

"I have not gone soft."

He pressed me back into the wall, his hips meeting

mine. "No, you're still as hard and hot as ever," he agreed. "Now stop avoiding the topic and listen to what I've said."

A growl vibrated my chest. "I've already told you I won't submit, Az. I meant it. So don't fucking force it."

"I'm not telling you to submit, Ajax. I'm asking you to *listen*. To hear my apology. To know how fucking sorry I am. To realize I'm willing to do anything and everything to make it up to you." He dropped his forehead to mine, his minty breath fanning across my lips. "We speak with our bodies, Ajax. Not our mouths. That's always been the way for us. So fucking destroy me if you have to. I'll accept it. Just…" He trailed off on a sigh that had me wanting to shove him away.

We didn't do this emotional bullshit.

We sparred. We fucked. And we sparred again.

None of this *talking* or admitting to *feelings*.

This… this was…

My jaw clenched. Because I couldn't define this moment. It felt vulnerable and far more overwhelming than moments ago when I'd faced my past.

What the hell is wrong with me? I wondered. *Why is this so much more impactful than Dakota's death?*

Because it's Az, some part of me whispered. *This is the future. The present. The way things will be from now on.*

We were connected via his Phoenix. Mated for life.

And we shared Cami, too.

A mate circle.

With Melek as well, I thought begrudgingly. *And Lucifer.*

Fuck, it was all too much. I wanted to rant, to rage, to… to *hit something*.

No. Not *something*. *Someone*.

Az.

And somehow he'd known. He knew this was the

emotional outlet I required. The fight I needed. The inevitable explosion I craved deep within.

Not because of my past or Dakota or the deaths of Emelyn and my parents.

It was because of *this*—the simmering passion between me and Az. The hum of my bond with Cami. The anger I felt toward Lucifer for leaving me on the outside for too long. The residual fury I felt toward Az for holding me at arm's length.

Understanding his reasons was one thing. Accepting them was entirely another.

Az was right. We needed this—our outlet. A communication between our bodies. A fight between our souls.

"Flames, I hate how well you know me," I told him. "Yet I feel like I know nothing about you at all."

"You know more than most," he conceded. "But you're welcome to get to know me better."

I grunted and shoved him off of me. "How? By chatting?"

"No," he returned, coming right back for me and slamming me against the wall behind me. "By fighting," he snarled, nipping my bottom lip and drawing blood.

Growling, I tried to shove him again.

He responded by grabbing my throat and squeezing it so hard I couldn't breathe. "By *fucking*," he went on. "Whatever you want, Ajax. Whatever you need. My body is yours. My mind and soul, too. So take me back to your room and do whatever the hell you want to me."

Az's grip lessened, allowing me to huff a raspy laugh. "Fuck off, Az," I ground out on a wheeze. "We both know you'll never submit in that way."

His Phoenix peeked at me through Az's eyes again, then disappeared entirely, leaving only violet flames in his wake. The palm on my throat shifted to the side of my neck as Az traced my jaw with his thumb. "Let me prove that I mean it. Let me apologize in the only way I know how—by giving you everything."

I shuddered, his words undoing something inside me. Because I could hear the severity of them echoing in his mind. He meant every word. Every promise. Every ounce of his need.

This was Az's method of giving me control, a gift he'd never willingly given to anyone before. Except for maybe Cami, and even then, deep down, he'd still guided her with his preferences.

But this... this was him truly handing me the reins. Telling me to do whatever the hell I wanted. Giving me permission to play.

I stared at him, looked deep into his eyes to his very fucking soul, and did the only thing I could think to do—I kissed him.

Hard.

Mastering him with my mouth and tongue. Tasting. Licking. *Owning.*

And he let me.

No push and pull. No fight. Just Az submitting to me and letting me lead.

When I moved back, he looked at me with eyes that radiated a mixture of arousal and pain. This wasn't Az. He needed control to thrive. To fight his past. To ensure he never hurt again.

However, for me, he was willing to swallow the discomfort that came with bowing to another's strength.

Because he trusted me. And on some level, he loved me.

Perhaps not in the same way that he loved Cami, but then, my feelings for him were different from my feelings for her, too. Az and I possessed a deep bond founded on brotherhood and friendship, and that bond was underlined by mutual attraction.

We enjoyed fucking each other.

We enjoyed fighting with each other.

Except, beneath the surface, we also cared deeply about one another. Cami had solidified that affection, turning it into so much more. Then Az's Phoenix had ensured we would be bound together for eternity.

Now I wanted to return the favor.

I'd already started without thinking, having accidentally drawn blood with my kiss.

Only that hadn't been from my teeth breaking the skin, but his. Maybe from the force by which I'd claimed him with my mouth. Or maybe he'd done it instinctively as a gift.

Whatever the cause, it didn't matter.

Because all I desired now was one simple outcome—*a claim*.

Between my soul and Az's soul.

Driven by my Midnight Fae instincts.

His Phoenix had bitten me.

Now it was my turn to bite him.

And make him mine.

CHAPTER 19

AZ

I sensed Ajax's intent a second before I felt his canines bite into my throat. A sharp gasp left me, followed by a groan as liquid fire blasted through my veins.

"*Fires,*" I hissed, losing myself to Ajax's vampiric kiss. How the hell had I gone a decade without feeling this? Had I known, I would have made him bite me the first time I fucked him.

Ajax pulled back, his blue-black eyes alive with hunger. "Your blood has always been empowering. But this…" He trailed off and went for the opposite side of my neck, biting down and sending another blast of heat through my insides.

"Fuck," I ground out, leaning into his touch and needing more. "This is making me so damn hard."

Not that I hadn't been hard already before he'd even begun.

Watching him handle Dakota had turned me on, which was all kinds of fucked up, but I'd enjoyed seeing him deliver her death sentence. I only wished he would have tortured her a bit.

However, that hadn't been what he'd needed.

And I respected his choice in how he dealt with the situation.

Just like I respected his choice now as he claimed me with his bite. "Fires, I want you to do that to my cock," I admitted on another groan. I knew it would hurt to feel his teeth sink into my hard flesh, but I was all for the pleasure that would follow. "It'll probably make me come."

Ajax growled, his mouth pulling away from my neck. "I'm not sucking your cock."

"I didn't ask you to suck, just bite," I replied.

His gaze narrowed. "You want me to kneel."

"I do," I confided. "But only if you want to."

"Always in control," he returned, making me wince.

"Ajax—"

His mouth covered mine before I could finish my reply. Not that I really knew what to say. He was in charge; I was just voicing my desires. But I understood why he thought it was me seizing the reins.

Because that was what I did. What came naturally to me and my Phoenix.

Although, I was trying to submit to him. To let him master me and—

Ajax jolted against me as the foundation below our feet shook. I tore my mouth away from his, my gaze instantly traveling the corridor of the dungeon.

"What the fuck was that?" I demanded, searching for whatever creature had caused that minor earthquake.

"I don't—" Another tremble cut Ajax off, causing both of us to face opposite sides of the hallway. His back brushed mine, our aroused states instantly forgotten.

Something was coming, but the uneven vibrations made it difficult to tell which direction it was coming from.

"It's several hours before curfew," Ajax said, wariness

in his voice. "There shouldn't be any prisoners out at the moment."

I grunted. "Unless the Hellhounds fucked something up. Garmr has been playing Warden in your absence."

Ajax made a noise that said how he felt about that. Garmr wasn't incompetent, but he managed too much in this realm, which often meant he had to delegate tasks to his Hellhound minions.

And those minions… were often incompetent.

"Fuck," Ajax muttered. "Time to hunt."

My lips curled. "Sounds like fun, actually."

"Says the Commander," Ajax drawled, his focus still on his side of the hallway while I guarded mine.

Only whatever was coming seemed to have disappeared.

Or gone above ground.

I glanced upward. "You don't think…"

"Fuck," Ajax repeated, clearly following my train of thought.

Both of us vanished at the same time, Ajax shadowing and me ashing, and arrived just outside of the detention dungeon. One glance toward the Candidate Headquarters confirmed my fears—the prisoners had escaped.

And not just a handful, but several.

Ajax instantly took out his wand as my sword formed in my hand.

"I've got the Minotaur," I informed him.

"Which one?" Ajax asked, causing my lips to curl down.

I glanced at him and saw he was focused on the nearby arena where two bull-like Nightmare Fae and various others were prowling around. "That's impossible," I said under my breath. "Typhos wouldn't have this many prisoners masked in Nightmare Fae mirages."

"Yeah, not to mention, last I checked, there was only one Minotaur in the cells," Ajax echoed. "Not two."

Shit. Something wasn't right.

A thought that was confirmed as multiple Nightmare Fae barreled out of the arena and headed straight for the snake-vined walls that surrounded the library and bridal dorms.

Feminine screams rent the air next, causing the hairs along my arms to stand on end.

This is chaos, I whispered, sensing the rise of magic filtering through the paradigm. *Typhos,* I said, switching my focus to the Hell Fae King.

Quiet followed. An eerie form of silence that had my instincts flaring to life.

Cami, I tried next.

Nothing.

Az, Ajax spoke into my mind, causing me to glance at him. *I can't hear Cami.*

Neither can I. Nor can I hear Typhos.

Ajax's jaw visibly clenched. *Vivaxia?*

Maybe, I replied, that static electricity mounting. *Likely.*

Ajax twirled his wand. *What do you want to do, Commander? Tame some beasts with me? Or ash out for reinforcements?*

And leave you here to have all the fun? I returned, huffing a mental laugh. *Fuck that.* My sword glowed with violet flames, my beast pacing inside. *This is our favorite foreplay, Warden.*

"It's always about sex with you," Ajax said out loud.

"Sex and blood tend to go well together," I returned, glancing pointedly at his mouth and the speck of my essence painting his lips.

He licked the blood off in response, then gave me a

chilling smile. "I'll take the gates by the library. You take the dorms."

"All right," I agreed, ashing before saying another word.

And immediately winced as I landed in a sea of nervous energy.

Several of the bridal candidates had gathered here, anticipating the incoming fight.

"Oh!" A female with bright red hair tried to hit me with a fiery ball of sticky magic, one I slashed with my sword. As soon as her hazel eyes met mine, she gasped out an apology, one I flicked away with a subtle head tilt.

When a second female nearly swung at me with some strange-looking flaming bat, I growled. "Get out of my way and let me handle this."

But as I stepped through the crowd and looked out through the gate, I saw it wasn't just a few Minotaurs and Manticores coming this way.

There were Centaurs, too.

Several Banshees.

Two Nagas.

And a fucking Sea Dragon.

What the fuck is going on? I wondered, my eyes widening as an Unseelie joined in the fun.

We're under attack, Ajax returned. *And they're not coming from the prison, Az.*

A portal door opened nearby, the power touching my senses and confirming Ajax's assessment. *This is definitely Vivaxia's doing*, I told him.

Not that I needed to.

We both knew what was happening here—another spell. Only this one was impacting all of the incoming Nightmare Fae.

And turning them feral.

I could see it in their expressions as they charged forward, their gazes set on the brides behind me.

They're going to destroy everyone here, I told Ajax.

They're going to have to get through us first, he replied.

Indeed. I crouched, ready. But already I knew there were too many for us to take on alone. And there were more coming.

The brides were going to have to fight. Some of the nearby Hell Fae, too. Assuming Vivaxia's spell didn't infect them first.

Fires. We needed Typhos, and we needed him right fucking now. "Who can teleport?" I demanded, my focus on the approaching Nightmare Fae while my words were for the candidates and lingering Hell Fae nearby.

A chorus of affirmations met my ears.

"All of you go to the Hell Fae Palace in the Hell Fae Kingdom. And shout for Lucifer." I didn't look to make sure they adhered to my command.

Someone would listen.

Hopefully more than a single person.

And hopefully they would be able to reach the Hell Fae Kingdom.

Because who the fuck knew what kind of spell Vivaxia had woven over this paradigm? Whatever it was, I hoped Typhos would feel it. *And soon...*

CHAPTER 20

CAMI

Several Minutes Earlier

"Gold ribbons?" Lucifer repeated, arching a brow at Melek. "I thought you wanted to use red rope."

"Only when it's a gift for you, my king," Melek purred back at him. "This is for me."

"And what do I get in return for this *offer*, hmm?"

"You get to watch," Melek replied simply, causing my cheeks to flame with heat.

I can't believe you're offering to tie me up in front of him, I whispered into his mind. *Without my consent.*

Your body is consenting, little angel, Melek returned, his arms wrapped tightly around my waist as he rested his chin on my shoulder.

A shiver traversed my spine as he kissed my neck, the affectionate act one he was doing for me and for Lucifer. I could hear the intentions inside his mind, the game he was currently playing.

This all started because of my thoughts about needing

a bath or a shower, and Lucifer's commentary about not rewarding brats.

Apparently, Melek saw this as an opportunity, one he was now using in his negotiation. "I don't see what any of this has to do with teaching," I muttered.

"He's showing you how negotiations can involve a third party," Lucifer responded as he folded his arms over his broad chest, his gaze on Melek even though his words were for me. "Typically, I'll allow this sort of discussion when the offeror has a claim on whatever or whoever he is offering."

"So you treat mates like property," I inferred. "And I suppose the same could be said about children since my father offered me—someone he had a claim on—to you in exchange for his freedom."

"No." He finally looked at me. "Negotiation is a skill, one I use to determine the goodness in others."

I frowned at him, not following.

Fortunately, he wasn't done speaking.

"I allow my subjects to use whatever they desire as collateral because their choices tell me a lot about them. In your father's case, his offering of you told me he was not only selfish but also a bad parent. Because anyone who is willing to give up his own daughter for selfish gains is clearly not a good father. Which meant the daughter—a fae of mixed origin—would likely benefit from being welcomed into my realm."

My brow came down, his words creating an avenue of thought I had not yet considered. "You thought I might need to be saved. That's why you made the deal."

"Not exactly. I thought you might need guidance or a safe place to hide from other fae. So I saw the trade as beneficial—I didn't want a Hell Fae tied to my Source who could so easily abandon his progeny, and I was relatively early on in the process of selecting female candidates for the Hell Fae Bride Trials. Thus, I accepted the offer."

It was a pragmatic approach, one I didn't want to acknowledge. However, his thought process made sense.

"You might not care for my methods, but the outcome was beneficial, Camillia." He glanced pointedly at Melek, making my heart race.

Because he wasn't wrong.

Without my father's deal, I would never have been taken to the Hell Fae Realm. *So where would I be now? Still at college? Earning a useless degree?*

No.

That had never been my fate.

My destiny was always to come here; whether as a candidate or something else, I'd been created to meet Lucifer. *To destroy him*, I thought, shivering.

All because of *Vivaxia* and her millennia-old vendetta.

"Now your mate is making me an offer, and an enticing one at that," Lucifer went on, returning his gaze to mine. "Unlike other propositions, this one is coming from someone I trust. I know his intentions. And deep down, you do as well. Melek won't hurt you, nor will he force you to do something you don't want to do. Therefore, I'm entertaining his game. Unless you'd like me to stop this lesson?"

"Oh, a safe word," Melek murmured, his lips caressing my thundering pulse. "Care to provide one, little angel? A single statement that'll end this delicious game?"

I shivered, recalling the last time I discussed a safe word. *With Az and Ajax.*

Thinking of them had me wondering if they'd resolved their issues yet. Or if they were still in the process of it. The temptation to link to them and ask was strong, but I didn't want to intrude.

Even if thinking of them fucking it out had me burning alive inside.

Because yes. Yes, please.

"Camillia?" Lucifer asked, drawing me back to him. He must have said something after Melek, something I'd missed because I was thinking about Az and Ajax.

Clearing my throat, I said, "My safe word is *camping*."

One eyebrow lifted. "Camping?"

"I *hate* camping," I emphasized. And I really didn't feel like elaborating on why. So instead I told him, "That's what I use with Az and Ajax."

His oceanic irises flickered to life with blue flames, the heated gaze making me swallow.

Wow, his eyes were pretty. Hypnotic, too. Twin pools of burning lust.

Because he's thinking of… of me with Az and Ajax? But he's not into them like that… right?

Hmm, maybe not. But he is into you like that, Melek whispered into my mind, his lips brushing my throat again. *And our king likes to watch, Camillia.*

"Gold ribbon," Melek went on out loud. "I'll bind her arms for you, behind her back. And I'll braid her hair, too. All while you watch."

Without taking his eyes away from me, Lucifer replied, "What are you asking for in return, little prince?"

"I want you to bathe her," he said. "She isn't a fan of my golden touch, and you know how to properly wash it off. So I'll tie her up for you, and then you'll cleanse her."

"Hmm," Lucifer hummed, taking a step forward and allowing me to feel the warmth radiating from his chest.

If temptation had a form, it was Typhos Lucifer.

Tall.

Broad-shouldered.

Tapered waist.

Dressed in a perfectly pressed suit.

I didn't want to crave him. Yet I doubted anyone could fight his magnetic pull. He was simply sin personified, his position here as the Hell Fae King not only worthy of him but appropriate for him, too.

"You want to watch me pet her," Lucifer said slowly. "And in exchange, you'll bind her for me."

"Yes."

"The bath part is for her," Lucifer added, moving even closer to me. "Because you're taking her needs into account as well."

"Yes," Melek repeated, his arms loosening until all I felt was his palms skimming my abdomen.

"Do you see how this works, little temptress?" Lucifer asked, his voice softening as he reached up to trace the line of my jaw with a single finger. "Your mate is making me an offer that includes you, but he's ensuring your contentment. That's the mark of a fae with good intentions." He cocked his head, his long hair falling over one shoulder. "So, is it an offer I should accept? Or should I counter?"

I tried to swallow, but my throat no longer seemed to work. I... I was frozen between them. With Melek gripping my hips and Lucifer lightly stroking my cheek.

So much heat.

So much power.

So much *male fae.*

Gods, I'd been trapped between Az and Ajax before, too. Yet this felt different. More intense somehow. More... more terrifying? But in a good way. Not that any of that made a lick of sense. However, I wasn't sure I wanted to embrace sane thoughts right now.

I kind of liked the idea of just... submitting.

Letting Melek tie me up.

And feeling Lucifer's hands on me.

"Well?" Lucifer whispered, his gaze falling to my mouth. "What would you do in my position? Accept or counter?"

"If I were you?" I breathed, then finally managed to swallow. "I would counter." Because I couldn't imagine that Lucifer ever accepted a deal on the first try.

His lips curved upward. "I do enjoy a good counter. Any ideas on what I should demand?"

"I..." I wasn't sure I understood the question. The way he was looking at my mouth had me thinking about him kissing me.

Which had me recalling what that felt like.

Because I had firsthand experience now.

No longer just a dream, but *real* practice.

"How long do you want me to bathe her?" Lucifer asked, his finger ghosting across my bottom lip.

"However long it takes to wash my golden sheen from her skin," Melek replied, causing Lucifer to chuckle.

"Oh, little prince, you'll have to do better than that." His eyes left my mouth to look over my shoulder at Melek. "Under those parameters, you could douse her for hours, thus requiring me to pet her for just as long."

Melek's amusement warmed my thoughts. "Are you telling me you wouldn't enjoy that, my king?"

"I'm sure I would, but a timeline needs to be defined. This is a deal, after all."

Gods, I can't believe this is happening, I thought, dizzy from their conversation. Or maybe it was their touch making me feel lightheaded. They were both radiating dark intent, the kiss of it a drug to my senses.

I wanted to drown in them.

Which was insane.

Lucifer and I... My eyes nearly closed, the thought

ending before I could finish it. Because I didn't know how to define my relationship with the Hell Fae King. It was tenuous. Hot. *Combustible.*

"One hour," Melek said, drawing me back to their negotiation. "But she'll only be tied up for thirty minutes of it."

Lucifer's eyebrow arched. "You want to give her freedom to touch me?"

"If she desires it, yes. However, I also want to ensure a slow introduction. An hour of being bound is too long for someone so new to the sensation of being tied up."

The Hell Fae King's eyes traveled back to mine. "Do you see how he's taking care of you, little queen?"

Fae, that nickname was going to undo me. "Yes," I admitted, my voice barely audible. There was just something so undeniably arousing by this whole situation. The two of them establishing terms on how they would handle me—*together.*

And this wasn't even sex.

It was just a bath.

Where I would be naked and have Lucifer's hands all over—

A chill swept over me, one that was at odds with the heat at my front and back. My lips curled down as invisible ice crawled over my skin, sort of like how the death magic did in the Netherworld.

I shivered, the frigid touch weaving through my veins at an alarming rate.

"Camillia?" Lucifer asked, his palm molding to my cheek.

He was hot. I knew he was hot. Yet I... I couldn't feel him at all. I couldn't feel Melek either. Everything was so cold.

What's happening? I wondered, my movements slow as I glanced around. *Why...why do I feel... like death?*

"*Camillia*," Lucifer tried again, the sharpness of his voice causing me to blink.

Had I missed something? Words? A question? I... I stared at him, noting the burning quality in his eyes. So intense. Yet that fire simmered for a different reason than before. It was no longer a result of arousal, but one of anger.

No.

No, not anger.

Fear.

My teeth began to chatter as the numbness spread.

I should be more concerned.

I... I should be trying to... to... *move*.

Yet a sense of contentment rolled through me, which made no sense, given that I was now shaking all over.

"It's like she can't hear me," Melek said, reminding me that he still stood behind me. His arms were around my torso, holding me tightly.

And he was... he was *burning*.

I could feel it, that heat. That delicious heat thawing some of my ice.

What the fuck is going on? I wondered dizzily. *Why... why am I...?*

I blinked as more warmth bled into my torso, the source of it Lucifer. Because he was holding me, too. Tightly. And his mouth... his mouth was against my ear, whispering something I couldn't hear. A spell, perhaps?

Magic prickled along my skin, stirring tingles from deep within. Then something *cracked*. Maybe not physically, but I heard it.

And suddenly I could *feel*.

Hear.

Sense...

My eyes went wide, my heart pounding in my chest.

Because what I was *sensing* wasn't here. It was somewhere else. It was… it was *in my soul*.

"Ajax," I breathed, his chilling essence pouring through me. "Something's wrong with Ajax!"

Lucifer caught me before I could disappear, my instinct to go to my mate overpowering logic. Yet something the Hell Fae King did held me in place, his power pushing down on mine. "Focus," he demanded. "Tell me what you're feeling."

"I… I don't know," I stammered out, vibrating beneath his dominance.

All I wanted was to go to Ajax.

But his mind was silent.

Just like Az's, I realized. "It's like when I was with Vivaxia and my mother," I whispered, realizing that I was strangely cut off from my mates again. "What's happening to me? Is Vivaxia here?"

"She's somewhere," Lucifer growled out. "And she's using you as a vessel of some kind."

"What do you mean?"

"We need to get to the paradigm," Melek interjected. "Garmr confirms everything has been cut off. The Hellhounds can't ash in or out. Which means Az and Ajax—"

"Are stuck there as well." Lucifer's wings flared to life, the burnt feathers making me gasp. "So we'll arrive the old-fashioned way. Are you taking Camillia, or am I?"

CHAPTER 21

AJAX

SEVERAL MINUTES EARLIER

A z's curse echoed through my mind, drawing my focus to an eruption of flames coming from the sky near the bridal dorms. *What the fuck is that?*

A very pissed-off Hellhound, he growled back at me. *No one can get out of the paradigm.*

What? I glanced at the portals opening all over the place in front of the arena. *They're certainly having no trouble getting in.*

It seems to be a one-way ticket, he replied.

Fuck.

Exactly, he returned. *Your dungeon is about to be full of pissed-off Nightmare Fae.*

I studied the field from my position at the gates of the library, my jaw ticking. *Yeah* was all I could say back to him as I stared, watching at least three new portals opening within the paradigm. Az had his hands full with the brides, leaving me to strategize. I needed to figure out where to begin.

Because this wasn't like the curfew games where Nightmare Fae roamed and the occasional one refused to go back to his or her cell.

This was a nightmarish mayhem.

It was on the tip of my tongue to call for my familiar, to ask for some assistance. Given the rising number of fae, we could use all the help we could get. But I didn't want to risk Kuro being trapped inside the paradigm with us, so I refrained.

Here they come, Az said just before a cascade of fire burst over the upper side of the paradigm. I trusted Az to handle the chaos at the dorms while I figured out a plan, but it did sound like he was having all the fun.

Fortunately, I wasn't to be left out. Two Minotaurs and one Manticore careened around the corner and spotted me, releasing roars as their footsteps shook the ground. I drew a circle with my finger and whispered familiar words intended to defend, not consume.

"*Hamaya Fuquay.*"

The Minotaurs charged me, as expected, with their bullish tendencies. They slammed into my defensive spell, cracking it but not breaking it.

The Manticore launched into the sky. His pronged wings lifted him from the ground, giving him an advantage, as did his scorpion-like tail. One strike with the tail might be enough to dismantle my spell. Instead, he dropped onto the top of the barrier, using his weight instead of his natural defenses, making me frown.

I'd never seen a Manticore do that.

How are the brides? I asked. *Are they okay?*

The majority of them are trapped behind a collapsed wall, but the ones out here are more than okay, Az replied with a wave of approval in his words. *Their training has paid off. They can handle themselves—for now. If this keeps up, though, we're going to be fucking overrun. We need Typhos.*

But we couldn't reach Typhos. Which meant Vivaxia didn't want him to be here for this.

What are you after? I wondered to myself, then glanced toward the fires flickering near the dorms. Dust and rock burst into the air as another wall collapsed, suggesting the goal was to separate our forces and pick us off one at a time. *The brides? Is that all you want?*

The remaining Nightmare Fae weren't necessarily heading for the bridal camp, though. Groups of them stayed right where they were, breaking apart buildings and tearing through Hellhounds.

Vivaxia was attacking this whole paradigm.

Why?

Simple destruction seemed… petty. And pointless.

From what I understood so far, everything Vivaxia did was calculated, so there was something I was missing.

The Manticores on the ground grew tired of slamming into the barrier, but if they kept going, they'd likely break it. Rocks and dirt sprayed into the air as one began to dig. The other simply stared at me, his nostrils flaring and his eyes wild and… full of agony.

You don't want to do this, do you?

This attack didn't seem to be organized or even mildly thought out. The sky burst with reds and oranges as a new column of fire climbed above the library. The snarl of Hellhounds followed as Nightmare Fae invaded the flames. One of the Hellhounds looked at me, but I gave him a nod. It was a universal gesture that said *I can handle this.*

The Hellhound left with his group to manage the loose Nightmare Fae rampaging down the street. Given that it was a dragon breed, it would take quite a few Hellhounds to corral it. A wall of Hellfire roared to life in their wake.

As if drawn to the blaze, the Manticore coming at me from above turned to the excitement and flapped his wings, heading for the moving target.

He dove right into the flames, not even caring that he might get burned. Manticores could handle high temperatures, but not outright Hellfire with their batlike wings.

The Minotaurs roared and followed him, which was once again entirely unlike the beasts. They didn't work in packs.

It's like they're just... feral. That was the term I had heard echoing in Az's deduction, but it wasn't like anything I'd ever seen.

Two small portals opened directly in front of me. One delivered a Siren, likely from the Underwater Kingdom. The other, a Naga from the Marsh Lands, but strange shadows flicked around its scales as it spilled through.

Both were intimidating, but it was the Siren that captured my interest most.

Because... because it was *male.* Not female.

There are male sirens? I thought, mostly to myself.

But Az must have heard me because he responded, *A few.*

Oh. I'd never seen one before. The Sirens in my dungeon were all feminine in appearance.

Of course, they weren't *real* Sirens. They were dark souls wearing a nightmarish mask.

This Siren, though, was the real deal. And he, along with all the other Nightmare Fae, had previously been cooperating with Lucifer, eagerly awaiting their new brides.

So why are you fighting on the wrong side? I wondered, taking a moment to look the Siren in his milky eyes.

And once again I found agony there that didn't align with the sneer on his face.

The Naga took advantage of my hesitation and went right for me, finally shredding my defensive spell in the process. A *pop* rent the air as the fae clawed its way through.

I barely sidestepped in time, taking note of the uncharacteristic full-frontal attack.

Nagas were Hell Fae, not Nightmare Fae, meaning they operated less on instincts and more on reason. And they were sly; they didn't just charge like a Minotaur.

And it was strange that those shadows were still clinging to it.

What is that?

Pain sent stars sprinkling across my vision when something hit me on the back of my head. I wasn't used to fending off multiple Nightmare Fae at once.

Hissing, I palmed the bloody wound, and then a blow from a second rock made me stumble to the ground.

On your knees already? Az teased. Despite his playful words, I picked up on his concern. He was worried enough that he was using our bond to tap into my mind and monitor my progress. A bond that was much stronger now that I had bitten him. Twice.

Don't worry your pretty feathered head about me, I purred in return as I found the male Siren picking up a rock in his hand. He gave me a toothy smile—or was it an apology?— before he hurled another one at my face.

I think I'm more worried about him, Az replied. *What's a Siren doing out here?*

I disliked Sirens, but I tried to set my personal feelings aside because Az was right. A Siren shouldn't be on land. Sirens could exist outside of their watery kingdom for short periods, but he wasn't going to last long like this.

Something isn't right, I told Az. And I wasn't just talking about the state of the paradigm and the portals.

I knew Nightmare Fae behavior, and they didn't act like this. Even the dark souls I had hunted and managed had an instinct for self-preservation.

The Siren's gills flexed and closed as he struggled to draw in the oxygen from the air. It was possible for him to breathe, but difficult. He was exerting far too much energy by forcing his powerful tail to prop himself up in order to face me.

I inched closer to him, examining him while he clearly struggled.

"Why are you throwing rocks?" I asked him. "Can't you sing? And what are you doing out here?"

He hissed at me in response.

Frowning, I drew my wand from my boot and gouged a hole in the ground with raw magic, then filled it with salt water that wouldn't evaporate. "Go on, get in," I told him.

He merely hissed again, ignoring the water, which didn't make any fucking sense.

Nor did the agony that continued to reflect in his flinching gaze, as if he were trapped inside his own head.

Which looked… familiar.

My eyes widened as I realized what was going on.

Vivaxia is using her magic on the Nightmare Fae, I told Az. *It's that damned pet spell.*

A flinch of hurt crossed my senses. I knew it was a sensitive topic for Az, and I still regretted using that spell on him. Even if I hadn't known his history, or the trauma I had been reopening for him, I shouldn't have taken away his free will like that.

But now… now I understood the depths of Vivaxia's depravity. She viewed Nightmare Fae and fae like Azazel as pets to be controlled.

She didn't give a damn about free will.

I know, Az replied, his mental voice softer than usual. *I recognize it. And I can also see that these aren't dark souls. At least, not all of them.*

My teeth ached as I clenched them. Of course Az could tell the difference between innocent and evil souls. He'd had that ability all along; he'd just never explained it to me.

I'd been left in the dark, not just by Lucifer but by Az, too.

You're not in the dark anymore, Az assured me, having likely heard my train of thought. *I share everything with you now. That's a promise.*

And I knew he meant it. The ferocity of his words left me craving him, not just to continue where we'd left off but also to show him with my body that I accepted his apology.

I accepted him. And I would show that soon by biting him for a third time.

Mmm, Az purred in my mind, obviously picking up on my intent. *Will Cami watch?*

If we all survive this, she'll more than watch, I promised.

Our foreplay would be taming these beasts, together. Not by defeating them.

But by saving them—at least, the ones who deserved to be saved.

As I circled the Nightmare Fae, giving myself time to analyze them, I could see the difference between the Siren and the Naga now.

The Naga had a dark aura about it that I had thought to be some strange shadow, but it wasn't a shadow. It was the aura of its soul.

The Siren did not have the same shadows.

It wasn't an ability I had before. But then again, I'd previously been the Warden in name only.

Lucifer had given me the key—a symbol of the true power that came with the role.

I was indeed part of his inner circle now.

The Siren was one of Lucifer's protected inhabitants, and Vivaxia was trying to confuse us, to get us to attack each other. The agony in his eyes was something I understood.

He didn't want to be here. Meaning this was an innocent trapped by Vivaxia's power.

Shit.

The Naga launched again just as I used magic to nudge the feral Siren into the pool I'd created and trap him there. I'd been distracted, leaving the Naga a chance to drag a claw across my leg. Blood seeped into the fabric of my pants, making me dizzy as stinging heat flushed through my veins.

Ajax, Az pressed. That heat grew and seared across my psyche as I tapped into Az's mind, sensing the battle he still waged on his end in the dorms. *It's getting worse out here. Tell me what to do, because right now I'm just stalling.*

Still, Az was trying to let me lead. But I wasn't doing a good job of it so far.

Fuck, how do I fix this?

I couldn't make a plan until I figured out how to separate the dark souls from the light ones—and now my leg was stinging like a bitch. Nagas could have poisons in their strikes, so I muttered a quick antivenom spell, but it didn't seem to work. The icy heat of the poison seeped over my hip bone and gave me a nasty pinch in my side.

What's the plan, Warden? Az pressed. He wanted to give me a chance to lead, meaning it was on me to handle this.

Az knew that was what I needed to accept my role as the true Warden, and I wasn't going to let him down.

Try to incapacitate or capture those under Vivaxia's pet-control manipulation until we can figure out how to help them, I replied. Az had broken the spell, so whatever alterations she'd made so far should be breakable as well.

We need to herd them all to the dungeon. We'll separate the light and dark souls once we get them there.

My dungeon wasn't just going to be a hall of nightmares anymore. Lucifer had trusted me as Warden, and I was going to make some changes.

I would fill it with those needing rehabilitation, not just torment.

But I would have to decide what we'd do with the dark souls once we had them secured in their cells.

Killing Dakota had created a conundrum inside me that I didn't have time to evaluate. But it was something I needed to consider as I moved forward in my role as the official Hell Fae Warden. Because I possessed the power now to remove mirages and end the dark souls trapped in those cells. I just needed to determine how to proceed and who deserved what sort of sentence.

Some souls, however, were innocent. Corrupted by a magic meant to manipulate and destroy. They didn't deserve the fate of being locked in those dungeons.

So, I would rehabilitate them. Those who deserved to be saved would be.

This was right.

This was the kind of Warden I wanted to be.

I whispered a spell that amplified the air around me, then I whistled. The sound drew the attention of several Nightmare Fae wreaking havoc away from the Hellhounds who were struggling with a Sea Dragon, as well as three other erratic fae.

And they homed in on me.

As I expected, their feral state made them more susceptible to loud targets.

"This way, wildlings," I coaxed them as excitement thrummed in my veins. The pinch in my side had lessened, or maybe I imagined that. It didn't matter; this would be over soon. Lucifer had given me the key, one that burned in my pocket and promised power to the Warden. To *me*. "Follow the noise."

This wasn't the typical hunt, but a sick part of me enjoyed the challenge that offered.

I had to capture, not kill. Every soul would be evaluated once we had tamed the beasts.

And once I drew the feral fae to the dungeons, I would use the power Lucifer had trusted me with to protect his people.

Our people, now.

I jumped as another portal opened right in front of me. Instead of fighting, I swirled my finger and summoned a defensive spell again.

What the fuck are you doing? Az demanded as I amplified my whistle while the newly arrived fae rammed into my defensive barrier. *I can hear that noise all the way from here.* The sound spell worked better than expected, likely because Vivaxia had done something to this paradigm to make it behave like an echo chamber.

I'm drawing them back toward the dungeon, I informed Az, but I didn't get a chance to explain further because a shrill reverberation of my whistle slammed into me, making me throw my hands over my ears as my barrier shattered like glass.

Az! I thought as the strong body of a Sea Dragon wrapped around my torso. The static electricity that had been perpetually humming bloomed until all I could hear was the throttling drone of magic that was foreign and wrong.

Whatever had separated me from Cami now stood between me and Az. I couldn't feel him or hear him at all.

A new sensation fluttered over my body, leaving me chilled even as I used my wand to force the Sea Dragon to release me.

Ice cold, just like Vivaxia's heart, I thought as my teeth chattered, and I glanced up at a broken sky while I stumbled into a run.

Literally broken, because cracks formed over the surface of the paradigm as if it was about to split apart.

"Fuck," I cursed as I forced power into my legs and continued running, because the Nightmare Fae were still on my heels.

All of them.

I tried to shadow to put some distance between them, but my magic sputtered around me and vibrated like opposing magnets trapped inside an iron spindle.

The throb from the wound across my thigh burned like frost, making my extremities go numb.

This wasn't like any Naga poison I'd ever encountered.

Because it's not poison, I thought as my vision started to turn an odd shade of brilliant white. *It's her.*

Vivaxia wasn't just finding a way into the realm; she was digging into the minds of innocent Nightmare Fae and trying to break us all apart.

Starting with Cami and her mates. I suspected the rest was just a bonus.

Killing the brides would set Lucifer back centuries.

Undermining me as Warden would be an embarrassment and seed further distrust and chaos.

This was how she won, by dismantling everything Lucifer had built.

By attacking his heart.

I was a part of that heart now, whether I was ready for

it or not. I was mated to Az, making me indirectly part of Lucifer's inner circle.

I might not be able to feel Az, but he was still there. Just like Cami was on the other side of the invisible barrier that was choking the life out of this paradigm. It wanted to keep me apart from her, to suffocate me, but there was one problem with that.

You don't understand the power of love, Vivaxia.

A strange sense of peace settled over me as I managed to summon one more defensive barrier. Even while Nightmare Fae corralled around me, hissing, and threatening to overcome me, nothing would take that truth away.

I thought I had understood love, experienced it, even, but it was nothing like the real thing.

Camillia was my heart and soul, and the entire power of Heaven and Hell couldn't keep us apart.

I looked up as if drawn to the paradigm's ceiling by instinct. The brilliant white light spreading across the sky wasn't just the invading magic that seared through my veins.

It was love itself.

Glass and sizzling gold stars broke through the cage surrounding the paradigm, and beyond the chasm was Cami's love radiating through.

Melek held her as he spread his impressive wings, making it seem like Camillia was the one who flew through the sky.

Like an angel.

My angel.

Our angel, a voice seemed to say as the vibrant sky slowly turned black.

And the feral fae attacked.

CHAPTER 22

CAMI

"*elek*," I breathed, urging him to fly faster, or to overcome this stupid spell and blink to Ajax's side because my mate had just *vanished* underneath a mountain of monsters. Or at least they were large enough to create a mountain from the dragon and two other large breeds of Nightmare Fae that had collapsed on top of him.

I had almost lost Az. I wasn't about to go through this again with Ajax, too.

"I'm descending," he promised me as my stomach turned from the drop. But it felt too slow, too stagnant as the campus stretched out over the broken horizon. "But we have to be careful, little angel. This is very likely a trap," Melek warned me as he took his sweet time delving into the paradigm.

Vivaxia's magic was everywhere, but so much of it was a harmless mirage. Some of the blocks had been real, preventing us from entering the paradigm, but once I felt Ajax's pain, I knew where to look.

Typhos seemed unconcerned with the spell now that I

had used my bond with Ajax to pull us beyond the wavering mirage that cloaked an otherwise delicate net. Or I had... siphoned a hole through it. I wasn't entirely sure.

Either way, the Hell Fae King had taken the opportunity to address a problem in his kingdom. The air sizzled as his powerful form blazed through, his confidence creating literal flames as he crashed into the ground.

Rock and dirt sprayed into the air, but it was a calculated landing. Not a single pebble strayed my way, and when Melek landed, I scampered onto the ground and my fingers twitched at my hip for a blade.

Of course, none was there. I hadn't exactly been *weapons* training a moment ago.

Keeping a weapon on me at all times had been my norm for many years. Even when I'd attended classes at the university, I kept one out of sight for the occasional supernatural nuisance or whatever shit my father surprised me with. But it seemed that ever since I had found myself wrapped in my destiny, I was constantly without a blade.

You don't need a weapon, little angel, Melek assured me in my mind. *You are one.*

I glanced at Typhos when he said that, because I was a siphon designed to tap into *his* power.

And what a power it was.

The Hell Fae King parted the gathering of wild Nightmare Fae with a wave of his hand. I'd spotted at least six so far, and fires and chaos in the distance suggested there were more to contend with.

The creatures in his immediate vicinity keened and cowered in his presence as a strange flickering energy swelled over them like a tidal wave.

What is that?

All beasts in the Hell Fae Realm bowed to their king, even ones that had gone feral.

At least, that was what Typhos had expected. The initial shock of our arrival had disrupted them, but only momentarily.

That foreign energy snapped right back into place, and that was when they coiled.

"Cami!" Melek shouted, both out loud and inside my head as my soul heeded the panic in his voice. I crouched and ducked out of the way just as a wall of scaly flesh slammed into the ground where I had been standing a moment before.

Is that a dragon?

"Stop!" Typhos roared. The power behind the single word slammed into my chest, and my body wilted as if it wanted to obey, but the command hadn't been for me.

The group of at least six Nightmare Fae, as well as a few Hell Fae types, simultaneously pounced on the Hell Fae King. He disappeared from view, but Hellfire spiraled into the sky in response. The heat swept upward, not actually aimed at any of the fae, but it served to spread them out.

He wasn't hurting them. Only driving them back so we could better manage their numbers. While there weren't exactly many of them, Nightmare Fae were... large.

But the Hell Fae King could handle a few beasts. This was his domain, after all.

Satisfied that Lucifer would be fine, my gaze tracked the broken ground, searching for the mate who had drawn me here, the one I still couldn't feel at all.

Ajax.

I spotted him crumpled on the ground and covered in blood. My eyes widened as my chest constricted. I couldn't feel him, but that didn't mean—

Pain splintered across my spine as a jagged claw raked

its way through my flesh. A scream followed, but it wasn't my own.

A Banshee slammed to a stop in front of me, her eyes wild and wrong.

Wait... not a Banshee, I thought, my brow furrowing.

A knifelike sensation pierced my ears, and I pushed the pain away as I struggled to see beyond the mask this creature wore. Her shriek felt real and made my knees weak. But it didn't mean this was a true Banshee. Dark souls were forced to wear Nightmare Fae forms, and that included access to some of those forms' abilities.

Those abilities were defensive in nature.

The Nightmare Fae weren't evil—quite the opposite, if I understood correctly—but this beast had a dark soul. Its cold, icy intentions didn't match what I had learned so far of the species that Lucifer's realm protected.

It made sense now as to why Lucifer had said there weren't any unmated females accepted by his Source.

Because there *weren't* many female Nightmare Fae in his realm, not real ones. They had been masked forms for dark souls to wear.

They sure look real, though.

The topless creature before me had scraggly hair and spindly wings with puffy down in the center arches, which were covered in spots, as well as long, twisted claws from otherwise human hands.

When I really studied her, I could see the true fae underneath. A twisted face on a fae boasting pointy ears and dull blue eyes shone through.

I didn't know who she was, but she wasn't one of Lucifer's Nightmare Fae.

Her nostrils flared as she swept one foot in front of the other and slunk closer to me.

Then her head was gone a moment later, severed in a flash of gold as blood splattered over my face.

I flinched, then glanced at Melek, who held out a sword I hadn't even seen him summon.

"Go to Ajax," he said, his voice more serious than I'd ever heard it. He kept his gaze on the headless body as it crumpled to the ground.

"Melek—"

His multicolored eyes found mine. "I know. I heard your thoughts. That's why I killed her before she…" His jaw flexed. "Go to the Warden. I'll keep them at bay."

I blinked. Melek hurting a creature seemed so unlike him. He was all sensuality and mischief.

But apparently he could be deadly, too. A finely honed blade at the right hand of the Hell Fae King.

"*Go, Cami,*" he said again, snapping me out of my thoughts.

Right. I took off toward Ajax, then slowed as I noticed the shimmering barrier around him. *Is that a protection spell?*

Yes, Az confirmed, my question clearly having been broadcast to my mates.

And is that a Siren? I wondered next.

No one responded to that.

But they didn't have to.

Because my eyes confirmed the answer.

A similar barrier shimmered around the creature, only it seemed to be containing it in an enchanted pool of water.

One sweep of my eyes over its form told me why. *There's no darkness surrounding this beast.* However, it appeared to be in pain, its milky eyes exuding a frantic kind of agony.

Panic, I recognized.

But it was safe.

I glanced at Ajax, in awe of his show of power. Not just his demonstration with the magical bubble, but his obvious deduction that this being wasn't a dark soul.

Praise graced my thoughts.

Praise that instantly disappeared as I took in Ajax's ashen state.

He looks...

I didn't allow my mind to drift any further into speculation. But it was clear why Melek had urged me over here.

Although, I wasn't sure what he expected me to do.

I wasn't even sure what had happened.

Ajax, I whispered, moving toward him.

Only to be intercepted by yet another Nightmare Fae, this time a Centaur. Its graceful, arching antlers speared into the sky, and the ground thudded underneath his hooves.

However, what was most noticeable was the lack of a dark aura surrounding him.

He's a good Nightmare Fae, I recognized.

Except his nostrils flared as he flexed his fists, his fury a palpable presence in the air.

Cami, Melek said.

I've got this, I promised him.

But Ajax—

The beast roared, cutting off whatever Melek had been about to say. The sound reminded me of the panic I'd seen in the Siren's eyes

Because he sounds agonized, I realized. *Like he doesn't want to be doing this... and has no choice.*

I could see it in the way his hooves hesitated on the ground, like he was trying to keep himself from charging at me.

Frowning, I crept toward him like one would a wild animal.

He released a furious snarl, one that was definitely threatening. Yet he didn't charge me.

That snarl lowered into a growl as I touched his torso. I wasn't sure why I chose to approach him like this; it just... felt right.

Except, what I sensed beneath my palm didn't *feel right* at all. His skin resembled ice.

The creature attempted to back up, but I followed him, intent on tracking the chilly strand of magic swirling around him.

Death, I thought, frowning. *Only not.*

It... it sort of reminded me of the energy I'd siphoned in the Netherworld Kingdom. Yet it was different, too.

Vivaxia, I thought. It'd been her manipulative spell I'd absorbed then. However, I'd ended up taking too much. I'd pulled in Nightmare Fae souls, too.

Innocents.

I couldn't do that again.

But if her enchantments were claiming these fae, I had to do something. Because this magic didn't belong here. It was wrong.

Very, very wrong...

I tried to delve deeper, to search for her specific strands of magic. The air hummed like a swarm of bees around me, causing all the hairs along my neck to stand on end.

But I had to find the strand... to... to *fix* this.

The Centaur growled again.

"I'm trying to help you," I told him.

A flash of understanding lightened his gaze, followed by a chaotic glimmer that didn't belong. A chaotic glimmer created by Vivaxia's magic.

Almost there, I thought, untangling the invisible cords with my mind.

Only to be distracted by a powerful blast behind me.

A blast that lit my veins on fire and drew a gasp from my throat.

I want that, I thought. *That power... I want to... to take it...*

My eyes instantly searched for the source of it.

Typhos.

Because of course it was his power my inner siphon desired.

He'd ensnared two Nightmare Fae in magicked chains, creating a line of Hellfire along their skin. The strands of vibrant electricity were wrapped around the neck of a Sea Dragon and the leg of a Manticore who was trying to fly, which was a magnificent sight to witness since he'd skillfully managed to imprison only the offenders, not the innocents caught in their clawlike grips.

A flurry of embers burst into the air as Az appeared and caught a new chain of fire from Typhos, the two of them working seamlessly to wrangle the Nightmare Fae around them.

Except... except several of them weren't dark souls.

Like the Centaur, I thought, my palm still against his vibrating chest.

When I looked back at him, I saw almost a plea in his gaze, like he was losing some internal fight.

"You're trying not to attack me," I realized aloud, my heart skipping a beat.

He blinked as though to confirm, some of that lightness coming through again. Only to be overrun by chaos once more.

Gods... It's the pet spell, I suddenly grasped. *Or a version of it.*

I wasn't even sure of the formal name.

Nor did it matter.

Because right now, these creatures were suffering.

And it was all because of Vivaxia.

I had to help them. To… to *fix* this.

By siphoning it off of them, I thought, my eyes widening. *I can siphon the magic.*

Just like I'd tried to do in the Netherworld, albeit with that death stone, but I… I was a siphon.

I didn't have to siphon just Typhos's energy, right?

I could… I could siphon Vivaxia's spell, too.

My fingertips tingled as I tried to locate the strands once more inside the Centaur. *Not his soul,* I thought. *Not his power. But the… the* disease *that doesn't belong.*

I had no idea what I was doing. I was just… *hunting.*

Sorting.

Chasing the darkness. The ice. That… that frigid familiarity.

I'd been exposed to this magic more than once. However, my understanding of it went deeper than experience. It… it was almost *ingrained* in my psyche.

Because it's Virtuous Fae magic, I realized. *And I'm… a Virtuous Fae. A siphon.*

I was literally created to *absorb.*

So that's what I'll do… I latched onto the darkest strand, the one that didn't belong, and started pulling. Unraveling. *Siphoning.*

It was slow at first, my tugs tentative.

But each second seemed to lessen the Centaur's agony, his eyes becoming clearer and clearer until… until he blinked.

"Thank you," he breathed. "*Thank you.*"

I took a step back, my body suddenly alive with the foreign magic. It hummed all over me, through me, *inside me.* Like it was searching for a valve, a place to go.

The Centaur took off while I focused on a few other Nightmare Fae, curious about whether I could unravel them from the poisonous spell without touching them.

It only took a few seconds of focus to find the source—that inky black strand—and tug it free.

More electricity vibrated around me. I shivered from the intensity but kept seeking out the spell, siphoning it from each Nightmare Fae I found with my gaze.

It was invigorating. *Empowering.* Yet I wasn't sure where to send the power. It... it just kept bundling inside me like an electrically charged ball.

Morphing.

Churning.

Curling.

Threatening.

I shifted my focus to the Siren next, the one Ajax had trapped with magic, and released it from Vivaxia's spell while carefully ensuring the barrier remained around it.

A shudder rippled through me as that final tendril curled around me, the power burning too hot inside.

It wanted to dig deeper.

Go inward.

To that place... the one that connects me to her.

No. I... I couldn't let it go there.

But I couldn't hold all this in either.

It was going to burn me alive. Suffocate me. *Kill me.*

I... I had to push it somewhere.

Somewhere safe.

My gaze flew to Typhos, to where he wrangled his beasts with wisps of burning power.

Or someone *safe*, I thought slowly. *His Source...*

I didn't think further; I simply acted, my heart opening as I connected to Typhos with ease.

Too much ease.

Because I'd been created to steal his light.

Only, I was going to fight that urge and do the opposite of what Vivaxia wanted of me. I was going to blast everything I'd taken from her—that horrible enchantment —and give it to her nemesis.

To Typhos.

To his Source.

I felt his eyes on me, but I refused to look at him. Refused to *hear* him.

He could accept this. Hell, he had to. Because I would not give anything to Vivaxia. If she wanted to bespell the fae who resided here, she would have to pay the price of losing that magic.

It belongs to Typhos now, bitch, I thought at her.

Not that she could hear me.

But I didn't fucking care.

I kept siphoning and sending.

Siphoning and sending.

Siphoning and—

Cami! Melek shouted into my mind. *You need to slow down and take a breath.*

I blinked, not understanding his concern. I felt fine. In fact, I felt *energized.*

I'm only taking Vivaxia's spells, I told him, certain of my actions. *No innocent souls.*

Because all of the strands I'd tugged on were dark cords of disease—manipulative to their frayed ends.

So much darkness, I thought, whirling around.

Only for my gaze to fall on Ajax.

Still unconscious.

Hidden behind his bubble.

Ajax, I breathed, momentarily knocked off-kilter as I realized I'd left him there to suffer. *Ajax!*

I ran for him, only slightly confused by how I'd ended up so far away from him.

Was I moving while siphoning all those spells? I wondered.

But I didn't have time to try to answer my own inane question.

All that mattered was Ajax.

And the copious amounts of dark magic covering his body.

Gods... How had I missed that before?

Or maybe I was just seeing the magical strands in better detail now as a result of being so hyper-fixated on them.

The *how* didn't matter, though. The fact was I could see them, and Ajax was infected with several strands.

This... this is going to be difficult to siphon.

He was riddled with power. So much so that he alone might push me over the edge and force that valve inside me to open.

No, I decided. *I can do this. I* have *to do this.*

I'd just... I'd just send even more power into the Hell Fae Source. If a little of me goes along with it, so be it.

I placed my hands on Ajax's far-too-cold body and tried to mentally unravel all the strands of magic strumming around him.

"Camillia," the Hell Fae King said, his voice carrying through the chaos. He was near the gates, while I was still closer to the library where Ajax had fallen, but it was as if Typhos's lips were right on the cusp of my ear. It was similar to the first time I'd heard his voice in the arena, only this time, all of his attention was on me.

He was surrounded by miraculous, fiery chains, the ends of which held various Nightmare Fae hostage.

He'd started lining them up for me.

Az and Melek, too.

Because they'd realized what I'd been doing, and now they were holding the fae there as hostages.

While waiting for me to release them from their spells, I thought, my heart warming.

Typhos had not only discerned what I'd started doing, but he'd also decided to partner with me in the effort.

And if he was mad at me for touching his Source, he showed no signs of it.

Instead, his expression only seemed marred with concern. Which was confusing, given everything we'd just unraveled together as a team.

He said something I couldn't hear now, my mind suddenly consumed by Ajax once more.

The darkness, I realized, feeling it crawling up my arms from where I'd touched Ajax. *It's spreading.*

Because it really was like a disease.

Only, I had the cure for it.

Me.

Ajax flinched as I began unwinding the invisible cords of darkness holding him captive.

You're going to be okay, I thought at him. *I just... I just have to...* I swallowed, the first kick of power nearly causing me to lose my balance. *Hold on...*

I wasn't sure if those words were for him or for me because it suddenly felt like I was flying. Soaring. *Too high.*

Gods, this is one hell of a spell... It practically choked me as I unraveled the first layer, the poison seeming to seep right into my spirit and head straight for that forbidden place—the connection to Vivaxia.

No, I growled, shoving it into Typhos's Source.

But it started to claw its way back, threatening to return to Vivaxia instead. *Via me. Like I'm some sort of fucking conduit.*

No! I shouted again, shoving it out of me with so much force that my breath left with it.

But I didn't care.

I was *not* sending any of this back to Vivaxia. Because if I opened that connection, who knew what she would do or accomplish? I had to *push.* To *shove.* To *unwind... and... let go.*

My eyes fell closed as a whooshing sound echoed in my ears, the intensity causing my pulse to race.

Someone shouted at me in my mind, but I ignored them, too focused on Ajax.

Next layer, I thought. *Almost... there...*

I forced myself to inhale, the icy bite of Vivaxia's power jolting me to my very core.

It sank into my soul, sucking and slicing its way down.

Cami! someone shouted again.

But I... I was lost in this web of power. Siphoning layer by layer off of Ajax. Along with... with other spells. All of them dark. All of them belonging to *her.*

It was heavy.

Intense.

Suffocating.

Ice prickled my being, like I'd suddenly been pulled under a crushing waterfall, the impact leaving me frozen beneath a barrage of powerful waves.

The spell, I realized. *It's breaking...*

Not just in Ajax, but in everyone around me.

In the entire fucking paradigm.

I was absorbing it all. Drowning in it. *Allowing those icy claws to scratch at the valve... seeking Vivaxia... desiring...*

No! I screamed at it, shoving it away yet again.

But the force of it was crushing me. Pulling me. *Breaking me.*

Only, I couldn't let it go back to Vivaxia, so I... I

pushed everything I could into the Hell Fae Source. Everything I could give. *Every piece of me.*

My breath squeezed from my lungs, and my soul itself seemed to detach from my body.

But I couldn't stop. I *wouldn't* stop. Not now. Not ever.

I had to keep going.

I can't let her win.

I won't *let her win.*

This power... belongs... to Typhos Lucifer now.

Every bit of it. All the magic. The energy. Even... even me.

Because I didn't have anything left.

Everything I am... is gone.

Every ounce.

Every spell.

Every breath.

Leaving me with nothing at all. Making me nothing. Creating... *nothing.*

Yet still I gave. Because I had to return all of it to the Source. To Lucifer. To the Hell Fae. To this realm.

None of it could go to the Virtuous Fae. To *her.*

I won't be a siphon for you, Vivaxia, I thought as the world blinked in and out of existence. *Because in the end, I'll choose death... Every. Fucking. Time.*

CHAPTER 23

TYPHOS

"Fuck!" Either Camillia couldn't hear me, or she was too stubborn to listen. Maybe it was a mixture of both, but if she didn't stop this, she was going to die.

I erased the distance between us and pulled her into my arms, then shoved the Source's energy back into her chest.

But the little brat pushed it right back, refusing to accept my power. Refusing to *siphon* it. Instead, she was giving all of herself to the Hell Fae Realm.

Sacrificing herself for my fae like a queen should.

My jaw clenched. "We need to get her back to the palace," I said before issuing a command to my Hellhounds to return the dazed Nightmare Fae to their realms. Then I vanished and let Camillia's mates follow us back to my chambers.

The teleportation only took seconds, but in that brief time, Camillia's skin had turned ashen and cold, her soul barely thrumming with life.

"You and I are having a long talk when I finish reviving you, little one," I growled.

A talk that involved a shift in methodology.

Because I was done playing the role of a slow and patient teacher. Camillia De la Croix needed a firm hand. Otherwise, she was going to end up dead.

And I refused to let that happen.

"She's not breathing," Az said as he appeared beside me, the scent of ash and fire heavy in the air.

Ajax arrived next, the Midnight Fae a little winded but otherwise mostly recovered, thanks to Camillia siphoning the Virtuous Fae spell off of him. Unfortunately, it was that act that had pushed her over the edge, Vivaxia's powerful magic having created a surge that had sent Camillia spiraling.

"I can't hear her," Ajax said, clearly more focused on his mate than on his lingering injuries.

Melek appeared right behind the Warden, his agonized expression stabbing me through the chest. He quickly masked it, but not quickly enough.

Fuck, that tormented look would forever be engraved in my mind. I *never* wanted to see it again. Although, something told me my own face would rival his if I didn't find a way to fix this.

Camillia had given everything to protect my realm, to protect *me*. Just like at that Interrealm Fae Ball.

This female was the opposite of a threat. She was a fucking beacon of hope. A Godsdamn *queen*. And I'd wronged her in so many ways.

Including in our training. I'd gone too slow, too *soft*, when I knew better. With Vivaxia as a threat, there was no time for gentleness.

Camillia needed to master her power. And she needed to do it *now*.

"She's rejecting my power surge," I said, irritated not only with Camillia but also with myself. I couldn't help feeling that her rejection was founded on distrust. But we'd address that after she survived this. Setting her on my bed, I focused on my Commander. "Azazel, I need you to—"

He pressed his hand over her heart, and electricity thrummed through the air, the Phoenix Fae inside him already charged and ready before I even finished my demand. Power rippled out of him, the palpable energy taking my breath away.

The pale quality of Cami's skin diminished, leaving behind a creamy glow. *Thank, fu*—

The color faded before I could finish the thought, my soul warming as a roar of fire hit my Source with a vengeance.

And Cami went back to resembling death.

I growled.

And Azazel tried again. "*Fires*," he hissed when the same thing happened after a handful of seconds.

Well, at least this isn't about rejection, then, I thought, some foreign part of me momentarily relieved. But I swallowed that temporary reprieve because we still had a big fucking problem.

"We need to drown her in power," I decided, voicing the solution as it formed in my mind. We didn't have time to think, only act. "And we need to distract her—to give her something else to focus on—so she can't just shove it all back into my realm."

Then, once she woke up enough, I'd take control and show her how a king tames a queen.

Azazel's hand still hovered over her chest as he asked, "What kind of distraction?"

"Anything that takes her mind off the energy coursing through her," I told him. "She's hyper-fixated on redirecting the power right now, even while unconscious. If we can shift her attention to something else, I should be able to help ground her."

My Commander nodded, then looked at Ajax. "Bite her."

The Warden arched a brow. "You want me to feed on her while she's weak?"

"I want you to make her body come alive while Typhos, Melek, and I flood her with power," Azazel said, taking charge.

Ajax gave him a skeptical look. "You think that'll be enough?"

"After what I experienced back there in that dungeon?" Azazel's gaze lit up with twin flames of golden lust. "Yes. Yes, I fucking do."

In the chaos, I hadn't realized what had transpired between the two of them until now—they'd deepened their connection. "Ajax bit you."

"Twice," Azazel said without looking at me. "Now bite Cami, Ajax." He ripped her tiny tank top clean off, exposing her bra—a bra that went up in flames in the next second as he seared it right off of her. "Arouse her. Make her pant. Drive her so fucking wild she can't think about anything other than our cocks being inside her."

Ajax was already moving before Azazel finished, his palm landing on one tit as his mouth sealed over the other. Azazel burned off the rest of her clothes, leaving her naked, a sight I would have enjoyed if she didn't resemble a fucking corpse.

Godsdamn it, Camillia, I thought at her, furious that she was sacrificing herself. But a part of me was also fucking aroused, which was really discombobulating.

I shouldn't want to punish her. Not like this. Not right now.

And yet, all I wanted to do was pull her over my knee and redden her pale ass until she screamed.

I grabbed her throat, my thumb pressing against her waning pulse. Melek joined me, kneeling on the bed by her head and threading his fingers through her hair. Then he leaned down and blew air into her mouth.

Air laced with power.

I felt the heat of it on my palm as I added my own brand of energy to his efforts.

Then Azazel placed his lips to Camillia's inner thigh with a low snarl that echoed through the bedroom suite. Energy hummed all around him, the Phoenix inside him building a surge that would burn us all. But I didn't fucking care so long as it overwhelmed the female lying lifeless in my bed.

"On my count," Azazel ground out, parting Camillia's legs to rest between them. His mouth shifted higher to the apex between her thighs, his touch hovering over her sweet little clit. A vision of him biting her there assaulted my mind, the desire to hear her scream an intrinsic need that had power rippling through me.

She'd deserve the sting.

Little temptress, I thought. *You're hurting your mates by playing the role of a sacrificial lamb. They'd better make you pay for that, Camillia. But if they don't, I sure as fuck will.*

Not that she could hear my threat.

We weren't bonded.

A fact that had me feeling a little out of sorts as I watched her mates combine their powers to revive her. I would be able to help as their Hell Fae King, but I could help so much more if I were Camillia's mate.

My jaw tensed. *That's not going to happen. Even if she's the perfect queen.*

And not because I didn't want to bond her, but because

she definitely didn't want to bond me. She didn't trust me or like me, something her body and soul had made apparent by rejecting my rejuvenating essence.

Unless... unless she's only rejecting me because she can't control it.

I shook my head, my musings devolving into a spiral of rhetorical nonsense.

Camillia De la Croix needed to fucking breathe.

Then I could... figure everything else out.

Flames erupted down Azazel's spine, burning through his shirt and sending tatters of fabric into the air. He ignored it, his Phoenix still building an inferno of cataclysmic vitality. It was unlike anything I'd ever seen from the Commander, his magic swirling in a way that appeared to be bolstered by his new Midnight Fae connection.

Violet and golden sparks danced around him, his hands running up and down Camillia's legs. He met my gaze from between her thighs, his expression borderline feral. "*Now,*" he said.

No countdown.

No warning.

Just a command, one I adhered to without hesitation.

A whirlwind of heat blossomed between the five of us, the maelstrom of electricity causing all the hairs on my arms to stand on end. Fire followed, the violet flames engulfing us in an inferno that should have burned yet didn't.

Because I countered it with my own power, tempering the fire and ensuring our safety while Azazel emptied every ounce of power into his mate.

Melek groaned.

Ajax growled.

And I basked in the glow of our circle.

It was intense. Beautiful. All-consuming. *Perfection.*

Fae, I wanted more. To feel this every fucking day for eternity. To exist in this bubble of fiery embers, lounge in the flames, and create a new throne for all of us to share.

Including Camillia, I realized, my heart racing as I felt her starting to filter that power back into my Source. But there was too much for her to balance, too much for her to consume and send on, too much for her to *siphon.*

Because all of us were flooding her veins with life, forcing her to rejuvenate, *to wake the fuck up.*

Those big eyes of hers opened as her lips parted on a scream, the sound so fucking delicious that I wanted to shove Melek out of the way and claim her for myself.

But he was already there, already breathing into her lips, his essence a decadent kiss that turned her screams into moans in a heartbeat.

Or maybe that was because of Ajax and Azazel. Perhaps a combination of all of the above.

Our Warden had switched breasts, leaving traces of blood behind on her opposite nipple. And our Commander had fully settled between her legs, his lips having sealed around her clit as he'd shoved all that power into her body.

Now he was driving her wild with his tongue, forcing her to focus on the sensations and ignore her siphoning powers. All while we pumped her full of our magical essence.

If only it was our seed, I thought, my hand threatening to clamp down harder on her throat. I wanted to see her bathed in cum, marked by all of her mates. *And me...*

Fuck, that was an unexpected desire. Or perhaps not unexpected at all.

I'd meant to deny this forbidden pull, to leave her to

Melek and the others, but watching her come undone beneath her mates had me panting with need.

Me. The Hell Fae King… fucking panting.

It was unheard of.

Melek knew how to taunt me, to make me harder than obsidian granite and crave his hot mouth. But this was a whole different level of lust. It was a calamitous yearning that ensnared me in a sensuous web that threatened my sanity.

I had to maintain order.

To be in *control.*

To dominate this female's power.

Yet her *scent* was invading my every pore, and her moans were the only sound I could hear. I'd wanted to drown her power, and now all I desired was to drown in her.

Fucking fae… I couldn't look away from the sinful feast unfolding before me. Power swirled, passion beckoned, and carnal needs flourished.

Camillia was awake now and drunk on the energy giving her life.

Not only that, but she was also distracted by her mates. Lost to their touch. Eyes closed once more. Indulging in Melek's kiss while fisting Ajax's hair as she held him to her breast.

All the while, Azazel *licked.*

And I… I watched. Captivated. Held in place by my hand around her throat. Leashed to the decadent display of uninhibited debauchery.

"Fuck, little warrior," Azazel groaned against her wet pussy. "I need to be inside you." His clothes were gone, his fire having eaten through them. And his cock was hard. Ready. *Roaring* with need.

Ajax released Camillia's breast, his gaze fixating on Azazel, his jaw tightening.

The Commander and Warden stared each other down, some silent conversation happening between them that had Camillia grabbing the sheets on either side of her hips in expectation. Melek finally released her mouth, causing her thick eyelashes to flutter open. But it wasn't my prince she looked at.

It was me.

Twin storms of intensity drilled into mine as a cyclone of energy whirled between us.

"If you push any more power into my Source, I'll choke you," I warned her. "And it won't be with my hand. It'll be with my cock down your throat." Because I was done playing nice. If she needed sex to focus on, I'd give her that. Fuck, I'd give her *anything*.

Her swollen lips parted, the reaction one I longed to interpret as an invitation. However, I suspected it was actually a reaction to my threat.

Only it wasn't a threat at all, but a promise.

Because right now, I wanted nothing more than to fist all that golden-brown hair and guide her mouth to my aching dick.

But we weren't ready for that yet. Fuck, I wasn't sure if she was ready for any of it.

Although, that didn't stop me from squeezing her throat and leaning down until we were eye to eye. "Test me," I dared her. "See what happens."

She swallowed against my palm.

Melek hummed in approval, his fingers skating over my hand before trailing down to play with her abused nipple. "Ty doesn't make false promises, little angel. But it could be fun to tempt him, hmm?"

Her eyelashes fanned across her reddening cheeks, her pupils dilating as she continued to hold my gaze. A war danced in those pretty eyes. A war between obedience and defiance.

Oh, she'd stopped flooding my Source with power.

But now she was considering doing it just to spite me.

I could see it in her expression and hear Melek's amusement as he read her thoughts.

"If you want my cock, ask for it," I told her. "Don't piss me off just so I'll fuck you."

Her gaze narrowed. "Maybe I don't want it."

I arched a brow, my thumb dancing along her now-thundering pulse. "Then what do you want, little temptress? For me to watch Azazel fuck you?"

I leaned down, wanting to be the only one she could see.

"Or maybe you want all three of your mates to fuck you at the same time," I continued, my mouth so close to hers that her breath kissed my lips. "Ajax in your ass. Melek in your mouth. Azazel in your slick cunt." I studied her features, saw the way her nostrils flared. "Mmm, you do want that, don't you, sweet queen? To have all three of your holes filled while I watch."

The way she shuddered in response confirmed my every word and had my lips curling as I slowly sat up again.

"All right, then," I murmured, meeting Melek's gaze before glancing at Azazel and Ajax. "Show me what I'm missing. Make me jealous. Better yet, make me *beg*."

It seemed like a good punishment.

A way to atone for being a fool all these months.

Maybe Camillia would forgive me in the end.

Or maybe she would spend eternity making me regret my choices.

And forever be… *my forbidden fruit.*

CHAPTER 24

CAMI

Fae...
I had no idea how this dream started, but I hoped it would never end. The last thing I remembered was surrendering myself to the inferno inside me and vowing to never be Vivaxia's siphon.

However, now...

Now I'm naked. On a bed. And surrounded by four hot-as-fuck fae.

One of whom just said he wanted to watch as all three of my mates fucked me.

Part of me knew this was real, not a fantasy. Yet it was all too incredible to be believed. Particularly as Typhos was here and issuing sensual remarks.

When he threatened to choke me with his cock, I nearly combusted.

Then he had to get all arrogant with me and taunt me with that line about asking for what I wanted. I couldn't admit out loud that I wanted him to follow through on his threat. That made me... made me... Well, I wasn't sure. It made me *something*.

Because I shouldn't want him.

Only, I was having a really hard time remembering *why* I shouldn't want him.

Especially when he looked at me like *that*. He'd been focused on my mates before, but he was staring down at me again, his hand still around my throat. "Azazel is going to lie down, and you're going to straddle him," he told me.

Part of me wanted to reject the command, just to see what he would do.

But then Az started moving, and I was suddenly hypnotized by all the masculine beauty on display. His muscular form was exquisitely defined, all sinewy lines and bulging strength. And that phoenix tattoo on his chest... Fae, it almost looked *alive*.

My tongue snuck out to dampen my lips as I caught sight of the impressive length between his legs, the desire to taste him hitting me right in the heart. Fae, I wanted to lick that drop of precum off his tip and indulge in the power that was all Az.

However, Ajax beat me to it.

The moment Az settled onto his elbows, Ajax leaned down, his gaze on our mate, and closed his mouth around the tip.

My heart kick-started, my lungs suddenly too tight to breathe. Because *fuck*, that was hot. But also... *You're okay*, I thought, connecting to Ajax's mind.

I'm more than okay, little rebel, he returned, his voice warm as he took Az deeper into his mouth. *I'm fucking phenomenal.*

I swallowed, my gaze skating over his nude form. I wasn't sure when he'd lost his clothes or... or when I had either. I suspected it had something to do with Az.

But it was all feeling so dreamy. So unreal. *Four sexy fae...* I nearly closed my eyes, wondering if I needed to wake up. Or if perhaps I'd died.

There'd been so much power.

Too much power.

I'd... I'd been unable to harness it.

And Vivaxia...

Shh, Ajax hushed into my mind. *Stay in the present with us, Cami. And don't even think about pushing our power out of you.*

Our power...? I echoed, shivering as a wave of electricity rolled across my skin. It took me a moment to realize it was Melek's finger sending shocks through my being, his gaze intent as I glanced up at him.

"You pushed too much into the Source," he murmured aloud, responding to my train of thought. "Ty told us to flood you with energy and coax you into taking it." His multicolored irises flickered with heat. "Now we're going to ensure you keep it." He lowered his lips to my abdomen, his expression filled with wicked delight as he began kissing a path downward.

Each touch lit my skin on fire, his power humming along my being and soaking into my spirit. "I didn't know you could do that," I whispered, every part of me feeling alive.

Melek had kissed me before. Touched me, too. But this... this was underlined in powerful vibrations that had my soul sighing inside.

Az hissed, drawing my attention to him as Ajax drew his teeth along his shaft. "You're fucking with me," my Phoenix Fae mate accused.

"I'm dominating you," Ajax returned. "So sit there and enjoy it."

My thighs tensed in response to their words, only for Melek to push my legs apart and settle between them. "Ty and I will prepare her to be fucked while you two play," he said, his mouth against my heated center.

Ty and I, I repeated, my gaze flying up to the Hell Fae

King. He was sitting beside me on the bed, his suit ruffled but otherwise intact.

While the rest of us were naked—including Melek—something I noted now as I ran my gaze over the tattoos decorating his chiseled torso before returning my attention to Typhos.

He canted his head, like he was pondering something.

Then he leaned down and pressed his mouth to mine as Melek slid two fingers into me below. I jolted, the combination of sensations underscored by a bolt of fire as they drowned me in their auras.

So much power, I marveled, shuddering. *If Vivaxia—*

No, Melek interjected. *Don't think about her. Focus on this— on* us.

But if she—

"No, little angel," Melek said, shifting to speak out loud again. "We're safe here. *You* are safe here. Let us heal your soul."

"No one can touch us here," Typhos added against my mouth, seeming to follow the conversation despite it having begun in my mind with Melek. "My Source is stronger than ever thanks to you, little siphon. So relax, enjoy, and let your mates worship you while I protect you all."

I trembled beneath the weight of his commentary. There was a hint of praise in there with his words of gratitude, but also a note of command underlining that last part.

Can I trust him to protect us? I wondered, staring into his eyes.

He'd stopped kissing me to speak but remained right against my lips. And now he was gazing at me with a ferocity that stole my breath.

He took dominance to a whole new level.

Suddenly, I simply wanted to let him lead. To give in to his need for control and enjoy, just like he'd told me to.

Questioning my faith in him was a moot point.

Because I already knew the answer. Of course he would protect us. It was what Typhos Lucifer did—he protected everyone in his realm, *especially* his inner circle.

Rather than respond verbally, I arched my neck and kissed him. It was almost like what I'd done in his bed the other day when I'd thought it was a dream.

But this was more than a fantasy.

This was me bowing to the Hell Fae King and expressing my gratitude for his guidance. For his leadership. For keeping me—*us*—safe.

I didn't want to fight this attraction anymore. I didn't want to fight *him*. I merely wanted to exist in the moment and let whatever this was happen.

His palm cupped my cheek, his responding touch gentle.

Until it wasn't.

He'd let me lead into it.

But the Hell Fae King sure as fuck finished it.

His tongue slid into my mouth, demanding reciprocation and compliance as he took possession of me in a way only Typhos could. And I let him. Oh, how I *let* him.

Flames erupted in my veins, his power flourishing inside me as Melek speared me with a third finger and closed his lips around my clit.

I moaned, but the sound was lost to Typhos's mouth. *My king*, I thought, bowing to his command while arching into Melek's touch. *My prince*.

A groan from Az had me adding, *My Commander… and my Warden*. Because I could *feel* Ajax pleasuring Az, taunting him, teasing him with his tongue and mouth.

Something about their embrace was different right now.

Because Ajax is leading. Az always told him what to do. Yet this... this was Ajax's choice. He was telling Az what to do. Not with his words, but with his actions.

And I could hear the intent in his mind.

His desire to be in control, to force Az to *submit.*

This was a battle of wills.

Only, Az wasn't fighting it.

He was letting Ajax take control.

This is... so... hot.

It's about to get hotter, Ajax replied, a smirk highlighting his tone.

I nearly asked what he meant as power blasted through the room... *from Ajax biting down.* Az's responding growl vibrated my entire being, causing Typhos's palm to slide down to my throat where he held me in place and continued devouring me.

I was panting.

Writhing.

So consumed by the magnetic burst of energy that I could barely breathe.

You just mated Az... The words resembled a pant in my mind, my ability to process what was happening barely registering above the chaotic current swirling in the air.

Yes. He's mine. And I'm his. And you, my darling little rebel, are ours. That final word echoed through my mind, or maybe out loud, I... I couldn't tell what was mental or vocal anymore. Nor did I care. Not with the sensations building inside me from Melek's ministrations below. At some point, he'd started prodding my ass as well, his hands working me over in a delicious way as Typhos owned my mouth.

Fae, I'm being burned alive, I thought, moaning into the

Hell Fae King's kiss while trying to move my hips. But a palm on my abdomen held me down.

Typhos's palm...

Part of me registered that I was no longer thinking of him as *Lucifer* but as *Typhos*. Then another part of me overrode the instinct to ask why and forced me to focus on his mouth instead.

Just let go, I told myself. *Stop thinking... and indulge.*

"Mmm, such a good little angel, letting us take care of you," Melek praised from between my thighs. "Just wait until our cocks are inside you, claiming you from the inside out."

A shudder worked through me, my mind fracturing beneath the onslaught of sensations and intrinsic need.

I could feel Az's pleasure mounting, Ajax's bite having nearly made him come. Only, the Warden wasn't allowing it. He was forcing Az to hold back, to wait until he was inside me. All the while, he stoked his desire, bringing him to the point of climax only to shove him back down again.

Because he wanted Az's eruption to be filled with the most potent energy imaginable, to force me to take it and keep it.

I swallowed, uncertain if I could handle it. *At least I can push—*

Typhos's palm tightened on my throat, his teeth skimming my lower lip.

"I felt that, little temptress," he breathed against my mouth. "Don't even think about touching my Source right now." His thumb traced the column of my neck as he pulled back to stare down at me. "I want you pumped full of so much energy that you're bursting like a star. And I want to watch your mates' seed drip out of your holes. Do you understand me, Camillia?"

His words stole the breath from my lungs. Hell, they

short-circuited my damn brain. Because no one had ever said such a thing to me before.

And now all I could imagine was being *filled*.

"Words, Camillia," Typhos said, his gaze narrowing. "Tell me you understand."

My throat worked against his palm, my heart beating so fast I was surprised I could hear him over the rapid thud echoing in my ears. "I... I understand." That was true, right? I understood what he wanted—to watch my mates fuck me.

But I... I wasn't sure I understood *why*.

Does it even matter? I wondered.

"Hmm, it's not perfect, but we'll work on your obedience, little one," he murmured, his lips ghosting across mine.

"You told her not to use titles, my king," Melek said, his lips brushing my sex and sending tingles through every inch of my body.

"I don't want her to use titles."

"Yet you're thinking about her calling you her king," Melek returned, the smile evident in his voice. "Which, I agree, would sound delicious on her lips, hmm?"

"Always meddling, little prince," Typhos replied.

"It's won me an orgy in our bed, hasn't it?" Melek sealed his lips around my clit before I could even process his words.

But Typhos certainly understood them.

And he chuckled in response, then claimed my mouth with a vengeance.

Flames danced across my being once more, heightened by the arousal and expectation of my mates. Melek sucked hard, drawing me to the edge of a climax that he halted by abruptly pulling away.

Only to repeat the action while Typhos held my lips

captive beneath his own, leaving me incapable of screaming in frustration.

I gripped the bedding, my knuckles no doubt white from how hard I clutched the silky material in my fingers.

Over and over again, Melek taunted me.

All while Ajax made Az *burn*.

It was torturous passion, making me so wet I was *dripping*.

Az's mind told me how hard he was, how badly he wanted to come.

But Ajax was relentless, his mouth pushing Az to his limits. He wanted to see if Az would snap and demand control.

However, Az was resolute in letting Ajax lead, his need to bow to his mate a gift wrapped up in an unspoken apology.

When Ajax realized that our Phoenix Fae mate wasn't going to grab the reins, he finally released him.

"You realize holding out this long is just another form of control, right?" Ajax asked him. "You're proving your own restraint." He kissed Az's cock—an action I felt, more than saw, through the bond. "So you're never truly not in control, but I appreciate the effort. Now let's go fuck our little rebel."

CHAPTER 25

MELEK

My lips curled against Cami's wet pussy, my anticipation heightening. I'd been torturing her with my tongue and fingers, waiting for Az and Ajax to cease their little game, and it seemed they were finally ready to *fuck*.

Ty met my gaze, his blue irises swirling with an arousal I knew very well. However, it felt deeper now, even more potent than ever before.

Yet somehow he released Cami and sat back to observe.

Ajax's comments to Az about control seemed to apply here as well because Ty was showing an extreme amount of strength by being able to pull away from the temptation on the bed. *You're punishing yourself*, I realized, my thoughts traveling to him via our connection.

No, little prince. You, Camillia, Ajax, and Azazel will be delivering this punishment.

Because you refuse to join, I acknowledged.

She's not mine to touch, he returned. *Yet.*

That last word appeared to be a whispered thought,

one my king hadn't meant for me to hear. The minor slip was the only thing that kept me from remarking on how he'd technically touched her already by kissing her.

Of course, Ty wouldn't see it that way. A kiss was an innocent caress in his mind. When he said *touch*, he meant something else entirely.

She's not mine to possess was what he'd truly intended to say. Followed by *yet*.

Knowing how he felt only made me that much more eager to play with Cami in front of him. Because I wanted to tease our king, drive him mad with envy, and show him what his stubborn side kept him from experiencing.

Camillia was no longer his future, but his present. He just needed to accept fate and indulge.

I demonstrated said indulgence by giving our female a long lick up her weeping slit, then hummed against her clit. Her resulting moan had Ty taking a deep breath, his struggle clear as he forced himself to remain in control.

"Are you ready for us to fuck you, little angel?" I asked against her slick skin, my focus shifting to her beautiful face. Her eyes were closed, her head tossed back a little as she tried to push her hips upward toward my mouth.

But Az's palm landed on her stomach to shove her back down, the Commander very much in charge as he sat up. His opposite hand went to Ajax's nape, then he dragged him in for a violent kiss.

Cami shivered.

And I smiled once more.

Ignoring Az's touch on her abdomen, I crawled upward and made my way to Cami's lips, needing to kiss her.

Her arms wrapped around my shoulders as she cradled my lower body between her splayed thighs. If she had any reservations about Ty being here, she didn't show it or think it. Instead, she was just enjoying the moment with her mates and reveling in the power flourishing through her veins.

Such a good little angel, I praised into her mind. *Letting your mates take care of you.* I'd already said those words out loud, but they were worth repeating. *I'm proud of you, Cami.*

I slid my cock inside her without warning, rewarding her with a punishing thrust that had her gasping against my lips. Ty had said that Az would be the one taking her pussy, but I'd primed her for our claim; therefore, I would be the first one to fuck her.

The Commander's palm flexed between us, his hand trapped between my abdomen and Cami's flat stomach. He could easily move but chose not to.

Which was fine by me.

Az and I might never have played together like this, but there was a first time for everything.

And I fucking loved that Cami was the star of that first.

She panted against me as I began to move, her nails digging into my shoulders to hold on while I possessed her in the most intimate way imaginable.

Mine, my body said.

Ours, Az's palm told us.

Mmm, Ty thought, like he was considering our claims. Or maybe he was just enjoying watching me fuck Camillia.

I ignored him and focused on worshipping her with my hands, my mouth, my *cock.*

Gods, she was phenomenal. So damn perfect. *My sweet love,* I thought, whispering the words into her mind. *You're the key to everything.*

Balancing power within the Hell Fae Realm.

Defeating Vivaxia once and for all.

Providing a reason to exist.

Giving me cause to fucking breathe.

I wasn't sure how to convey all of those cherished reasons, so I simply channeled them into my touch. Her pussy squeezed around me, her orgasm mounting all over again.

She clamped down on my ass with her ankles, trying to force me to keep moving, ensuring I didn't withdraw.

But she wasn't in charge here.

This was about power exchange. Flooding her with so much sensation and energy that she couldn't even consider giving it back.

Which was why I pulled out of her before she could explode.

She screamed in frustration, her nails resembling claws as she made me bleed. "*Melek.*"

"You haven't earned the right to come yet, little siphon," Ty interjected. "Rewards are earned. Now let your mates fuck you and work for your pleasure."

Cami tore her lips from mine to glare at Ty. "You are not in charge here." The words came out breathy, undermining the intention behind her declaration.

"I'm not?" he countered, arching a brow.

He was the picture of bored elegance, leaning back against the headboard beside her, his long legs crossed at the ankles. But I could sense the heat simmering beneath his suit.

He was barely holding on to his control.

Something he didn't let her see but allowed me to feel. His need was a brand in our bond that seared me from the inside out.

If Cami wasn't careful, he'd lose all manner of self-restraint and pin her—a reaction I very much wanted to witness.

So I carefully crawled backward, freeing her. She sat up instantly, her breasts beautifully aroused and swaying with the movement. "I could tell you to leave," she informed Ty.

"You could," he agreed. "Would you like me to?"

My heart rate slowed as I waited, my stomach tightening with an emotion I didn't want to name.

"N-no," she stammered out. "I just..."

"You just meant...?" he prompted her, his eyebrow winging up even higher.

"That I have the power to make you leave," she said, her voice lowering to a whisper.

"Of course you do," he murmured, lifting his hand to cup her cheek. "Your safe word ensures you have the power any time we play. But that doesn't mean you're in charge, Camillia De la Croix. The ability to stop a scene and the concept of controlling it are two separate entities."

"Did you share your safe word with him, Cami?" Az asked as he drew his finger down her delicate spine.

"Yes," she told him.

"Say it," Az told her, his own dominance coming out to play.

She swallowed, her gaze still on Ty. "Camping."

"Good girl," I said, leaning over to press a kiss to her shoulder.

"What's your nonverbal safe word?" Az continued, ignoring me.

Cami lifted her hand into the air and formed a fist, the motion causing the Commander's lips to curl. "Now you can praise her, Melek."

"I can praise her whenever I like," I returned. "She's perfect and beautiful and mine to worship."

"Ours," he corrected.

"Sure," I agreed. "But she's mine to praise as I please." *And I will praise you every moment of every day,* I added via our bond. *Because you are seraphic, Cami.*

I still don't forgive you for denying me my orgasms, she replied without missing a beat.

I'll endeavor to make it up to you, little angel, I promised.

Only, Az moved before I could try, his fingers locking in Cami's hair to tug her away from Ty's touch. "I know Typhos said to take your pussy, but I want your ass. Then Ajax is going to fuck your sweet cunt while I hold you in my lap."

Cami's eyes widened, her pupils dilating and then disappearing from view as Az used his grip on her hair to yank her toward him. The abrupt move had me wanting to reach for her, to ensure she was all right, but the moan that left her mouth told me she not only approved but also *liked* Az's rough-handling.

Hmm, I mentally hummed to Ty. *That reaction bodes well for you, my king.*

He didn't reply, causing me to glance at him. However, he wasn't watching me at all. Only Cami. His nostrils flared at what he saw, which had me returning my focus to our little angel just in time to see Az thrust into her ass.

No gentle handling.

Not even a test to ensure she was ready. He just took her the way he needed to, the feral movement drawing a gasp from Cami's plump lips.

Then he sat back on his heels and pulled her down into his lap, just like he'd threatened.

All while maintaining his grip in her hair.

Her eyes glazed over with pleasure, her expression one of wanton delight.

A delight that only deepened as he released her blonde tresses and gripped her legs. He didn't waste a second, parting her thighs to show off her glistening pussy for all of us to see.

Fuck, Ty thought, the curse echoing through our mental

bond. Yet outwardly, he remained calm, his expression only slightly heated.

I smiled, intrigued by his waning restraint. I'd never seen him like this, and I wasn't surprised at all that Cami was the one pushing him to the edge.

"Take her," Az said to Ajax, his palms on Cami's inner thighs as he presented her like an erotic gift. "She's very ready."

Ajax knelt before them, his palm on his cock as he gave himself a firm stroke. "She's always fucking ready."

Az chuckled. "True." He pressed a kiss to her neck. "You love being fucked, don't you, Cami?"

She visibly trembled, her thighs clenching as though she wanted to close them and seek friction. "Yes," she breathed. "Fuck me, Ajax."

The Warden grinned. "Az has trained you well, little rebel."

Indeed, I thought, my pulse racing as Ajax moved between Cami's legs and aligned himself with her entrance.

She let out a beautiful sound as he slid into her, a sound that had my balls tightening in anticipation. Because I wanted to join them and the look Az tossed my way said I could. Not only that, but he was also looking forward to it.

This was a new game. A new experience. A rarity for someone our age.

Cami moaned again, her head falling back against Az's shoulder. He released her thighs, one hand going to her hip as the other grasped her chin. "You heard the Hell Fae King, Cami. He wants to see you take all three of your mates. So part those lips and invite Melek to fuck you next."

Her alluring sea-gray eyes landed on me, her expression reminding me of a succubus. *You're like the angel of lust,* I told her with a thought. *Not even a saint could deny you in this state.*

Cami's lashes fanned her pinkened cheeks, her tongue sneaking out to lick her pretty mouth. "Melek," she beckoned, her sultry voice resembling sex. "Let me suck your cock."

Ty growled, not vocally but internally, causing my dick to pulse in response to his desire and Cami's words. "Anything for you, little angel," I murmured, moving toward her.

I stayed on my knees and brushed my knuckles against her cheek.

A move that was apparently too soft for Az because he took hold of her once more and pushed her face toward my groin. "Lick him," he demanded. "Taste your sweet arousal mingling with his, and give us all what we want—pleasure."

"I've always thought it would be fun to watch you and Ty fight for dominance," I mused, my words for Az as I kept my gaze on my angel and her delectable mouth. "Now I think it would be even more fun to watch you both dominate Cami."

She would absolutely need her safe word then.

Because they might actually destroy her with their commanding presence.

But if anyone could take it, it was Cami.

"She can't handle my brand of dominance," Ty said, causing Cami to frown as her lips neared my cock. "I told her what I wanted to see, and she's yet to obey. And you know how I feel about brats, little prince."

I nearly smiled. "You love a good punishment," I reminded him as I slid my touch away from Cami's face to the back of her head. Az released her, allowing me to take over as I locked gazes with Ty. "So yes, we both know how much you adore bratty subs."

I pressed my dick to Cami's pouty lips.

"Prove him wrong, little angel. Show the Hell Fae King how perfect you are by swallowing my cock." *And drive him insane with envy,* I added mentally, my words for her alone.

I felt her spark of interest, her need to put on a show and make Ty wish she was his.

Because Cami loved a challenge.

And Ty had just issued one with his commentary.

Let the sensual games begin…

CHAPTER 26

CAMI

I wasn't sure why I translated Typhos's words into an expression of doubt, but I did. He seemed to think I couldn't handle my mates, which only made me want to pleasure them all that much more.

If Typhos experienced a little envy in the process, then, well, good. I'd consider that a bonus.

Or maybe it's my actual goal, I thought as I parted my lips around Melek's cock. *Maybe I want to make the Hell Fae King beg…*

Just like he'd said earlier when telling my mates to fuck me. To fill me with their cocks and their cum. *So he can watch their seed drip out of my holes…*

That hadn't been his exact phrasing, yet the concept played through my mind now as all three of my men started to move in and out of me.

Fae, what I must look like, I thought, shuddering as Melek slid deeper into my mouth.

"A Goddess," Melek said, his fingers in my hair and tugging on my already tender strands.

Az had been rough with me, his Phoenix riding him

hard after Ajax taunted him with his vampiric bite. Now both men were fucking me like I was unbreakable, their cocks hitting me so deep that I swore they were going to rip me apart.

But I didn't care.

Because it felt so good.

So powerful.

So *right*.

"You look like a Goddess," Melek reiterated, praise underscoring his tone as he stared down at me with admiration in his gaze.

I'd already forgotten about my inner musings, how I'd wondered what I must look like. But I loved hearing his comment now. I almost preened. Only a particularly harsh thrust from Az had me moaning instead.

"Can she take more?" Typhos asked, sounding bored. "Or is this the best she can do?"

My nostrils flared, my nails biting into Ajax's hips. I'd been holding on to him for balance, letting him and Az lead with their movements while I tried to focus on Melek in my mouth. But now I wanted to punch Typhos in the face, too.

"She's taking me just fine," Melek told him, that note of praise still there as he continued to hold my gaze.

"You're not even halfway in her mouth," Typhos returned. "Don't tell her she's doing fine or that she's a Goddess when she's not even trying to take you down her throat. That's not worthy of praise, Melek. That's worthy of *teaching*."

Melek sighed, his gaze leaving mine to look at Typhos. "Her tongue feels like fucking heaven, Ty. I don't—"

His voice cut off on a curse as I took him deeper into my mouth, all the way to the back of my throat.

Because fuck Typhos.

And fuck his comments.

I can take more, I thought. *I can take everything my mates give me.*

I proceeded to prove that by blowing Melek's mind while using my grip on Ajax to thrust my hips upward and back into Az.

Growls echoed in response, my men reacting to my movements and driving me onward. Forcing me to accept every bit of them and give all of myself in return.

To move.

To swallow.

To lose myself entirely to the sensual dance created by my mates.

"Fuck, Cami," Melek bit off, his neck straining as I all but choked on his cock. *Just like Typhos threatened to do to me,* I thought. *Only it's Melek's dick in my mouth instead.*

And I was very much enjoying showing the Hell Fae King what he was missing.

Ajax grasped my hips, encouraging me onward, while Az palmed my breast with one hand and slid the opposite between my legs to thumb my clit.

Sensation rippled up and down my spine, my body possessed in every way imaginable.

So full, I marveled. *I'm so... so full.*

Of Ajax. Of Az. Of Melek.

My throat worked around my Hell Fae Prince while my lower half squeezed my Warden and my Commander, and I felt *invigorated.* Reborn. So damn *alive.*

I couldn't remember how any of this had begun, nor did I care. All that mattered was this moment, this claiming, this *experience.*

Masculine need flourished all around me, in the way my mates touched me and in their minds. I could taste their lust. Feel their building climaxes. Sense their burning desires.

It stoked my own carnal passion in kind, lighting me on fire from within and causing me to lose my mind to the ferocity of our embrace.

So much heat.

So much virility.

So much energy.

The latter swirled in the air, threatening to drown me in its powerful kiss. And I welcomed it. Welcomed the cataclysmic end to this madness. Welcomed my mates' savage possession.

Because they were the ones building that raging inferno, their combined yearnings creating a cyclone of hot need mingled with scorching intensity.

I was going to explode.

Absolutely combust.

Perhaps even die from the thunderous eruption.

But I trusted my mates to ground me. To revive me. To *love* me. Because I could feel their adoration beneath the brutality, their need to protect me even while they defiled me.

All while he watches, I thought, my insides clenching. *Typhos is going to see me fall apart.*

A jolt hummed along my spine, one born of trepidation and something else. Something electrifying. Something *empowering.*

"Don't hide from this, Camillia," he said, sending sparks to all my nerve endings. "Open your eyes and embrace this. Because you're the little temptress who seduced all her mates. And now they're going to drown you in their power and cum."

Every part of me vibrated in anticipation, his words making me burn that much hotter as I obeyed him.

I couldn't believe he was here, watching this. Watching *me*.

I also couldn't believe my mates were sharing me like this.

I couldn't believe this was my reality. My life. My *fate*.

But I wouldn't trade any of it for anything in all the realms.

This was my world. My mates. *My existence.*

"Melek was right," Az whispered against my ear. "You're a fucking Goddess, Cami."

"A queen," Ajax added as he thrust into me at the same time as Az.

"A Goddess queen," Melek groaned, his head tipping back as he forced himself into the back of my throat. "One who'd better *swa*—"

Melek exploded into my mouth, his seed warming my throat as I did exactly what he'd been about to command —I *swallowed.*

I swallowed every ounce of Melek's powerful essence.

I swallowed even as I needed to breathe.

I swallowed until there was nothing left.

Until a palm around my throat made me stop and pulled me off of Melek. Then a tongue entered my mouth as energy pulsed below.

Az; I recognized, even with my eyes closed.

Typhos had told me to open them and I'd listened, but the moment Melek had started to come, I'd closed them again.

And now I was lost to Az's kiss.

But Ajax wasn't one to be outdone, his fangs skimming my throat before sinking into my neck.

Just as Melek touched my clit—a caress I recognized because of his simmering power. His energy rippled through me, causing my thighs to clench as Ajax and Az fucked me into oblivion.

I lost my mind, sensation overtaking my entire being. Until pleasure ripped through me with a force that stole my breath.

The orgasms Melek had denied me earlier seemed to have combined into a catastrophic climax that annihilated every piece of me.

I couldn't inhale. I couldn't think. I couldn't *see*.

Yet power rushed through me like a wave, drowning me in a sea of intensity that refused to let me go.

I clawed at the whirlpool around me, trying to break free. Only for another crash to send me down, leaving me writhing in an obsidian-like abyss.

But oh, it felt good. Like I was being reborn. Recharged. *Possessed*.

Because all my mates were here, their auras swirling around me in an erotic claim.

I sighed.

I screamed.

I trembled.

And then I flew higher, bursting with a pleasurable aftershock that had me coming all over again.

It was unlike any embrace I'd ever experienced and left me more satisfied than ever before.

By the time I came down, I was a sweaty, shimmering mess.

Covered in a fresh wave of Melek's golden glitter.

Dripping from Ajax's and Az's arousals.

Bloody from Ajax's bite.

Overpowered from Az's explosion.

Exhausted from taking all of their cocks.

And...

And taken aback by the look on the Hell Fae King's face...

I blinked up at him, somewhat startled to find him so close to me. Then stunned to realize he wasn't just staring at me but also holding me.

I glanced around, searching for Melek, Az, and Ajax, but they were nowhere in sight. Instead, all I saw was marble.

A shower, I realized, my eyes widening and flying back to Typhos.

He was no longer wearing his suit.

In fact… in fact, I didn't see any clothing on him at all.

"I owe you a bath, little siphon," Typhos said, his deep voice echoing in my mind. "But you're covered in cum and Melek's mark, so let's start with a shower instead."

CHAPTER 27

TYPHOS

Camillia's expression exuded a mixture of confusion and concern, two emotions I didn't really want to see in her features right now.

"Just relax," I told her. "Let me take care of you."

She'd been thoroughly taken by her mates, something that had been an absolute pleasure to observe. But that level of intensity came with a certain level of needed aftercare, something I'd volunteered to provide.

Well, I hadn't really volunteered. I'd more so seized the opportunity while Melek, Ajax, and Azazel basked in the afterglow of their power explosions.

By the time they realized I was stealing their mate, it'd been too late. "She deserves a reward," I'd informed them. "And I'm going to deliver it."

Camillia hadn't heard my declaration, too blissed out from the energy roaring through her body and soul.

But her mates had understood.

And they hadn't tried to stop me. Not even Ajax.

"I don't understand you," Camillia mumbled, drawing my gaze to her swollen lips. "One minute, you hate me.

The next, you…" She trailed off on a wince, suggesting she hadn't meant to voice any of that out loud.

"I've never hated you, Camillia," I murmured back, a bit perplexed by that pronouncement. I'd felt threatened by her, yes. But hatred? "I don't think such an emotion is possible where you're concerned."

"But you…" She trailed off again.

"But I what?" I asked as I turned on the water.

She curled into me like she feared the cold spray, but it was instantly warm. A perk of being in the Hell Fae Kingdom, I supposed.

Camillia didn't immediately move, but once she realized the shower was already up to temperature, she started to relax once more.

"You're naked," she whispered, causing one of my eyebrows to wing upward. Because I highly doubted that'd been the sentence she hadn't finished before. But I didn't remark on it, choosing to focus on what she'd just said rather than press her on the other item.

"I'm not completely naked," I informed her softly. "Just stripped out of most of my clothes. The shower would be uncomfortable otherwise."

And the whole point of this was to help her recover.

"Oh." She closed her eyes and leaned against my chest like she was considering a nap.

It was kind of endearing to see her like this. It was almost like she trusted me.

But the second I sat down on the shower bench, she stiffened. I tried angling her to receive more water, thinking that maybe she was cold. However, she remained frozen in my lap.

"Talk to me, Camillia," I requested, doing my best to maintain a calm tone. "I can't read your mind." Which wasn't exactly true. I could try to push into her thoughts via her bonds with Azazel and Melek, but I refused to violate her or them in that manner.

When she still said nothing, I sighed.

"I can't help you recover if you don't talk to me, little queen."

She shivered in response. "Why?"

"Because your commentary helps me learn your needs," I explained.

"No, I… I mean… why are you being nice to me?"

I frowned. "Why wouldn't I be nice to you?"

"Because you don't like me."

I huffed a laugh and maneuvered her onto the bench with her back against the wall and her legs over my thighs. Her gaze instantly tracked over my shirtless state to my black boxer briefs, where she remained glued to the erection concealed by the tight fabric.

A note of fear entered her gaze, killing my humor.

"I'm not going to fuck you, Camillia."

Not today, anyway, I added to myself as a thought.

But that fear didn't leave her gaze. It darkened her entire expression and threatened to destroy my giving mood.

"Why do you think I dislike you?" I finally asked, needing to regain control of my sanity before I did something we'd both regret—like kiss her until that fearful look left her pretty gray eyes.

It was a bad idea, one that probably wouldn't work. But her expression was making me feel desperate. And I was already ramped up from watching her take three cocks at once.

Sex seemed like an excellent solution to the stress created by her expression.

Except it directly conflicted with the promise I'd just made regarding not fucking her.

"You wanted to kill me," she muttered. "Which... which I get. But you also didn't seem all that impressed by me either."

My brow furrowed. "You think I'm not impressed by you?"

She made a sound that resembled a scoff. "Is this the best she can do?" Her voice deepened to an almost comical level as she attempted to impersonate me.

I smirked. "You think that was me being unimpressed?"

Her stormy eyes finally met mine, the fear replaced by an emotion that was much more arousing—anger. "Yes."

I didn't hide my resulting smile. "Look at my dick, Camillia. It might be covered by my boxers, but I'm certain you can see how *impressed* I am."

"Attraction is different from being... being, well, *impressed*," she said. "I'm naked, so of course you're reacting to me. But that's not the same as finding me good enough or worthy enough or whatever it is I need to be for you."

Okay, I was frowning again. "Camillia, I am constantly in awe of you. Which makes me want to test you."

A desire that had come out in force while watching her play with her mates.

It had taken physical effort to feign boredom and keep my hands to myself. But I'd been enthralled by her movements, her moans, her fucking arousal.

"All I wanted was to seize control and force you to take my cock," I confided out loud, aware that my admission didn't fully make sense with my previous statement. But this female threatened my sanity. "I said those things to placate my urges. The words weren't meant to belittle your worth or suggest I dislike you, Camillia."

She stared at me, her forehead crinkling a little.

"I enjoy challenging you," I added. "I want to push your limits and see how much you can take."

Although, as I observed her now, I realized how much I'd held back these last few months. And how restraining myself had impacted my needs in the bedroom.

"I've been soft with you," I acknowledged in a low voice, one that barely registered over the pouring water. Primarily because the confession was more for me than for her. "Not exactly soft, but... but not straightforward either. In truth, you've been exceptionally difficult to master." Something that both intrigued me and scared me.

I ran my hand up and down her leg, very aware of her nude state beside me. And equally aware of how close her calves were to my aching cock.

But I was too focused on this conversation to be distracted by her sexy limbs. However, I massaged her tense muscles, my need to exude some sort of self-care controlling my actions.

Meanwhile, reason controlled my mouth.

"I need to be harder on you," I told her. "Vivaxia isn't going to give me time to properly train you. I knew that, and yet, I went easy on you. Tried to start at the beginning and explain things. But that's not how we work, Camillia. I *push*. And you push back."

It'd been that way since the moment she first arrived. Hell, it'd started before that when she'd challenged my Hellhounds and forced Ajax to hunt her down.

Then she'd captured Melek's intrigue, ended up in my Warden's dungeon, and met every fucking challenge along the way.

I reiterated all that now, continuing into what came next.

Her falling into my book, my Commander and my

Warden tracking her down, how she ensnared them in her web, the inevitable punishment...

"That was me pushing you and everyone else," I confided. "I wanted to test your mettle while observing Ajax's, Azazel's, and Melek's reactions. And I'll admit, that dress was meant to punish me, too. To make me admire what I could never have." I lifted my hand to brush my thumb along her jaw. "My forbidden fruit."

She hadn't said a word since commenting on her worth, giving me freedom to elaborate on my response. To explain to her how worthy I found her to be while also going into my faults and missteps.

It was a lot, our history riddled with life-altering moments and misunderstandings.

But all of it was necessary.

Just as our next steps were paramount. "Vivaxia will attack again, and soon. She's using her link through you to weave ancient spells through my realm. Which makes it imperative that I teach you how to stop her. And not by redirecting your power to my Source."

That'd been Camillia's solution in the paradigm—to shove all the energy back into my realm after dismantling Vivaxia's spell.

"I suspect Vivaxia wanted you to lose control, similar to how you did in the Netherworld. And I think she's playing on your emotions, too. She saw how you reacted to Azazel's injuries, and attempted to replicate the act with Ajax. However, you felt something today, something that had you redirecting your influx of power. And you managed to siphon only her spell, not the Nightmare Fae essence."

Which was really fucking impressive. But equally frustrating since she'd acted as a damn martyr.

"What you should have done was use that energy to

form a weapon that you could send back through your link to Vivaxia, something to harm her. However, we'll work on that." Because now that I knew Camillia could sense the connection, she could use it.

"You know she's using me," Camillia whispered. "I... I didn't even... I just sensed it and reacted."

"I know."

"But *how* do you know?" she asked, blinking at me. "How did you...?"

"I felt it," I told her. "And I felt the connection the moment you returned to my realm. She'd activated something inside you, something to do with your siphoning ability, and I realized what it was the moment you started redirecting your power to me and my realm."

"I just knew I had to push it away from her."

"So you latched onto the only other outlet you could find—your connection to my Source," I told her. "Which would have been fine had you not shoved your own fucking soul into it."

She flinched. "All I was thinking about was countering Vivaxia. And I had no idea how to hold on to the power, so I just... shoved it away to the nearest trusted outlet."

"My Source," I murmured, my hand sliding up her thigh to her hip.

"Your Source," she echoed, causing my lips to curl a bit.

"Yes. But as for holding on to the power, you can and you did." I tilted my head as I held her gaze. "Azazel unleashed a catastrophic amount of energy into you, and you not only accepted it, but you *kept* it. So it is possible, Camillia. You just need practice, something I'm going to give you. Because, unfortunately, Vivaxia knows what you can do now, and she'll be ready to thwart your redirection during her next attack."

"Which will be soon," she muttered warily.

I nodded. "You likely weakened her by absorbing her spells and feeding them into the Hell Fae Realm, but she'll regenerate quickly."

"So we need to figure out her next move before she makes it," Camillia replied.

"And ensure you're ready for it," I told her. "Which leads me back to my role in all this—I have to be hard on you. It's the only way to prepare you for Vivaxia's true power."

Camillia frowned at me, her storm-like irises swirling with thoughts.

I waited, aware that I'd thrown a lot of information at her in her already exhausted state.

Yet her pinkened cheeks and alert gaze told me she didn't mind. She was considering everything I'd said, and perhaps even more.

"Why bother with all these smaller attacks?" she asked slowly. "What's her true goal here? If she's powerful enough to face you head-on, why bother with everything else?"

"Because she's not powerful enough to face me," I told her. "You're her conduit. She's working through you— trying to provoke *you*—to do what she couldn't."

"Mate you?"

My lips twitched. "No. She wants you to steal my light and feed it back to her. But you're proving to be a bit of a rebel, Miss De la Croix. And I'm certain it's royally infuriating your dear grandmother."

Camillia growled, the sound going straight to my cock. "Do *not* call her that."

I smiled. "Not a fan of the family connection?" I lifted my hand to her neck, my palm fitting perfectly around her slender throat. "While it's unfortunate, it's also fortuitous."

She narrowed her eyes, wariness filling her features. "Why is it fortuitous?"

"Because your familial line is what will make you the perfect Hell Fae Queen."

Her wariness vanished behind a look of astonishment. "What?"

"You heard me just fine, Camillia," I murmured, my gaze falling to her lips. "But in case you didn't understand them, allow me to demonstrate what those words mean— by worshipping you as your Hell Fae King."

CHAPTER 28

CAMI

ell Fae Queen.

The three words echoed in my mind as Typhos set my legs aside so he could stand and reach one of the shower wands.

I just... stared at him. Admired his back. All those muscles. All that strength. Then took in his torso when he turned, my mouth going dry at all the defined lines on display.

He was a work of art.

And he just called me a Hell Fae Queen.

He'd been using *queen* as an endearment, had even said a few times that he wanted to turn me into *a* queen. But he hadn't said *Hell Fae Queen*. Nor had he ever referred to himself as *my* Hell Fae King.

Yet...

Allow me to demonstrate what those words mean—by worshipping you as your Hell Fae King.

I licked my lips, my body seeming to come alive at the prospect of what he intended to do. It didn't matter that I was still recovering from what Az, Ajax, and Melek had done to me. I was already heating up at what might happen in this shower.

Except, Typhos didn't lose the boxer shorts. He simply stepped forward with the wand and started rinsing my hair.

Okay, maybe he has something kinky in mind for after...

No. Nothing kinky.

Just shampoo.

Followed by conditioner.

My lips twisted, my mind trying to process that the Hell Fae King was *bathing* me.

Okay, yes, he'd said something about that before. And he'd claimed he intended to worship me now. So maybe this was what he'd meant? By thoroughly washing me off?

As the soap slid into his hand and he knelt before me, I realized it was exactly that. "You're taking care of me," I marveled in a whisper.

"That's what I said I would do," he replied, glancing up at me. "Surprised I meant it?"

"Just... surprised you want to."

His sapphire gaze darkened to twin oceanic pools. "You're surprised I want to touch you, Camillia?" He pressed the bar of soap to my abdomen, then slipped upward to my breasts. "You're my forbidden fruit, little temptress. The first female I've desired in eons. And I've told myself I can't have you."

"Why?" I asked on a breath, trying to understand him. Trying to figure out how we'd gotten *here*, to this intimate place where we expressed our desires.

I'd dreamt of him for weeks. Or was it months? Time was elusive here.

And all the while, I'd told myself I didn't want him. Yet it was a lie. It'd always been a lie.

Just like the lie I'd believed about him hating me.

Melek kept telling me it wasn't true, but I refused to believe him. Because believing him meant embracing the idea that Typhos might feel something else for me.

However, the Hell Fae King wasn't hiding now. He was letting me see his desires and not even trying to hold back.

Except he said he wasn't going to fuck me…

"Are you listening to me, Miss De la Croix?" Typhos asked, making me blink.

"I, uh…" I licked my lips, my brow furrowing.

"Hmm," he hummed. "I didn't think so. You asked me why I told myself I couldn't have you—and I just admitted that you're not mine to touch." He brushed my nipple with the soap, stirring a gasp from my throat. "You belong to Azazel and Ajax and Melek. And they belong to you."

I swallowed as he began massaging my breast with the bar, lathering the soap in slippery suds.

"But Melek wanted me to bathe you, to show you how to remove his mark. So I suppose that means you're temporarily mine"—he switched to my other breast—"to caress."

"Only temporarily?" I echoed in a whisper.

"Unless you choose otherwise," he murmured. "Then yes, only temporarily."

"But what about what you want?" I wondered out loud. "Why is it my decision?"

"Because you're our queen, Camillia," he replied. "That means you're in charge."

I arched a brow at him. "That's not what you said in the bedroom."

"Because I'm in charge there," he returned, the soap bar slipping south to my abdomen.

I gave him a look. "Pretty sure you're in charge everywhere, Typhos."

His lips curled. "A good king knows when to bow to his queen."

"And that's what I am?" I asked, still trying to understand this shift in our relationship. "Your queen?"

He paused, his eyes holding mine as the bar remained against my lower abdomen.

I shivered, his kneeling position exceptionally intimate. He'd left me on the bench, just maneuvered me as needed and used the wand to rinse the shampoo and conditioner from my hair.

But now he was using that soap like some sort of sensual toy, stroking my overheated skin as he knelt between my sprawled legs.

It left him with an uninhibited view of my core, yet his gaze remained focused on me.

"Yes."

A single response.

No elaboration.

Just uttered with a resolution that sent a tremble down my spine. "Okay," I whispered. That was all I could say, merely a simple word of consent, something I knew he needed.

Which I supposed was the point. He'd said I was in charge, that the decision was mine as to whether this was temporary or absolute. And all it took was a few seconds of conversation to realize what he meant.

He considered me to be his; it was my choice whether or not I wanted him to be mine.

But we were already linked via our mates.

Which makes me a Hell Fae Queen, I realized. Not just because of my bonds, but because of my siphoning ability.

A talent that came from my Virtuous Fae ancestry.

A talent that rivaled Typhos's gifts.

A talent that made me an ideal mate.

"Our souls are compatible," I marveled aloud, the truth hitting me right in the heart. "They always have been."

He nodded, his touch resuming once more as he drew the soap down to my hip and lower to my thigh. "Melek realized that the moment he saw you reading Vita in the library. He knew then that you were meant to be our queen. And I think he's loved you ever since."

I snorted. "Love might be a bit of a stretch." Fated mates existed amongst some fae species, but not all. And definitely not for me.

"Obsessed is probably more accurate," Typhos agreed. "However, he knew your potential as a mate, while I denied the possibility. I know he thinks I created the trials to find an ideal match, and maybe I did. But I didn't do it intentionally. Honestly, I was too caught up in the demands of my realm to even consider my needs."

After everything I'd witnessed with Typhos, I believed that. "You put everyone and everything above yourself."

"As do you," he replied, his gaze searching mine. "You couldn't control your export of power because your focus was on everyone else's survival, not your own. It's a selfless response, the kind made by a queen. But if you're going to survive in your role, you need to master the art of balance."

He drew the soap down my inner thigh to my knee and lower to my shin, momentarily distracting me from the weight of our conversation.

"Can you stand up for me?" Typhos asked after a long beat, his touch near my ankles now.

He didn't back up, just looked up at me with silent expectation.

Swallowing, I reached for his shoulders and used them for balance as I slipped off the bench to stand, the action placing my intimate flesh within inches of his mouth.

However, he still didn't look there, just up at me as he circled his hand around to my heel and drew a sensual path up my calf.

My nails bit down, this erotic dance undoing me inside.

I used to have reservations about Typhos, concerns about trusting him, worries about what he might do to me... to Ajax...

But seeing the Hell Fae King on his knees like this... it...

My throat worked, my heart hammering in my chest. I couldn't find the words I needed to articulate my feelings. Everything was jumbled. A chaotic mess of sensations. Of needs. Of fears. Of *desires*.

And that gentle touch, I thought, my eyes nearly closing as he switched legs. *Gods, I never knew Typhos could be like this...*

I half expected to hear Melek in my head, telling me that he always knew, but my mates were oddly silent.

A realization that had my forehead crinkling and my mind instantly seeking them out. *Ajax?* I whispered first, his name and connection the ones that made the most sense in this moment.

Because he didn't trust Typhos.

Or, well, he hadn't before, anyway. But now... now I wasn't so sure.

Hey, little rebel, he replied softly, his mental voice sleepier than I expected.

Where are you? I wondered, confused.

In the bed I just fucked you in, he murmured, sounding a little more awake now. *Are you all right?*

I... I blinked and looked down at Typhos again, only belatedly aware that I'd broken our stare. However, he was no longer gazing up at me but instead focusing on my legs, his expression lacking the heat and intensity of earlier. Almost like he'd chosen to hide behind a mask.

Did I hurt him? I asked myself. A strange question, one I never thought could be possible where Typhos was concerned. Yet... the clenching of his jaw suggested...

Cami? Ajax inquired, drawing me back to our mental conversation.

I'm okay. I was just... trying to figure out why you all are being so quiet, I admitted.

Lucifer said he wanted to take care of you, so we're giving you privacy. But we can hear you just fine, Cami. You're in the bathroom only about fifteen feet away from us.

Oh. I knew that. Or, well, I assumed that, anyway. Inferred it? I nearly shook my head to clear it, the inane babble unimportant. *Thank you,* I told Ajax.

Then I released one of Typhos's shoulders so I could grasp his chin and pull his gaze back to mine. His eyes were just as blank as his expression, giving me nothing.

Yet somehow I could sense the hurt beneath the surface. Maybe Melek was projecting it to me. Or maybe... maybe my soul just knew.

Still, I felt compelled to say, "I'm sorry."

His brow furrowed. "You don't need to apologize to me, Camillia. I understand your distrust. And not only that, but I deserve it."

"I..." Now I frowned. "No. It's not about distrust. I was just distracted by the silence in my head. It made me seek out my mates, to make sure they were still there and okay." An instinct likely born from the few moments I'd been cut off from them.

Not that I thought Typhos would have separated me from my mates, but with Vivaxia's endless mind games, I had to check on them.

Who knew when she would attack again or how?

Typhos had suggested that she might be weakened by me absorbing her magic and redistributing it to his Source, but I suspected she wasn't weakened much at all.

In fact, she was probably already working on her next attack.

So what would it be? I wondered.

"What are you thinking about?" Typhos asked, making me realize that I'd wandered off again. Only this time, I'd held his gaze while pondering Vivaxia's intentions.

"Her next move," I whispered, frowning. "Vivaxia's, I mean."

He drew his touch up to my hip, then slowly stood before me. My gaze followed his along the way, causing my head to tilt back to maintain our eye contact.

Gods, sometimes I forgot how tall Typhos was, but I certainly felt it now.

He had over a foot of height on me, something that used to intimidate me. However, I felt safer than ever in this moment. Because this male exuded strength and protection. I suspected he always had; I just hadn't been open enough to accept before.

Everything had changed between us.

A part of me should probably still be scared, yet the fluttering sensation in my lower abdomen had nothing to do with fear and everything to do with interest.

"You could probably use your connection to her to determine her next move," Typhos said, his comment at odds with my mental musings but reminding me of what I'd said seconds ago.

Gods, I seem to lose all sense of reason around this man, I thought, quivering a little inside. The varying topics in my head were giving me whiplash. "How would I do that?" I asked him. "Try to follow the link she created and... invade her head?"

I frowned as my words shoved another realization into my mind.

"If I can do that to her, can she do that to me?" I stiffened, my heart skipping a beat. "Can she—"

"Breathe, Camillia," Typhos interjected, his hands suddenly on my cheeks as he pulled me beneath the shower spray.

I sputtered as water hit my face, my desire to shove him away slamming into me. But he had me up against the shower wall before I could even process what was happening. "Calm down for me," he commanded.

"*Calm down?*" I repeated on a shriek. "You just tried to drown me!"

"I just snapped you out of your panic," he bit back.

I growled.

And he growled back.

"You're impossible," I snarled at him.

"I could say the same to you, Camillia De la Croix."

"What the fuck even just happened?" I nearly shouted. "You were being all gentle, and now… now you're…"

"Taking charge?" he asked, arching a brow.

I tried to fold my arms, but he was too close for me to maneuver them up to my chest.

Gods, he has me pinned… I hadn't even realized it, but his palms were on the stone wall behind me, effectively trapping me between his muscular form and the hard surface at my back.

I glared up at him.

And he glared right back. "You need to learn control, Camillia."

"And you're going to teach it to me by dominating me?"

"Yes."

I huffed a humorless laugh. "Okay." Again I almost

crossed my arms but couldn't, which just... just pissed me off. "*How?*" I demanded.

"By making you fight me, my queen," he murmured, his lips curving upward in a taunting smile.

Then he kissed me before I could reply, his tongue invading my mouth in a quest for dominance that left me winded and a little dizzy.

Because *fuck,* I wasn't expecting that. But I probably should have been after all this touching.

Except he said he wasn't going to fuck me.

Gods, this male is maddening.

But so were the mingled feelings inside me. Fear mixed with yearning. Anger mixed with intrinsic need. *A hatred that was never really hatred... but lust in disguise.*

I wrapped my arms around him, my nails digging into him for an entirely different reason now. Because I wanted to climb up his big body and plaster myself to his exquisite form.

Except his hands went to my hips to hold me against the wall as his mouth continued to own mine.

Taunting me, I realized. *Trapping me beneath his power, his form, his very being.*

Because he wanted me to *fight.*

I had no idea what brought this on, how he'd anticipated my panic before it'd truly begun, but I didn't care.

All I wanted to do was annihilate him with my touch, bring him to his knees with my mouth, and prove that I really was a queen. One who was not only compatible with him but also capable of battling him where it counted.

His teeth skimmed my lower lip, a hum of approval seeming to emanate from his chest. "I enjoy you like this," he told me. "All feisty and pissed off."

"I don't even know why I'm mad," I admitted. "But I am."

"Because I yanked you out of a downward spiral," he returned, his mouth against mine. "If you worry about how deep Vivaxia can go into your mind, you'll basically pave a path for her to follow to your innermost thoughts. Instead, you need to locate that link inside you and use it to your advantage. But you'll need training on how to do that."

I stilled, his words bringing back my concerns. "But what if she's already—"

"Shh," he hushed. "If she's already done it, then it's too late to stop her. So let's not invite her in and instead find a way to push her out."

My head spun. "How?" I demanded. "How do I shove her out?"

"That's the question, isn't it?" he murmured, his nose brushing mine in a tender movement that contradicted the rough way he'd handled me. "It's a puzzle we'll solve together, but you're going to have to trust me, Camillia. Do you think you can do that? Can you trust me?"

I gazed into his eyes, the answer coming to me without hesitation. "Yes." Because I already did.

It was insane. And maybe even borderline suicidal.

But I trusted this infuriating male. This Hell Fae King.

With all my heart and soul… "I trust you, Typhos Lucifer."

"Then let's begin, Camillia De la Croix…"

CHAPTER 29

CAMI

SEVERAL DAYS LATER

I*f Typhos hits me with one more blast of power, I'm—*
A scream ripped from my throat, one born of fury and pain as fiery energy overwhelmed my being.
"Ty—"

"Stay out of it, little prince," Typhos said, his voice radiating a coldness that contradicted the heat flourishing through my veins.

"Typhos is right," Az added. "This is between them."

Traitor, I thought with an internal growl. But another wave of furious energy wiped out my ability to think. All I could do was *absorb* and fight like hell not to *expel*.

That was the point of this—to siphon Typhos's power without giving it back.

And without giving it to Vivaxia.

"The key is to isolate the source of her connection," Typhos had said the other morning when this hell all began. "To do that, you need to figure out where that link exists inside you."

307

"Okay," I'd replied slowly. "So how do you want me to go about finding this link?"

He'd merely smiled. Then uttered two words that had been repeating in my mind for the better part of a week. *"By surviving."*

All the tenderness I'd witnessed in that shower the other day had vanished behind the Hell Fae King's mask and had quickly reminded me why I'd once mistaken my lust for hatred.

At least until *after* his torture exercises ended. Then he let me witness that male again—the one who had shown me care and compassion—thus conflicting me all over again.

But right now? Yeah, right now, I *hated* him. And he knew it, too. Because I kept saying it.

Unfortunately, he didn't care.

As evidenced by the inferno growing around me.

I could feel Melek's growing unease. This was unlike the previous days, Typhos having decided to escalate our training session to a catastrophic level.

All in his Hell Fae Palace Courtyard.

Where everyone could see me being annihilated by his power.

Where everyone sees you becoming the Hell Fae Queen, Ajax corrected in my mind, his mental voice flat. *They're all gaping at you in awe, Cami. Now show them what you can do by swallowing the power down.*

As if it's that easy, I thought back at him with a snarl.

You swallowed Az just fine this morning, he returned. *And we both know how big his explosions are.* His amusement would have made me smile any other day.

But not today. *Glad you're finding some humor in this.*

It's the only way to accept this, little rebel. Otherwise, I'll be tempted to punch Lucifer in the face.

Now that *is a plan I can support,* I thought as I wove

invisible bands of power around my arms and legs in an effort to ground myself.

Typhos said something in response, words that sounded mysteriously like *praise*. But I wasn't interested in that from him right now. I just wanted to show him I could do this.

Then drown him in a wave of heat afterward, I decided.

Only, I suspected that would defeat the purpose of our training. He'd accuse me of releasing all the power back into his Source.

Another growl rumbled through me, frustration mounting as he hit me *again*.

There was a piece of me that longed to open, a cavern I desperately wanted to fill. *A place I avoided...* Because it was my link to Vivaxia. Or the cusp of it, anyway.

I could sense it now, but I didn't know how to manage it. Or thwart it. Or *break* it.

However, I did know how to block it. Which was a start. Except I had no idea where to expel the excess power. And Typhos was pumping me full of too much.

I can't take this, I thought, my insides beginning to *burn*. *I'm going to combust*.

You can take it, Az returned, his mental voice reminding me a little too much of Typhos. *He's only pushed you a little harder than yesterday*.

I barely survived yesterday, I gritted back at him.

Which earned me a snort from the Commander. *Are you talking about training with Typhos or all those orgasms I gave you last night?*

I snarled at him through our bond.

But I also warmed for an entirely different reason.

Because yeah, he and Ajax had taken turns making me come, the two of them trying to drive Melek mad with envy.

All my mates might have played with me together the

other day, but a hint of rivalry remained. Although, it seemed to be more of a playful game now than a serious competition. Because once Ajax and Az were done, Melek had scooped me up for a bath.

A bath Typhos had supervised.

I shivered, the action at odds with the intensity flooding through me. But thinking about Typhos and water had me craving another experience.

One where we did more than kiss.

Because that was all we'd done this week. But oh, that male's mouth was positively divine. I was addicted to him.

Which meant I didn't totally hate him.

Not even as he hit me with yet another wave of ferocity.

Oh, but it was close. Because this was just... *too much.*

I needed an outlet. Somewhere to push my excess power. *Somewhere that isn't connected to Vivaxia,* I told myself.

The whole point of this exercise was to force myself to handle influxes of magic, to control my siphoning ability, and to try to find a way to permanently push Vivaxia out.

So there were a lot of goals. But I also required a redistribution point, one I could manage.

Like Typhos has with his Source, I thought. *And Vita...*

He pushed memories and power into Vita, and took some out as needed. The book served as a gateway of sorts, one that was probably less consuming than his Source.

So I need a Vita, I decided.

Except I didn't have one.

But maybe Typhos could help me create one...

I considered that for a moment as the inferno inside me grew even larger, swirling like a cyclone of intensity that threatened to take me into the sky.

Perhaps not literally.

Or perhaps I'll grow wings, I mused deliriously.

"Ty," I heard Melek say again, a hint of urgency in his tone.

"I see it," Typhos replied, sounding disappointed. It was a tone I didn't like. One I wanted to change by doing something unexpected. By... by *surprising* him.

But I can't keep all this energy inside me... It was making me lightheaded, to the point where I felt like I might fall despite the roots of power I'd created around my limbs. *Think, Cami, think...*

However, I already had an idea. An act that would be a statement, one I could then explain as I asked Typhos for help...

What's the worst thing he can do? I thought with a mental snort. *Chastise me?*

Or maybe he'll punish me, another part of me considered with an anticipatory quiver.

Okay, enough of that, I told myself, focusing instead on my plan.

It was about time I called for Vita. That damn book always plopped down at inopportune times for me, getting me into trouble and taking me on unexpected journeys.

Well, now it could do something for me.

"Cami," Az said out loud. "Don't—"

But it was too late for me to listen to him or anyone else. This was me taking charge and doing what I needed to do with all this excess power.

And I would prove to Typhos that I could not only handle an outlet, but control it, too.

I hoped, anyway.

Pushing the doubts aside, I focused on Vita. *Come here, you troublesome book,* I demanded.

"Camillia," Typhos growled.

I ignored him, all my desires centered around his infamous text.

Which appeared right before me on the ground, the pages already spread to reveal an image of a bedroom.

Probably not something I want to know, I thought at Vita.

A fact that became a reality as a strand of inky black hair appeared like a beckoning ribbon. It was too dark to belong to Typhos, and it certainly wasn't from Melek.

Ignoring that disturbing picture—a former conquest, no doubt—I knelt and pressed my palm to the pages. Then unleashed everything Typhos had given me.

His roar of fury echoed in my ears.

But I didn't stop.

It was his power anyway. He might as well take it back. *Maybe this will create a memory for him,* I thought darkly. *A memory where I take charge of my own training and prove that all this power handling is futile.*

Az and Melek both spoke at once, their words melting into the background as I closed my eyes.

Because this required focus.

I didn't want to give Typhos any part of me, just the power he'd provided today. Which meant I had to decipher his energy from mine, an action I found oddly simple. Because I could see his strands of power, the ribbons warm and full of intensity, just like the man himself.

I unbraided his essence from mine, carefully giving it all to Vita, then sighed as my soul balanced once more.

As soon as the last tendril left my fingertips, I pulled back, triumphant. *"There,"* I broadcast, smiling. "I didn't give too much, just enough."

But when I looked up at Typhos, I didn't find pride in his expression. Instead, I found a hint of wariness. "That's not how Vita is supposed to work, Camillia."

"It's not?" I asked, my brow furrowing. "But Melek

said you store your memories in the book, and memories are power, right?"

His lips curled down, his palm going to the back of his neck. "Yes, I suppose they are, but that's still not Vita's purpose. She holds my memories because I've lived too long to keep them all inside my mind. Any power I feed her is tied to those experiences, not everyday energy exchanges."

My brow furrowed. "Okay, but you still use it—er, *her* —as an outlet?"

He squeezed his nape like he was trying to work out a kink. Then he dropped his hand and squatted before me and Vita. "She's an outlet for my mind, not my power. They're different exchanges."

"Oh."

"Oh," he echoed, but there was a soft smile teasing his lips. "It was a clever idea, though, little queen."

My eyebrows lifted. "You're complimenting me?"

"Would you rather I chastise you?" he countered, arching his own brow in return.

"Well, I mean, Melek has told me you like punishments…" *Gods, I'm flirting,* I realized, my cheeks burning. *I'm flirting with the Hell Fae King.*

And I couldn't be prouder of you for it, Melek drawled into my mind. *I'm sure it hasn't escaped Ty's notice at all that you're on your knees already, little angel.*

Typhos's heated gaze suggested that Melek was right.

Or maybe the Hell Fae King just liked my not-so-innocent comment.

"I see you're in the mood for another kind of lesson today," Typhos murmured, his eyes lowering to take in my tank top and jeans.

He, of course, was in a pair of dress pants and a

button-down shirt, the sleeves of which he'd rolled to expose his delicious forearms.

I'm starting to wonder if you're into exhibitionism, Ajax whispered into my mind. *Because the way you're looking at Lucifer right now suggests you want to give the lurking Hell Fae a different kind of show.*

I swallowed, aware that his words should snap me out of the moment. Yet they didn't. Instead, I... I kind of liked the idea of kissing Typhos in front of all these fae. *I'm losing my mind.*

Or you're simply finding your true self, Az replied. *Your future is here, Cami. With us. And I think you're finally accepting that fate.*

I think so, too, I agreed as I leaned toward Typhos.

But the clearing of a throat had him looking away, his gaze instantly zeroing in on a nearby Hellhound. He stood a second later and started toward the newcomer.

Payan, I recognized, my teeth snagging my lower lip to keep from smiling. Because unlike the last time we'd shared space, he was looking at me now. And his sharp gaze told me he *definitely* recognized me.

Feeling bold, I gave him a little wave. "Hellhounds regenerate, right?" I asked, feigning innocence.

Typhos glanced at me. "Why? Are you thinking of stabbing Payan in the balls again?"

This time, I couldn't hide my smile. "Do I have a reason to?"

"Did you the first time?" Typhos countered, a hint of teasing in his tone.

"I think so," I told him honestly.

"Hmm," he hummed, a flicker of laughter dancing in his intense blue eyes. However, the look disappeared before he focused on Payan. "Yes?"

The Hellhound stared me down for another minute,

causing me to stare right back. Just because I was on my knees didn't mean I was about to submit.

Not to him, anyway.

Payan finally looked away and cleared his throat. "You're being requested in the Morpheus Kingdom, Your Majesty." Payan glanced around, then lowered his voice as he added, "It's King Nos, sire. They say he has hours left."

A few lingering Hell Fae whispered nearby, clearly having overheard Payan's news.

Typhos cut the trio a lethal look. "Stop eavesdropping and go do something useful," he demanded. Then he returned his attention to Payan. "Thank you. I'll take it from here."

"Of course, my lord," Payan replied, bowing so low that I thought he might kiss Lucifer's dressy shoes. Only, he blinked out of existence before that could happen.

"Nos has been ill for some time, but I have heard reports that it's grown worse over the last few weeks," Melek said, moving to stand before Typhos. "I assume it's related to Sabre's disappearance."

Typhos sighed and ran his palm over his face. "That damn Monsters Night excursion created a lot of fucking problems."

"I think we've barely skimmed the surface on that one," Az agreed, folding his arms. "Maliki knows more than he's said. Hades, too."

Typhos shook his head. "We'll handle them in time. But it sounds like Nos is at the end, which means I need to pause our training for today." He looked at me, a hint of apology in his expression. "I originally planned to take you and Ajax with me to the Morpheus Kingdom, to introduce you to some of the Nightmare Fae politics in this realm, but I fear I need to handle this issue on my own."

I nodded, understanding. "It's fine. We'll go with you next time."

He cupped my face, his thumb tracing my lower lip. "Melek will take over while I'm gone." He glanced at our princely mate, who was impeccably dressed in a full suit, as per usual. "Teach her everything you know about Vita, including how you acquired the book." He looked down at Vita on the ground. "There's a reason she showed Camillia that scene of Vivaxia's bedroom. Dig into why."

Melek bent to pick up the book, closing her pages and tucking the leather-bound text under his arm. "Consider it done, my king."

Typhos smirked, then returned his focus to me and the thumb he'd left near my mouth. "When I return, I want you naked and waiting for me on your knees, Camillia. I think it's time you learn how I handle brats."

My lips parted in response, surprised and aroused by his unexpected comment.

Then he disappeared before I could even fathom a reply.

And he calls me a temptress, I thought, trembling from his lingering touch.

Only a temptress could bring a king to his knees, little angel, Melek murmured via our bond. Then, out loud, he added, "Stop daydreaming and follow me back to the palace. Professor Melek is about to deliver a lecture."

Ajax grunted. "If Professor Melek is going to talk about himself in the third person, then I'm going to pass."

"That's fine," Az cut in. "Professor Azazel has a lesson of his own to deliver." His gaze snagged on Ajax. "And I will absolutely be forcing you onto your knees, Warden."

My blood heated for a whole new reason as I watched Ajax narrow his gaze in challenge.

"Sparring?" he asked.

"Sparring," Az repeated.

"Limits?"

"None."

Ajax arched a brow. "Well, sounds like a fun lesson."

"Doesn't it?" Az drawled, then he grabbed me and pulled me in for a long, unexpected kiss. "Come find us if you'd prefer our brand of pleasure over Typhos's punishment games. You know where we'll be."

I did.

They'd taken over one of the palace's inner courtyards located in Typhos's private wing. Or I supposed it was our private wing now.

A strange concept.

But I'd get used to it… eventually.

As Az had somewhat suggested, I was starting to feel at home here.

However, there was a lot more for me to learn.

Which was why I shifted back to Melek and accepted his extended arm. "All right, *Professor*. Let's go learn about Vita."

CHAPTER 30

MELEK

Camillia hummed with excitement beside me, something I assumed was related more to Typhos's licentious promise than my upcoming "lecture."

In truth, it wouldn't be much of a lesson, just a story.

Because Vita was very much Typhos's secret. However, I knew enough to provide her with background information, as well as important context.

Leading her into one of my favorite reading nooks of our private wing, I settled into a well-used love seat and patted the space beside me. "Sit down, angel student."

She scoffed a bit at the ridiculous nickname. "I'm not calling you *Professor*, Melek."

"Not a kink you're into?" I wondered aloud. "Because you certainly seem enthused by the concept of Typhos's dominance, and I have to tell you, professor-student relationships are very much defined by their power-exchange dynamics."

She gave me a look. "I'll call you *My Prince*, but I'm not into the whole schoolgirl thing. Plus, if you saw the professors at my college, you'd know immediately why that kink was never unlocked for me."

My lips twitched. "Fair enough, little angel." I leaned in to brush a kiss against her cheek. "All right, where to begin…"

"You could start with opening that textbook," she suggested, glancing pointedly at the text I still had tucked underneath my arm. Then, in her most seductive voice, she added, "*My Prince.*"

I narrowed my gaze.

I could see why Typhos kept calling her a *little temptress.* I also understood why he considered her to be a brat. Her sensual lilt, coupled with the way she now ran her foot up my leg, was very distracting.

And positively delightful, too.

I'll absolutely be helping Ty punish you later, I told her. *Maybe I'll tie you up for him.*

He told me to be naked and on my knees, she reminded me.

Not that I needed the reminder. I was very aware of what he'd said. *But he didn't list any other parameters, which means ribbons are allowed. But I digress…*

"I'd be careful calling Vita a textbook, little angel," I said, switching from our mental conversation to a verbal one instead. "Vita is so much more than a simple book. I'd even dare to call her unique."

Cami crossed her arms as she frowned down at the magical book I had pulled onto my lap.

"The physical trip through Typhos's memories was a pretty good hint at her *uniqueness,*" Cami deadpanned.

My lips twitched. *You really are a bit of a brat, hmm?*

She didn't reply, just arched a brow like she was daring me to repeat those words out loud.

I didn't.

Instead, I smoothed my hand over Vita's cover. She

vibrated with power, likely from Cami's explosion. Or maybe she liked our conversation. With Vita, it was hard to know for sure.

"Well, when I say *unique*, I'm thinking more about her origin. She was actually a journal, not a book." A very important journal at that.

"Okay, it's a journal." Cami's brow pinched. "Er, *she*. But, um, why is it a she?" Her eyes widened. "Wait, she's not some poor soul transformed into an inanimate object because of a reneged deal, is she?"

A laugh bubbled out of me. "No, she's not a dark soul." I slid Vita onto the glass coffee table in front of us and unfurled her pages, some of my humor dissipating. "She's more like... a memory."

She was a book of memories; that much Cami had been told already.

But she only knew about Typhos's memories. *Not the original owner's...*

I waited for Vita to show what I desired, aware that my thought would prompt a picture.

Only... the pages remained blank.

Odd.

I frowned.

Vita always depicted something, even to me. But now the parchment simply glowed with power residue, giving off red and gold sparks.

Hmm. Perhaps she was still recovering from the energy blast, which both made sense and also concerned me. *Something to talk to Ty about when he returns.*

But in the interim, I'd teach. Just like he'd requested.

"Vita used to belong to Typhos's mother," I began, a small smile twisting my lips. "It was her journal. That's why I refer to her in the feminine form."

"Oh," Cami whispered, her playfulness gone. But a

note of interest shone in her stormy eyes, prompting me to proceed.

"Long ago, Typhos asked me to retrieve the journal for him. He'd said it was important to her and filled with memories he never wanted to forget. And I think that's why she eventually evolved into being his memory keeper, too. Only, his version of journaling was a little different from his mother's."

Cami smiled. "That's actually very sweet."

Humor touched my heart, making me want to chuckle. Because *sweet* and *Ty* didn't usually go together.

But I supposed she wasn't wrong.

Ty had wanted to honor his mother. And he had. In a very special way.

"What was his mother like?" Cami asked softly.

"I never met her," I admitted. "But from the memories I've seen through Ty, I know that she was a good mother."

"She died?" Cami asked, her brow crinkling. "Virtuous Fae... can die?"

"Not in the typical sense," I told her. "It takes a very powerful event to remove a Virtuous Fae's soul. And even then, their energy can't truly be destroyed."

I had no proof of that. Although, Typhos's accident certainly provided a significant clue as to what happened in a Virtuous Fae's version of the afterlife.

"My kind is often likened to angels for a reason," I mused aloud, finishing both my reply to Cami and my train of thought.

"Do I want to know what happened to his mother?" she asked warily, her mind telling me I was being cryptic again.

But it wasn't on purpose. I just... I didn't have all the answers where Virtuous Fae deaths were concerned.

However, I did know the response to this particular query.

And it wasn't one I wanted to voice.

Alas, Cami needed to know because the incident defined Ty's existence. His very purpose in this realm. "Ty…" I trailed off on a swallow, then sighed before forcing the sentence to leave my lips. "Ty killed his mother."

Cami's eyebrows flew upward. "*What?*"

"By accident," I added. "He was young and didn't realize what he was doing." My lips twisted. We'd deviated off topic a bit, which I should have realized would happen when bringing up Vita's origin. "This is really Ty's story to tell…"

But given the look in Cami's eyes right now, it'd just become my responsibility to tell her about Ty's past.

She'd only recently begun to trust him.

I couldn't let *this* be the reason she backtracked. Especially when it wasn't his fault.

"You remember how he said he used to be a siphon like you?" I asked.

"Yes," she said, her face paling as her mind no doubt anticipated where I was heading. She'd nearly killed a dozen or so fae in the Netherworld Kingdom recently. She knew what her power could accomplish. "He… he lost control?"

"He had no control," I replied. "He didn't even know he was a siphon. He just knew something he was doing weakened his parents until… until they simply no longer existed."

"Parents?" she echoed, making me realize that I'd only focused on his mother because of the journal.

"Yes. He siphoned the energy out of his mother and father until their physical bodies disappeared," I explained.

"I wasn't there, but from what I understand, their souls fractured and are now a part of Typhos... forever."

It wasn't a pretty tale.

It also wasn't one I could share many details on, as I hadn't been there and I wasn't a siphon.

But I went on and told her what I did know.

Which was that Ty had fed on their energy for years as a child, his soul consuming theirs as sustenance. And while they clearly knew what was happening, they didn't try to stop him.

"His mother's journal had several entries about it," I said, explaining Vita's importance. "Many of those entries were written in the form of letters to Ty, letters she knew he would one day need. Letters of forgiveness and understanding. And assurances that she would live on, through him, and she'd always be with him. But physically, she would be gone and they'd never talk again. Hence the importance of her journal."

Cami lifted a hand to her mouth, her eyes filling with tears. "That's horrible."

"It's love," I countered. "The love of two parents willing to give their child everything to survive, even their own lives. Some would say that's the ultimate sacrifice."

"Or incredibly unfortunate," Cami countered. "Why didn't they help him?"

"They didn't know who could assist him," I replied, shrugging. "And no one wanted to help. Virtuous Fae create, and many saw Ty's gift as destructive, which is the opposite of our nature."

My lips twisted, my mind spinning through the agony I know Ty must have experienced back then.

"In truth, though, it's an entirely new form of creation," I went on slowly, processing my words as I spoke them. "Ty can take energy and *create* something completely new. He can *transform*." Just as he'd done to himself. That day he'd fallen, he'd changed his Virtuous Fae energy into an entirely new manifestation.

That was the day he had become a king.

"So what happened? After his parents died? No one... no one helped him?"

"Not at first, no," I confided, the history a sad one to recount. "His family wasn't royal, and he didn't have any relatives. So he handled the loss alone, and eventually, he left, thus leading him to me. And... Vivaxia."

Cami stared at me. "He must have been so sad."

"Sad. Angry. Bitter. Broken." I winced, hating to use that last word, but it was apt. "Typhos felt a lot of ways, but guilt was probably the most prevalent emotion. That guilt is actually what guided him in creating his Source."

"Guilt?" Cami repeated.

I nodded. "Yes. He wanted to find a way to siphon power for good, to atone for his past sins. And he did that by manifesting an outlet for his power, an outlet for all of his *light*. But the key was, he didn't use that energy. Instead, he gifted it to others. Primarily those who needed protection."

"The Nightmare Fae," she translated.

"Yes. Now, it's the Nightmare Fae. Then, it was Virtuous Fae and others he saw as needing an extra boost." I shrugged. "What you see today is several thousand years old. Trust me when I say that he started small. Though, he's always been powerful."

"So how did he learn to do that?" Cami asked. "His parents obviously didn't teach him. Not because they didn't want to, but because it sounds like they couldn't. So who helped him?"

"Vivaxia," I replied. "In a roundabout way, anyway."

"Oh." Cami's expression darkened. "She taught him how to siphon his power... for good?"

"Not exactly." I paused, considering how to explain this. "After everything that happened with his parents, he more or less throttled his siphoning ability. But it wasn't a permanent fix because the power still existed within him. So he found a new outlet, one born of his lessons with Vivaxia on how to craft deals. While the outlet might not have been the purpose of those lessons, it was something he taught himself while mastering the art of negotiating with others."

"So she didn't actually help him master his siphoning talent," Cami replied.

"No. I'm not even sure she knows about it. Ty says she doesn't." But I'd always wondered deep down if she knew the truth and if it was his ability to siphon that she longed to exploit. Because it was that ability that allowed him to manifest his creative energy.

"That makes more sense to me," Cami said slowly. "But even with teaching him the art of making deals, I assume she had an ulterior motive."

"Oh, she absolutely did. She wanted his light, as you know. But she helped him master his ability and watched as his power grew. Basically, she groomed him and his gift, knowing all the while that she intended to one day take it."

"Except the deal didn't go according to plan," Cami said.

"Correct. And that deal brings me back to Vita," I murmured, pleased that I'd finally reached the whole point of this discussion—to explain Vita's history, just as Ty had requested. "The day I retrieved that journal is the day he penned that infamous deal with Vivaxia."

Cami sat forward a little, like she was eager to hear more.

"Ty sent me to find that little book, saying he needed it for nostalgic reasons. Of course, I knew the purpose was deeper. By that point, he'd perfected his skills and was using deals as a way to fuel his Source."

"By collecting debts," Cami said.

"Yes, exactly that," I replied as I stretched my arm out behind her along the top of the love seat. "I had thought he might want the journal to pen some of his deals, or maybe just as a keepsake. I later learned that the purpose was to have a place to guard his memories and ensure no one could access his mind."

Her face expressed confusion, telling me I needed to clarify what I'd just said. Which I supposed was the entire point of this lesson and what Ty truly wanted her to understand.

"He's been alive a very long time, which often increases the risk of immortal insanity. But Vita allows him a safe space to expunge some of his vast knowledge and experience, which is imperative for someone in his position."

"But not imperative for you?" she hedged.

I smiled. "I'm not the one with an entire realm under his sole protection."

"Yes. However, you are mated to the one who is," she pointed out.

"True," I agreed. "And if I someday feel a weakening of my mind, I may seek a similar outlet. Ty has simply chosen his method early, which again makes sense for one with his responsibilities."

She considered me for a moment. "So he didn't actually need Vita yet?"

"Maybe, maybe not. The point is that he created her in case he does need her, because the safety of the realm will always come first. And he knows the importance of safeguarding his thoughts."

"Which is what Vita does for him. It's not a power exchange for him. It's an outlet for his memories, one that allows him to keep an, uh, open mind."

My lips twitched at her apt description. "Actually, yes. That's exactly what Vita is to him. Although, I didn't know that would become her purpose that day. At that point, we weren't fully mated yet, so I couldn't read his mind or his intentions."

A fact that I hadn't liked at the time. But I'd understood it.

"Ty couldn't fully mate me until he mastered his power," I went on. "He hadn't wanted to risk hurting me."

Cami swallowed. "He'd already lost his parents; he didn't want to lose you, too."

"Yes," I agreed, warmth filling my chest.

Of course, that warmth vanished as I recounted what came next... *after* I'd found the journal.

I told her how Ty had given me directions, thus making it an easy search-and-retrieval mission. "But while I was gone, he penned that deal with Vivaxia."

A deal whereby he'd agreed to mate her.

A deal that had broken my heart... for a few seconds in time. At least until I'd realized his true intentions.

He'd wanted to free Az. He'd also wanted to free himself. Which meant he could finally be with me.

So I'd played along by pretending to betray him. I'd thrown that journal onto Vivaxia's nightstand after telling him I'd bedded her. Then I'd left.

"And later that day, he fell," I concluded, having provided the entire summary of events out loud.

Cami said nothing, her gaze on me as she processed everything I'd told her.

"To save him, you orchestrated his fall," she finally commented.

Everything that had happened was because of what I'd put into motion that night. Vivaxia had groomed Ty to the point where he'd thought he was winning.

But I'd known that the game had been rigged.

So I'd done what needed to be done.

"Sometimes, it's in the darkness that we can finally see the light," I said, suddenly needing a drink.

I pushed away from the love seat and glanced down at Vita in the process. She was still blank.

Very strange.

I closed her cover, wondering if that would help process that power surge better. Then I wandered over to a bar in another nook.

Cami followed, her steps quiet but her presence very much noted.

"Hey!" she snapped, causing me to frown and face her just as a quill flew past her face. "Ugh. I remember that thing. You told me not to touch it." She ducked as it buzzed around her, causing my lips to curl.

"Like Vita, that, too, is riddled with magic. It must have heard us talking about Ty and Vivaxia's agreement."

Cam raised a brow. "What?"

"That's the pen they used," I explained as the quill whirled around her again.

"Oh." Her body stiffened. "No wonder you told me to stay away from it."

"Yes, it very much has a mind of its own." As did most objects from the Virtuous Fae Realm. Although, this one seemed to be trying to say something now, which was odd.

The feather quill twirled in front of Cami's face, causing my eyes to narrow. It was always performing tricks, the magic very much a personality of sorts.

Similar to Vita, I thought, glancing at the book again. I'd left her closed on the table, but her pages were spread again.

Only, they were still blank.

What is going on? She should have had enough time to recover by now.

And Vita always had something to say.

Because she has a mind of her own, I told myself, something about that nagging at me. She'd always been a unique object, her existence very much tied to Ty.

And the quill... I looked at it again, noting its increasing velocity as Cami backed away. *The quill is tied to Vivaxia.*

Ty had used it to sign their legendary agreement, but it'd been his, not hers. Same with Vita.

But she touched both. My eyes widened. *She* touched *both.*

"Oh, fuck," I breathed, pieces coming together in my mind. Pieces that should have been obvious before but weren't. Because I'd never considered that she might have left her mark in—

Pain exploded in my chest, stilling my train of thought and drawing my gaze downward.

To where the infamous pen had just lodged itself... *in my chest.*

CHAPTER 31

CAMI

"**M**elek!" I screamed as his knees hit the floor.

The quill danced inside his chest, taunting me with its golden feathers.

Melek had once told me not to touch it, a reminder he'd issued just moments ago.

Well, fuck that. It'd *stabbed* him!

I grabbed the twirling weapon and yanked it out of him. Which was probably the wrong thing to do, given the blood gushing from the wound, but surely he'd heal. He... he was immortal. *Right?*

His eyes captured mine, sheer terror shining in his multicolored depths. It was a look I never thought I'd see on his face, one that had me grasping the quill even tighter as it tried to writhe out of my grip. I didn't trust it not to stab him again.

Cami, his mind whispered to mine. *Vivaxia... touched the... and Vita, Cami... You have to... warn Ty...* His eyes rolled into the back of his head as he fell silent.

"Melek?" I reached for him, noting the blood still pooling from his chest, and winced as the damn quill tried to spin out of my opposite hand. It seemed hell-bent on flying again, but I wasn't in the mood to let it go.

Only, its golden feathers turned sharp, trying to slice its way free.

"Oh, no, you don't," I growled at the damn thing, my siphoning ability kicking in as I started absorbing the magic from its metallic edges.

It was such a natural response.

One that had my brow furrowing after a moment because I... I *recognized* the essence.

Vivaxia, I thought, blinking. Melek had said this was the pen Typhos had used to sign his deal with her. *Is that why I sense her?*

No. It... it went deeper than that. Her power was embedded in the enchanted item. Almost like she'd wielded it herself...

My eyes widened. *Az! Ajax!* I screamed their names, needing to ensure our connection still existed.

Nothing.

Fuck!

She was here again, this time choosing to hurt Melek. *To play with my emotions,* I realized, growling to myself.

That must have been what Melek had been trying to say about warning Typhos.

Except... I frowned. *What does that have to do with Vita?*

I siphoned the last bit of energy from the quill, causing the golden shine to die in my hands. Then I let the object fall to the ground with a soft thud. It was no longer empowered, the glittering magic inside me instead of the pen.

Rather than expel it, I kept it, knowing I was probably going to need that energy boost to battle whatever enchantment Vivaxia had woven across the Hell Fae Kingdom.

But what about Vita? I wondered again, hearing Melek clearly in my head.

He was unconscious on the ground, his wound still fresh.

Glancing between him and the book, I bit my lip. *He's immortal. He can't die.*

But that had been no ordinary pen.

What if…

No. I could still feel him. Sort of. I couldn't hear him, but I… I sensed his life strand inside me. *Is it weakening, though?* I swallowed, trying my best not to lose my mind. To keep calm. Because losing control of my emotions was Vivaxia's goal.

Is she attacking Az and Ajax, too?

Their life strands were just as alive inside me.

But that didn't mean they weren't hurt.

Fuck. I closed my eyes and focused on breathing. *Don't let her mess with your head. Just… just think, Cami.*

Hell Fae Rule #3: Know Your Enemy Before Engaging.

Hell Fae Rule #13: Nothing Is What It Seems.

My eyes opened. Those rules were taught to me by my parents. Parents I'd never trusted. Parents I would never trust.

But my mates… I trusted them. Typhos, too.

And they lived under their own guidance, making their own choices and decisions as each moment presented itself.

Hell Fae Queen Rule #1, I thought. *There Are No Rules.*

I needed to stop thinking inside a box and consider all potential avenues in a problem.

Melek is immortal. A Virtuous Fae. He can't die.

Except he was stabbed by an enchanted Virtuous Fae item. However, I had that magic inside me now, which meant I should be able to determine the spell's intentions.

Closing my eyes once more, I focused deep inside

myself and called on that strand of magic, evaluating it for any deadly properties. Yet all I found was creationism undertones. And a note of possession.

Like the pet spell, I recognized. *Vivaxia simply enchanted the item to allow her to use it from afar. But it's not deadly. It's just... a very sharp pen.*

One that had obliterated Melek's heart with all that spinning.

My eyelashes fluttered as I refocused on his chest. *He'll survive.*

I was sure of it.

Okay. Now what about...? I looked at Vita again and forced myself to breathe. It wasn't easy, especially with my mates being blocked from my mind again, but if I'd learned anything from my new life here, it was how to properly focus.

Melek had said something about Vita. Something important. *Vivaxia touched... and Vita.*

"Were you talking about the quill?" I wondered out loud. "The quill... and Vita?"

He'd just finished telling me how the book had been in her room.

And Vita had shown me that scene, too.

There must have been something it—*she*—wanted me to see.

"What about now?" I asked as I walked toward her. "Anything useful now?"

But as I reached the text, I found simple, blank pages.

I arched a brow and bent to close the book. However, I jolted back as my finger was met with an icy touch.

What the fuck? I thought. "Why—"

"Cami!" Az shouted from somewhere in the distance. "Where the fuck are you?!"

"I'm in here!" I yelled back, my heart kick-starting in

my chest from both the panic in his voice and the chilled book on the table. "Vivaxia…" I trailed off, not sure how to finish my sentence. Nor did I want to yell my suspicions out loud. I might be in our private quarters, but I didn't trust her not to be close by. Or to have one of her enchanted minions nearby, anyway.

Thus far, she hadn't entered the realm. Typhos had said he would have felt it.

And I believed that.

She emitted power, just like he did.

I'd *felt* that energy around her. Experienced it in my own soul. *Recognized it now,* I thought, frowning. *Why does it feel like she's all over this room?*

It hadn't felt that way before. Or… or maybe it had and I hadn't noticed it?

"Cami," Az breathed, seeming to appear right in front of me. I wasn't sure if he'd ashed or if he… if he'd just run really fast.

But I was in his arms in the next moment, his hands roaming all over me like he was trying to assure himself that I was real.

Ajax joined him in the next second, his lips suddenly in my hair. "Fuck, little rebel," he whispered. "We… we couldn't hear you—"

"We thought…" Az added, trailing off. "*Melek.*" He released me and leapt toward the fallen prince. "What the fuck happened?!"

"The quill stabbed him," I said numbly. "I… I think he's alive, though?" It came out as a question. Because everything felt so unreal. *Like a dream,* I marveled, blinking. "Vivaxia did something." I couldn't define it, but I felt it.

Frowning, I tried to trace the strands of energy—the ones that seemed to be intensifying with each passing second—and found myself staring at Vita again.

Why are you cold? I wondered as I slipped free of Ajax's arms and knelt by the table.

Lifting my hand, I hovered my fingers about an inch away from the chilled text. "I can't feel Typhos," I whispered. Which was strange. Every time I touched this book, I sensed heat; I sensed *him*.

Yet right now, I felt nothing.

Just… ice.

My frown deepened as I flattened my hand on the pages, determined to solve this puzzle.

Az and Ajax said something in response, or maybe to each other. I wasn't sure, as I couldn't hear them over the rhythmic beating of my heart.

Thud.

Thud.

Thud.

Cold.

Cold.

Cold.

It didn't make sense. I'd just pushed all that energy into Vita. She should be thriving with life, not resembling ice.

I flipped the pages, searching for anything useful. But she revealed nothing.

Why can't I read you? I demanded, closing the book to scowl at the cover.

A cover… that looked tattered and old. *So, so old…*

And so unlike the Vita I knew.

She… she looked like a normal book.

No, a journal, I thought, my heart stalling in my chest as a whooshing sound echoed in my ears. *No…*

I opened it again, my gaze scanning the first page.

A page filled with a script I didn't recognize, the language ancient. *Typhos's mother's words,* I thought, blinking at it. "That's impossible," I whispered. It was like Vita had reverted back to her original form. "Where did all of Typhos's memories go?"

And what happened to the energy I'd pushed into it?

Vivaxia... touched the... and Vita... Melek had said to me.

Vivaxia touched the pen and Vita, I put together. *Warn Ty...*

"She did something to Vita." And Vita had been trying to tell me. "That's why she showed me the bedroom." As well as that strand of black hair.

Vivaxia has black hair.

My lips parted.

What if I wasn't the first siphon?

What if... what if she'd put something in Vita?

Something I'd triggered...

By flooding the book with energy.

"Oh, shit," I breathed, looking up for Az.

He was there, standing beside Ajax, both of them watching me intently. "What is it, Cami?" Az asked.

"Can you feel Ty?" I asked him.

Az shook his head. "I can't feel any of you. Vivaxia's clearly fucking with the Hell Fae Kingdom, just like she did with the paradigm."

"Or she's fucking with the entire Hell Fae Realm," I told him, the chilled book spreading ice through my veins. "Something's wrong with Typhos."

It was the only explanation for how she'd gained this much, this quickly.

"She's here somewhere," I went on. That was why I could feel her now, sense her magic all over this palace. "She's infected the realm." I swallowed. "And I... I think it's because I gave her the access she needed to break through the gates."

By being the key, I realized.

Melek had called me that before.

If only he'd realized how accurate he was...

339

Because I'd unlocked Typhos's mind by releasing his memories.

By absorbing his essence.

And shoving it all into Vita.

Vivaxia's original siphon…

CHAPTER 32

TYPHOS

My ethereal wings disappeared as I landed in the Morpheus Kingdom—specifically just outside the Strigoi Palace.

While I assumed Nos was waiting for me somewhere inside, I'd opted to take the longer route. It would give me a chance to gather my bearings, a pause I greatly needed.

Because I didn't feel right.

Maybe it was the power burst Camillia had sent through Vita.

Or maybe it's because I know what I'm about to face, I thought, aware that I'd been away from this kingdom for far too long. Specifically, the Strigoi side.

There'd been a lot of turmoil here.

Turmoil founded on the lack of available mates.

Strigoi needed Sigils to thrive. And my Source—*my gates*—had made that rather difficult since females weren't typically granted entry into this realm.

Sighing, I took in the courtyard around me.

The disturbing scent of wilting flowers assaulted my senses. *Roses dripping with blood,* I noted, eyeing the towering fountain situated in the middle of the violent red scene. A blood-red moon hung behind it, framing the picture in a gruesome display suitable for a vampiric playground.

I frowned at it. The Strigoi were like vampires in that they fed on blood, but they weren't normally so… *dark.*

The land around me felt melancholy.

Sickly.

My heart squeezed in my chest. Because this was only going to get worse once Nos died. He was the Strigoi King, one of my prized lieutenants.

Though, he hasn't been all that reliable lately.

When was the last time he even attended one of my lieutenant calls? Toward the beginning of the trials, perhaps?

I wasn't sure.

Which… which said a lot about how I'd performed as this kingdom's Hell Fae King.

Another sigh escaped me as I followed the petal-laden path around the palace toward the front entrance. The flowers actually seemed to crunch beneath my shoes, a grinding that echoed eerily in my ears.

Since when do roses even make that sound? I wondered, glancing over my shoulder. A trail of bloody footprints littered the ground, causing my lips to curl downward.

Surely that's a bad omen…

Fuck. This was going to be a long and exhausting visit.

"Your Majesty," a Strigoi guard greeted when I reached the cathedral-like doors of the Strigoi Palace. His dark eyes didn't hold any of the characteristic red they should have had, suggesting he was hungry. "King Nos has been asking for you. He's in the throne room." The door creaked open without him having touched it. "If you'll follow me."

The throne room? I wondered. *If he's expected to pass today, then why isn't he on a deathbed?*

I pondered that as the guard took me through the uncharacteristically empty halls of the dark palace.

I remembered it being more... vibrant... the last time I was here.

"Where is everyone?" I asked the guard after he had taken me through a series of staircases. The throne room was near the top of the palace, if memory served.

The guard paused at an ornate door, his hand resting on the handle.

"The Strigoi have been dying, Your Majesty. The blood fields have been withering from Rot, so many of us are being forced to hunt in other realms. And, well, most Strigoi have not been successful in alternative methods of survival." His fingers tightened on the handle, making his dull veins bulge. "Now that you're here, hopefully that will change."

My chest constricted at his words. Strigoi operated like a hive mind with their royal bloodline being their primary source of power. And the blood fields were what empowered that bloodline.

If they were rotting, like this guard claimed them to be, then all of Strigoi kind was at risk of death. Because if the royal bloodline perished, they would die, too.

Why hasn't Nos reported any of this to me? I wondered.

I'd disciplined the Morpheus Kingdom and the Netherworld Kingdom after the whole Monsters Night incident by disqualifying them all from the Hell Fae Bride Trials. My thought had been that since they'd run off to another realm to find their own mates, they no longer needed what I had to offer.

Cruel, perhaps. But it'd been a logical punishment, too.

A few of my lieutenants had complained.

But not Nos.

In fact, I hadn't heard from him at all.

Which was strange since apparently his son, Sabre, the heir to the Strigoi throne, had relocated to another dimension—a development I'd learned from Hades, not from Nos.

So why have you been so quiet about all of this? I wondered as the guard opened the ornate doors to reveal Nos sitting alone on his throne.

I blinked, taken aback by the scene while memories danced through the familiar space. It was a bizarre sensation. Like hundreds of souls frolicked throughout the room. Only, it was bare. *And so very… dead.*

The bloody rays of the Strigoi moon clashed against the dust in the air, as if this were the inside of a crypt. It was more reminiscent of a graveyard than a throne room.

Which it shouldn't be. This wasn't the Netherworld Kingdom; it was the land of dreams.

The Morpheus Kingdom could play tricks on the mind, but this wasn't an illusion. The decrepit scene before me was the result of a neglectful Strigoi King.

It was his job as the head of the royal Strigoi bloodline to maintain the blood fields, to ensure their life and prosperity in exchange for an abundance of energy.

But he'd clearly failed in that task.

And many others, I thought as I stepped into the room.

The stench of wilted flowers wafted around me even though we were far away from the courtyard now. I searched for evidence of any discarded bouquets but only found a massive dais at the end and silver vines threaded through bare marble. Those vines gathered around a blood-red design that glowed on the ground just beneath Nos's tattered boots.

The hairs along my arms stood on end, my nerves prickling with every step I took through the room.

Nothing had felt right since I'd arrived.

Hell, I was pretty sure this sensation had begun before I'd left. *When Camillia altered Vita.* It was like a jolt to my mind, the energy coming at me from the wrong direction and leaving me off-kilter.

I'd hoped the longer flight and walk here would have helped clear some of that fog from my mind, but it was only getting worse.

And the dropping temperature of this room was not helping.

My dress shoes clicked across the chamber floor as the icy bite of the air prickled across any exposed skin. The Morpheus Kingdom wasn't usually *warm*, necessarily. But I was certain it'd never been this cold before.

Nos's red eyes watched me as I approached. He definitely didn't appear to be dying. Actually, he was almost *glowing*.

Because he's drawn in all the power of his territory, choking off his own people to keep himself alive, I realized. It was the only conclusion that made sense.

And here he sat on the very throne I'd gifted the Strigoi. The one I'd crafted from magic to serve as a power source in the absence of a Sigil.

"Whoever sits upon the throne controls the Strigoi Royal Bloodline," I'd announced long ago.

Then I'd left it up to the Strigoi to determine their fate.

Nos was the most recent victor, with many kings having sat on this throne before him.

Yet seeing the Strigoi King like this now, all gluttonous and unrepentant, had me regretting my choice not to monitor the situation more closely over the millennia.

I believed in free will. Allowing my Nightmare Fae to thrive. But this was not thriving. This was *dying*.

I've greatly neglected my role as guide and protector here.

I've been too busy. Too overloaded to notice the Strigoi slipping right out from underneath me.

And now what power remained in this territory glowed at Nos's feet, seemingly the only sparkle of life in the otherwise suffering territory.

At least until he removed the mirage cloaking the room —a mirage I'd felt when sensing the lingering souls in the room.

They were real.

And very, very dead.

Dozens of bodies appeared as his veil continued to rise, all of them fallen Strigoi. *With one lone woman*, I noticed. *Did she come from that infamous Monsters Night?* I wondered.

"You finally grace me with your majestic presence," Nos sneered in a tone that had me arching a brow.

He might not be truly on his deathbed, but I could change that in a blink.

Of course, I wasn't sure there were any Strigoi left to take his place on that throne.

Which had me reining in my temper and narrowing my gaze instead. "What have you done, Nos? Why would you do this to your people?"

Because I was certain that he was responsible for the "rot" the guard had mentioned.

But I'm the one who was responsible for him, I thought, a pang touching my chest.

A pang that just continued to grow rather than abate. The same pang that had been with me since Camillia had blasted Vita.

Frowning, I stroked my Source but didn't find anything unordinary.

Yet I felt… weakened.

Is it this room? This decaying territory?

"You have the audacity to ask why I've done this when you knew the Strigoi were starving?" Nos bit out, recapturing my focus. "You did nothing to stem our hunger, *my* hunger. Nothing to cure our fields or tend to our weaknesses. Perhaps I took a page out of your book, hmm? Maybe I chose *my needs* over everyone else's."

"I told Onyx to supply replacements for the damage any Corpse Fae might have caused to your fields," I reminded him, recalling the conversation and solution clearly. "But I don't think that's the real problem here."

Because something else was going on.

Something beyond Nos and his mishandling of his role as the Strigoi King.

Payan had said he was dying, I thought. *Had made it sound like he had hours left.*

Which had obviously been a lie.

But why?

Why coax me here? Because he knew this had gotten out of hand? Or had someone else put Payan up to this?

Regardless, this territory needed my help. Which was something I should have recognized well before it reached this point.

Fuck. Melek was right. I was stretching myself too thin, and my fae were suffering for it.

Nos steepled his fingers, causing his long fingernails to tap against one another. "Yes. That five-minute conversation with the Corpse Fae King was such a generous gift of your precious time."

I narrowed my gaze again. "Are you trying to antagonize me, Nos?" I asked him. "Challenge me for some sort of power gain? Because I can assure you, that would be a very bad decision on your part."

He smiled. "No, Your Majesty. I'm just doing my part and holding your attention."

What? I glanced around as the hairs along the back of my neck stood on end.

Everything had felt wrong since the moment I'd arrived. *Before* that moment, actually.

And I'd thought… I'd thought it'd been related to Vita.

But that… that wasn't the case at all.

It was related to whatever mirage Nos had developed here.

A mirage that was beginning to shift. "Who are you working with, Nos?" I asked warily.

However, I feared that I already knew.

A wounded king was just the sort of soul *she* would prey upon.

"With me," a feminine voice murmured, one that reminded me of long nights twisted in the sheets.

A seductress.

A witch.

An evil fucking bitch.

And she now stood before me in the flesh.

Right behind Nos's throne.

Oh, the Morpheus Kingdom was known for its dreams and its nightmares, but the devastating vision of Vivaxia herself was too real to be a dream, even for this place.

A curtain of dark hair framed her deceptively angelic face, one that hadn't aged a day since the last time I'd seen her. Broad wings spanned from her back, the golden-tipped feathers flickering between white and black. One was real; one was a mirage. Her heart was as black as pitch, so I knew Vivaxia's true colors, no matter how hard she tried to hide them.

What I didn't know was how the fuck she'd managed to enter my realm.

"How the hell did you break through my gates?" I demanded as the stench of dead roses grew.

Vivaxia's scent.

It was everywhere now, confirming this wasn't her first visit.

No, she'd been here long before.

Playing her games. Twisting the minds of my fae. *Manipulating my lieutenants.*

"Oh, I didn't need to break your gates, Typhos," she purred as her gray eyes glittered with triumph. "I only needed a *key*."

CHAPTER 33

AZ

A Few Minutes Earlier

"Cami?" I whispered, her skin abnormally pale. "You said you gave Vivaxia access to break through the gates. Explain what that means."

"It's the book," she said, her glassy gaze meeting mine. It was almost like she'd fallen asleep while awake, her expression oddly dreamy. "Vita, Az. I pushed all that power into Vita, and Vita was the original siphon."

My brow furrowed as I tried to decipher what she meant.

But it was Ajax who said, "I don't understand. How is a book a siphon?"

"Typhos turned it into an extension of his power, one meant to hold his memories. But Vivaxia had the book in her possession *before* he enchanted it." Her expression cleared a little, her eyes less glassy than before. "What if she left some sort of trigger inside it? Like the one she put in me? Something that... that would *open* and feed the power directly to her..."

"If provided with enough of an energy boost," I finished for her, understanding her logic now. "You think Vivaxia left behind an old enchantment."

Cami nodded.

"One you activated," I added.

Another nod, this one with a slight tremble. "The book is no longer enchanted," she whispered. "It's... it's his mother's journal again."

Frowning, I finally looked at the book in question, as did Ajax.

"That's Vita?" Ajax asked, sounding uncertain. "I don't remember it looking like that."

"Because it used to be layered in Typhos's essence," I said, my voice softer than intended, as I was in shock. "Cami's right." And not just about Vita, but about everything she'd said. "Something's wrong with Typhos." They were the exact words she'd uttered mere moments ago, but now I felt it in my soul. "*Very* wrong."

Because he was no longer inside me at all.

The palace trembled around us, like it was agreeing with our assessment. Or perhaps warning of a catastrophe to come.

"Melek's wounds are a distraction," Cami said, her focus on the Hell Fae Prince. "A way to tamper with my emotions and force me to react. All while Vivaxia hides whatever it is she's really doing."

"How do you know that?" Ajax asked.

"Because it's what she's been doing the whole time," Cami told him, her voice regaining some strength as frustration broke through. "The portals, the chaos, hurting you and Az... It was all a distraction. Or maybe it served as a layer in her plan, to instill distrust in others. Regardless, she's been up to something for a very long time."

She pointed at the book and then at a quill on the ground.

"Vivaxia never stopped playing this game with Typhos," she went on, sounding angrier by the second. "And whatever is happening right now is her real play. Because she's here. I feel her *everywhere*." That last part came out on a growl.

I studied Cami, concerned. "Tell me what it feels like, Cami. Because I don't sense her at all." Which meant whatever Camillia was picking up on might be related to her link with Vivaxia. Or perhaps it was linked to whatever had happened with Vita.

How did we miss it? I wondered. *If Vivaxia had put something inside the book, why did none of us sense it?*

Because we thought it was over.

Typhos had fallen, and she'd remained in her precious Virtuous Fae Realm. It wasn't until recently that we'd even realized she was the one behind all the portal attacks.

Her goal seemed to be founded on revenge. But Typhos had wondered if perhaps she'd merely been playing the long game.

Which would only add credence to Cami's assessment regarding Vita.

"Cami?" Ajax prompted as her eyes took on a dreamy quality again.

Nothing. Like she hadn't heard him at all.

"We need to wake up Melek," Ajax said after a beat.

I glanced at him, then down at where Melek lay prone on the floor. "Wake him up how?"

"By flooding him with energy," Cami replied, suddenly with us again. "Help me, Az."

It wasn't a request but a demand. And it was like my question and Ajax's concern hadn't been heard at all.

"I can channel some of the magic I absorbed from the

quill back into him, but I don't know if it'll be enough. So I need your inner Phoenix to blast him, okay?" She wasn't looking at me while she spoke, but it was clear she was talking to me.

"Okay," I told her. Though, I was trying to figure out what she meant about the *quill*. *As in the* quill *that had stabbed Melek?* I wondered, noting the old-fashioned pen on the floor. The feathers appeared to be wilted, like the object had recently died. *Because she siphoned the spell out of it.*

Wait...

I looked over to the corner, my eyes widening.

That wasn't just any quill; it was *the* quill. The one Typhos had used to sign his deal with Vivaxia.

A quill that had been riddled with magic for eons.

Just like Vita...

I blinked, the puzzle pieces finally starting to fall into place as I realized what Cami had been trying to say— Vivaxia had enchanted both of those items. Then left them in plain sight, all while what? Waiting for her endgame?

An endgame that Cami had triggered... I slowly comprehended. *When she shoved the energy into Vita...*

Oh, fuck.

It made so much sense. *Too much sense.*

Vivaxia adored these kinds of plays, her immortal mind not caring much for the passage of time. She would wait an eternity if it meant she would win.

She'd desired Typhos's light from the very beginning. His siphoning ability was so incredibly unique, to the point of being one of the most powerful talents in existence.

Because his power was a step beyond creation.

He literally transformed negative energy into something positive, something *vital*.

His Source.

It was contrived from raw energy, one that had created

a whole new world. Which was something Vivaxia could never do.

Or I didn't think she could, anyway.

I assumed this was what fascinated her about Typhos, why she craved his power.

A power that was probably even more expansive than any of us realized because he'd locked most of it away after accidentally killing his parents.

Typhos focused his ability now by applying it to deals, where he siphoned power for the greater good and redirected it to those who needed it most.

That was how he'd created the Hell Fae Source.

A Source of power that had slowly become something too vast for him to manage. Melek and I had felt that imbalance but trusted Typhos to manage it.

And thus far, he had.

Alas, Vivaxia... She'd been waiting for this moment to take everything from him. Waiting for his light to burn so fucking bright that it would explode and she'd be there to pick up the pieces.

She'd just needed an instigator.

And that instigator was Camillia De la Croix.

A siphon created to steal his power. A being who nearly functioned as his equal. A fae whom Vivaxia had planted her own seeds inside, allowing her to become the ultimate puppet master.

But she couldn't have foreseen my reactions to Cami, let alone the reactions of Melek, Ajax, and Typhos.

Which meant her plan wasn't foolproof.

Hence Cami's reactions now. She wasn't allowing Vivaxia to control her emotions or her responses. Instead, she was focused on problem-solving.

However, that dreamy look in her eyes... I swallowed at the thought, concerned by what that could mean. *Is that her fighting Vivaxia's control?*

Typhos had said the outlet inside her was what Vivaxia had planted in her. But what if it was more? What if it was a switch of some kind that none of us could sense? Not even Camillia herself?

"On my count," Cami said, oblivious to my runaway thoughts. "Three, two…"

I called upon my Phoenix, the power pooling in my fingertips.

Just to lose my balance as the floor shifted.

And the sound of claws on marble followed.

Fuck.

"Hellhounds," Ajax muttered, his wand falling into his hand. "I'll handle this while you two revive the prince."

Except, as they rounded the corner, their wolfish features didn't display feral madness, only panic. I stood, blocking their view of Melek on the floor.

Of course, they would still be able to smell him.

But it was my job to stand in as their Commander, especially with their king and prince being out of commission. "Report," I demanded, causing Garmr to shift into his human form.

"We're under attack by an unknown entity," he informed me in his gravelly voice.

"An unknown entity?" I repeated.

He nodded. "We can't see it. But… but buildings are imploding, like bombs have been set from within. And some of the kingdoms claim their skies are falling apart."

"From portals?" Ajax guessed. "Similar to what happened in the Underwater Kingdom?"

Garmr shook his head. "No, Warden. This… this seems different from that."

"It's the Source," Cami said. "It's… it's self-destructing."

I blinked and looked over my shoulder at her. "What do you mean?"

"You can't feel it?" she asked, seeming confused. "You can't feel what she's doing?"

"No, Cami. All I feel is the palace shaking." I didn't voice it in a snarky tone, just a straightforward one. "I don't sense Vivaxia at all."

She stared at me, her throat working on a swallow. "I feel her everywhere."

"Yes, you mentioned that. What does it mean?"

"I don't know," she replied in a whisper. "I…" Her brow furrowed, her focus falling to Melek. "You need to wake up," she told him, her hand covering his chest. "I need you coherent *right fucking now*."

Electricity singed the air as Camillia exploded with power.

Shit. I took a step forward, ready to intervene, but her power pushed me back.

Ajax cursed out loud, the two of us trying to reach her now.

But in the next breath, everything went silent.

And Melek opened his eyes.

I gaped at him and then at his bloody chest. His hand flew upward to the wound, his shoulders jolting with the effort. "Fuck, little angel," he rasped out, wincing. "That hurt."

"Sorry," she whispered. "But I need you. *We* need you."

The palace trembled around us, underlining that claim.

Yet all Melek did was smirk a little and say, "It's nice to be needed, little angel."

Of course he would be carefree about being zapped

back to existence while recovering from a chest injury. "How the hell did a pen do that much damage, anyway?" I demanded, looking at all the blood again.

"It twirled," Melek told me. "*A lot.*"

"I siphoned the magic out of it," Cami informed him. "It won't hurt you again."

Melek arched a brow, then shot her another smile. "My little hero."

Ajax palmed the back of his neck and blew out a breath. "Right, well, Melek is clearly fine. What do we do about everything else?"

"We rely on Cami's instincts," I said without hesitation. "She says this is from the Source and it's something Vivaxia is doing to it or to Typhos. So I say we find Typhos, but as a team. We can't split up. Not when we can't hear each other. And we need Cami's guidance."

She stared at me for a beat, her throat working again. Then she nodded. "Did Typhos make it to the Morpheus Kingdom?" Her eyes widened as she finished the question. "Yes. Yes, he did. That's why I feel so out of it. It's a kingdom of dream creatures, right?"

"Not quite accurate," Melek coughed out.

"Strigoi dreamwalk but need blood to survive. Kind of like vampires. And Ghouls primarily eat nightmares," I added but quickly reverted back to the topic at hand. "What do you mean by *out of it?*"

"Everything feels muted," she told me, her brow furrowing. "Like I'm too calm. Like everything is, well, a *dream*. I..." Her frown deepened. "Az, I think the Source is trying to tell me that the Morpheus Kingdom is in danger. I can't explain why I feel that way; I... I just do."

"A queen's instincts," I murmured, nodding. Then I shared another look with Ajax. "You feel anything?"

"Not a thing." He glanced at our Hellhound audience.

"Have you heard anything from the Morpheus Kingdom?" he asked Garmr.

The lead Hellhound shook his head, causing his long silver hair to dance along his bare shoulders. "Want me to see what I can find out?"

"No," I replied, taking over the conversation and facing him head-on. "But I do want you to help us find safe passage to the Netherworld Kingdom."

From there, we would use the tunnel to reach the Morpheus Kingdom.

Because if something was happening to Ty there, I suspected we wouldn't be able to just ash in. We needed to approach this carefully. Evaluate the situation. And figure out our next move.

Vivaxia might be a queen on her side of the board, and she might have captured our king.

But we had our own queen to play. One Vivaxia would likely underestimate. She'd created Cami, probably considered her a puppet in this game.

However, we knew the truth.

Camillia De la Croix was our Hell Fae Queen.

Which made it our job as her protectors to maneuver her through the realm. Get her there unharmed. Properly charged.

And ready to fight.

Because it was time for Vivaxia to fall, once and for all.

CHAPTER 34

TYPHOS

MEANWHILE...

Vivaxia trailed her manicured nails down Nos's throne—a throne that once glowed with power. Power I'd given the Strigoi to help them thrive.

Now it simply resembled *death*.

How fitting that Vivaxia would choose this relic to stroke. Perhaps it was prophetic.

Melek, I called mentally. *Vivaxia is in the Strigoi Palace.*

I waited for him to react, to feel his surprise.

A surprise I very much echoed.

Because this shouldn't have been possible. She'd claimed to have a *key*.

"What key?" I asked her. Though, I knew better than to expect a straightforward reply, or really any at all.

Vivaxia favored riddles and lies.

Which meant this was a puzzle for me to solve.

I could only assume she was referring to the magic she'd left inside of Camillia. However, I had to wonder if there was something else going on here. Because her presence here felt… *permanent.* Like she'd been lingering in this kingdom for much longer than a handful of minutes.

Nos had said he'd been trying to *hold my attention.* What had that meant? And why would he be working with Vivaxia?

She'd created so many of the Nightmare Fae in this realm. Nightmare Fae who all loathed her and what she'd done to them long ago.

Perhaps his ancestors hadn't passed on enough of a warning, thus leaving him susceptible to her influence.

"Hmm," Vivaxia hummed, those long nails of hers still dancing along the throne as energy vibrated in the air.

An energy I recognized.

More mirages.

More tricks.

More mind games.

It had me wondering if she was truly even here. This whole kingdom was renowned for its illusions. Perhaps someone was fucking with me now.

But who? And why?

My primary nemesis was the woman standing mere feet from me. *In my realm,* I thought again. *Because she found a key.*

Naturally, she didn't elaborate. She just tilted her head in a playful way, a move that sent her dark hair to one side. "I brought you a present. A belated housewarming gift, if you will."

I arched a brow, my arms folding over my chest. "I'm not interested in your *gifts,* Vivaxia." Because they always came at a price.

A price I was not willing to pay.

Melek, I tried again.

His lack of a reply was uncharacteristic of him. It had me going deeper, searching for his mental state.

When I found nothing, a chill swept down my spine.

Azazel, I thought, shifting to my connection with him.

Only it was just as quiet. Just as *still*.

My lips threatened to tighten, my heart stuttering a little in my chest. *Is this the* gift *she'd mentioned? Has she done something to my mates?*

Was this another one of her spells, similar to the experience the other day?

Or had she done something worse?

My soul didn't feel all that wounded, which told me Melek and Azazel were very much alive. But that didn't make me any less concerned.

Vivaxia had been fucking with my realm for months, perhaps even longer. Her being here—in the flesh—suggested we were about to end the final round of her games.

Unless she's just getting started, I thought, my blood running cold. Nothing with Vivaxia was ever final. I'd learned that the hard way with her agreements.

One of which she seemed to produce now as she waved a delicate hand.

Only this parchment didn't bear my signature on it. However, I recognized her loopy scrawl. "It seems some of your fae are not all that faithful to your design," she murmured as she sent the document my way with a magical little current from her fingertips.

I almost didn't take the paper from her, aware that she'd probably enchanted the text. But when I saw the date on top, I snatched it out of the air.

Because I recognized that day.

Camillia's birthday.

My gaze flickered to Nos—the one who had *signed* this deal—before returning my focus to the agreement. My eyebrow arched, the terms almost laughable. "You betrayed me in exchange for a queen?" I looked at him. "A queen who could never properly survive in this realm?"

My Source was very particular about whom it empowered. Bringing someone here who didn't belong was a death sentence for most fae. Not because I would kill the intruder—or the being responsible for said intruder—but because my Source wouldn't allow them to prosper.

Faedoms and the fae inside them all required energy to survive.

That was how our worlds worked.

"My gates exist for protection, Nos. They keep unwanted visitors out but also ensure that only those my Source can properly nurture are allowed in," I went on. "And your failure to understand that has earned you a death sentence."

Which officially explained the Rot in his territory.

My Source had stopped feeding him life, hence his need to steal the souls of everyone else around him. Including the female I assumed he'd claimed as queen— the one lying dead at his feet.

Or maybe she was another casualty.

Regardless, it didn't matter.

He'd betrayed me.

And it seemed the date he'd chosen to do so also held vast significance.

Because it was Camillia's birth date—the exact day she'd been created.

That was obviously not a coincidence.

But now I wondered if Camillia had merely been a decoy and if Vivaxia's true intentions rested in this kingdom.

On Nos's throne, I thought, noting the way her hand had ventured right back to the conduit, as though she needed it to remain stable inside my gates.

It was also entirely possible that everything served a purpose, that Camillia wasn't a decoy so much as a layer in Vivaxia's plans.

She always operated several steps ahead, a fact that used to enchant me many eons ago. But I'd learned her tricks, mastered them for myself, and fully intended to use them now to unravel her current play.

Except, something was nagging at me.

A lagging thought.

A... I frowned. *A buried memory.*

Something about striking deals at the right time in the right place.

Why is that important? I wondered. *And why can't I grasp the full intention of that thought?*

"What is it, Ty?" Vivaxia asked, her use of Melek's nickname for me grating on my nerves. "Struggling to understand my gift? Need some help to decipher it?"

The condescending undertone of her questions had me wanting to growl. It was like she was in my head, dancing right along with me as I tried to untangle her motives.

I'd always despised that sensation, and she was one of the few who had ever made me feel this way.

Yet it seemed worse somehow. Which was impossible. I'd spent thousands of years away from her. She had no idea what I was capable of now.

"I have to say," she went on, "I'm not surprised. You really have stretched your powers to the brink of self-destruction." She sounded sad, as though she actually cared. But I caught the glimmer of malice in her cruel gray eyes. However, she chased it away as she glanced down at Nos. "I mean, he hasn't even noticed that you've failed to reply at all. Isn't that just so typical?"

She tsked, the sound one that echoed throughout the too-quiet room as she drew her nail across Nos's throat.

He gurgled in response, causing my brow to pinch.

Then blood pooled from a fresh cut that went far deeper than should be possible from such a simple touch.

"Thank you for your service, Nos," she said, her lips suddenly at his ear. I hadn't even seen her bend. It was like she'd been in two places at once.

Because she's playing with mirages, I realized as she whispered something to my dying lieutenant.

I stepped forward, only my feet didn't move.

I frowned down at my legs, confused by their lack of a response.

"Is it that you can't move?" Vivaxia asked softly. "Or is it that you don't want to move?"

My gaze returned to her, my jaw clenching. "Stop fucking with my head."

"Oh, so it's my fault now?" She was the picture of innocence as she looked at Nos in disbelief. "Can you believe him?"

Nos released a tortured sound, one that had my teeth grinding. "You've made your point, Vivaxia. He betrayed me. But his life isn't yours to take."

"Actually," she said, drawing out the word. "It is." She gestured to the contract still clutched in my fist. "I gave him a queen and an heir. In return, he agreed to be mine, a deal we struck using a spell you may or may not remember."

My hands nearly tightened into fists, my ire mounting

Because yes, I knew the spell. I knew it well. It was the same one she'd used on Az to turn him into her personal slave.

She'd owned his life.

His every move.

His every breath.

His right to free will.

I'd fought for his freedom, agreed to countless deals until I'd finally crafted the perfect one. But I was beginning to doubt my success.

Which was probably exactly what Vivaxia wanted.

That'd been the point of her letter, the one where she'd insinuated that I hadn't given her a proper blood sacrifice.

But did you bleed the way I wanted, sweet Typhos? Or did you grow into a being with so much more to lose? To **sacrifice***?*

The memory of our deal played through my mind, the terms ones I knew by heart and would never forget.

And yet, something about them felt murky at the moment.

Which was strange. I often revisited that history with Vita. It was my way of ensuring nothing like that ever happened again.

Every deal I made contained specific parameters, most of them driven by my experiences. The ones with Vivaxia were the most important of all.

So why am I struggling to recall the most significant one in our long history? I wondered, frowning.

Because that bitch is in my head, I realized in the next instant.

But how? How the fuck did she…? My eyes widened. *Vita.*

Vita housed all my memories.

And Camillia had shoved all that energy into—

"I told you he wouldn't help you," Vivaxia murmured, her cooed words dragging my focus away from my own thoughts.

Because a fog had crept into the room.

A lethal one.

"I warned all of you, didn't I?" she went on, her words seemingly pointed as the smog thickened. "And now you see it for yourselves, hmm? Your king has *weakened*."

What? Who the fuck was she even talking to? Nos?

He was almost dead.

And not from the slit to his neck.

It was Vivaxia's *power*. She owned his soul now. His very being. And she was extinguishing his essence through her own force of will.

A horrible way to die.

Painful, too.

While he might deserve it after what he'd done to the fae under his command, it wasn't her punishment to give.

Yet I couldn't move. I was being forced to watch her dismantle his soul right before my eyes.

What the fuck is happening? I marveled. *Why does it feel like she has control over me?*

I hadn't agreed to one of her *pet* spells. Nor was I a creation she could control. Our deal had never been about *ownership*. Just a soul-bond. One that my soul had rejected, thereby nullifying the entire agreement.

Which was where her *blood payment* clause had come into effect.

Regardless, that didn't grant her authority over my spirit. *So why the fuck can't I move?*

"See how he struggles?" Vivaxia infused a hint of sadness into her tone. "It's so disappointing to watch, is it not?"

The fog began to lift, revealing the room once more.

And all the Strigoi inside it.

Breathing Strigoi, I realized, noting that over half the bodies on the ground were no longer there. They were standing inside, their alarmed gazes fixated on me.

"What game are you playing?" I demanded, my words for Vivaxia.

"It's not a game so much as a trial," she replied. "A trial of your strength. And I think you might be failing, sweet Typhos. Just like you failed to extinguish those portals in the other realms. Just like you failed to handle the whole Monsters Night debacle correctly. Just—"

Just like I failed to protect my mind, I thought, cutting off whatever she'd been about to add. She kept talking, but I stopped listening.

Because I suspected this was also a distraction—hence the reason Nos hadn't died yet. She could have ripped him apart in seconds.

She wanted this to last, which implied she possessed a nefarious purpose for this prolonged charade.

So what are you really up to? I wondered, trying to decipher her motives.

The fae in the room all appeared to be real, yet they were clearly being controlled. Perhaps because of her ties to Nos.

She'd bound him by that slave spell, and they were bound by the hive mind.

Or had Vivaxia done something to turn them all into puppets?

Virtuous Fae were creationists. She would have the ability to master any being she'd created in the past, including her Nightmare Fae.

But Vivaxia hadn't manifested the Strigoi. Another Virtuous Fae had done that.

So how is she controlling them? I pondered, still ignoring whatever she was saying to the room.

Her words didn't matter.

Her actions, however, spoke volumes.

She'd somehow ensnared me and all these Strigoi.

I ran my gaze over her, searching for clues, and again noted how she stroked the throne with those deadly-looking fingernails. *My conduit.*

I'd been considering it earlier, realizing that her

connection to Nos was clearly purposeful. *Because he uses my power in place of a Sigil*, I thought.

But it had to be deeper than that. I hadn't granted him enough energy to enslave me. So she was garnering her strength from something else. Something even more powerful.

Something like Vita, I thought, my heart stopping. *Camillia pushed my essence into Vita and...*

I frowned, my mind trailing off into nothing.

Which didn't make sense.

It was like my brain had formed a wall that I couldn't pass through.

Because of Vita... something with Vita.

Something with these fae.

Something with Vivaxia controlling everyone and everything in this room.

Not just by the power of the throne, but... but by the power of various Virtuous Fae.

I blinked, that concept seeming to come out of nowhere.

Yet I felt it now, the strands of energy she was manipulating—strands that didn't belong to her. Or they shouldn't, anyway.

It was as though she'd *absorbed* the essences of others.

Like I did with my parents, I realized, the memory assaulting me with a vengeance.

A memory that had once been locked away in Vita. I'd released it recently, but not quite like this. The vision now hit me like a punch to the heart.

I must have visibly reacted to the invisible hit because Vivaxia tsked, the noise reminding me of nails on a chalkboard. "I wonder how many more of you have to fall before he'll even try to retaliate," she asked, drawing my focus back to the room and noting three fresh bodies on the floor.

One belonged to Nos, his shriveled skin reminding me of a husk.

The sight of it stole my breath as another recollection assaulted me.

A recollection that starred my own parents in a similar state. They'd resembled husks, too. Husks that had broken apart under a soft breeze, turning their remains into dust on the wind.

As though to remind me of that moment, Vivaxia bent and blew out a breath in Nos's direction, causing bits and pieces of him to flake off his dried-up form.

Then a fourth body collapsed, the Strigoi gripping his throat as agony spilled from his lips.

The guard, I recognized, his eyes meeting mine.

Betrayal and agony lurked in the depths of his dark eyes, his words from before playing through my mind.

"Now that you're here, hopefully that will change."

My failure to do so echoed in his expression, accusations seeming to linger on his lips.

Why aren't you doing anything? he seemed to be asking. *Why aren't you helping me?*

My teeth ground together, my power flickering deep inside.

Only to quickly be extinguished by a wave of foreign energy.

Energy that shouldn't be there.

Energy that belonged to *Vivaxia*.

My gaze cut to hers.

"You've amassed so much power since your fall, Typhos," she said, her gray eyes glittering with cruel intentions. "It truly has become your heart, hasn't it?"

My chest squeezed as though she had her hand

wrapped right around my organs, her nails digging into me without her ever having moved.

Real or a mirage? I wondered. *Physical or mental?*

Because I couldn't tell.

She was suddenly everywhere, her essence infecting my very being.

Vita, I thought again. *She... she...*

There was something there. Something I had to grasp. Something... something that escaped me again.

The guard took his last breath, his soul crying out to me to intervene. To *help*.

I could hear it deep in my head, hear my Source screaming for an opportunity to react. To respond. To *punish*.

Just as it had punished Nos.

Because deep down, my power had recognized the betrayal and the infection that betrayal had brought with it.

Somewhere, somehow, I'd known she was here all along. Weaving her magic through my realm, corrupting my fae, manipulating them to do her bidding through her links to their souls.

Creationist magic.

Creationist magic that she's siphoned *from others.*

She's a siphon. Like me. Like Camillia.

Is that possible? I thought, dizzy from another twist of my heart. *Did Vivaxia understand my power all along? Is that why she sought me out? Taught me about deals? Because she saw herself in me?*

She'd said that before, told me how I had the potential to be as great as her, if not greater. And I'd always caught that glimmer of envy in her eyes when she'd said those words.

I'd thought she'd been talking about my inner light, the

power I possessed that helped others. *A power crafted from my ability to siphon and harness energy.*

It had shifted over my lifetime, my parents' deaths acting as a catalyst that had turned my talent into something else entirely. My fall had heightened the burning energy when part of the Virtuous Fae Source became mine. Then I'd fostered it throughout the millennia, ensuring it protected the Hell Fae Realm.

And now Vivaxia wanted what it had become. Or perhaps she'd always wanted it. But she'd bided her time, waiting for me to create the ultimate Source before she stepped in to take it.

The Source being my heart. My core. My very reason for existing.

She'd promised to make me bleed, and this was what she'd meant—by forcing me to watch her extinguish the lives of everything and everyone under my protection. All while she absorbed my light.

This ultimate consequence of a nullified deal.

But she wasn't the only one who understood the importance of layers and contingency plans.

She'd taught me well, after all.

I knew never to go into an agreement without thinking several steps ahead, thanks to her endless games.

And this was no different.

Something she seemed to know, as her smile dimmed now. "Typhos…"

She must have heard the intention in my mind or seen the glimmer of promise in my gaze. I wasn't sure, and I wasn't about to pause to evaluate how she knew what she knew. She'd clearly breached my thoughts, but I was *never* going to let her breach my Source.

I'd die first.

Closing my eyes, I activated the protocol I'd hidden deep inside myself for this very moment.

And let my Source *engage*.

Vivaxia screamed as blinding light filled the room, the echoes of it resembling fire beyond my closed eyelids.

I let it engulf me. Become me. *Push me.*

Then I relaxed into what came next, welcomed the pain, and gave myself to the darkness of the fall.

It was the only way to protect the realm.

To protect my mates.

To protect Camillia.

Because Vivaxia couldn't take my Source if my mind was no longer sound.

But as a member of my inner circle—as a mate to my mates—Camillia could. She could absorb all of it. Create her own light. *And save us all...*

CHAPTER 35

CAMI

A Few Minutes Earlier

Chills trickled down my spine as we walked through the Netherworld Courtyard. There were trees everywhere. *Skeleton trees*. Their bony limbs creaked in the wind stirred up by the turbulent sky above, the village surrounding us a literal ghost town.

"The Corpse Fae are all hiding in the crypts," Maliki said as he wandered alongside us. "And the Death Fae are in their castle. First time I think I've ever seen this place empty."

He'd met us in front of Death's Den, having seen Melek flying us all into the crater that the Netherworld Kingdom called home.

Or maybe he'd felt Ajax's protective energy; he'd created a massive shield around Melek to ensure he wouldn't weaken too much in the Netherworld Kingdom. "Can't have your wings giving out mid-flight," he'd said to my Virtuous Fae mate.

"Thanks," Melek had replied, giving Ajax a small smile. "Once we reach the tunnel, I'll be fine."

That'd been the end of the conversation, all of us too somber to talk on the journey.

But Maliki didn't seem to share that melancholy feeling.

As evidenced by him facing Az now and asking, "So, want to tell me what's going on, big brother? Or shall I guess?"

"What you should do is go grab Hades and see if he wants to help us take down a Virtuous Fae," Az returned.

Maliki considered it for a moment, his finger tapping his chin. "Hmm, no, I don't think he'll be of much use. He has his knot in a twist over something at the moment. But maybe Morpheus will be interested? I saw him playing in the tunnel a bit ago."

Az paused and looked at his brother. "Do you just perch up on a mountaintop all day and spy on everyone?"

"When I'm bored, sure. Don't you do the same when in bird form?"

"It's a Phoenix, not a bird, and—"

"A Phoenix has feathers, ergo, *bird*," Maliki interjected.

"—no, I do not," Az finished, ignoring his brother.

"Look, if you have nothing useful to add, then can you fuck off?" Ajax asked, sounding exhausted. It made me wonder if maybe he was feeling dreamy like I had a bit ago. However, a glance at him told me he wasn't exhausted, just exasperated.

"We're trying to make a silent entrance into the Morpheus Kingdom," Az added, his tone exuding a patience that resonated deep inside me.

Because despite the chaos unfolding in the sky above, I felt right about our path. Which only further confirmed that the Source was the one drawing me forward.

I no longer felt dreamy or tired, simply focused.

There were no hints of being overwhelmed. No fear. No true concern. Just a sense of purpose. Of *rightness*.

This was where I needed to be.

With my mates.

Ready to face Vivaxia.

Was I ready? Probably not. However, given her age and experience, I would never be properly prepared to face her.

But I had something she didn't—*love*.

And that love was what drove me forward.

Provided me with a goal. An *aim*.

This realm was falling apart.

Everything Typhos had created for his Nightmare Fae and Hell Fae. I could feel it crumbling, see it fracturing high up in the sky. Ajax had asked Garmr about portals, and I supposed the holes above somewhat resembled a similar concept. Only, those holes bled into nothingness. A void. *The destruction of the Hell Fae Realm*.

I could feel it deteriorating all around me, causing my feet to move faster.

Vivaxia was absorbing all of this. *Siphoning* it. Creating her own... *something*.

A new Virtuous Fae Source? Her very own light?

I wasn't sure.

I just knew I had to take it back.

And find Typhos.

How did she wound you? I wondered, ignoring whatever Maliki was saying to Az now. *How did she get the upper hand? Is it because of what I did to Vita?*

I'd pushed a lot of power into that book.

I'd shattered something. Broken a veil. Given Vivaxia exactly what she'd needed.

Part of me wondered if that had been the plan all

along, if the valve she'd placed inside me had been a red herring.

It made sense. We'd all been so focused on ensuring I didn't feed any power to Vivaxia via that connection that we hadn't even discussed other potential threats.

If the portals were all a distraction, I thought, *then maybe I was a distraction, too.*

I wasn't actually sure the portals had been a distraction; it just... felt right. She hadn't really accomplished much other than stirring temporary chaos.

Well, and hurting Typhos's image as a protector, I thought as we walked out of the courtyard and into what looked like another village. Or maybe it was the same village and it just framed the courtyard.

Regardless, the flickering blue flames were dimming ahead, suggesting we were nearing the end of this very long path.

And hopefully entering a tunnel.

"They're losing faith in him to lead, Az," Maliki said, his softly spoken words piquing my interest. "The portal incidents haven't helped."

"One of which you were responsible for," Az reminded him with a growl.

"Yes, but that had nothing to do with Vivaxia."

Az considered him for a long beat. "You'd better hope I never find out otherwise, Mal. Brother or not, I'll be forced to side with Typhos's judgment."

"As you should," Maliki replied, his voice more serious than I'd heard it before. "However, back to what I was saying—they're losing faith. That incident at the Den was the final straw for a lot of the Corpse Fae. Being manipulated with that spell..."

"Fucks with you," Az said when Maliki didn't finish his statement.

"Yeah." Maliki's expression darkened. "Yeah, it does."

I frowned, wondering if Maliki had lived through an experience similar to Az's. Except Az had said his brother was born in the Hell Fae Realm, not the Virtuous Fae Realm. So perhaps it was something else he'd experienced.

I would have asked Az if I could link to him, but our mental bonds still seemed to be fractured. I wasn't sure what had caused it because it didn't feel like a spell so much as a protective barrier. Like our minds were purposely not speaking to each other.

How I knew that, I wasn't sure. But as Az had said before, he was trusting my instincts, and so I was doing the same.

Thus far, it seemed to be working.

"Now this," Maliki went on, his voice even lower. "This isn't good, Az."

"I know."

"Morale is already low—"

"Mal," Az interjected, pausing beside me. "*I know.* Fuck, *we* know. And there's nothing I can do about it right now. We need to find Typhos."

Maliki stared at him for a beat and nodded. "All right. I'll… I'll see what I can do here."

Az arched a brow. "Will you really?"

His brother tilted his head, a cocky grin gracing his full lips. "Have I ever let you down before?"

"A thousand times."

Maliki's grin only grew. "Then maybe I'll surprise you this time."

Az grunted.

Maliki winked. And then he vanished.

"Well, that was helpful," Ajax deadpanned.

"It was, actually," I said slowly, thinking through everything Maliki had said. He'd commented on the weakening morale, which had me thinking about the point of the portals and Vivaxia's attacks again.

Rather than remark more out loud, I let those thoughts circle around me as I continued our journey toward the tunnel that connected the Netherworld Kingdom to the Morpheus Kingdom.

"How was it helpful, little angel?" Melek asked after a few moments of silence. He didn't sound doubtful so much as intrigued.

"I'm not sure yet," I admitted, aware that I probably sounded a little crazy. "I'm not done puzzling it all out. Vivaxia wants Typhos's light. That's always been her goal. But why instill distrust in his fae? To make them turn against him?"

I paused as the path ended and turned back toward the silent village.

"If her goal was to create a rebellion, I think she failed. The Nightmare Fae don't seem angry so much as scared. They're not vengeful. So was that not her goal?" I looked at Melek. "And if it wasn't her goal, then why create all those portals? Was it really all a distraction?"

I was being repetitive. I knew that. But I needed to understand her motives. To see through every trick. Uncover the details.

Because that was what made Vivaxia tick.

She'd been playing with Typhos Lucifer for thousands of years. And from what I understood, she kept undermining him at every turn.

This is no different, I thought.

"She wanted to destroy their faith in Ty," Melek murmured, his irises glittering with a mixture of anger and sadness.

"Yes, that's why she attacked the brides, too," Az added. "Typhos spent a millennium planning that event, all to appease his fae. Only for her to undermine it and make him look like he was losing control."

"Another hit to their faith," Melek said.

"Exactly," Az replied.

"But why?" I pressed. "What end purpose does it serve?"

"Guilt," Melek answered simply. "Losing the faith of his fae makes him feel like a failure, which induces *guilt*."

I frowned. "Guilt."

He nodded. "If there's one thing Vivaxia is good at, it's exploiting guilt in others. And guilt is one of Ty's weaknesses. He doesn't like to fail others, not when he's spent an eternity repenting for his perceived sins."

The deaths of his parents, I realized. That'd been the catalyst that had caused him to shift his power into something else, to use his talent to help others rather than harm them. It was why he no longer considered himself a siphon, and yet, he was still siphoning power... just in a very different way.

Melek had said Vivaxia didn't know about his ability, or that Typhos *thought* she didn't. But I was starting to wonder if that was true.

She'd mentored him in the art of deals, something he'd used to foster his energy-absorbing talents. Surely she'd noticed.

And we all knew she hadn't helped him out of the goodness of her heart.

She'd just wanted him to master his skill so he could amass more power.

Power that had become his inner light.

A light she'd wanted to steal.

And now I realized that she'd determined the best way to do that was to exploit his weakness—*his guilt*.

Guilt was a building block of his Source, his need to protect others with his power born of his desire to repent.

Vivaxia had left him alone for thousands of years while he'd created the ultimate light. She'd waited until he was bursting with power, nearly knocked off-balance, to swoop in and make her final play.

And she built her final act around his guilt.

I stared at the tunnel, my heart suddenly in my throat.

Whatever we were about to walk into was going to hurt. I could feel it in my soul.

We're coming, I wanted to tell Typhos as I resumed our journey, only with a faster pace. *We're coming!*

I started to run, my spirit suddenly filled with an urgency I couldn't define. But Az had said to follow—

The world shifted as I fell into the tunnel entrance, my palms flying upward to catch myself before I face-planted onto the cobblestone path. "Ow," I groaned, my foot throbbing from whatever I'd caught it on.

Az and Ajax were instantly there, both of them saying my name in unison. I winced, feeling like a complete klutz.

New Hell Fae Queen Rule Number One, I thought to myself. *Watch. Your. Step.*

That should be common sense. But apparently I'd let my emotions control me... *again.*

Maybe that should be the first rule, I mused. *Don't Get Emotional.*

Of course, I wasn't supposed to have any rules.

Yet my mind was clearly focused on—

"She tripped over the death stone," Molok said, interrupting my mental gymnastics and causing me to frown.

"What?" The death stone had shattered into pieces after I last used it. "I tripped over pebbles?" And why the hell were they on this path?

"It re-formed," Melek said, stepping around to squat in front of me. I was propped up by my palms, looking like a clumsy fool. But the moment the rock came into view, I forgot all about how I'd fallen.

Because Melek was right.

The rock had *re-formed* itself. "Or is it a new stone?" I whispered, my brow furrowing. "What's that with it?" I could see a little piece of what looked like scrap paper in his hand.

"A note," Melek said.

He stood as I went back to my knees, then held out the "note" for me. It was small, reminding me of a business card.

But the words were very clear because they were glowing like literal fire on the white parchment.

"Glad you finally got my message, Queen Camillia," I read out loud. "A mutual friend said to give you this. In dreams, M."

My brow furrowed.

"What the fuck does that even mean? *In dreams?* And what message is he or she referring to? And who the hell is *M?* Maliki?" I guessed, pushing up to my feet to spin around and look for the meddling fae.

"Morpheus," Melek said, giving me pause. "I can feel his essence all over that note."

"That explains the dreamlike sensations," Az added.

"What?" I looked at him. "What do you mean?"

"He's the God of Dreams, and the Morpheus Kingdom is where he resides since it's, well, *his*. He must have been trying to coax you here with his magic." Az sounded irritated.

It was an irritation I felt, too. "Why not just call?"

"That's not how Mythos Fae work," Melek replied, amusement underscoring his tone. "They're cryptic."

"Then you must be best friends," Ajax deadpanned.

"With Morpheus? No. But I am fond of him," Melek told him. "However, I'm much more interested in the *mutual friend* he's mentioned. I assume that's Zenaida?"

"Considering he left Cami a death stone that's either the same one Zenaida gave her or similar to it, then yeah, I'd agree with that guess." Ajax drew his fingers through his thick hair, his expression darkening. "Or it could be Shade. Morpheus seems like the type of fae he'd befriend for fun."

My jaw clenched, my mind whirring.

So if Morpheus was the one who drew us here, it had nothing to do with Typhos's Source.

Why does that feel wrong? I wondered as goose bumps skated down my arms. *Because I can still feel his Source calling for me...*

Maybe... maybe both assessments were true.

Morpheus had inspired the dreaminess while the Hell Fae Source called for me.

That could explain the calmness that had settled over me, the need to rein in my emotions and *think*.

Or perhaps it was just me and I was learning what it meant to lead.

To be a queen.

But not just any queen—the Hell Fae Queen.

I took the stone from Melek and said, "Let's go."

We could analyze what this meant all day and night, or we could act.

And something told me Typhos needed us to act... *right fucking now.*

CHAPTER 36

MELEK

Cami took off down the tunnel, forcing the rest of us to chase after her.

She had no idea where she was going, yet she sprinted as though she traversed this tunnel every day. She deftly dodged right, narrowly missing a pit of skulls, then continued forward while Az ashed several feet in front of her.

An "oomph" left her as she ran right into his chest. Then she growled and tried to maneuver around him, but he grabbed her by the hips and hoisted her into the air.

"Now you listen to me, little warrior," he began.

"Put me down!"

"Cami, this tunnel is riddled with traps," Ajax said, joining them with an exasperated sigh. "We have to tread carefully down here. You have no idea what kind of hole you might fall into."

"Or portal," Az added. "There's one just over there that goes to the Human Realm; it's frequented a lot down here."

"Yes, that. And there's the tunnel split to consider, too."

"Split?" Cami repeated, her tone tinted with irritation.

I could barely make out her face in the shadows—the flickering blue candles nearby casting only enough light to illuminate the enchanted path through the mountain—but I suspected she was scowling.

However, she'd stopped trying to fight her way around Az.

"Half of the tunnel sits under the Netherworld Kingdom Mountain. The other half splits into two enchanted paths, one of which leads to the Ghouls and the other to the Strigoi," Az explained. "They don't really commingle the way the Corpse Fae and Death Fae do. And, well, the Morpheus Kingdom is… large."

"Understatement," Ajax muttered.

Cami heaved a sigh. "Fine. Then you lead, Commander."

Az didn't immediately move, likely mulling over how to reply to the impatience underlying Cami's tone.

But after a beat, he did the smart thing and started walking down the tunnel.

Had this been any other time or place, he probably would have challenged our mate for sassing him.

But we were all concerned about Ty.

And rightly so.

I could feel the power shift in the air. This was bigger than all the previous incidents combined, yet so much less *violent*.

That alone told me this was no ordinary attack.

After all these years, it seemed Vivaxia was about to deliver her final play.

Or maybe it was just the beginning.

It was hard to anticipate her moves. She was never forthcoming, and her plans were always layered.

And time meant nothing to her.

I curled my hands into fists at my sides, my stomach twisting. Ty had grown a lot, his power immense.

But Vivaxia would always be older. More vindictive. More *flexible* in terms of what and whom she was willing to sacrifice.

That was precisely the difference between them.

Vivaxia approached life as though she had nothing to lose. Because she didn't. She had no ties to anyone or anything other than herself.

While Ty... Ty had grown roots everywhere. They were all around us now in these enchanted tunnels, the very fibers of each kingdom born from his robust power. Crafted via his will. Protected by his heart.

And Vivaxia would use that against him.

She'd use *everything* against him.

Hurt whomever she desired. Torture whatever poor creature stepped into her path. Dismantle his beautiful creation right before his eyes.

Because that was what Vivaxia did. That was who she was.

A fact that became even more evident as we entered the Morpheus Kingdom.

The vast fields that usually greeted visitors from this angle were nowhere in sight due to a thick, cold smog that had settled into the air. I couldn't even see the dark spires of the Strigoi Palace, only a haze of reddish clouds illuminated by the blood moon above.

The stench of decaying roses assaulted me as I stepped out of the tunnel, the scent one I knew well.

Vivaxia hadn't always smelled like a dead flower bouquet. She'd once radiated a rather pleasing floral aroma. But as her intentions became clearer, so did her natural perfume.

She was rotten from the inside out.

Yet she masqueraded as an angel in disguise, her beauty an allure that seduced many Virtuous Fae to her side.

At least until they realized the evil lurking beneath all that pale skin.

But by then, it was usually too late. They'd already been ensnared by her infamous deals—deals that were always drafted in her favor.

Ty had learned from the best but chose to use that knowledge for the greater good. That was why Cami's negative commentary about his arrangements had hurt him; he didn't want to be seen in the same light as his former mentor. He wanted to be a leader his fae respected, not a king they feared due to distrust.

"Does it always smell like this?" Cami asked, her voice low.

"No. Vivaxia is here," I replied, my gaze scanning the concealed scenery once more.

This wasn't a natural fog, nor was it enchanted. It just felt like an ominous cloud of death.

Surely that's a bad omen...

The words echoed in my mind, sounding more like Ty than me. Somewhere deep in my soul, I sensed that he'd recently shared that thought.

Where are you, my king? I wondered at him. *Why can't I feel you?*

I couldn't remember a time when we'd ever truly been cut from one another. It concerned me, but I also couldn't sense Cami. Yet she was fine and standing right in front of me.

So Ty is probably okay, too, I told myself.

Although, deep down, I knew that wasn't true at all.

The sky and fog proved that. His Source was breaking,

his power shuddering through the very ground we walked upon now.

Az still led the way, his steps sure as he moved us in the direction of Strigoi territory.

Ty had gone to meet with Nos, which made this his last known destination. And given that the entire kingdom now reeked of dead roses, it seemed like the right move.

Unless Vivaxia is fucking with us...

My eyes narrowed as my footsteps slowed.

Cami must have noticed because she matched my pace, her gaze finding mine. "Not being able to connect to your mind is rather inconvenient right now," she muttered.

My lips twitched. "You miss my thoughts, little angel?" I sauntered a step closer. "The dirty ones? My wicked promises? Maybe my praise?"

Her eyebrows lifted. "Seriously? You're flirting? Now?" She gestured to the eerie smog thickening around us. "*Here?*"

"That's just who I am, love," I murmured. Besides, flirting with her was a nice distraction from the darkness growing inside my head.

Alas, I couldn't smile for long.

Because that darkness only grew as the red moon above turned into a murky haze that spread across the sky like a diseased cloud. *That explains the absence of fae,* I thought, noting the unguarded tunnel exit.

I swallowed. "I can't tell if Vivaxia is really here or if she just wants us to *think* she's here."

Cami followed my focus upward, her own throat seeming to bob in a motion similar to my own. "I take it that's not normal for this kingdom either."

I shook my head. "It's usually a clear night, illuminated solely by the blood moon above. Although, it is the Dream Realm. So illusions are not necessarily uncommon either."

"And you think Vivaxia might have crafted the illusion of her presence?" Cami asked.

"I think it's possible," I hedged, looking over her shoulder to meet Az's violet gaze. "What do you think?"

"I think there's only one way to find out, and it's not by standing here discussing poss—"

A crack rent the air, one that had dozens of lightning bolts splintering across the sky.

My lips parted.

And my heart fucking stopped.

Because I *knew* that crack. I'd lived through it before. Experienced the outcome. *Saw a Virtuous Fae fall...*

I was running before I even processed where I was going, my soul screaming in agony for the male I called *mate*. Cami screamed my name, her terror an invisible ribbon that wrapped around my core and nearly caused me to stumble as my spirit literally split in two.

One half going to Ty.

The other back to Cami.

My king.

My queen.

I... I... I started to shake. Everything was... was so fucking cold. Yet hot at the same time.

Hot because of Cami, I realized, her hands suddenly on my face. *Cold because of Ty.*

My angel wrapped herself around me, her eyes giant orbs of terror and concern. She must have felt what I'd felt. Knew... understood...

Except...

My brow furrowed. *Why are her hands covered in blood?*

Her hair, too.

I reached for her as horror ripped me to shreds. "You're hurt," I whispered, searching her for a cause.

But she shook her head. "No. It's the rain."

"The rain?" I blinked. "What...?" I glanced up, then winced as a glob hit my eye.

It... it wasn't rain. Not in the traditional sense, anyway. Because that hadn't been water.

With a flick of my hand, I pulled it away and found it smeared with *blood*.

Blood I knew.

Blood I recognized.

Blood I'd *tasted*.

"*Ty*," I whispered, agony shredding me from the inside once more. "*Ty!*"

But I... I couldn't run to him. I was glued to Cami, her warmth the only stable presence in my life. The only thing keeping me upright.

She grabbed my hand, her mouth moving with words I couldn't understand. Because the rain—*the blood*—had turned into a downpour.

It was loud.

So. Fucking. Loud.

And it became all I could hear.

Yet somehow I started to run. *Because of Cami.* She had her hand in mine, her body pulling me toward a fate I didn't want to face.

Not again. Fae, not again.

But it was inevitable.

I knew that. Sensed it. *Felt* it.

However, nothing could prepare me for the scene before us. The scene that had haunted my nightmares for eons...

Oh, the background had changed.

Instead of pristine palaces with too-perfect white sidings, I saw a gothic, cathedral-like palace instead. A courtyard sprawled out before it... just like the one in my memory. Except that one had been layered in flawless greens and pebbled with crystallized flowers.

This one was *dead*.

Black.

And centered around a bloody fountain.

A bloody fountain that's been shattered, I thought, my stomach twisting. *Shattered by the fall of a king...*

Because half of it had been taken down into a hole.

A crater.

A pit.

Cami said something that I couldn't hear, my mind caught somewhere between reality and the past. I saw a black hole, one shaped like a vortex that had sucked my intended mate down, down, down...

But he wasn't my intended now.

He was *mine*. My mate.

I also couldn't define the vortex here. *Because it doesn't exist,* I realized.

Only crumpled rocks. Dead flowers. *And blood.*

So. Much. Fucking. Blood.

Ty... Ty's wings had been burned to near ash during his fall. Harmed beyond repair. But I... I didn't recall there being this much blood at the site of his fall.

Was there this much near his landing site? I wondered, trying to remember.

Yet I couldn't. It was as though that memory had been stolen from my mind, or perhaps *blocked*.

Or stolen, I thought, purposely repeating that word. Because it seemed important. It reminded me of something.

Of... of *Vita*.

My eyes widened. "When you shoved the energy into Vita..." I looked at Cami, only she wasn't where she'd been before, her touch having left my face.

And we were no longer running.

We'd stopped near the edge of the courtyard. Or maybe only I had stopped. Because I couldn't see Cami now. She'd disappeared.

As had Az and Ajax.

I spun around, trying to find them.

"It's Ty's memories!" I shouted, hoping like hell they could hear me. "Vita protected his mind. But Vivaxia hid a funnel inside it—a funnel that Cami activated when she hit it with power!"

No one replied.

It was like they'd abandoned me in this courtyard. But I knew they wouldn't do that.

This is another illusion, I realized. *Does that mean the crater isn't real? Is this my own personal nightmare?*

I growled, my gaze narrowing. "You and your fucking tricks," I said, my words for Vivaxia.

"I seem to recall you once being quite fond of them," the witch whispered in my ear.

I whirled around, trying to find her. But I was just met with more fog.

More blood rain.

More *emptiness*.

And that fucking crater.

"Do you remember the last time we played this game?" I asked, a taunt in my tone. "I believe it ended when I introduced a blade to your heart." Which had happened right before I'd jumped after Ty and followed him to literal Hell.

Vivaxia had physically died. But it'd only been temporary. It hadn't been a death like Typhos's parents had experienced—one caused by his siphoning ability, not a mere blade.

Thus, Vivaxia had easily regenerated and brought her

corporeal form back to life. Only, the Virtuous Fae Source had forever changed in that moment.

It'd shattered.

Created all the realms.

And became part of Ty.

He always said it was because I'd killed her to avenge him. But it was his easy explanation. Deep down, we both knew the truth—the Virtuous Fae Source had shattered *for him.*

I stared at that familiar crater once more, my gaze narrowing as the past mingled with the present.

There was only one way to determine if this was an illusion or not.

One way to *break* whatever mirage Vivaxia had woven through my mind.

By facing my fear.

I didn't think; I just ran.

Closed my eyes.

And jumped.

CHAPTER 37

CAMI

"**A**z!" I screamed, my lungs burning from my lack of air. "Ajax! Melek!"

I couldn't see them. Couldn't hear them. Couldn't *feel* them.

One moment, we'd been running toward the courtyard and then... *chaos*.

There was no other word for it. The eerie atmosphere had parted to reveal dozens of fighting Nightmare Fae, all centered around a large crater-like hole.

When I'd spun around to avoid the battle ahead, I'd realized I was alone. Which made no sense. I'd been holding Melek's hand. My fingertips were still warm from his touch.

Yet he'd vanished.

My eyes narrowed. *This has to be some sort of—*

I ducked as a spiral of flames came straight for my head.

From a dragon's mouth, I thought as the beast responsible started charging toward me.

Now my eyes narrowed for an entirely different reason.

"Well, that was rude," I told the Nightmare Fae. I assumed this was an Air Dragon since it had just released a torrent of fire from its snout. Or maybe Water Dragons could do that, too.

I didn't know.

And it didn't matter.

Because neither creature belonged in the Morpheus Kingdom.

Just like the Naga and Griffin battling a few feet behind the approaching flamethrower.

Another spiral of fire came for me, forcing me to dodge left. The sudden action nearly sent me to the ground, but I managed to balance myself at the last second with an unintended hop.

The fire-breathing creature wavered with the movement, causing me to frown. Because he'd... he'd blinked in and out of existence for a second. Almost like a hologram.

What in the...?

I twirled and tilted my head at the same time, the movement probably making me look absolutely ridiculous, but it caused the Nightmare Fae to flicker again.

I straightened. "It's a mirage," I whispered aloud. "Just like the first trial."

No one heard me. Or, if they did, they didn't react to me.

Are they even here? I wondered.

They had to be.

But maybe not in this mirage. Maybe they were seeing something completely different.

This was the land of nightmares and dreams. Who knew what was real and what was fake?

Yet something told me this illusion had nothing to do with the Strigoi or the Ghouls of this realm. Because they weren't the only ones who were fond of manifesting false realities.

Vivaxia excelled at it, too. I'd seen her version of it in the Virtuous Fae Realm when she'd crafted that false utopia.

A utopia I'd seen through, thus revealing the decaying world beneath.

She'd fixed the vision a few times, but I'd caught enough of the truth to realize her version was a lie.

Just like this, I thought as I glanced around again.

The blood splatter was real. I saw it in both visions—the battle façade and what I assumed was reality.

The courtyard appeared to be real, too.

Same with the crater-like hole near the fountain.

So how do I break the mirage? I wondered as I jumped sideways to avoid yet another fireball. While the vision might not be completely real, I didn't want to test my theory by letting myself be burned.

But I really needed that damn dragon to stop trying to kill me.

Glaring, I focused my siphoning ability on him to see if there was a way to temporarily douse his fire.

And found him covered in Vivaxia's magic—a magic I recognized, thanks to that spell I'd absorbed in the paradigm. Only this enchantment felt different. It wasn't compulsion-based like the one I'd felt on the Centaur. This... this felt... heavier. More deeply ingrained.

Frowning, I tugged on the essence and startled as the entire world around me jolted in response.

It feels deeper because it's tied to this mirage... I yanked on the magical strands once more, causing the entire world to tremble in response.

The dragon roared in annoyance, or maybe that was

Vivaxia growling. Regardless, I gave another harsh yank—one that sent the beast tumbling to the side.

I didn't wait for him to get up or for Vivaxia to think of something new for this little game of visions. Instead, I engaged my inner siphon and started pulling all the energy into my being.

A shriek pierced my ears, the fae before me vibrating in and out of existence. Pain stabbed my heart in the next blink, freezing me in place.

I'm killing them, I realized, my breath stalling in my lungs. *Just like in the Netherworld Kingdom.*

Is this…? Is this real?

I…

I swallowed, my ability lessening its hold on the magical strands and allowing the visage to exist once more.

The fae seemed to sigh in relief, then all turned toward me at once with hatred burning in their gazes. I'd hurt them, and now they were going to make me pay.

But… but is it real? I wondered as I stumbled backward. *Did I get it wrong? Is this not a—*

The ground shook as the fae started toward me, their combined powers a force that had my eyes widening in alarm. *So much anger. So much hate. All directed at me…*

It was like a nightmare come to life.

And my feet… my feet *refused to move.*

I wheeled my arms like that might help my legs, yet I remained glued to the trembling ground below.

A scream lodged in my throat, panic overtaking logic.

I need to run! To fight! To… The thoughts trailed off as the visage shook again, reminding me that this… this wasn't real. It couldn't be.

I'd been walking with my mates, searching for Typhos. There was no physical way these creatures had just *appeared* out of thin air and begun fighting. Not without us having heard them in the distance.

Gritting my teeth, I grabbed hold of the magical strands once more and siphoned the energy.

Shrieks erupted in response, the Nightmare Fae throwing fearful looks my way. Words spilled from their lips, pleas and accusations rending the air.

I closed my eyes, blocking them out and *focusing*. Because I could *feel* that this was a mirage. *These are not innocent souls. They're not innocent fae. In fact...* I opened my eyes once more, my brow furrowing. "There are no souls," I whispered to myself.

They possessed neither light nor dark auras, confirming my analysis.

"You're not real," I told them. That didn't make me any less remorseful to watch them disappear, though. Because a small part of me kept wondering, *What if?*

What if I'm wrong?

What if they're real?

What if I'm killing innocents?

But as the scene dissolved completely, reality settled before me.

Or what I assumed was *reality*, anyway. It could easily be another mirage. However, I didn't feel Vivaxia's enchantment lurking in the air anymore. It was deep inside me instead, revolving with power that begged to be released.

Only, I kept it captive, letting it fuel my steps as I wandered into the courtyard. It was littered with dead roses that framed a bloody fountain and the crater beside it.

Truth or fiction? I thought as I tiptoed closer to the massive hole outlined by burnt edges. I'd seen something similar once... in a dream. Or what had felt like a dream, anyway. However, it'd actually been Lucifer's memory, one Vita had forced me to witness firsthand.

The day of his fall.

I crept forward and peered over the edge into an ominous abyss.

Seems like a good time for a rule, I decided. *Hell Fae Queen Rule #2: Don't Jump.*

Gods, I was losing my mind.

This might still be a mirage, too. Which would explain why my mates were nowhere to be seen.

"Az!" I tried yelling. "Ajax! Melek!"

Silence.

Because of course they weren't here.

It's another illusion.

Gritting my teeth, I stepped away from the black hole and searched the murky landscape for energy strands. I didn't have to look far because Vivaxia was everywhere.

In the dead roses.

The fountain.

The blood falling from the sky.

The cobblestone paths.

And especially in that palace, I realized, eyeing the gothic spires of the cathedral-like structure bordering the courtyard. *The Strigoi Palace.*

Why would Vivaxia's presence be particularly potent there? Had she bespelled them all to do her bidding? Perhaps they were the cause of these illusionary games.

It would be just like all the other incidents where she'd bespelled the Nightmare Fae to act on her behalf, like a puppet master controlling her minions.

Which suggested that walking into the palace would be a bad idea.

Yet my feet were already moving in that direction because some part of me knew that was where I needed to go. The Hell Fae Source had guided me this far. Why stop relying on my instincts now?

Whatever was going on here, the cause of it was in the palace. I sensed that more and more with each step, the energy seeming to buzz along my skin as though warning me to turn back.

Not a chance.

I wanted this illusion to shatter. And more than that, I wanted my damn mates back.

I hated not feeling them. They were *mine*. This blocking spell—or whatever the fuck had cut me off from them—needed to be taken down.

Except, I couldn't sense any enchantments lingering inside me. Well, any *new* enchantments, anyway. The funnel was still there. Although, it felt quieter now. Less eager. Something that was strange, considering I'd just imbibed a lot of energy.

Maybe all that work Typhos had done this week was paying off.

Or maybe the funnel is no longer needed, I thought, prodding it as I followed the path to the front of the palace. A sense of déjà vu settled over me, like I'd just done this recently. Which was impossible. I'd never been here before.

Yet, I could swear that at some point in my past, I'd seen those doors. That I'd felt the heavy atmosphere around me. *That I'd sensed the wrongness of this kingdom.*

Frowning, I paused and glanced up at the blood moon. It was clear now, the fog seeming to have lifted. And it was no longer raining.

However, I wondered if what I was seeing now was even real. Because I could feel magic tickling the air, the presence threatening my sanity.

I really miss having you in my head, I thought at my mates. *Even you, Melek.*

An inappropriate joke would make me feel a lot better about all of this. So would a scoff from Az or a taunt from Ajax.

Alas, nothing.

I couldn't even sense our bonds. *Just like when my mother took me to meet Vivaxia.*

My teeth ground together as I started up the stairs, only to jump as the stone in my pocket released a heated sensation against my thigh. I pulled it out, ready to toss it away, but paused as the rock turned cold in my palm.

What in the world…? It'd burned me mere seconds ago. Now it resembled ice. *Was it just trying to remind me to use it? Or was it warning me about something?*

I'd nearly killed all those Netherworld Fae the last time I'd used this stone. It had amplified my power to a point where I couldn't control it.

Is it trying to warn me that I might do that again?

If that was the case, then why had Morpheus left it for me in the tunnel?

I frowned down at the stone. Morpheus's note had said a mutual friend had given it to him to leave for me. I'd assumed he'd meant Zenaida.

Only…I'd never met the Fortune Fae.

So is she really the mutual friend? My eyes widened. *Did he actually mean Vivaxia?*

My heart stuttered, my hand nearly releasing the stone.

This might all be a trick. I didn't know Morpheus. We'd never met. Why would he help me?

But none of my mates had thought he meant me harm. Had they suspected that, they wouldn't have let me keep the stone. And Melek had said he was fond of him, which held a lot of weight.

My jaw clenched again. *This is ridiculous.* I needed to

rely on my instincts, to press forward, to get rid of this damn mirage. And find my mates.

Which meant I had to go through those doors. Because the source of power was emanating from inside the creepy palace.

More like a haunted mansion, I thought, shivering at how barren this place felt. It was as though only ghosts existed here.

A sensation that sent another stroke of familiarity down my spine.

It was the strangest experience, knowing I'd never been here and yet suddenly being aware of exactly what I would find beyond the threshold.

Something—or *someone*—was guiding me forward.

To the throne room, I thought, blinking as my feet began to move again. *I need to go to the throne room.*

I didn't know how I knew that; I just did.

But I wasn't sure if it was the Source guiding me now... or Vivaxia.

Only one way to find out...

CHAPTER 38

AZ

Everything was dark.

Too dark.

My Phoenix paced inside me, disturbed by our surroundings. This endless tunnel resembled a cage, which brought back painful memories of our past.

Not being able to sense my mates only worsened the sensation of feeling lost.

I also couldn't remember how I'd gotten here. One moment, I'd been walking with Cami, Ajax, and Melek, and the next thing I knew...

I'd woken up here.

Alone.

Deep underground.

It was cold. Damp. And *contained*. A tunnel with a low roof that skimmed the top of my head and walls that brushed my arms on either side as I walked.

A nightmare, I recognized. *One derived from my past*.

Only, I wasn't sure how I'd landed in this tight space. And I was determined to escape it. To find my mates. To be *free*.

A tremble tickled my spine, that final word one that reverberated through my head. *Free.* I'd longed to experience liberation many moons ago, when I'd been trapped by Vivaxia's spell.

I'd tasted independence since, been allowed to exist of my own free will.

However, I felt... weighed down again now. Like she'd somehow tightened her noose around me once more.

My gaze narrowed. *No.* I would *never* be hers again.

She could play. Flaunt. *Threaten.* But I was my own Phoenix. My own fae. My own *man.*

"You'll have to do better than this to trap me," I told Vivaxia. Because I had no doubt she was the cause of this nightmare.

I'd sensed her presence the moment we'd entered the Morpheus Kingdom. It was as though she'd taken over, her aura thickening the air with her familiar perfume and nearly making me gag. Melek had picked up her scent, too. I'd seen it in his expression.

We both recognized her brand of immortal madness.

And this mirage she'd created was just the beginning of her games.

Fuck, I hope Ajax and Cami are okay. They'd never played in Vivaxia's mental mazes. *If they didn't see through her tricks...*

No. I couldn't think that way.

Cami had proved very capable of identifying mirages while in the bride trials. She'd recognize this for what it was.

And Ajax... My lips twisted. Ajax should be able to figure it out, especially in his role as Warden. Typhos had done something to bolster his power. Surely it would—

Energy swirled in front of me, causing me to jump back, the bright light nearly blinding my sensitive eyes.

"Thank fuck." Ajax's familiar voice had me blinking in

confusion, my eyesight still hindered by the unexpected light. "I was beginning to think Kuro had lost his mind."

A huff came on the heels of that pronouncement, followed by the ruffling of feathers.

I blinked again and again, my vision slowly registering the sight before me.

Ajax stood just outside of a portal, his wand in one hand with his familiar perched on his opposite shoulder.

I frowned at the owl. "When did he get here?"

"Around the time you all vanished into thin air," he told me. "Vivaxia tried to ensnare me with her spell as well, but my defensive instincts kicked in before she could pull me into her paradigm-like enchantment."

Paradigm-like, I repeated to myself. "She cast a mirage."

"Yeah. One I couldn't see but could feel." He glanced around. "Although, I guess she stuck you down here. Because this is real, not an illusion. That's why I was able to find you. Or Kuro was, anyway. He can still sense you."

I stared at the owl. His golden eyes held mine, his expression one of indifference. "And here I thought you didn't like me."

The owl huffed again, as though to say, *I don't.*

"We need to get above ground," Ajax said, ignoring my standoff with his familiar. "Cami's up there somewhere, so I need you to help me hunt her down."

My inner Phoenix perked up, his desire to track instantly engaged.

Except... no. That wasn't quite right. My Phoenix had already been tracking someone.

Typhos.

I'd been tracking him above ground with Melek, Ajax, and Cami, searching for his power. We'd reached the Strigoi Palace Courtyard, and everything had shifted.

Vivaxia's influence had been everywhere at once, and these walls had appeared.

Because my Phoenix took me deep underground.

Not Vivaxia. My animal. He'd *ashed* us here. To protect me. And to continue our hunt.

But why would you leave Cami? I asked him, confused by his choice.

He purred inside me as Ajax said something— something I didn't hear because I was too busy trying to understand my beast.

We need to find Typhos.

I understood that much.

However, I didn't understand why we'd abandoned—

Power flooded my soul, causing flames to explode from my fingertips. Ajax jumped back with a sharp curse, one that echoed in my ears as I focused on that inner fire. *Typhos's Source.*

My Phoenix paced again, urging me to move, his impatience curling deep within me.

This was his way of helping Cami—*we need to find Typhos and his Source... for Cami.*

I wasn't sure how he knew it, but the jolt of energy seemed to confirm that knowledge somehow. If I didn't know better, I'd say the Source was talking to my Phoenix.

Just like it'd been communicating with Cami as she'd led us to the Morpheus Kingdom.

"Typhos's emergency protocols have been triggered," I realized aloud, aware of his strategy because I knew him. I'd been inside his mind for so long that I knew how he *thought*. "We need to find him." *That* was why my Phoenix had insisted on ashing us down here. He'd been leading me to Typhos until Ajax had interrupted our hunt with his portal.

Unless Vivaxia is fucking with my mind, I thought in the next instant.

But I was already shaking my head in denial. Because no, this direction felt too right. Typhos's Source had taken over. It was in self-preservation mode. I could feel it now, my energy swirling inside me and connecting to the beacon of power with a single thought. Just like I always had.

Typhos had gifted me with that connection, providing me with an outlet.

It might not be *my* Source, but we knew each other well. Because I was mated to it as much as I was mated to Typhos.

As well as Cami.

"I can feel her," I whispered, noting the way her energy curled around inside Typhos's Source. "I can feel Cami."

"Where is she?" Ajax demanded.

I shook my head, unable to answer that. All I could say was "She's okay." I looked at him as I repeated, "We need to find Typhos. *Now.*"

I didn't wait for him to reply; I just started running into the darkness.

Ajax cursed behind me, then cast a spell that sent some sort of firefly racing ahead of me to light up the tunnel.

He knew how my beast worked—once we had a scent, we couldn't be stopped.

I'd been dazed before, confused by how I'd ended up in the tunnels. Perhaps I'd even been fighting off a hint of Vivaxia's magic—one I'd narrowly escaped, thanks to my Phoenix ashing me out just in time.

Whatever the case, my head was clear now, and I knew where to go.

These were the caverns Typhos had created after his first fall, the land deep under the Hell Fae Realm that no one but him ever traversed.

Except for maybe Melek. I suspected Typhos allowed him to venture down here. But knowing Melek, he hadn't visited often.

And as for me, I'd only been down here once—the day of Typhos's fall.

It didn't bode well that he was underground now because it suggested he'd fallen... *again*.

I picked up my pace, determined to find him. My upper body protested, the tight walls scraping my bare arms, but I pushed through it.

Because time was running out.

I could feel it in my bones. In my heart. *In my soul.*

A countdown had started.

The Source ticking away like a time bomb.

It's going to implode.

And if that happens before Typhos wakes... the entire realm is going to go with it.

CHAPTER 39

CAMI

Into the creepy-as-fuck palace I go, I thought as I crept up the stairs. *Because it's totally normal to know where I'm going in a place I've never been before.*

There was probably a rule I should be thinking about, but I couldn't exactly go back now. Not when I was this close to learning what power was drawing me here. *And who…*

The hallways were vacant, but the scent of decaying roses lingered in the air. Not the most inviting aroma. Yet it drew me forward, my flat shoes silent against the marbled ground.

Actually, no.

My steps… weren't silent. They seemed to whisper along the floor, the sound echoing softly in my ears. Which was strange. *I'm not dragging my feet, so why…?*

I slowly stopped walking, the line of thinking trailing off as the sound continued to float around me. I'd just traversed the stairs alone. There'd been nothing around me. Nothing behind me. *So where is that noise coming from?*

Turning, I searched the space for the source and found nothing but dying candles and dusty mantels.

My eyes narrowed. Because the whispering remained. *Maybe I can't see it...*

That thought suggested this might be another mirage, a consideration that had my gaze narrowing even more. Because fuck this. And fuck Vivaxia.

I started toward my quarry again—that beacon of energy that warmed all my senses—just to pause as a gust of frigid air hit me from behind. Accompanied by that sound...

Spinning around, I tried to catch the cause of it but only found the soft flickering of candlelight once more. My jaw clenched. Either a ghost was playing with me, or I'd missed some sort of opening.

Like a portal, I thought, scanning the bare walls for clues.

My father had taught me all about those, how they could blend into anything, especially in the Hell Fae Realm. There were codes that activated hidden ones, too. But some didn't require passwords at all. It just depended on where the portal led.

Tiptoeing backward, I listened for that raspy sound again and froze when a breeze ruffled my hair. Frowning, I followed the source of that airflow to a mirrorlike shimmer coming from the top of the staircase—a mirrorlike shimmer that hadn't been there when I'd ascended moments ago.

It blinked out of existence as I approached, only to appear once more as soon as I stood in front of it.

My lips parted at the image on the other side, the familiar face one that seemed to make the stone in my hand pulse. Or maybe it was my own heartbeat coming through as I gripped the rock tighter than I should.

But I couldn't help it.

Because it was my mother staring back at me, mouthing something I couldn't hear.

After a beat, she held up her hand and pressed it to the mirror.

I studied it warily.

This was absolutely a trick, some sort of distraction from where I needed to be.

"You taught me never to fall for something like this," I told her, folding my arms with that rock clutched even tighter in my fist. "Hell Fae Rule #8: If It Sounds Too Good to Be True, It Probably Is. Oh, and Hell Fae Rule #13: Nothing Is What It Seems."

Her nostrils flared in response, suggesting she could hear me just fine. "Camillia," her mouth seemed to say. "Trust. Me."

I snorted. "Fat chance of that, *Mother*. The last time I *trusted you*, I ended up in a fake utopia and met my *grandmother*." A shudder worked through me at the term. I never wanted to use it in relation to Vivaxia ever again.

She's my nemesis and nothing more, I thought.

"Camillia," my mother tried again. But the mirror disappeared for another long blink, and when it came back, it was to reveal an image that had my lips parting for an entirely new reason. The visage before me was... dystopian. A wasteland. Dead trees—and not like those I'd seen in the Netherworld Kingdom and the Midnight Fae Realm. These trees were shriveled into strands of ash.

Feathery wisps danced around them, their gray quality causing my lips to curl down. They... they kind of looked like *ghosts*.

A strange visual.

But as my mother appeared again, I realized what I

was seeing. *Souls*. She held up her arm—or what was left of it—to show me the translucent strand that should be a wrist and a hand.

Her blonde hair blew in another gust of wind, causing several strands to just fly away. But it was her wings that captivated me.

The last time I'd seen her, they'd been a brilliant white color, their beauty nearly taking my breath away. Now they resembled skeletal branches with smokelike ends.

"I…" I didn't understand. "Is this real?" Was I looking into the true Virtuous Fae Realm? Not the mirage she and Vivaxia had created, but what actually remained of their glorious world?

A memory nagged at me, one of me seeing Vivaxia's wings—the tattered ends blending with her gorgeous plumage. In one visage, she possessed beautiful white wings with golden tips. And in the next, her feathers appeared worn and dead.

Just like my mother's, I thought, swallowing as another breeze stole more of her essence. The smoky tendrils seemed to be crawling up her forearm now, morphing her skin into a husk-like texture.

Sadness rimmed my mother's ice-blue eyes, the color appearing paler than usual. "Run," her cracked lips mouthed as a tear slid down her cheek. "Camillia… *Run!*"

The mirror shattered on that final word. My arms flew upward just in time to protect myself from the glass splintering all over the hallway.

Followed by an icy breath of wind that whirled up and down the halls.

A *tsk* followed, the echo of it sending a chill down my spine. Because that tsk had been *here*. Real. Not beyond a veil or a portal. But in this very corridor.

And as I peeked out from behind my arms, I found the owner of that condemning sound. *Vivaxia.*

The stone heated in my palm, almost as though it were angry. But when my fingers loosened in response, it instantly cooled. Maybe it wanted to remind me of its presence. Or perhaps it was a sentient form of energy like Vita.

I couldn't discount anything at this point, including my own vision. Because while Vivaxia certainly appeared to be real, it could easily be another trick.

However, the cuts on my arms certainly felt real.

"Mystika always was dramatic," Vivaxia drawled, sounding disappointed. "At least she served her purpose." With that pronouncement, she disappeared through a threshold.

To the throne room, my mind somehow knew. *A throne room riddled with secrets.*

My brow furrowed as a memory played through my mind of Vivaxia standing behind a throne holding a dying Strigoi King. It was a vivid reimagination, one that felt like my own experience. Yet I knew I'd never been here.

So how am I remembering this? My arms slowly fell to my sides, the stone still in one hand.

More of the memory rolled inside my head, showing me the Strigoi King's death—at Vivaxia's hand. Only it hadn't been the cut across his throat that had killed him, but Vivaxia's power over him. *The pet spell.*

She'd owned his soul... because he'd struck a deal with her.

A deal that involved granting her access to the throne in exchange for a queen.

I blinked. This was all too specific to be my own imagination at work. Yet I possessed the knowledge as though it were my own.

Was Melek here? I wondered.

But no. That didn't feel right.

This… this visage and the information that accompanied it felt like it came from Typhos. *Why am I suddenly aware of his…?* The question trailed off in my thoughts as another replaced it. *Vita.*

I'd shoved all that energy into Vita, breaking some sort of lock inside that had allowed those memories to go to Vivaxia. Or perhaps she'd just inherited the power.

But I, too, was linked to Vivaxia.

And Typhos's Source.

So something… something had caused a feedback loop. Or maybe the Source was the one sending me these details. Or perhaps it was Vita fighting her way back to Typhos via my connection to Vivaxia.

Regardless of the how or the why, it was happening. Because I could feel the energy humming through me now, the strands far too powerful to be my own. And they weren't linked to the spell I'd siphoned outside.

However, I could still feel the lingering effects of that magic humming in my blood. Just as I could see the remnants of it all over this palace.

The strands seemed to ripple around me as I moved, my feet automatically taking me to where Vivaxia had disappeared through the threshold.

I wasn't at all surprised to find her standing on the dais, her fingertips playing across the decrepit throne. A vision in my head told me what that opulent power symbol should look like, and it was nothing like this broken-down chair before me. Even the blood-veins decorating the stage appeared to be dry, the formerly polished golds darkened to a deep bronze.

This platform looked nothing like it used to.

And the same could be said about the Strigoi lingering

nearby. Gone was their vampiric presence and in its place, shadows of ghosts.

Oh, they were still alive. I could see their souls clutching onto their corporeal forms. But they were on the verge of death.

All because their king—the one meant to *lead*—had failed them.

He'd struck a deal with the real devil. With *Vivaxia*. And the Source had turned on him in response.

I could feel that punishment thriving inside me, the concept one I instantly understood. Because it was exactly as it should be. He'd betrayed Lucifer and the Hell Fae Realm. Why would the Source continue to empower him and his people after something like that?

I almost nodded, like I was agreeing with some figment lurking in my head.

Maybe I was. Maybe I'd lost my fucking mind. Yet I'd never felt more knowledgeable in my life.

It was as though something had cracked open inside me, allowing all the details of this world to flow through the membrane of my mind and into my very soul.

The Hell Fae Source is empowering me, I realized. *Or maybe I'm siphoning all of this information...*

But no. I hadn't activated that part of myself. This was coming from somewhere I couldn't define. A link I had no idea existed. A *connection* created by my soul.

If Vivaxia saw it, she didn't comment. Instead, she blew the dust away from the throne—dust that used to resemble a king—and sat on it with a sigh.

She needs the conduit to stay in this realm, I deduced. *That's Typhos's power, and it's operating as a leash.*

For now, anyway.

Because I could see her absorbing the power of

everything and everyone around her, could feel her testing my own aura with her ability, too.

Mentally, I redirected her effort, her energy oddly tangible in my mind. Just like everything else around us. I couldn't tell if I was just more in tune with my siphoning talent or if this was a gift from Typhos's Source.

Vivaxia arched a brow. "Well, that's new." She crossed her long legs and leaned back in the throne, her wings nowhere in sight. She seemed to be recovering from something.

Had the walk into the hallway drained her of energy? That would make sense with the throne being her proverbial leash. *So what happens when the conduit runs out of power?*

It seemed to be fizzling out near the base, Typhos's energy barely hanging on.

What would happen then? Would she start absorbing the souls of the Strigoi? Was that their purpose here?

I suspected she needed Typhos for something. Only, he was nowhere in sight.

Because he fell, I realized, noting the hole in the wall. A hole that was framed with burn marks similar to those of that crater out by the fountain.

All the pieces seemed to come together in my mind—Typhos knocking himself out and relinquishing his hold on his Source. Which allowed his Source to prosper without his influence.

And now his Source was talking to me.

Filling me with knowledge.

Granting me access to Typhos's memories.

Turning me into a live version of Vita.

Only it was more than that. With each passing moment, I felt more and more powerful. Like the Hell Fae Source was forcing me to absorb energy, just as Typhos had done while pushing me to my limits this week.

Except this was more gradual. More *intentional*.

However, I had no idea what to do with it. If the Source fed me too much, I'd be at risk of opening that connection deep inside me to Vivaxia.

Is that actually the point? I wondered. *Is she doing this?*

My head spun with theories, making me miss whatever she'd just said out loud.

Several things, actually.

She'd been talking this whole time, and I'd been too lost in my thoughts to hear her.

And the thunderous expression on her face told me she didn't appreciate it one bit.

I cocked my head. "You don't like being ignored, do you?" I wasn't sure why the taunt left my mouth, but it felt right.

This bitch had created me to be her little toy. Her *siphon*. And I really wasn't interested in playing along.

My parents had taught me to fight authority. To think of only myself. To put myself first.

Hell Fae Rule #6: Only Look Out for Yourself—No One Else.

A whole slew of rules followed that one in my mind.

Hell Fae Rule #3: Know Your Enemy Before Engaging.

Hell Fae Rule #4: Don't Trust Anyone.

Hell Fae Rule #5: Be Prepared for Anything.

Hell Fae Rule #1: Don't Die.

That last one echoed the loudest. It was a rule I fully intended to take to heart.

So I guess the rules still apply, I thought.

Maybe it'd been seeing my mother that had triggered them to possess more meaning. Maybe it was just my own rebellious spirit. Or maybe I needed the reminders to ground me in the moment.

All the power swimming around me was enough to

make me feel a million miles away, to toss me into a torrent of energy and never resurface.

But I had to focus.

To find Typhos.

To save the Hell Fae Realm.

I nearly blinked at that last notion. It'd come from a deep part of me, the part connected to Typhos's Source.

Whatever Vivaxia was doing on that throne was threatening the realm's existence. Typhos's Source. Typhos himself.

Which meant she was threatening my mates.

And me.

I narrowed my gaze. "You don't belong here, Vivaxia."

She released a surprised laugh. "You're just as ungrateful as your mother," she informed me, her voice seeming to caress every inch of the room.

The stone in my palm burned again, reacting to her voice. Or maybe reacting to her words.

I again wondered at its sentient-like response, but I was too focused on Vivaxia now to ponder it more.

"You two only exist because I created you," she went on, sounding imperial as fuck. "That means I own you both. Your souls. Your mind. Your *power*."

Pain rippled from my chest on that last word, the term seeming to strike me physically in the heart.

"You're *mine*, Camillia De la Croix. Just like Nos and all his Strigoi. Just like Azazel. Just like every other creature I've ever brought into existence."

My knees threatened to buckle as she *twisted* her hold on my insides, the protective shell I'd imagined no longer in existence.

It was as though she'd penetrated my very being with a simple thought.

Because she had.

Because she *could*.

I'd been so seduced by Typhos's influx of power that I'd felt invincible. But Vivaxia had fixed that naive notion with a single fucking word.

Agony shot through my being as she canted her head, the simple motion seeming to curl her power inside me more. "It's really quite simple, darling," she murmured, her tone turning matronly. "I'm your *Goddess*. The one you're meant to worship. To *serve*. All it takes is a thought, and suddenly you'll forget how to breathe."

My hand shot up to my throat in response, my lungs ceasing to function.

All the while, the death stone thrummed against my opposite palm, reminding me of its existence. But I wasn't sure how the hell it was supposed to help when I couldn't inhale or exhale.

"Another thought could stop your heart," she went on, her tone underlined with boredom. "It's just so easy. And, actually, it's not only my creations that I control, but every single one manifested by my fallen Virtuous Fae." A little giggle escaped her as she lifted her hand to reveal a swirl of gray energy. "Their essences reside in me now, as do the strings to their nightmarish puppets."

It took me a moment to process what she was saying, my mind somewhat preoccupied with my frozen lungs.

But slowly, I began to weave together her words with what I'd seen of the Virtuous Fae Realm. *And my mother.*

Parts of her had resembled a ghost.

A husk.

That'd been the wispy sounds I'd overheard—the *husks* of fallen Virtuous Fae.

Similar to the one mere feet from me now, only those ash-like remnants were the remains of a Strigoi King.

She's absorbing all their powers and killing their corporeal forms.

Like Typhos did to his parents.

Only she was doing this *intentionally*.

And she clearly had no interest in using her power for the greater good.

She was a dark soul.

An evil being.

A true fucking monster.

And I have no idea how to stop her.

CHAPTER 40

AJAX

Kuro bristled on my shoulder, his sense of alarm telling me something was very wrong.

Az froze at the same time, his head cocking in a way that told me his Phoenix had taken over. "*Cami,*" he breathed as a pang echoed in my chest.

He spun around, his large form resembling a shadow, thanks to the light being at his back. But I didn't need to be able to see him to know his heart was breaking.

Just like mine.

Our mate was in trouble.

We should never have stayed down here. But I'd followed Az's lead, just like I always fucking did.

Now isn't the time to cast blame, I thought. *Now is the time to align and find our fucking mate.*

"Kuro," I demanded, my familiar fully aware of what I needed.

Using my wand, I created a portal based on his instincts—just like I'd done when trying to locate Az moments ago—and stepped through the opening without looking back.

Az's Phoenix practically burned at my back, the two of us still shirtless from our sparring earlier. We could have changed before heading to the Netherworld Kingdom, but we hadn't bothered. Just like Cami hadn't wasted time changing out of her bloodstained tank top.

Flames, she'd better be okay. But I could feel in my soul that she wasn't. She needed us, and we...

"We're still underground," Az said, sounding as confused as I felt. "I don't—"

"Wake up!" The demand cut off Az's words and sent us both running toward the owner of that voice. *Melek.*

Az entered the cavern first. I made to follow but jumped back as a spout of flames shot up from the floor right in front of me. Another burst to the side and several more up ahead. Az either didn't notice them or didn't care. Being a Black Phoenix, he was basically fireproof.

Me, not so much.

Another geyser of fiery liquid shot up, the whooshing sound nearly drowning out Melek's plea for Az to help him.

The light from the fire allowed me to see why he needed help—Lucifer was unconscious on the floor, his suit burned in various places and his face a bloody mess.

"What the fuck happened?" I breathed, looking around the violent cavern before peering up into a black abyss.

"He fell," Melek gritted out. "*On purpose.*"

"He's protecting his Source," Az replied.

"I know. But Cami..." Melek looked at Az with more fear than I'd ever seen in his expression. "He has to wake up and help Cami!"

Another pang went through my chest, causing me to twirl my wand again to create a second portal. But it only led here. "Damn it, Kuro!"

"Melek's right—we need Typhos," Az told me. "Your owl knows it, too."

I growled. "Cami's hurting."

"I feel her as well," Az said, looking back at me. "But we need Typhos. So get over here and help us power him up."

Power him up? I repeated to myself. But there wasn't time to debate or contemplate what that meant.

Cami was in trouble. I could feel it in my soul. My heart. My *everything*.

And I would do whatever I had to do to save her.

"Tell me what to do." My words were for Az and Melek as I forced myself into the cavern. Flames shot up to my right—flames I doused with a spell from my wand. Sweat dotted my brow, my limbs instantly overheated. But I pushed onward, then knelt beside Az at Lucifer's side.

Kuro bristled, clearly not liking the fire either. However, he was the one who'd brought us here, so I considered it his punishment to bear.

"Bite him." Az's command had me blinking up at him.

"What?"

He didn't repeat himself, just put his hand over Lucifer's heart and pushed energy into him. Similar to what he'd done to Cami after the incident in the paradigm.

The phoenix tattoo on his chest rippled as his power filled the cavern, all of it focused on the unconscious fae.

"Even if this doesn't work, it'll empower his Source," Melek said, his hands also on Lucifer. "And the Source will give that vitality to Cami."

I wanted to ask how he knew that. But I knew better than to question his knowledge.

If biting Lucifer was going to give Cami strength, then I'd do it. I'd do fucking anything. *Even mate the Hell Fae King.*

Grabbing his arm, I pushed his sleeves up, then

brought his wrist to my mouth. "If Lucifer kills me when he wakes up, tell Cami I did this for her and that I'll love her... *forever.*"

I didn't wait for Az or Melek to acknowledge me, just sank my fangs into Lucifer's veins. And hoped like hell we could wake him up in time.

CHAPTER 41

CAMI

The world spun in spirals of darkness and chaos.
Darkness and life.
Darkness and death.

I... I couldn't see. I couldn't breathe. But I could *hear*.

Vivaxia's voice was everywhere, in my ears, my mind, my fucking soul.

My fingers curled into fists, causing a chilly bite to shoot up my right arm. I didn't understand it at first, the temperature change at odds with the numbness stealing over my body. But a pulsing in my palm reminded me that I still held the death stone.

And it seemed to be trying to communicate something important.

Something *vital*.

What is with this damn stone? I wondered, dizzy from my inability to breathe.

A responding energy pulsed in my chest, one that felt oddly familiar. Like it was important. Like I should focus on—

"You'll thank me later," Vivaxia murmured, her words loud in my head despite the whispered quality of her voice.

Ugh, she'd been droning on and on about the Virtuous Fae Realm, how she intended to restore it to its beautiful state.

And it seemed she wasn't done.

"I'll re-create you and your mother," she went on. "Then you'll worship my Source. Obey me. Exist to amuse me."

I wanted to frown at her, to ask how that sort of *existence* would be enjoyable for anyone. But it seemed all Vivaxia truly desired was to be revered as some sort of creationist Goddess. She wanted minions to serve her in every way imaginable.

Except, no. She'd had that in the past, when she'd owned Az. When she'd tried to manipulate Typhos.

I... I remembered some of it. *Because of Typhos's memories...*

The stone pulsated again, grounding me as my knees finally gave out. I was surprised I'd lasted this long. *When was the last time I took a breath? How am I even still alive?*

"And I shall be inside the Source," Vivaxia continued. "Showering you with power while I observe from my ascended place from above. It will be glorious."

What? I wanted to ask her. *Ascended place from above...?*

That sounded divine in nature, like she was trying to become some sort of supreme being. A creator from the sky. But in a non-corporeal form. *Magic redefined.*

That last thought reverberated through my mind, stirring something deep inside me. A knowledge. An understanding. *A realization.*

Typhos redefined his magic.

After siphoning his parents' essences.

And creating his own light.

442

He thought Vivaxia didn't know about his past, that she wasn't aware of him being a siphon.

But she'd known all along.

She'd planted a virus inside of Vita, a corrupt little morsel that had allowed her access to Typhos's mind for millennia. He hadn't sensed it because it'd been deep inside Vita's pages, lost in his mother's entries.

Every time he'd released a memory for storage inside Vita, Vivaxia had been there to review it. And a handful of those memories—very specific ones regarding Vivaxia— had been tucked away for good.

Such as the day he'd realized that she knew he was a siphon and she was one, too.

Part of him had always known that, of course. He'd felt her presence over the years, testing his gates, playing with those portals. But he hadn't considered her a significant threat because a few key moments from their history had been hidden from him.

Memories from the day of his fall.

I saw them now, playing out in real time.

"Oh, sweet Typhos," Vivaxia had cooed, her palm on his cheek, her expression affectionate. "I knew your soul would reject mine."

Typhos had said nothing, his expression not giving anything away.

But I was in tune with his mind now. His memories. *His life.*

And I felt that thread of uncertainty inside him, the thread that worried he'd missed a detail. Because he *always* missed something when it came to Vivaxia and her games.

Her lips curled into a grin, one that suggested she, too, knew his thoughts.

"Now you owe me a sacrifice. One underlined in *blood*." She drew her sharp nail across his cheek and down to his mouth, her gray irises following the movement. "You're going to fall for me, Typhos. You're going to assume that's the price I require. And I'm going to let you believe that for a very, very long time."

My heart skipped a beat as I watched—*learned*—this history. It... it was so strange to hear and see. Because I knew I still stood in the Strigoi throne room, yet every part of me was tuned in to this history. Reliving it. *Observing* it.

"Your power needs some fine-tuning," she went on. "But you're well on your way to greatness, my love. I can feel it in your light, see it in your strength. Your fall is going to irrevocably alter the Virtuous Fae Source. Well, that and Melek reneging on his deal with me."

Typhos's jaw clenched. "What deal?"

"The one that says he has to pay homage to me." She cocked her head. "In exchange for me not mating you. Little did he realize I already knew our bonds would fail. But he's going to be very upset indeed when you fall. And I fully expect him to react appropriately—by betraying our deal."

"Homage?" Typhos repeated. "How was that term defined?"

"Oh, Typhos." She drew her nails down along his bare chest. "You know the kind of *homage* I enjoy."

My jaw clenched, her little purr on the end of that final word making me want to break out of this strange little recollection and kill her.

But she wasn't done speaking.

"The offer was for one single instance, at a time of my choosing. No longer than sixty minutes. Only me and him. And he defined the limits." She arched a brow. "You taught him well, darling. However, there were some fine-print details that he may have overlooked—such as the one that states *no violence*."

Her gray eyes seemed to glitter with triumph.

Meanwhile, all Typhos felt was dread.

Because he already saw where this was headed.

"He thought I meant it as a sensual limit." She smiled. "Can you believe that? Me? A sadist?" She laughed a little, the sound grating on my nerves. "Does he not realize how alike you and I are?"

Typhos remained silent, his expression still giving nothing away.

However, I felt his emotional state. Experienced it as though it were my own. Yet somehow I could see him.

Or maybe…

Maybe I couldn't see him. Maybe I just felt the image he thought he was exuding.

He was clamping down his external reactions, ensuring that Vivaxia couldn't sense anything on the outside. And therefore his memory showcased him as such.

Except, I couldn't help wondering if that was true at all. His viewpoint was somewhat unreliable.

Hell, everything about him was unreliable. Not because he desired to be cryptic or mercurial, but because Vivaxia had manipulated him in this manner.

She'd tampered with his mind.

Even now, I could feel the effect of her weaving her essence into his and redefining this moment.

Making him forget every word.

"As I'm sure you've deduced, our sweet Melek is about to feel quite violent." She glanced off to the side. "And wouldn't you know? Our hour has just begun, as it was by *my* choice, after all. Which means even the slightest punch will nullify our agreement. And, well, you know how the Virtuous Fae Source feels about betraying our vows."

Typhos's mask began to slip, his fury a hot wave to my senses that had me quivering inside. *God, this feels so real.* Yet

I could still sense the Strigoi Palace around me, even while seeing Typhos standing in this idyllic scene. *Right in the center of a beautiful courtyard.*

One I recognized.

Because I'd been there with my mother. While lost in Vivaxia's mirage.

Is that what this is now? Another visual trick?

But no. No, this didn't feel like an illusion at all. Not like the ones I'd seen and previously experienced.

"Do you think Melek will be cast out?" Vivaxia went on. "*Indefinitely?* I mean, we are beings of peace, are we not? Our deals are founded on loyalty. To break a vow risks our very foundation."

Typhos scoffed at her words, despite his inner turmoil mounting. "Our games are for us to enjoy, Vivaxia. Leave Melek out of them."

Her long lashes fluttered as she gave him a coy look, one that contradicted the malice brewing in her gaze. "You invited him to play when you sent him for this." She held up a journal, one I recognized as Vita's past.

And everything suddenly clicked.

This isn't an illusion. This isn't Vivaxia's doing, either.

This is Vita.

She's showing me her history.

Showing me how this all began.

Because this is the moment that changed everything.

Typhos eyed the journal, confused as to how she had it in her hand. He'd taken it from her nightstand earlier in the day.

Or had he?

Vivaxia was a fan of her illusions.

What journal did I actually take home? he wondered, the words echoing through our strange little bond, like he was here now, thinking those very words.

"You're going to change everything, my sweet Typhos," Vivaxia murmured, her voice affectionate and warm. She palmed his cheek again, her eyes crinkling. "One day, you'll remember this moment, darling. Realize how I've been ten steps ahead the whole time. And instantly understand *why*."

He attempted to step away, but Vivaxia's hand moved to the back of his neck to hold him near.

Then he jolted as the journal touched his palm, his fingers automatically closing around it.

"Use it as a vessel for your mind," she whispered to him. "You'll need the outlet with all that power growing inside you. Share your memories. Your burdens. Relinquish your fears. And grow."

The words were clear and understandable, but a hint of magic wove through each of them, the hum of a spell forming beneath the commands.

I could taste it.

See it.

The strands were all Vivaxia's, her smoky tendrils clear to my eyes but seemingly invisible to Typhos's.

Those ribbons wove around him, forming his decisions, taking charge of him in a way Vivaxia had done to so many others. *A version of her infamous pet spell*, I thought, watching in horror as the magic seeped into Typhos's being, melding with his spirit.

Fury grew inside him.

Part of him understood what was happening, knew that Vivaxia had just betrayed him in the worst of ways. She was forcing her magic into him, awakening his siphoning power, and making him absorb part of her essence.

So she would always be with him.

Framing his mind.

Masking his memories.

Stroking his hatred.

Everything he'd become, everything he'd done, was rooted in this experience. His distrust of women went far deeper than this mere moment of betrayal. It was a seed Vivaxia had planted in his soul.

She hadn't wanted competition.

Melek was fine. She'd even given him Azazel, too.

But not a female mate.

Never a *queen*.

Only, she'd sent me to him. I was a woman. A female. *A potential mate.*

However, she'd groomed me in her own light. Had carved me into a weapon, one she'd fully intended to use. *To unlock Vita. To grant her access when the time was right.*

I saw it all, her plans, her intentions, the wicked web she'd woven.

Because the Source knew. It had felt her intrusion. Sensed her intentions. Knew she'd crafted the perfect plan to take down its master. *Typhos Lucifer.*

Which meant Typhos knew, too. On some hidden level, he'd been aware of her endgame. And he'd crafted his own retaliatory moves.

I understood everything now, this game of chess, the strategy at play. The *power.*

Yet, in a blink, I was back in the Strigoi Palace, balancing on my knees and gasping for breath.

A breath that Vivaxia had allowed me to take.

No, I realized. *No, she hadn't allowed any of this.*

The stone in my hand was cold. Dead. Drained of power.

Because it's inside me now. I could feel it warming my veins, the energy familiar, yet not.

And Vivaxia… wasn't even looking my way.

How much time has passed? I wondered. Because it felt like several lifetimes in my head, but I suspected it'd only been mere seconds.

Time was elusive when delving through a memory of the past.

Vivaxia's power swam all around me, holding me on my knees like some sort of doll she'd placed for her amusement. Energy compressed my chest, her mental grip still wrapped around my heart.

I could see those infamous strands again, the signature smokelike tendrils circling my being.

All the Strigoi nearby wore similar bands, the magic clear to my eyes now. And not just because of my siphoning ability.

I simply *saw* her. The vitality she wielded. Her creationist gifts. It was everywhere. Suffocating the room. Drowning out the free will of the Nightmare Fae.

And it stretched for miles.

Kingdoms.

Throughout the entire realm.

I knew that from the Source, could *feel* it with my own being.

My gaze narrowed.

This female was heartless. She possessed no compassion for the beings she and her kind had created. Considered everyone her servant. Took lives for her own personal amusement. And all because she wanted to become some insane Goddess with a creationism complex.

She had destroyed the Virtuous Fae Source. Not Typhos. Not Melek. But *her*. With her derisive games meant to tempt her fellow fae to *sin*.

And I once thought Typhos Lucifer was the devil.

He was the true angel of this story.

The hero.

The one who bore the world on his back and saved the innocent.

This female—this *bitch*—was the one who deserved to *fall*. For good.

I pushed to my feet, causing her to glance at me in surprise, one wicked eyebrow rising. "Well, that's interesting." She tilted her head. "Trying to use the gifts I've given you against me?"

The stone pulsed back to life in my palm, surprising me, as it'd been dead moments ago.

But it felt very much alive right now.

And it was trying to tell me something.

Energy hummed inside me. Energy I recognized. Energy that came from my *mates*.

Not the rock.

However, the stone shot a similar jolt up my arm to meet the power warming my being.

Vivaxia said something about giving it my best shot, but I ignored her and instead focused on the competing energies inside me.

My mates were empowering me. I could feel them deep inside. That pulse to my heart before had been them. And something about it had triggered Typhos's memory.

Or... or maybe that had been the death stone.

It's a siphon. Typhos is a siphon. I'm a siphon.

It was all related.

My mates were sending power into Typhos, and it was coming directly to me. *Via the Source.*

Such a convoluted mess of power, but it allowed me to see and feel so much. It granted me the keys to my kingdom. My realm. *As the Hell Fae Queen.*

Vivaxia sat on the throne, looking regal as fuck, likely feeling as though she'd already won. Because all these beings were under her spell, their souls tied to hers as she forced them to do her bidding.

But what happens when the strings are cut? I wondered, stroking her power. *What happens when a siphon swallows the spell whole?*

I canted my head, just like she'd done countless times in Typhos's memories, and even in my own. "You made a mistake, Vivaxia," I told her. "And that mistake is going to unravel thousands of years of planning."

My words were intentional, my power already seeking out every strand she'd woven through this realm. Every hint of magic that didn't belong. Every speck of vitality that belonged to *her*.

"Oh?" she asked, leaning forward. "Do share."

"I'm not yours," I said simply.

Then I yanked on her ribbons, my siphoning ability fully engaged.

Her enchantment began to fray at the edges.

And in a blink, her sinister web started to *unravel*.

CHAPTER 42

TYPHOS

My eyes flew open as power rippled all around me. Through me. *Inside me.*

"Camillia," I breathed, sitting up and nearly knocking heads with Melek. He was quick, though, jumping back with Azazel and Ajax, the three of them kneeling around me. "What the fuck is going on?" The question came out as a rasp, one that had my brows drawing downward.

Then a pang went through my head as a screech rent the air.

A furious. Feminine. *Screech.*

"*Fuck*," I muttered, grabbing my head. It sounded like a Banshee. Except it wasn't. It was *Vivaxia.*

I could sense her everywhere. In my head. My soul. My heart. *My realm.*

But it wasn't just her I felt—it was Camillia, too.

Her presence was just as potent as Vivaxia's, her essence touching every part of my being as she unwound invisible strands from my core.

I stole a deep breath, my heart suddenly beating with

renewed purpose as my Source heaved a sigh of palpable relief.

I had no idea what Camillia De la Croix was doing, or how she was doing it, but it felt right. It felt *good*.

And the shock wave of fury that followed from Vivaxia told me she did not approve.

"Where is she?" I asked, looking around the dark cavern, my brow furrowing once again. "Why the fuck am I down here?"

"You fell," Melek said, sounding irritated. "*Again*."

"It was from some sort of fail-safe," Azazel added. "You—"

"I was blocking Vivaxia from sinking her claws deeper into my mind," I interjected, remembering now.

And it wasn't just that incident I remembered.

It was *everything*. My full history with Vivaxia and so much more.

"That bitch has been playing with my memories for far too long," I growled. The ire underlining my words was directed more at myself than at Vivaxia.

Because I should have known what she was doing to me. I should have *felt* her. Though, I supposed that on some level, I had. Which was why my Source had reacted to the intrusion.

Not just today, but on every other occasion where she'd attempted to tamper with my realm.

It'd all been a way to instill distrust in my fae while also keeping me on guard. She'd wanted me to be emotional and reactive.

And I had been to an extent.

But not to the lengths she truly desired.

Which was why she'd escalated her endgame. Why she'd manipulated my Strigoi King and engaged in her final move.

Only, she hadn't anticipated her pawn becoming a queen. And a few weeks ago, I wouldn't have expected it either.

However, the men around me had forced me to see Camillia's worth. Her true potential. Her *power*.

Which had my lips curling now despite the furious energy warming my veins. Because, unlike Vivaxia, I'd known Camillia could be a queen. And not just any queen, but *my* queen.

Another wave of hot energy washed over me, dismantling Vivaxia's aura before it could even touch me again.

She's still trying to sink her hooks into me, I realized, sensing the clawlike sensation of Vivaxia's gift lingering in the air.

I'd forgotten how potent her ability could be, how *suffocating.* She'd stolen those memories from me, altered their foundations, and coaxed me into being her little puppet. Grooming my power. Guiding my instincts. *Ensuring my failures.*

I sensed it all now. Her purpose. Her goals. Her desire to *ascend.*

Fuck, she was a crazy immortal bitch.

And Camillia is battling her alone.

I pushed up off the floor, urgency flooding my veins. There wasn't time to explain everything out loud, so I shoved the knowledge via my bond links to Azazel and Melek... *and Ajax.*

Blinking, I turned slowly to look at the Midnight Fae, one eyebrow arched.

He held up his hands, his mind telling me he was wary of how I was about to react. "They told me to bite you."

My eyebrow arched higher.

"It was the best way to force my power into you."

"By forcing a bond on me?" I asked, clarifying his

statement. Because he'd bitten several times, ensuring we were fully mated.

Ajax bristled. "It's not like I wanted to do it."

My eyes narrowed, my mind instantly interpreting his desires from his thoughts. "That's a lie, Warden."

His jaw clenched. "We'll discuss it later."

"We will," I agreed.

With that, I granted him full access to my thoughts, feelings, history, and everything else I could.

Because I didn't mind this mating at all. What I did mind was his lie about not wanting it.

However, as he'd said, *we'd discuss it later.*

The blue outline in his eyes seemed to pulse, nearly overwhelming his mostly black irises. I saw myself in that color change, my power obviously having claimed him as mine, too.

Good.

He needed the energy boost. We all did. "Let's go find Camillia."

I didn't wait for agreement, just flared my wings to take off, and froze when I felt the feathery sensation at my back.

"Ty," Melek gasped, his eyes widening at what I could already feel.

No more embers or burnt strands. Just a full set of black plumes with golden tips. *Camillia... healed my wings.*

I had no idea how that was possible. But I felt it in my very soul. She'd pulled me out of some sort of web, untangled me from Vivaxia's influence, and set my soul free.

Except, no. It was so much deeper than that.

It's my Source.

Camillia was... changing everything.

Rewriting my power. My realm. Crafting a new balance, one free from Vivaxia's creative control.

You'll never touch these fae again, I heard her thinking, her mental voice a kiss to my fucking spirit. *They're under our protection now.*

Our, I repeated, curious about that term.

And everything stopped. *Typhos,* Camillia breathed. *I...*

Don't stop, I urged her. *Don't you fucking dare stop, Camillia De la Croix. Keep cleansing the realm. Keep saving us all.*

I could swear I heard her heart skip a beat at my words, could feel the sweat perspiring down her spine. Could *taste* her confusion.

But perhaps most importantly of all, I could hear her resolution. Her determination. Her *power.*

It hit my senses with the force of a thousand suns, burning me alive inside and out. And I fucking bathed in that light. In *her.* In her power. Her presence. Her *everything.*

Gods, that feels fucking amazing, I told her. *Keep going.*

A shiver of pleasure traveled through our new bond—a bond that I didn't fully understand but absolutely supported.

The world blinked in and out of existence around me as I *ascended* to her side, her soul a beacon my spirit couldn't deny.

She stood where I had in the Strigoi throne room, her focus on a furious Vivaxia as power whipped around the room.

I reached out a hand, placing it on Camillia's shoulder as I helped anchor her. It was the most natural of movements, a response to a need she hadn't spoken aloud but conveyed with her soul.

Her eyes closed, her lips parting as more energy whirled around her. Through her. *Inside her.*

I have no idea what I'm doing, she whispered.

You're creating a Source, I told her. *One that appears to be mated to mine.*

"What?" she asked out loud, seemingly drawn out of her daze as she looked right at me. "How—"

Power jolted across the room, hitting Camillia right in the chest and shoving her backward.

Melek and Ajax appeared just in time to catch her before she went crashing into the wall. But flames erupted all over her as Vivaxia's toxic magic engulfed every inch of Camillia's body.

Azazel roared with fury as he arrived, his sword appearing in a flash as he attempted to drive it into Vivaxia. However, she caught the sharp end, twisted it from his grip, and seized him by the throat. The movements were so quick I barely caught them.

She'd always been powerful. But this was so much more than that. *How many Virtuous Fae souls reside inside her?* I wondered, recognizing the magic I saw spiraling through her aura now.

It seemed she was what was left of the Virtuous Fae Realm, her power nearly as robust as a Source.

Only, she wasn't able to control it. It simply orbited her in waves of chaos, ones she absorbed energy from, but it wasn't... it wasn't the same as what I did with my power outlets.

Unfortunately, though, it still empowered her.

As it did now when she began mouthing a spell, one Azazel knew well. One that had me growling in fury. One that had Camillia... *screaming*.

No. That was the *fire*. It was eating her alive.

Melek shouted something, as did Ajax, the two of them trying to douse the flames. But whatever magic Vivaxia had cast was too strong for them to battle. Or too unknown.

Azazel hissed in fury as the pet spell began to take hold. A spell that shouldn't be allowed to exist. Because it went against our original deal, the one that had set Azazel free.

Which could only mean one thing—Vivaxia had found a new spell to use on him. One that wasn't subject to the bounds of our original agreement.

Or maybe she just doesn't care about our terms anymore, I thought.

Then another blast shot out of Vivaxia toward Melek, the rope of fire catching around his neck as she yanked him away from Camillia.

It all happened so fast, *too fast.*

My heart splintered at the sight, my soul torn between an impossible choice. *Melek. Azazel. Camillia.*

And now Ajax.

Because the fire had spread from Camillia to him, the flames supernatural in nature and seeking to *destroy.*

I growled, the sound rumbling across the floor in an echo of torment. Pain. *Fury.*

Vivaxia had sought to force an emotional reaction from me, and she'd finally won. Because seeing my mates—*all four of them*—in agony had my heart cracking wide open. And with it, my Source.

"You want my light?" I asked Vivaxia, my voice deeper than ever before and riddled with unspoken *power.* "*You can have it.*"

Energy flowed from my fingertips as I raised my hands in her direction, my Source empowering my rage as *light* shot from deep within.

All my being.

All my vitality.

My entire fucking soul.

Because I was more than willing to die for my mates.

Camillia would survive. She'd hold them together. She'd be their queen.

And together, they'd serve as her kings.

The ultimate sacrifice.

A true fucking fall.

All in the name of love.

Not just for my circle, but for my Nightmare Fae. My Hell Fae. *My realm.*

I die for you, I told them, my eyes closing. *All I ask is that you survive… of your own free will.*

Because the gates would forever be open now.

No more rules. No more discrimination. No more false undertones of protection.

My Nightmare Fae and Hell Fae deserved to *live.* To prosper. *To reign.*

I closed my eyes as my Source flowed through me and out of me, and into Vivaxia. Overpowering her. Teaching her what true *light* looked like.

It was a gift she'd never be able to handle.

Because leading required sacrifice. Compassion. *A heart.*

And Vivaxia had none of those things.

She'd forever be alone. Ascending into her own personal hell. *A place where she can no longer create.*

Enjoy, I thought, my knees giving out. *You've earned this fate just as I've earned mine.*

Melek shouted my name. Azazel, too.

They knew what I was doing and how this would end.

But it was too late to stop it now.

You were right, little prince, I whispered to him as my palms hit the floor. *Camillia's the key. Our Hell Fae Queen. Love her for me, please. Love her fiercely. Cherish her. Protect her. And know… know that I'll always be there, little prince. I'll be smiling from the stars. Brightening the Source. Existing forever inside you all…*

CHAPTER 43

CAMI

Typhos!

His power exploded around me, causing the fires to burn hotter, faster, more *intensely*. But they weren't burning my skin. They… they were pulsing around me and Ajax.

Beneath a slender barrier of fire… Which was counterintuitive to battling a flame, yet it served as a shield that kept us warm and protected.

Did you create this? I asked Ajax, our minds suddenly linked again.

Though, I realized now that it hadn't been Vivaxia's magic blocking our mate-bonds, but Typhos's Source. It'd gone into protection mode, ensuring we were not connected mentally to protect us all from Vivaxia. She'd breached the confines of Typhos's mind, making us vulnerable. The Source had known that, and it'd reacted appropriately.

No, Ajax said, answering my question about the fiery shield. *It's coming from you.*

I frowned. *It's not...* I trailed off as I tracked the origin of the energy to the stone in my hand. *The death stone...*

It was fighting fire with fire. *Just like what I'd done on those camping trips...*

I swallowed, my mind torn between the present and the past, but as another sizzling wave washed over me, I was solidly grounded in this moment once more.

Typhos is detonating.

Melek's sharp cry of pain hit me right in the heart. Because I felt it, too. The sense of loss. The understanding that Typhos was sacrificing everything to save us.

His Source.

His life.

His realm.

He was shoving it all into Vivaxia with the force of a million shooting stars, all aimed at giving her exactly what she craved—*his light.*

I understood his logic, saw how he thought it would overwhelm her and send her into an existence she could no longer manage.

Because she was already showing signs of having siphoned too much.

The Virtuous Fae souls, I thought. *She absorbed too many of them, creating a beacon of power around her that swirled and provided energy without actually granting her true control.*

Managing a Source required a heart. It required knowing how to *love.*

But Vivaxia only cherished herself.

She could never truly lead.

Except, Typhos can't sacrifice himself either, I decided, needing to do something. To stop him. To *help* him.

He'd said I was creating a Source—a Source that had *mated* his. It'd startled me and I'd lost focus. A ridiculous reaction, because in the next breath, I'd known it was true.

I'd been siphoning all those spells, stripping Vivaxia's control away from the Hell Fae Realm, and channeling the power into a new form. A beacon of compassion. A renewed sense of power that would grant the Hell Fae and Nightmare Fae the ability to fight Vivaxia.

I'd wanted them to have *free will*. And in doing so, my sphere of energy had mated with Typhos's Source.

It'd been so natural, so right, that I hadn't even realized what I'd been doing until he'd mentioned it.

Now, I need to do it again, I thought, my mind focusing on the fire engulfing me and Ajax first. It fizzled and cracked, the dark strands of magic trying to avoid my mental touch. I felt it wiggling, writhing, and trying futilely to escape my siphoning ability.

My jaw tightened. *I will not be defeated by fire.* I'd been in enough infernos to know how to fix this.

Rather than pull the energy into me, I used the death stone to amplify that thin layer of flames and blasted it outward.

Right into Vivaxia.

She drew it inside her, just like she was doing with Typhos's power.

Free from her fiery prison, I focused on Melek's flaming leash and sent that back to its creator as well—to Vivaxia.

Azazel was next. Only, he wasn't engulfed in flames but trapped in a spell that had forced him into his Phoenix form. His dark eyes captured mine, and what I saw burning inside him was unadulterated ire. He was furious. And he was fighting from within. But whatever Vivaxia had done had imprisoned him.

Not for long, I thought, narrowing my gaze and unwinding the invisible ropes around him. Vivaxia accepted them back into her growing ball of energy with ease. It was as though she didn't even realize what she was taking into her soul; all she desired was *power*. And she didn't care where it came from.

She wasn't paying any attention to me at all.

Because I was merely her pawn.

Meanwhile, Typhos thought of me as a queen. *His* queen. And I was about to serve by his side.

I'd start by taking back that throne, the one she still touched like her survival depended on its existence.

With a thought, I crushed the metal and stone, destroying the conduit she'd taken control of, and smiled as she stumbled, her eyes blinking as though coming out of a daze.

I didn't give her a chance to recover, instead hitting her with a dose of my own light. If she wanted to ascend so badly, she could soak it all up and explode like a fucking star.

The death stone pulsated in my hand like it agreed, the rock amplifying my gift with a force that took my breath away.

It wanted me to use it to expel power, not siphon it.

Yet it was a siphon. Just like me.

Fight fire with fire. Make it burn hotter.

Fight a siphon… with a siphon.

Even though it didn't make sense at all, I understood the purpose.

Hell Fae Rule #13: Nothing Is What It Seems.

Is it possible that my parents had groomed me for this moment? I whispered to myself, thinking back on all our experiences. All the impractical solutions to catastrophic events.

I'd thought they'd meant to prepare me for the trials.

But now… now I wondered if it'd been for this. *To battle Vivaxia. To save Typhos. To protect the Hell Fae Realm.*

Did they know? Were they fighting Vivaxia all along?

My mother had seemed distraught in that mirror, her

eyes wild with panic. Had Vivaxia been controlling her before? Controlling my father, too?

I swallowed, my head spinning with questions and no answers.

And there wasn't time to contemplate more.

I had to help Typhos.

He was all but depleted on the floor, his light almost entirely extinguished.

Yet he still continued to pummel Vivaxia with power.

I ran to him, my free hand finding his beautiful wings as they folded over him like a black-and-gold blanket, and shoved some of my vitality into him.

You're mine, I told him. *I won't let you die. Not now. Not after…* I couldn't finish the thought. Rather, it trailed off as he took my energy and gifted it to Vivaxia.

I growled at him and fisted my hand in his wings to hit him with a heavier dose.

Don't fight me, Typhos, I thought at him. *Work with me instead.*

A fierce surge of possession followed my words, but it didn't originate from me. It came from him, from his *soul.*

I felt it inside me, all around me, in the core of my existence. It was as though his essence had reached out and seized my very being, claiming me on a level that shouldn't exist.

And yet it did.

Because my spirit bowed to his, accepting the ownership without question.

Power exploded between us, our spirits winding together in a binding way that secured our future. Our present. *Our past.*

Melek was suddenly there, too, his arms wrapping around me from behind as Az—now in his human form again—fell to Typhos's other side. Their energy mingled with ours, creating a surplus of strength and vitality that whirled inside Typhos to replenish his reserves.

Ajax was last, his Midnight Fae essence a kiss to my senses that helped ground me in the moment. It gave me focus.

And focus I did.

On blasting Vivaxia into her own fucking universe.

I clutched Typhos with one hand and the stone with the other and allowed them both to amplify my siphoning talent. I absorbed the rest of Vivaxia's presence in the Hell Fae Realm, absorbed all the negative energy I could find anywhere nearby, and absorbed the gifts provided by my mates.

By Ajax.

By Az.

By Melek.

By Typhos.

They were all mine and I was theirs. Just as this realm was mine and I was its queen. I wanted to protect the fae here. Honor them. *Free them.*

I'd felt the gates deteriorate as Typhos had begun to overload Vivaxia with power. He'd opened his realm for the first time since he'd created it. Because the bride trials didn't count. Those females had been selected by his Source and provided special permission to enter.

However, now his realm would be available to everyone.

His Source would protect those who chose to remain, but he would no longer decline entry to others. Specifically, female fae.

Because something he realized was that he'd failed all the female Nightmare Fae that existed. He'd blocked most of them from entering his realm because of whatever seeds Vivaxia had planted.

Now he would rectify that.

If they even still exist, I heard him thinking, his mind a whisper against mine.

If they do, we'll help them together, I promised him as the stone burned hot in my hand. I nearly dropped it but held on when an echo of power zipped up my arm.

It felt oddly familiar.

My mind searched for the cause of that familiarity, but Typhos took a strangled breath, his mind seeming to blink in and out of existence.

Because he was still feeding his light to Vivaxia and keeping nothing for himself.

It reminded me of my experience in the paradigm when I'd been hell-bent on pushing all my power away from Vivaxia and into his Source. Only, he was doing the opposite now and trying to overwhelm her with his essence.

At the expense of himself.

I filled him with more power, as did Az, Melek, and Ajax. But he didn't accept any of it. All that energy simply spiraled around him and... *and flowed back into me.*

My eyes narrowed. *Stubborn fucking king.*

I tried again.

And again.

And again.

Each time, he returned it to me while giving up the last of his light to Vivaxia.

His corporeal form was dying, his energy moving on to a new phase of life.

I shook my head, furious with him for doing this. Furious with myself for not knowing how to stop him. Furious with Vivaxia for being the cause of *everything*.

The bitch was standing by the destroyed altar, looking wind struck with her tattered wings bent backward at odd angles and her hair whipping around in some sort of invisible breeze.

She was ascending, just like she wanted. I could see it. *Feel it.* And while I knew that was the point, I... I couldn't...

There has to be another way.

But I don't know how... or what... or...

An explosion derailed my broken thoughts, causing me to jolt as power flowed through me and into Typhos.

What was that? I wondered, looking around.

The Strigoi, Az replied, sounding awed. *They're adding their energy to ours.*

My eyes flew open, my mind whirring. "But they can't," I said aloud, taking in the sight of the weakened Strigoi around us. "You have to stop," I told them. "This... this will hurt you. It might kill you!"

They'd been abused and battered for too long. I could feel the frailty of their kingdom, see the withered energy reserves of inner souls.

It's their choice, little angel, Melek said into my mind, his internal voice strained. *They're supporting their king and queen.*

Not like this, I thought, ready to force them to stop.

But another geyser of strength soon followed, the owner of it outside.

Ghouls, my soul whispered. Or maybe it was the Source. Because I could see their energy strands now, my heart recognizing their origin.

Just like I saw the Strigoi now, too.

It all came to me in an array of light and color, the magic beautiful and unique as it wrapped around us and flowed into its fallen king.

I was momentarily struck by the sight, unable to respond, and only more taken aback when additional currents of energy flowed up from outside as portals began to open.

My connection with Typhos and the Hell Fae Realm helped me identify them, my mind sensing their auras and recognizing them instantly.

Because I was married to this world now. Mated to the Hell Fae King. Bonded to his Source through one of my own.

It was utterly unexpected. But all I could do was embrace it and *use* it.

My mind connected to everyone here, their essences flowing into me like I held some sort of beacon. And maybe I did. Maybe it was the stone. Maybe it was just me. But I let their power build mine into a maelstrom of energy that I released back into the realm, into the Source I'd been creating.

It just kept building and building, creating a new light. A new purpose. *A new star.*

But that star desired *more*.

My soul required all of my mates.

Typhos, too.

Because a queen needs her king...

With a snarl of fury, I sank my fingers into his plumes again with one hand and pressed my opposite over his chest with the death stone near his heart.

I closed my eyes and commanded my mate to return to me.

To be here.

To wake the hell up.

And be my fucking king.

CHAPTER 44

MELEK

Cami was fucking magnificent.

The way she took charge and mastered the powers around her, intertwining them through the air and into a breathtaking star of power was... *perfection*.

I held her in my arms, feeling her energy mingling with everyone else's auras, weaving a masterpiece for the Hell Fae Realm.

All while Ty continued to sacrifice his light.

But I felt Cami's intentions, understood what she planned to do.

You're not going anywhere, my king, I thought at him. *Because our queen needs you. We need you. And Cami isn't going to let you die.*

I could sense it in her resolve. The Hell Fae King had met his match in Camillia De la Croix. She wouldn't let him sacrifice himself and become a martyr. She was going to reinstate him as our king and make him her mate.

It was the most amazing sensation in the world to observe and experience. I wasn't sure how Cami had done it, how *they* had mated, but I felt it in my heart. They were joined, not just by the Source or their royal statuses in the Hell Fae Realm, but by their *souls*.

It was a bond unlike any I'd ever witnessed. Not Virtuous Fae. Nor was it Hell Fae. It was simply them.

Ty and Cami.

Our king and our queen.

I kissed the back of Cami's neck as my wings formed to curl around us in a protective cocoon. Ajax nestled in as well, one hand on her hip as his other rested on Ty's thigh.

Power hummed between us all. Az, too, from his position across from me. His hands were on Ty, but his violet eyes were on Cami.

She was the center of our universe. Our world. *Our Goddess.*

And she was reviving our king.

Ty pushed back, his energy dwindling. But Cami leaned down and pressed her mouth to his to literally breathe life back into him.

He fought her, his light blinking in and out of existence.

I swallowed, my heart slowing with his. *Come on, Ty. You're a sadist, not a masochist.*

He didn't react other than to take one final breath, the sound far too quiet. Far too ominous.

Ty, I snarled at him. *I will never forgive you if you do this. And you can forget me loving Cami for you. That's your responsibility. She's* your *queen. So wake the fuck up and take her the way a king should.*

"*No,*" Cami said, making me blink. "You're not doing this. I refuse." She fell over Ty, her breasts pressing against his back as the two collapsed on the ground with me right behind them. Feathers and skin and *fire* blended in a mystical mix of redefined power.

Ajax and Az were there, too.

All five of us were locked in some sort of starlike swarm of energy that was growing violently around us.

Cami was at the center of it, her essence spinning in waves of fiery *light*.

The Source, I thought, amazed.

She'd... she'd tugged it out of existence, into this very room—assuming we were even still *in* a room. Actually, we might have left it. I couldn't see anything beyond the blinding white star that was Camillia De la Croix.

Whirling.

Burning.

Forming a cyclone of intensity.

One she shoved into Ty with a force that had his back bowing in response.

With a sharp inhale, he spun their positions around on the floor and grabbed Cami by the nape, his eyes open yet narrowed. "You do not command me, my queen," he told her as he settled between her parted legs.

"Yes, my king, I do," she replied as she shoved more energy inside him with her palm.

No.

Not with her palm.

With the death stone.

I blinked at it, confused by how she was using it in this manner. That stone contained souls. It was a literal prison, one that *siphoned* spirits from a corporeal host and captured them inside the rock.

She'd used that stone before to amplify her power. However, this... this was on a whole different level.

Ty growled, but she kept hitting him with power.

He shoved it back.

So Cami did it again.

The two of them engaged in a duel underlined in

vitality, their souls manifesting a star so bright it blinded my eyes.

A new Source, I realized.

Or rather, a *renewed* one.

More robust. More powerful. More *balanced*.

Because it came from all of us.

Az. Ajax. Ty. Cami. *All of the Hell Fae Realm.*

It was being fed by everyone's sacrifice, everyone's willingness to work together, everyone's cohesive love for their world and what it represented.

Holy fae, I thought, admiring the stunning display of togetherness. Of respect. Of a realm joined by mutual goals and affections.

This was the world Ty had created. A world where everyone was accepted. A world where everyone *cared*.

And now they were showing him what that meant to them.

They'd never doubted him as their king. They'd worried, yes. But their worry had been founded on love for the fae that had protected them all their lives.

It was the most unselfish and divine coming together of a faedom that I'd ever seen.

It's what the Virtuous Fae used to be, I realized, feeling the warmth from that world shining down upon us now. *A realm of love, peace, and equality. Our very own utopia.*

Unfortunately, the screech that sounded in the distance told me Vivaxia didn't appreciate this development.

She'd wanted all of Ty's light.

Yet Cami had prevented him from giving her the last sliver, and it seemed the Source was returning to Ty with a vengeance.

Not just Ty, I thought. *Us…*

It was reviving every part of the realm that Vivaxia had touched.

Replenishing the Nightmare Fae with their inner lights.

Strengthening Ty.

And emboldening Cami.

All while they fought on the floor, their competing natures creating more light. More energy. More *life*.

They were both so fucking stubborn. Ty with his resolve to sacrifice himself. Cami with her determination not to let him.

A balance of purpose.

The grounding of a union.

Our Hell Fae Queen and Hell Fae King.

Ty growled. Cami growled back.

And then they were kissing, their mouths seeking dominance over one another.

Ty would win. But Cami wasn't going to make it easy on him, something she proved by palming his chest and driving even more power into him.

He responded by mastering her with his tongue and flattening her to the ground as flames shot up all around them.

Az sat back to admire the show, as did Ajax.

But I kept my eyes trained on the scene, trying to decipher exactly *where* we'd ended up.

Not in the cavern. Yet we were also no longer in the Strigoi throne room.

And that ground I thought Ty had pinned Cami to… wasn't the ground. It was a wall of power.

My eyes widened. *We're in the sky.*

My wings instantly splayed out at my back as I locked a hand on Ajax's arm, preparing to fly for us both if needed. However, the Source simply rolled around us, guarding us in its light, and gradually returning us to the hard surface below.

Where Ty continued to devour Cami on the actual ground.

Either they couldn't hear Vivaxia shrieking from somewhere nearby, or they didn't care.

I lifted my hand to shield my eyes as the Source brightened even more, only to disappear in a flash.

Except it hadn't actually vanished. It'd... returned to the realm's core.

Spreading love throughout the kingdoms, creating safety, and empowering its beings once more.

It was invigorating and perfect and utterly *virtuous*.

Just like Cami.

Although, the way she was kissing Ty right now wasn't all that innocent. She bit down to draw blood, causing him to growl against her mouth. "I'll never submit," he said against her lips.

"I know," she breathed. "You're a king."

"I'm *your* king." He kissed a path to her ear. "Which means I'll bow occasionally. For you."

I arched a brow. *Oh? You've never bowed for me, my king.*

We both know that's not true, little prince, he replied without missing a beat.

Then he started kissing Cami again, like he couldn't help himself. *Perhaps now you see why we all fell for her,* I drawled.

Magic fucking pussy, he returned. But I heard the humor in his voice, as well as the underlying groan. Because he wanted to be inside her. To fuck her. To *claim* her.

And she desired the same.

However, her mind was also processing their surroundings and paying attention to the electric currents in the air.

Fascination stole over me, only to turn to horror in a

blink as I sensed Vivaxia's darkness coming right for Cami and Ty.

Their names left my mouth as a shout, but the two of them were already moving. Ty's wings flared around him and Cami, his hands on her hips as they faced the incoming swarm of angry energy.

It didn't even look like Vivaxia, just a mess of hornet-like spheres buzzing in a fiery hive.

But it was her.

Her essence.

Her *soul*.

She wasn't welcome here. The gates may no longer exist, but this realm protected its own. And the Hell Fae Source was the ultimate beacon of power.

A beacon of power that Cami and Ty owned.

A beacon of power that Az, Ajax, and I guarded.

And that beacon of power didn't approve of Vivaxia's presence.

However, we couldn't let the Source push her out. It might take thousands of years for her to recover, but she would be back. She was obsessed with Ty's light, and Cami would be just as much of a target.

Which meant we had to find a way to imprison her. To *destroy* her corporeal shell and encapsulate her soul.

Ty, I started.

But a hush from his mind told me not to interfere. He was helping Cami focus.

I listened as she realized what she needed to do, the stone in her hand guiding her. Ty's thoughts helped her understand what the rock was trying to say, too. I couldn't hear him, but I could imagine what he was saying.

It's a death stone because it imprisons souls and prevents them from moving on.

Which suggested she might be able to trap Vivaxia

inside it, a realization that Cami was now making as the hissing hive neared us all.

She straightened her shoulders, her gaze on the ghastly sight while she clutched the rock in her hand. "Fight a fiery portal with heat," she said. "Douse Hellfire with warmth. Take down a dark soul with *death*." She held up the stone while she spoke, her words not making sense to me until I saw the lines she'd drawn in her mind, her history linking to the present.

All those camping trips with her parents had served a purpose.

Hell Fae Rule #13: Nothing Is What It Seems.

The rule rolled through her mind, along with a dozen others. Including one that caught my attention now, one that didn't quite fit with the rest.

Hell Fae Rule #6: Only Look Out for Yourself—No One Else.

That'd been about survival. But Cami realized now that worrying about others was what made the Source thrive. Typhos had created a new light that supported everyone and everything under his control. She'd emboldened that power with her own strength.

And through the guidance of her parents. Of who they'd helped her become.

Culminating in the death stone she now held in her hand.

Hell Fae Rule #7: When You Can't Win a Fight, Run into the Shadows.

Vivaxia couldn't be defeated in the traditional sense.

But her darkness could be contained in *shadows*.

Cami lifted her hand as power swirled around her, the ribbons invisible to me, yet I could hear her processing them in her mind. She was unraveling Vivaxia's essence and siphoning it into the stone... while simultaneously freeing all the souls inside.

Souls that had been trapped for fae only knew how long.

Energy and vitality swirled in response as the lost spirits joined a new form—the Hell Fae Source.

It was so natural. So *invigorating*. I could sense their presence around us, their existence possessing new meaning. These were beings who had died and hadn't been allowed to move on. But they could reside in our realm, in our beacon of power, and *thrive*.

Cami shivered, their cool essences slithering all around her. Or one in particular. One she recognized.

Dad, she thought, a tear pricking her eye.

But the furious hive vibrated too close by for her to focus on the spirit for long. Though, I swore it wrapped around her in a hug as it guided her hand higher toward Vivaxia's form.

A whisper of a kiss graced Cami's being, eliciting another tremble, then the presence disappeared and left her to finish this.

Her jaw set, her gaze narrowing as she took in the seething mass vibrating in the wind.

It wasn't just Vivaxia, but the power she'd created, the souls of hundreds or maybe thousands of Virtuous Fae. Cami could see them all, hear their screams, and feel their pain.

Ty sensed it all, too, his ire mounting by the second.

The Source tried to shove the furious energy out, to remove Vivaxia from our realm, but Cami connected to Vivaxia via an invisible strand—her own essence reaching out to *siphon* the furious swarm of energy.

Only, she didn't pull that energy into herself.

She *unraveled* it.

Freeing the souls that didn't belong to Vivaxia while ensuring the darkest thread remained. The swarm shifted and writhed, the mass lessening by the second, until only smoke persisted.

"You'll never be *free* again, Vivaxia," Cami said in a voice underscored with determination. It was the voice of a queen. *Our queen.* "No choices. No independence. Just a life inside a rock where you won't be able to move, breathe, or *speak*. Because that's what the death stone desires and you are its new *pet*."

A scream wavered from the mist, or what I assumed was meant to be a scream. But it came out as a raspy whimper instead.

A whimper that slowly disappeared as the stone absorbed every wisp of Vivaxia's form.

Cami didn't move for a long moment, her focus on the place the Virtuous Fae had just been. Her brow furrowed, her lips quivering a little. "I... I guess those camping trips were more important than I ever realized. And yet, I *hated* my parents for... for *everything*."

Ty slowly turned her in his arms, his palm reaching for her cheek. "They were under Vivaxia's control, Camillia. There's no way you could have known."

His words were kind for her, but his thoughts weren't so kind for himself. Because deep down, he felt he should have sensed it. At least in Pierre De la Croix.

Vivaxia was in your head, my king, I reminded him softly.

I should have sensed her, too, he muttered.

Maybe, I agreed. *But it's over now.*

It's over now, he echoed.

"Your parents are free now," he added out loud to Cami. "All the souls Vivaxia had imprisoned and controlled are free. Because of you."

"You mean they're dead," she replied, swallowing.

I frowned. *Not all of them*, I nearly said.

But then she continued, her words clarifying what she

meant. "I *feel* them, Typhos. I feel my dad... and my mom. They're... *everywhere*. Their essences. Their history. Their *thoughts*."

Our king remained quiet for a moment, his mind whirring with knowledge and intuition as he deciphered what she was feeling. What she was *hearing*.

I couldn't pick up on the same essences, my ties to the Source very different from hers and Ty's. But I absorbed the information from Ty, the details making my heart ache for our little angel.

Vivaxia had siphoned the souls of so many Virtuous Fae, Cami's mother included. But not her father's. He'd been trapped in the death stone—on purpose.

Her mother had put him there to hide him from Vivaxia. And then Mystika had given the stone to Zen. Or rather, left it somewhere for her to find.

That history—that *memory*—resided in the Hell Fae Realm now.

Because her parents were here now. *In spirit.*

I shivered, realizing what that meant. They'd sacrificed their lives for Cami. Though, it could be argued that their lives had already been forfeited due to Vivaxia's manipulations.

Still, they'd fought for Cami.

And in the end, they'd saved their daughter by giving her the tools she'd needed to destroy one of the most powerful entities in existence.

"Mystika and Pierre are part of our Source, Camillia. Just like my parents," Ty whispered, summarizing aloud everything I'd just learned. "And I guarantee they're not only at peace but also proud of the queen you've become."

He leaned down to kiss her again, softer this time.

Grief radiated from our queen, her mind processing everything she'd learned, everything she'd now become, and the relationships she would never have with two people who should have mattered so much more.

Except, they had. They'd mattered so incredibly much. Because they'd ensured their daughter knew how to survive. And in doing so, they'd saved us all.

Ty gradually pulled away from Cami, then released her to Az and Ajax, who quickly embraced her.

I would have gone to her as well, but Ty turned to me, his blue eyes holding a note of amusement in their depths.

I arched a brow, focusing on him while keeping my mind very in tune with Cami and her thoughts. The moment Az and Ajax stopped kissing her, I fully intended to take over.

Ty would sense that desire, too. And the look in his eyes said he wouldn't fault me for it at all. She was our heart now. Our future. *Our mate.*

"It looks like you've won, little prince," he murmured.

"Oh?" I asked, feigning innocence. "And what game were we playing, my king?"

His lips curled, his amusement deepening. "A dangerous one, Melek."

"Hmm. Would I engage in such an activity?"

"You would," he replied. "For the right prize."

Now it was my turn to smile. "I have many prizes in mind, my king."

"I know you do."

My eyebrow winged upward. "Are you saying it's time to collect?"

"Perhaps. I believe I also still owe you a boon," he murmured, his hand clasping my nape as he jerked me into his embrace. "So I suppose we'll be playing with ribbons?"

"Red ones," I confirmed. "When our prize is ready."

"When our prize is ready," he agreed, his lips brushing mine. "Perhaps on her coronation night."

My heart skipped a beat. "Oh, I do like the sound of that."

"I thought you might." He kissed me with a lot less force than I'd anticipated, his touch abnormally sweet. As was his mind when he mentally whispered, *Thank you, little prince. Thank you for loving me. Thank you for protecting me, even from myself. And thank you for seducing Camillia De la Croix.*

I chuckled a little at that last line. *Trust me, the pleasure was all mine.*

I have no doubt.

She's mine, too, you know.

I do. His tongue traced my lips, seeking entrance. *She's ours.*

Ours, I echoed. *Our mate.*

Our mate, he whispered back. *Now let's make sure the realm welcomes her properly. And afterward, we'll show her what it means to be our Hell Fae Queen.*

CHAPTER 45

TYPHOS

I stood back as Melek kissed Cami, his hands roaming over her beautiful form as though ensuring every inch of her still existed. Az and Ajax had done the same thing, but now they stood beside me, their gazes on the diseased Strigoi blood fields.

A sigh left me as I took in the damage. "I should have visited sooner."

"It wouldn't have changed the outcome," Az replied. "King Nos betrayed you and his people."

"And a lot of Strigoi died as a result," I muttered. I had to fix this. To help them. To rebuild the kingdom. But I didn't want to overstep again.

The throne had been my way of helping them survive without a Sigil. While it'd worked for a while, it'd clearly bred resentment, too.

With the gates no longer existing, they would be free to find mates and establish a proper hierarchy. However, they wouldn't be able to accomplish anything without a royal bloodline to keep their hive-like energy alive.

Which meant I had to give them something to hold them over.

Something to help them thrive and survive long enough for a Sigil to be found and crowned as the Strigoi Queen.

Cami's mind stroked mine, our thoughts aligning as power rippled out of us over the deteriorated fields. The black rot spread far and wide, the decaying plants wilting with death.

"They used to be sturdy and tall with blood fruits on the ends," I told her, describing what the area around us should look like.

"There are humans down below," Ajax said, his vampiric senses no doubt picking up on the live blood bank used to power the field. It stemmed from a combination of human lives in stasis and the power from a Sigil. When one failed, all failed.

"They're not in pain," I assured him. "Just... frozen."

"Because that's a better way to live," he muttered, clearly not pleased by this development.

"Humans are food," I replied, glancing at him. "As a Midnight Fae, you should understand that."

His black irises flickered, the blue rim around the edges seeming to pulse. "I prefer to bite."

My lips curled. "Yes, you do," I agreed. "*Mate.*"

Cami pulled away from Melek to face us both, her gaze assessing. I could feel her searching for how and when Ajax and I had mated. I didn't make her hunt for it, instead sharing that he'd bitten me to make me wake up.

Approval radiated from Cami, surprising me.

But on the heels of that approval came a wave of disapproval as she surveyed the fields. "Holding human life in stasis like this isn't okay."

I'd already pointed out that humans were food for

Strigoi, so I didn't repeat the explanation. Instead, I folded my arms and stared at my pretty little mate. "Without the blood fields, the Strigoi will die. And the blood fields require two things—a Sigil and the human essence energizing the crops. So what would you propose we do?"

It wasn't meant as a taunt, but as a legitimate question. I wanted to hear what my queen desired in this situation. Because I couldn't exactly disagree with her thoughts right now. The term *barbaric* kept floating through her head, and, well, she wasn't necessarily wrong.

"Is it really the only way they can survive?" she asked after a long, thoughtful moment.

I considered her question. "As far as I know, yes. But that doesn't mean we couldn't ask them to find an alternative."

It didn't even have to be a direct request, just an implied one with whatever solution we devised for the Strigoi Kingdom. Perhaps we'd put a time limit on our assistance, or reevaluate in a few decades once things had calmed down throughout the kingdoms.

Camillia's power brushed over me as she explored the fields with her mind, her ability to feel sources of energy and souls taking over as she learned more about the land. The people here. *The Nightmare Fae in need.*

They'd been lost in a state of necessary survival for far too long.

But with a queen at my side, perhaps now they could *thrive.*

Melek stepped back to give her room, his expression one of acute adoration. That look would have irritated me a few weeks ago.

Today, I understood it.

Hell, I probably exuded a similar appearance.

You don't, he murmured, clearly in tune with my thoughts. *You're as stoic as ever, my king.*

My lips curled. *Stoic?* I didn't want to be *stoic* around Camillia. I... I wanted to be adoring to a point. Supportive. Protective, too. But not *stoic.*

You've mastered that regal look, Ty. It's just who you are. But your mind tells us all how you feel. He met my gaze. *As do your eyes.*

I hummed, unsure if that was enough.

I wanted the realms to know how much I'd fallen for our new queen, to understand that she was the cause—*the key*—to our existence. She'd saved the realm from a horrible fate. Saved the Nightmare Fae from being leashed. Saved me from giving up my light.

The Source belonged to her now as much as it belonged to me.

Which made her their monarch, their *Goddess*, and they needed to know how their king felt about their queen.

Camillia's power warmed our bond again—the unique connection created by our souls—and I felt her testing her vitality on a nearby stalk. She siphoned a little from the Source to embolden the human roots and watched as the plant grew tall and proud. Red bulbs—*blood fruits*—blossomed in a blink, causing her to cant her head to the side.

"This is the realm of dreams," she murmured. "These humans can at least be given pleasant visions while they sleep. Perhaps even full lives. But this can only be temporary. The Strigoi need to find another way."

Her words carried on the wind, our Source informing the kingdom that their queen had spoken. And not only that, but she was issuing an edict of sorts.

It would be an easy one for the Strigoi to agree to since the humans beneath the stalks already dreamt. Though, they might also be experiencing nightmares. So perhaps the Strigoi could guarantee pleasant sleep for their mortal fuel.

Either way, I would honor my queen's wishes and ensure the remaining royal bloodlines in the Strigoi Kingdom understood her demands—by sending a missive to their homes.

We'll help you for now, I thought, translating her words into a script that I would later draft on paper. *However, we will be back, and we expect to see changes. So find your mates. Locate a Sigil. And claim your title. Then fix your territory.*

"The Ghouls can feast on the dreams of these humans, too, right?" Camillia asked, her power spreading through the fields.

I nodded to confirm her question. "Yes, they feed on nightmares and dreams."

"Okay, then these humans can serve multiple purposes," she replied. "But I expect them to be treated with kindness. And I want them all to eventually be released."

"Do you have a timeline expectation?" I asked, arching a brow. "Other terms to add?"

"Are we crafting a deal?" she returned, glancing at me. "Or am I creating a ruling?"

I smiled. "That's entirely up to you, my queen."

Her eyes narrowed. "Terms and timelines sound like a deal."

"Yes, but edicts often require similar traits." My arms fell to my sides, and my hands slid into my pockets, which weren't really there. Because apparently my suit hung around me in tatters.

A consequence of the fall and everything else.

Actually, we were all a little worse for wear. Cami, too.

Her tank top torn and spotted with blood, her jeans ripped, her hair wild.

Az and Ajax were shirtless, their chests painted in ash and dried blood.

Even Melek was less than pristine, his suit torn open at the chest to show off some of his tattoos, which appeared to have dried blood streaked across them.

Hmm.

We all very much needed a shower and some rest.

As well as a good fuck.

I'd waited long enough to claim my female. Yet she wasn't done testing the boundaries of her new role, learning where I would bend and how deep-seated my dominance went.

I raised a brow, daring her to press harder. "Which is it, little mate? An edict or a deal?"

Her power continued to spread, the stalks throughout the field rising in waves. "I'm not ready to define more terms or a deadline. For now, I'll give the Strigoi time to recover and strengthen their kingdom. However, I expect the humans here to be treated well. They might be *food*, but that doesn't mean they need to suffer."

I nearly pointed out that they weren't suffering today, just utterly unaware.

But I'd save that history lesson for another day.

Instead, I simply nodded. "As you wish, my queen."

Now she arched a brow. "Really?"

I stepped forward with a smile. "Are you wanting to see what else you can demand of me and our realm?"

"It's not really a demand. It's—"

I caught her by the nape and pulled her into me, the sharp movement abruptly ending her statement. "It's a gift that you've given them," I rephrased. "But you seem to want to test my dominance. So what would you like to demand of your king, Camillia?"

She stared up at me. "I can ask for anything?"

"Always," I told her, meaning it.

"So long as I'm willing to pay the right price, yes?"

My grip tightened, my dick suddenly taking an interest in the direction of this conversation. "I think that depends on the desire, my queen."

Her pupils dilated as the last of her power spread across the field. She pressed one palm to my chest, the other still at her side. "Our souls are mated."

"Yes."

"I think our bodies should mate, too," she whispered, her gaze boldly holding mine.

My lips curled once more. "You're asking me to fuck you."

"No, I'm *telling* you to fuck me."

"Hmm." I drew my thumb up the column of her slender neck as I wrapped my other arm around her. "Terms?"

That eyebrow of hers winged upward again. "We're negotiating sex?"

"For our first time? Yes. Yes, we are. I need your limits, Camillia. Otherwise, I'll do whatever I want to you."

Her breasts met my chest as she inhaled sharply, her cheeks reddening. "Okay."

"Okay what?" I asked when she didn't say anything else.

"You can do whatever you want to me." She cocked her head. "I have a safe word. But I don't think I'll need to use it."

"Oh?"

She gave me a sexy little smile that sent a fresh stroke

of sizzling fire through my veins. "I can handle you, Typhos Lucifer."

Apparently, our queen is ready, I thought at Melek, recalling our conversation about waiting.

I think we are all ready, my king, he returned. *But I'll save the rope play for coronation night.*

Mmm, red silk...

That is what I promised you, he replied.

The way Camillia's blush deepened even more told me she'd either understood our mental conversation or was perhaps being enlightened by Melek.

Either way, it had me very eager to play.

However, I'd introduce her slowly. She'd claimed she could take me—and I believed her—but that didn't mean I'd rush this between us.

I wanted to make it memorable for us both.

A king taking his queen.

Claiming his mate.

And joining their souls in the most intimate of ways.

I reached for her hand—the one at her side, not the one against my chest—and took the death stone from her. "Warden," I said while holding Camillia's gaze. "Can you find a safe place to put our prisoner?"

He stepped up to my side and held out a hand. "I think I know who to ask for advice."

Zenaida, I heard him think.

I nodded and set the stone in his palm. "Can you go with him, Azazel?" Zenaida would never hurt Ajax. But I preferred the pair to travel together, especially when visiting the powerful Fortune Fae Omega.

"Trying to keep Cami to yourself?" Azazel asked. "Because she's *ours*, Typhos. You have to share."

I glanced at him, amusement touching my chest. "I can

share. However, you've all played with her for months. It's my turn."

"It's not our fault you took so long to claim her," he pointed out. "So you can have her tonight. But she's ours in the morning."

His tone told me this wasn't a negotiation.

Unfortunately for him, I didn't care. So all I said was "We'll see."

Then I grabbed Camillia and whisked her to our suite in the palace before anyone could stop me.

My love, Melek murmured. *Would you like me to play emissary here for a bit? Make sure the Strigoi and others are all right?*

Yes, I replied, my forehead falling to Camillia's as I closed my eyes. *But join us after. I'll have our queen wet and ready to be fucked by then.*

Amusement mingled with intrigue as Melek whispered, *Enjoy, my king.*

Oh, I will, little prince, I promised. *And so will Camillia…*

CHAPTER 46

AJAX

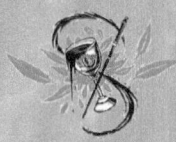

"**D**o you remember that coin toss? The night Payan went after our final Hell Fae Bride Candidate?" I asked after materializing outside of Zenaida's house.

Kuro followed, landing right on my shoulder. He'd disappeared during the energy storm in the Morpheus Kingdom. But now that things were calm again, he'd apparently decided to come back.

Or maybe he just wanted to see Zenaida.

"You mean the coin toss that you lost?" Az drawled before his eyes darkened to black orbs and narrowed at my owl. It seemed his inner Phoenix and my familiar were still not on the friendliest of terms.

"Yeah, that bet," I said, my lips quirking up a little at the memory. It was the night I met our mate. "Kind of glad I lost now."

"But was it truly a loss? Or fate playing her hand?" a musical voice asked as the door opened to reveal Zenaida holding a plate of her famous cookies. "Hungry?"

"I'm sure he's starving after all that power-sharing," a more masculine tone replied.

I rolled my eyes. "I should have known you'd be here, too," I told my oldest friend.

Shade poked his head out from behind his grandmother. "I see you have the death stone again," he said by way of a reply, his gaze on my hand as he brought a cookie to his mouth. "Does that mean you finally went out on that date with your mate? To play with zombies?"

I blinked at him, then recalled how he'd mentioned something about that when originally giving me the rock in my hand. "There were no zombies."

He frowned. "That's a shame. I've heard so many fun tales about the Netherworld Kingdom that I just assumed."

"They're Death Fae and Corpse Fae, not zombies," a cultured tone replied from behind us.

I turned to find a tall male with long silver-white hair standing with his hands clasped behind his back, his vibrant gaze locked on Shade inside.

"I'll be sure to share your expectations with my cousin," he went on, still talking to my oldest friend. "Hades will be absolutely fascinated, I'm sure."

My eyes widened. *Cousin* and *Hades* could only mean one thing. This was a Mythos Fae. Or a God, as the Nightmare Fae often called them.

Zenaida sighed. "Well, you might as well all come in, now that everyone has arrived."

"And why is Morpheus here?" Az asked, the name sending a chill down my spine. "Or is stopping by for cookies more important than properly governing a kingdom?"

"Last I checked, I have no such responsibilities of *governance*," Morpheus replied, his focus now on Az. "I am simply an icon to be prayed to. Sometimes I answer those prayers. Often, I do not." He glanced at Zenaida. "What is it you Fortune Fae always say? It's frowned upon to interfere with fate?" He shrugged. "Seems like as good an excuse as any, yes?"

Az folded his arms across his bare chest, his phoenix tattoo seeming to bristle in response to his mounting irritation. "You let a Virtuous Fae into your kingdom."

"No, the Strigoi throne did that. Which, if we want to be particular about it, was created by Typhos. Ergo, *Typhos* let the Virtuous Fae into the Morpheus Kingdom. So I suppose I should be displeased, but I'm in a forgiving mood." He waved to the door. "Shall we enter? I hear it's the polite way to respond to being invited in."

Az suppressed a growl, one I heard echoing in his mind.

I understood that urge, as I wanted to growl, too.

"Lucifer nearly died," I told Morpheus. "Would you have stepped in had that happened?"

The Mythos Fae blinked at me, his blue-green irises even more intense as he captured my gaze. I nearly startled at the force of his stare, his features almost too perfect to be real.

I suddenly understood why they called this male the God of Dreams.

"I would have been severely disappointed had that happened," he informed me. "Especially since your mate had the death stone. Fortunately, she figured out how to use it." He again looked at Zenaida. "You know, for a Fortune Fae who says she doesn't tempt fate, you certainly have a knack for finding ways to alter paths."

"I'm certain I have no idea what you're talking about," she replied.

Because of course she didn't.

Why would she know anything at all?

Fucking flames, we're surrounded by riddlers, I thought. *This really is hell.*

Indeed, Az returned, sounding just as irritated.

"Perhaps you're right," Morpheus mused, walking around Az toward the house and taking a cookie from Zenaida's plate. "No need to posture, Kodiak. I have no plans to play with your Omega's dreams tonight."

Grumbling sounded from inside the house, causing Zenaida to sigh again.

Fortune Fae Alphas were particularly possessive of their Omega mates.

And I supposed her Alpha mate wouldn't be all that keen on a Mythos Fae Alpha walking into his Omega's nest as a result.

I almost hoped the meeting would end in a brawl. It would make for a fitting climax to our very long day.

Though, I also really just wanted to return to our mate.

I trusted Lucifer to take care of her, particularly as I could hear his intentions through our new mating bond. But that didn't stop me from missing Cami.

If anything, it actually made me crave her more.

Because I could hear *what* he was doing to her right now.

A bath, I thought, somewhat amused. *He's bathing our mate.*

And feeding her, Az replied.

He really enjoys delayed gratification, doesn't he? Because I definitely wouldn't have had the patience to bathe a naked Cami after months of holding back my attraction to her. *She's practically begging him to fuck her.*

I could feel her desire. Hear her mental demands.

And hear his responses, too.

He was insisting on taking care of her first, something that had Cami growling about not needing to be coddled.

But Lucifer's dominance was winning, leaving our mate panting for him. *Fuck, she's making me want to shadow back right now,* I admitted to Az via our mental link.

Same. As soon as we're done here, we're joining them.

I thought we were giving Lucifer the night with her, I returned as I glanced at him.

I've changed my mind.

I smiled. *I approve.*

I assumed you would, Warden. He stepped away from me to enter Zenaida's home. Unlike Morpheus, though, he didn't take a cookie.

I opted out as well, though I thanked her with a smile as I moved by her in the doorway. "I presume that you know why I'm here," I said.

"I do," she replied, following me inside and closing the door.

Her dining room and kitchen often entertained large parties of eight or more, but something about the space felt smaller today. I suspected it was because of the two Alphas in the room.

Morpheus had taken up a position against the wall, his hands in the pockets of his dress slacks.

Meanwhile, Kodiak and Vadim—Zenaida's mates— stood near the kitchen island, their narrowed gazes on the God of Dreams.

I hadn't heard them speak yet, something that was an anomaly for them. They weren't exactly loud, but they weren't necessarily quiet either. In truth, they were usually much friendlier. Especially Kodiak. But his cold stare suggested he did not consider Morpheus to be a friend. And Vadim clearly felt the same.

"I don't actually know why you're here," Shade interjected. "But when I heard you might be visiting, I came by to check in. After all, the last time I saw you, your mate had been sucked off to another plane of existence. During Aflora's ball, in case you need the reminder."

I winced. "Yeah, sorry about that."

He shrugged. "Florica creates paradigms full of violent snakes daily. It's fine. But a little note saying you were okay might have been appreciated." He glanced pointedly at my owl. "Same with you, Kuro."

My familiar ruffled his feathers, his head lowering a little in response to the chastisement.

"Anyway, I'm glad you're alive," Shade went on. "Oh, and before I forget, Aflora wants me to invite you and your queen over for dinner. Given the state of certain things, I suggest that it be sooner rather than later. You're about to be very distracted with your new roles."

I frowned. "Why does that sound like a riddle?"

He gave me the most innocent of looks, which only further confirmed my suspicions. "Would I do such a thing?"

"You're Zenaida's grandson. So yes. Yes, you would."

He smiled. "Well, just get back to me on the dinner soon, hmm?" He looked at his grandmother. "Sorry to eat and run, G'ma. I need to go help Kols escape Florica's fiery ropes."

"Yes, I do believe you've left him to suffer long enough," she replied, her gaze narrowing. "You should consider—"

"Nope," Shade cut her off. "No prophecies or advice today. Maybe tomorrow. Or next year." He shadowed out of the room without another word, clearly in a hurry to escape his grandmother's meddling.

I felt similarly.

Which was why I quickly cut in and said, "I need a safe place to keep this stone, and since you gave it to me, I assume you already have an idea for me."

Her blue eyes practically shone in response, her long, dark hair seeming to wave on an invisible breeze. "In fact, I do." She looked at the God of Dreams. "Morpheus will take it."

Rather than comment, he merely held out a hand for the stone.

I scoffed at this suggestion. I'd expected Zenaida to recommend a paradigm or perhaps help me create somewhere to hide the stone for eternity.

But this?

No.

"Why the hell would I trust you to handle this after you allowed Vivaxia to blatantly manipulate the beings of your realm?" I demanded.

He arched a silver brow, the expression almost reminding me of Lucifer. Probably because he looked haughty as fuck, all while boasting a regal flair. "Because I have access to a prison in my home realm that was specially built to hold immortal fae like Vivaxia."

I folded my arms. "Tell me more about this prison."

"It's Pandora's Box," he replied, the name meaning nothing to me. "It houses the worst of Mythos Fae kind. And my brother Ares is the Warden there. He'll find an appropriate place for that death stone."

"I realize you don't know each other well," Zenaida interjected before I could reply. "But giving Morpheus the stone is my recommendation. He knows how to handle it and the contents inside of it."

"Forgive me for not being all that confident in this solution," I drawled. "He left his kingdom to die."

"Just because one doesn't intervene in fate doesn't mean that being doesn't care about the outcome," she replied with a soft smile. "Many of us have our roles to play, Ajax. And in my experience, being the watcher is the hardest role of all."

I flinched at her choice of words, her comment bringing back a memory of the day I'd been forced to *watch* as my loved ones died. If anyone understood the horrors of that role, it was me.

But I didn't understand why she felt the need to mention it now.

Was she trying to imply that Morpheus had been forced into a similar situation?

I doubted it. He was an all-powerful fae God. He could have intervened if he'd wanted to.

Unless it would have altered fate, I thought, glancing at him again. The events of today—of the last few months—had changed everything in the Hell Fae Realm.

Those events had turned Cami into a queen. Helped us find our mate-circle. Made me a true Hell Fae Warden. Allowed me to bond to Az and Lucifer. Brought me closer to Melek.

I swallowed.

While I could fault Morpheus for not assisting more, I had to wonder what would have changed had he been involved. Would today have even happened?

I could ponder it all day and night. But at the end of it all, it wouldn't matter.

Because the changes were already done.

What mattered now was assuring that Vivaxia never returned. And it sounded like Morpheus had a way of securing that fate.

Part of me wanted to confirm this decision with Lucifer.

But he'd named me as his Warden for a reason. He'd also trusted me with the stone.

Which meant this choice was mine.

I glanced at Az.

He simply stared back. *I'll support whatever you want to do,* he told me with his gaze more than his mind.

Zenaida was a lot of things, but she'd never steered me wrong. I trusted her, despite her penchant for riddles.

She was also the one who'd given me the death stone in the first place. Via Shade, of course. But that still counted.

That death stone had basically allowed Cami to save us all and master her siphoning power, too.

Which meant Zenaida had been helping us all along, from very early on in my time with Cami.

"You had Shade give me the stone, then ensured I had it again recently," I said to the Fortune Fae Omega before looking at Morpheus. "And you left it for Cami in the tunnel with that note."

Both of them looked at me yet said nothing. No acknowledgment. No confirmation. Just expressions of expectation.

I sighed. "I can see why you're friends."

"They are not friends," Kodiak inserted. "They are acquaintances who share similar goals."

"Some might call that the basis of a friendship," Morpheus replied, smiling at Zenaida. "Or the foundation of a mating."

Kodiak stepped forward, but Zenaida had already moved into his path. "Please don't," she whispered.

The Alpha bristled, then wrapped his arms around her and pulled her backward into a possessive embrace. Vadim shifted to their side in a fluid movement that was more predator-like than anything else.

Why does it feel like I've just seen our future? Az asked me via our bond.

I think it's our present, I replied, thinking about that note from Morpheus. He'd said something about seeing our mate in her dreams. Which had better not fucking happen.

Cami had four very alpha, very possessive mates who were all obsessed with her.

Including the fucking Hell Fae King.

God or not, we could take this asshole down.

"You probably shouldn't visit the Hell Fae Kingdom anytime soon," I told him as I handed him the stone. "Wouldn't want you falling into the wrong dream and turning your reality into a nightmare."

The flicker of amusement in his expression told me he knew exactly whose dreams I referred to.

"Not to worry, Warden. I'm currently preoccupied with a pretty little dreamer in the Netherworld Kingdom. So your mate's mind is safe for now." He held up the stone. "I'll see that this makes it to Ares for safekeeping." He moved closer to Zenaida to take another cookie. "Delicious as always, little one."

Kodiak growled, but Morpheus was already gone before he could even react to the flirtatious comment.

Zenaida shivered, her pupils dilating at the commanding sound from her Alpha.

"See you again soon, Ajax," she said, no doubt sensing my desire to leave. *Immediately.*

Because I didn't want to witness whatever was about to happen with her and her mates. She might look thirty years old in physical appearance, thanks to immortal genetics, but I still saw her as a grandmother.

Ugh.

"Thanks, Zen," I managed to choke out, her nickname all I could say before I shadowed back to my room in the palace.

Az followed, a subtle laugh echoing in his mind.

"It's not funny," I muttered.

"It is," he countered. "Because that really was our future. Thousands of years from now, we'll still be just as attracted to Cami. Just as dominant. Just as possessive." His tone deepened with each statement. "We're going to fuck her for eternity, and I can't fucking wait."

I looked at him. "Are you wanting to start now?" Because I sensed her finally getting out of that bath and I wouldn't mind helping her towel off.

But Az shook his head. "We'll give Typhos a little more time. Then we'll join." He stepped into me, his bare chest touching mine. "And in the interim, we'll spar."

"Foreplay?" I countered.

"That is what I said," he replied, making me roll my eyes.

"The adventures today weren't enough to whet your violent appetite?"

He smiled. "That barely took the edge off."

I stared into his eyes, noting the flicker of black as his Phoenix gazed back.

Vivaxia had leashed him again. Just for a few minutes. But it had been long enough.

Az wasn't saying it, but he needed a little violence to work through what had happened. And he was choosing me for that outlet... to protect our mate.

"One match," I told him. "Then I will want to shower and eat some—"

His mouth captured mine before I could finish, his kiss so abrupt and harsh that he drew blood.

I growled and kissed him back with just as much force.

Then I let him take me down to the floor and submitted to his needs.

Because that was what mates did for each other—we helped each other in times of need. We provided protection and a safe place to heal. *And we loved one another unequivocally.*

CHAPTER 47

CAMI

I glared at Typhos's bare back, his wings having vanished soon after we'd arrived. Now his muscles created an erotic display that had my thighs clenching with need.

A need he'd stoked for the last hour while in the bath.

While forcing me to eat.

When all I wanted was to devour him instead.

Our Sources had joined, our mating bond fully intact. I needed to fuck him and complete our connection. To finally feel that thick dick of his inside me.

But he was prolonging my torment by trying to take care of me instead. While I appreciated the effort, there was a part of me that he was very much neglecting to touch.

And I was really fucking tired of it.

"I can hear you over there pouting," he murmured, his back still to me. "I told you, Camillia. This is a lesson in dominance." He turned around as he finished wrapping a towel around his waist, the cotton material hiding his impressive erection from my view. "You can't command me, little one."

I narrowed my eyes again. "You're punishing me for saving your life."

"This isn't punishment, little siphon," he said, sauntering toward me. "This is me ensuring that you know I'll take care of you." He cupped my jaw and leaned down, our gazes locked together in an intense stare. "I don't want you to forget how gentle I've been. Because when I take you, I'll be anything but."

If he weren't so close, I would have folded my arms across my bare chest and scowled at him. But he was only a hairsbreadth away from my mouth. So all I could do was say, "You're teasing me."

"No, I'm warning you," he returned. "The things I plan to do to you are going to make you question my intentions. But I need you to know and believe that I cherish you. Because you might feel otherwise very soon."

I shivered. There was a threat lingering in those words, a threat I very much wanted to experience. "Yes, please."

He chuckled, his lips ghosting over mine. "So eager to be destroyed." His hand slid down to my neck, his touch turning harsh against my throat. "What's your safe word, Camillia?"

"Camping," I said, the word coming out a little choked, thanks to his tightening grip.

"And if you can't speak?" he asked, his palm cutting off my ability to breathe.

I lifted my fist in the air. He studied it for a moment, like he was assessing whether he liked it or not.

But after a beat, his grasp lessened and he murmured, "Good girl." He grabbed my thighs and parted them, then yanked me forward to where I teetered on the edge of the counter.

I took hold of his shoulders to keep myself from tipping backward.

"It's been a very long time since I fucked a woman," he told me. "Thousands of years, Camillia. So when I say that I'm going to take every part of you, I mean it. I want your mouth. Your cunt. Your ass. Every fucking hole. And you're going to let me use you." He drew his nose across my cheekbone to my ear, where he nibbled the lobe. "And you're going to *beg* for more."

I shuddered, my nipples beading against his chest. "Yes, my king."

"Mmm," he hummed, approval radiating from his chest. "Such a good little mate, letting her king master her."

His lips skimmed down to my throat, his teeth threatening against my skin.

I swallowed, my heart hammering in my chest.

He was barely touching me, and I was already on the verge of an orgasm. I could feel it curling inside me, demanding release.

Gods, we'd only been in the bath for an hour, yet it felt like years of foreplay were finally coming together for the climactic act.

So much teasing.

So much *yearning.*

So many dreams.

But this was real. Typhos was here. Touching me. *Owning me...*

"Outside of these walls, we're equals, Camillia," he whispered. "But in here, you kneel when I tell you to kneel. You spread those long legs when I ask you to. And worship my cock like it's your fucking deity."

Another shudder worked through me, my legs

squeezing around his hips. "Yes, my king," I told him, aware that he wanted a response.

Because I could hear his mind.

Feel his intentions.

Understand his expectations.

Fae, he really is going to destroy me...

But the Source—*our* Source—would put me back together again.

He released a low growl, the sound vibrating every inch of my being. His hands left my hips to grab the marble counter, his mouth still lingering against my throbbing pulse.

I waited, my breath stalling in my chest.

Yet all he did was inhale. Then exhale. Then inhale again.

My lungs began to ache, my need for air finally taking over. But right as I parted my lips, he *struck*. His palm encircled my throat as his teeth sank into my neck.

I tried to scream, but I couldn't. His grip was too tight.

His opposite arm came around my waist to pull me even farther off the edge and into his chiseled torso. Then his mouth captured mine, and he pushed air into my lungs. *His* air. Breathing for me. Mastering me. Making me *his*.

Oh, fuck... My insides turned molten hot in response to his dominance, his essence, his *everything*.

I wanted to climb this man and make him mine. Bite him. Mark him. *Please him....*

He carried me from the bathroom to the bed in his suite, his mouth against mine. We weren't kissing, just breathing. Just existing. Just... *mating*.

Gods, I could feel him in every inch of my being. Yet the space between my legs had never felt so empty.

Part of me wanted to beg.

But Typhos didn't give me a chance to speak or even

think as his tongue invaded my mouth. Suddenly, all I could do was try to keep up with his demand, his mouth possessing mine in a way I'd never experienced before.

I barely felt the mattress meeting my back. I was too consumed by his touch, his heat, *his hands*... They were roaming up my sides, tracing my curves, and ending at my breasts.

A gasp escaped me as he pinched my nipples with a little too much force, but that gasp quickly melted into a moan as he massaged the hurt away.

His hips settled between mine, the damn towel blocking me from truly feeling him. My hands went to his toned sides and down to the fabric, my desire to rip it away taking over. But the second I tugged on it, he caught my wrists and sent my world spinning.

I released a groan as my face met the pillows.

Then froze as Typhos pressed my tender breasts into the mattress by placing his hand between my shoulder blades and pushing down.

What...?

"Apparently, I wasn't clear," he said against my ear, his heat bathing my back. "In the bedroom, *you* bow. *I* lead."

A resounding smack filled the air as his palm met my ass, causing me to jolt. "*Typhos.*"

He tsked as he shifted backward. "What happened to *my king*, hmm?"

Another slap had my thighs squeezing in protest while my insides curled into something hotter. Something... *exciting*.

"Ask me for another," he said, his lips brushing my ear again. "*Beg me*, Camillia." His hand caressed my tender backside, causing a strange sort of moan to slip from my mouth. "Mmm, not quite good enough, little one." His fingers slipped down between my legs to stroke me where I desired him most.

I gasped, my insides seeming to pull tight with excitement as he neared my clit. Only for him to withdraw in the next breath.

"So fucking wet for me already," he murmured, drawing his touch back to my other hole. "Maybe I'll spank you, then fuck you raw here, just to take the edge off. Perhaps then you'll be ready to beg me for more."

I turned my head so I could look at him, only to jump as he smacked my other cheek. The burn spread up my spine while heat curled in my lower abdomen. *Fuck...*

"Trust me, little one, I'm considering it," he responded, obviously having heard my thoughts. "But if you don't start cooperating, I'm going to ensure the *fucking* is for me, not for you. Because I only reward good girls with orgasms." He leaned down again, his lips at my ear once more. "And you, Camillia De la Croix, have been trying to top me from the bottom for far too long."

Gods, I couldn't tell if I wanted to punch him or mount him.

Az was dominant.

Typhos... Typhos was on another level completely. A level I didn't know how to counter. I wasn't even sure if I wanted to try, either.

"Don't fight me, Camillia," he whispered, his teeth skimming the shell of my ear.

I almost laughed at his choice of words; I'd spoken similar ones to him when he'd been trying to sacrifice himself like some sort of martyr.

However, I felt his need to lead now. His desire to dominate me entirely. And his promise to take care of me... if I submitted.

As well as his threat to force my submission should I choose to continue challenging him.

I shivered, the juxtaposition between the two options making me hot for very different reasons. Part of me wanted to see how far I could push him. While another side of me just wanted to let him take charge and enjoy the ride.

Typhos drew his finger up and down my spine, waiting for me to decide. All while my ass stung from his previous ministrations.

"What's it going to be, my darling little queen?" he asked softly. "Are you going to let me use you in a way that benefits us both? Or are you going to make me turn you into my personal plaything?" His finger dipped between my cheeks to slide into me, creating a slight sting from the lack of lubricant.

I arched, the sensation not fully unpleasant, but not nearly as welcome as when he'd dipped his hand between my thighs to nearly reach my clit.

"I don't care if this is our first time together," he went on. "I have expectations, and either you will meet them or I will *take* them."

I bit down on the pillow as he inserted a second finger, the burn deepening inside me.

"Decide, Camillia," he demanded. "Or I will choose for you." He scissored his fingers, making me groan at the pleasure-pain sensation.

Fuck, I shouldn't like that. But I did.

Just as I enjoyed the feel of his teeth sinking into my neck, his dominance washing over me in a hot wave of passion.

Fighting him was fun. Fighting him felt right.

But this... this felt even better.

My shoulders loosened as his bite shifted into a kiss.

Then my limbs turned to liquid as he laved the teeth marks with his tongue.

Fae… I'd never experienced anything like this.

His fingers were still moving inside me, twisting and turning in a way that sent sparks to my nerve endings. It hurt. But his mouth on my neck seemed to distract me from the pain.

However, the sting returned in full force as he shoved deeper and took his lips away from my skin. I jolted as a third finger was added to the mix, the stretch causing my back to arch. "*Typhos,*" I hissed, the agony nearly too much.

"Last warning, little one," he said, not letting up at all. "Submit or I'll make you submit."

Fuuuckkk…

I grabbed the silky sheets beneath me, a scream leaving my lips as he forced me to take another thrust. The burn was that much more intense. That much *harsher.* "*Please…*" I whispered.

Only, I wasn't sure if I was begging for more… or begging for something else.

Because suddenly the ache morphed into a new sensation. It still fucking hurt, but it… it felt good, too.

Gods, what are you doing to me? I wondered, feeling dizzy from his roughness as well as the gentle kiss of his scruff against my neck as he pressed his lips to my jaw, just below my ear.

"I'm teaching you how to pray to me," he murmured, his minty breath seeming to reach every one of my senses. "I'm your *God* now, Camillia De la Croix. So worship me the way I desire, and maybe I'll reward you."

A rebellious part of me wanted to hate him for those words, to fight the very meaning behind them. But as he started kissing a path down my spine, I couldn't find the strength to even try to speak.

Because while he was telling me to worship him, it certainly felt like the opposite was happening—that he was priming me to be cherished. To be fucked into another existence.

Now you're getting it, he hummed into my mind. *I'm your God, but you're my Goddess, too. So let me take you to the stars, my queen.*

He nibbled one sensitive globe, the skin smarting from his previous strikes against my ass. But it felt good, too. The strange mixture of passion and torment was making me dizzy, my mind struggling to focus on what I should say or do.

All I wanted was to bow to this male and let him do whatever he desired.

It would be so much easier. No worries. No responsibilities. Just... just endless oblivion. Following his orders. Pleasuring him.

And being pleasured in kind.

I quivered, the tremble seeming to traverse my entire being, to the point where I pushed my hips into the bedding below. Because I needed friction. I... I needed *more.*

But another swat to my ass had my back arching instead. "Your pleasure is mine to give, Camillia," Typhos said from between my legs. "And you haven't earned it yet."

I nearly snarled in frustration. However, I somehow channeled the angry energy into my hands as I clutched the bedding once more.

That must have been the right decision because his tongue traced the crease of my cheek, right where it met my leg. Then traveled upward... to a place... I'd never been... *Fae!*

His wet caress instantly chased away the sting his

fingers had created, causing my heart to skip in my chest. Because wow. *Wow.* I… I didn't know how…

I moaned, the sensation unlike anything I'd ever felt before. It had hurt more than I'd realized. But now… now he was healing me. Warming me. Making me feel so, so *good.*

"Typhos," I whispered, his name leaving me for entirely different reasons now. "*My king.*"

He hummed, clearly pleased with me for using his title.

At some point, he'd told me it wasn't necessary. But I heard in his mind now that he enjoyed me saying it while in bed with him. It was about power. Respect. And mutual understanding.

Because, to him, a king and a queen were partners. Not one above another, but a pair who governed *together.*

So it wasn't about rank or any sort of traditional hierarchy.

It was about *leading.*

As a unit.

But knowing when to succumb to the other.

Such as here… in the bedroom. My king needed my submission. And deep down… I needed to submit. To give him the power and just accept his dominance.

I'd given all of myself to the realm today. To the fae. To my mates. To this world.

Now it was time to recover. To let my king thank me in a way only he could. To indulge in our new bonds. And simply exist.

I understood now, the purpose of all this. Why trust mattered so much to all my mates. Why Typhos had insisted on caring for me before properly claiming me.

Because he needed me to feel safe.

Protected.

Secure.

So that he could push me to my limits. Take me to the stars. And fuck me the way a king should.

"I'm yours, my king," I told him as I fully relaxed beneath him. "You can take me however you want. Wherever you want. In whichever way you desire."

He speared me deeper with his tongue, then slowly withdrew.

"Good choice," he said, kissing my abused flesh before sliding back onto his knees behind me. "Now turn over and spread your legs for me. I want to taste that magic little pussy of yours. The one that enslaved all my men. The one that brought me to my knees."

The threat was back in his voice, his tone deepening to a low growl that had my toes curling in response.

"After I'm done memorizing your sweet cunt with my tongue, I'm going to make you come for me, Camillia De la Croix. As many fucking times as I demand. Because this is my pussy to please. And you, my darling little queen, are going to take every fucking thing I give you. *And more.*"

CHAPTER 48

TYPHOS

Camillia's submission tasted sweeter than I could ever have anticipated. My strong, stubborn queen had finally let go and let me truly lead.

It was a gift, one I intended to reward.

But first, I wanted to touch her. Explore her. *Learn her*.

Because Godsdamn, she was a sight to behold. Her long legs spread. Her pussy glistening. Her clit swollen and needy.

It took restraint not to lean down and take her. To force my tongue inside her and drive her over the edge into oblivion.

However, my little siphon needed to be utterly out of her mind before I let her fall. It was the only way to properly introduce her to the beauty of submitting.

Kneeling between her thighs, I took hold of one foot to lift her ankle to my lips. Her eyes fell closed as I kissed her there, my mouth moving slowly up her calf to her knee, and then along her inner thigh all the way up to her weeping slit.

However, rather than lick her like I wanted to, I repeated the actions on her opposite leg.

She squirmed a little but didn't protest. Nor did she try to command me. "You're doing very well, my queen," I told her softly as I returned her foot to the bed.

Camillia swallowed in response, her skin flushed with heat. It was a pretty sight, the blush traveling down to her beautiful tits—a sight that made my mouth water.

Humming, I crawled over her, my towel still tucked around my waist, and settled between her splayed thighs. It wasn't at all what I said I was going to do, but her breasts desperately needed my attention.

So I bent my head to take one hard nipple into my mouth. *And sucked.*

Her back bowed in response, her hands fisting in the sheets. But my obedient queen didn't try to force me to do anything else. She just let me play. Explore. Lick. Nip. *Bite.*

I rewarded her by lavishing her tits with my affection, my mouth memorizing every inch of her soft skin before tonguing her stiff little peaks.

She whimpered, her thighs tensing against me. I sank my teeth into her breast, right above her rosy tip, and smiled at the gasp she released.

Her pleasure-pain tolerance was high, which suited the sadist inside me. I fully intended to test those boundaries in time. But for now, I just used my mouth on her to create little love bites all over her chest.

She started when I moved up higher to kiss her, my lips claiming hers in a bruising demand that left her breathless when I finished.

"Such a good queen, letting your king worship every inch of you," I praised her as I palmed her tit and gave it a not-so-gentle squeeze. "I think I could play with your breasts all night, Camillia." I pressed my lips to her ear.

"Do you have any idea how long it's been since I touched a woman like this?"

I started a path downward now, my lips caressing her throat and her breasts again before dipping to her belly button and further to her soft mound.

"Thousands of years," I told her, answering the question I'd asked her.

My mouth hovered right over her clit as I glanced up to find her eyes wide as she stared down at me.

It seemed my response surprised her. Though, it really shouldn't have, as I'd said as much a few minutes ago. But perhaps the information still shocked her.

Melek had been my only lover since my fall, a truth she could no doubt hear in my mind.

Just as she could hear my intentions now.

Still, I voiced them out loud by saying, "You'll have to endure thousands of years of thirst, Camillia. Because it's been a very, very long time since I feasted on a woman's flesh. And your pussy is the most divine of them all."

I didn't give her a chance to process my words. Because I couldn't wait a second longer to properly taste her.

Melek had given me a hint of her decadence when he'd fed me her pleasure with his tongue. But it was nothing compared to the real heaven between her thighs.

Holy fucking Hellfire, I thought, my eyes damn near rolling into the back of my head. Camillia's cunt was my own personal ambrosia. A forbidden sweetness I was never supposed to be allowed to savor. Yet our souls had other plans for us.

Our Source had married us for eternity.

And the selfish part of me was thrilled.

Deep down, I knew I didn't deserve her. I'd wronged her in so many ways. But I would spend eternity apologizing—preferably like this—if it meant she would find me worthy of her.

Rather than voice all that into her mind, I told her with my tongue against her clit. I sealed the promise with my lips. Secured the vow with my teeth. And drove my intentions home by thrusting my fingers inside her.

Both holes.

Because I wanted her full. Prepared. *Ready*.

I'd promised to take her every which way, and I'd meant it.

But she needed to come on my tongue first. *Over and over again*.

It didn't take much, her taut little body already strung tight from all my stroking and kissing. A little pressure to her clit coupled with my fingers twisting inside her sent my queen soaring with a scream that echoed off the walls of our suite.

My cock throbbed in response, eager to join the fun.

However, I wasn't done.

Nowhere near it.

I needed her panting. Fuck, I wanted her *begging* me to stop.

Only then would I drive inside her. Hitting her swollen, abused little clit with my hips while I took my pleasure and forced her to feel more. To explode with a climax so intense that she lost her fucking mind for a minute.

Then I'd take her again.

From behind.

Gods, I was ready to come just thinking about it. This woman had me in knots, her magical hold over me resolute.

But I no longer cared about the cause or the reasons.

I just wanted to indulge in our present and embrace our future.

Which included driving her over the edge again, something I did by biting down on her clit while pushing deep inside her with my fingers.

She bucked and tried to move, the agony mingling with her ecstasy and releasing beautiful sounds from her pretty lips.

When she tried to squirm out from under me, I removed my hand from her ass and pressed down on her stomach to keep her in place.

Then I devoured her with renewed vigor. *I told you to take it, little one,* I reminded her with a thought. *Now be a good girl and come for me again.*

Typhos… I… I can't…

You can, I promised her, then bit her again as a soft reprimand.

She jolted, my name leaving her lips followed by "My king…"

I smiled and gave her a little lick. *That's better, my queen,* I returned and renewed my purpose between her thighs.

By the time I finished, she was a weeping mess of passion and incoherence, the sight one that had me ripping the towel away from my thighs as I climbed up her gorgeous form.

My heavy cock fell against her well-prepared cunt, making her jump as the head landed right against her clit. I grabbed her before she could get away from me, my hands holding her hips while I slid through her damp heat.

"Grab my shoulders," I told her.

She did, her nails biting into my flesh. "Typhos, I—"

I slammed into her before she could finish speaking, causing her to break off on a scream that went straight to my balls. "Fuck, Camillia," I whispered, her tight pussy clamping down around me in protest of my intrusion. I was thick. I knew that. But Gods, I couldn't remember anything ever feeling this good around my shaft.

Maybe Melek's mouth.

However, there was something about Camillia that heightened this experience to a new level of existence. It made our joining feel unique. Divine. *Otherworldly*.

I slid out to the tip and thrust back in again, wondering if it was just the initial heat that had my mind spinning with outlandish thoughts.

But no.

It was *her*.

This female.

My mate.

I couldn't get enough. I needed to fuck her for eternity. Live inside this beautiful cunt. *Mark her with my seed.*

She said something I couldn't hear over the rhythmic beating of my heart, my ears echoing the sturdy sound.

It took physical effort to try to focus, to listen to her. To make sure she was all right.

But one look at her face told me she was fine. Her flushed cheeks and swollen lips were the markings of a well-pleased woman. The way her nails claimed my shoulders suggested she wanted more. And as I leaned down to kiss her, her tongue informed me that I'd better fucking *move*.

This woman was topping from the bottom again. I'd punish her for it later. Right now, I was a slave to the urges inside me, the need blossoming between us, the urgency warming our bond.

Take. What's. Mine.

That was all I could do.

It was a savage desire, one echoed by the way I began to punish Camillia with my hips. But my beautiful queen took my movements with the grace and vigor of an equal.

She accepted me inside her, clenched around me in warm welcome, and met my kiss with enviable force.

I'd tried to take her into oblivion, to force her to lose her mind with lust. Yet I was the one who had fallen over the edge into a rapturous state, unable to think of anything other than taking us both to the stars.

Our pants mingled with our groans, our bodies dancing to our own erotic beat.

It was a mating for the heavens.

A joining that would empower our Source.

A fucking so exquisite I might actually die…

"Fuck, Cami," I breathed, using her preferred nickname. It wasn't what I usually called her, but in the moment, it felt right.

This was my queen.

My partner.

My mate.

I'd do whatever the fuck she wanted, call her whatever she desired, so long as she let me live in this fucking pussy for the rest of my days.

"Gods, you're… so… fucking… *tight*," I breathed, my grip bruising on her hips. "I need you to come, Cami. I need you to come all over my cock like a good fucking queen."

She started to shake her head, her mind telling me she didn't think she could climax again, not after how much I'd already put her through.

But I wasn't accepting that as an answer.

My mate was going to fucking come, even if it took me hours to make her do it. I'd hold out for as long as it took. And I told her that with my mind before reclaiming her mouth with my tongue.

Some of the magical hold she had over me seemed to

snap, my dominance taking the reins as I forced her to accept more pleasure. More thrusts. More *everything*.

She exhaled my name as tears glistened in her eyes.

But she knew her safe word.

If she wanted this to stop, she'd use it.

I kept pushing, driving deep, hitting that spot within her that she couldn't ignore, all while moving my hips in a way that engaged her clit.

It was the most natural of movements, our bodies coming together in a way that confirmed our fate. We were always meant to fit this way. To be together, just like this. *For-fucking-ever*.

Her body tensed, her insides seeming to spasm violently, and I felt her orgasm coming.

She started to shake her head like she couldn't handle what was about to happen.

It was probably going to be so intense that it would hurt.

But I'd see her through it. Fuck her through the pain and indulge in her euphoric aftermath.

"T-Ty... I-I..." Her eyes seemed to roll back into her head in the next instant.

And then she was coming.

Hard.

Her body clamped down around me in waves of intensity as her voice gave out from screaming too hard. I didn't stop moving, my shaft enjoying the trembles and tightness as I fucked her even harder. Hitting that point to prolong her agony and ensure the most exquisite bliss.

Tears escaped her eyes.

Her lips parted in a silent shout.

Her body quivered violently.

I reached between us to stroke her clit, drawing it out

even more, until she started begging me to stop inside her mind.

That still wasn't her safe word.

Which was why I didn't completely remove my touch, instead choosing to simply push down on her sensitive nub as I pumped into her slick heat. "Keep coming for me," I demanded. "I want you writhing while I empty myself inside you."

She shuddered, a decline rolling through her mind. She didn't think she could handle any more.

But I proved her wrong by forcing her to take more. To feel me possessing every inch of her cunt. *By coming so deep inside her that I was certain she could taste my seed in her throat.*

I detonated with the thought, my shaft exploding with an orgasm unlike any I'd ever experienced. It was so fucking intense that I nearly blacked out, my body shaking violently in response.

"*Fuck,*" I breathed, burying my head in her neck. "*Cami...*"

I couldn't stop coming.

It was like I'd saved thousands of years' worth of cum for this female, my seed needing to fill her to completion. To own her. *Possess her.*

I bit down on her neck, needing something to ground me, and tasted blood.

Power hummed in response, our bond somehow deepening, like I'd just fucking claimed her all over again. Maybe I had. There'd never been a mating like ours. It was one of a kind. Just like her.

Which made it fucking perfect.

Another wave hit me, my body still coming undone.

Then awareness tickled the back of my neck, a soft voice humming approval into my mind. *Little prince,* I barely managed to think.

She's amazing, isn't she?

All I could do was grunt. Because yes, she was. So much more than amazing, though. There wasn't a term that captured Camillia De la Croix's brilliance. She was simply… a Goddess.

I cocooned her trembling form, her body well used and sated.

But she had another lesson to learn.

I kissed her softly, bringing us both down. Then slowly rolled until she was straddling me, my dick still inside her.

"I promised Melek that you would be wet and ready for him when he returned," I told her, my voice holding a gruff note to it that wasn't like me at all. But I didn't care. She deserved to hear how much she'd impacted me.

"She's certainly wet," Melek murmured from beside the bed.

Camillia glanced his way, a lust-drunk expression on her face. I really liked that look on her. It was fitting, given what was going to happen next.

"Open yourself for him, Camillia," I told her. "I want him to take your ass while I'm still inside your pussy."

Her eyes widened like she couldn't believe I would tell her to do this.

I simply arched a brow back at her. *You have four mates, Camillia darling. And we all like to share.* In fact, I could hear Az and Ajax thinking about joining.

Which meant our girl was about to prove her queenly abilities… all fucking night.

Melek lost his clothes—the suit one I noted was different from the bloody outfit he'd had on in the Morpheus Kingdom. He'd obviously showered and changed somewhere.

Not that it mattered.

He was about to get really fucking dirty with our mate.

His tattoos glittered a little as he slid onto the bed, his Virtuous Fae magic radiating off the runes embedded in his skin. One day, he'd tell Camillia the story behind those protective markings.

Perhaps when he drew some onto her skin as well.

I reached around her to spread her ass for his view as he settled behind her, causing Camillia's eyes to widen even more. "You can take it," I assured her. "Just like you've taken everything else. And more than that, you're going to fucking enjoy it."

Melek took a fistful of her hair and twisted her neck a little so he could kiss her on the mouth. She trembled again, but the way her nipples beaded told me she wasn't afraid. She was aroused. *Excited*, even.

And that excitement only grew as our prince positioned himself at her back entrance.

"She's ready," I told him, aware that I'd mostly prepared her for this.

Oh, it'd sting a little.

Fortunately, our queen enjoyed the bite of pain, something she proved now by moaning as he thrust inside her.

Az and Ajax chose that exact moment to walk in, their gazes instantly falling on the bed. Camillia didn't react, but I knew she felt their presence. Just as she sensed their intentions to join.

Melek released her mouth as Az kneeled on the bed, allowing the Commander to take over by yanking her into his own kiss. Ajax settled on the other side, his hand reaching out to stroke Camillia's side like he was checking on her physical state.

The fire in his eyes radiated interest, his pupils dilating with expectation.

Camillia's pussy clamped down around me again, telling me she more than approved of the night to come. Though, a stroke of her clit had her wincing.

You'll recover, I whispered into her mind. *Trust the Source to rejuvenate you, my queen. And trust your mates to take care of you.*

I brushed her clit again as Melek pumped into her ass, our prince indulging in her tight little hole. My dick flexed in response, the thin barrier between us allowing me to feel his movements. It was making me want to come again.

Which I would, and soon.

Because I wasn't leaving this cunt for the rest of the night.

Her mates could take her other holes. Her pussy was fucking mine.

Then tomorrow, I'd indulge in her ass.

And definitely her mouth, I thought as Ajax turned her head toward his waiting cock. He'd stripped while Az had been kissing her.

I eyed the pierced tip with interest, then watched in fascination as it disappeared between Camillia's plump lips.

She moaned around him, clearly enthralled by the metal. Or perhaps it was just the taste of our Warden on her tongue.

Regardless, it painted a very pretty picture. "You look so fucking good with all your holes filled, Miss De la Croix," I informed her. "But I think you'll look even better when you come while the three of us fuck you."

Az reached between us, his fingers taking over for my thumb.

Then I gripped Camillia's hips and started to fuck her again.

If this became too much, she'd let us know.

But I suspected our rebellious little vixen would be just fine.

She was made for this. Made for us.

Because she was our very own... *Hell Fae Queen.*

CHAPTER 49

CAMI

I *'m pretty sure I'm dead,* I thought, my eyes refusing to open.

You're not, a deep voice returned. *You've just been lost to an orgasmic high for a few hours. But you're slowly resurfacing.*

I frowned. *Typhos?*

Mmm, he hummed, confirming it was his voice in my head.

Warmth spread over me in the next instant, followed by the sensation of being in water.

My frown deepened. *Are we in the bath again?*

We are, yes.

Had my eyes been able to open, they would have blinked. *You know, for a Hell Fae King, you seem to have a strange obsession with water. One would think you'd prefer fire or brimstone.*

He chuckled, and I felt the motion against my side, suggesting I was curled in his lap. "I do like fire," he replied out loud, his lips brushing my forehead. "But water is more effective for washing off Melek's glittering claim."

His words slowly registered in my head, the meaning

behind them causing me to growl inside. *He turned me into a fucking disco ball again, didn't he?*

Male laughter filled my head, the origin coming from Ajax and Az as they confirmed that yes, Melek had covered me in his infamous golden jizz.

Well, they hadn't called it that.

But that was how *I* referred to it.

Some mates bite, Melek murmured into my mind. *I prefer angel dust.*

Angel dust, I repeated with a mental scoff. *It makes me glitter, Melek.*

I know. I find it pretty, he replied.

I sighed. There would be no reasoning with him on this one.

At least Typhos was helping to clean it off.

I floated in the bliss of his touch for a while, somewhat lost to my dreamlike state. One where I relived hours of pleasure in my mind.

Gods, my mates were insatiable.

I could still feel them all inside me. Especially Ty...

My brow furrowed. *Wait.* My thighs clenched, my lips parting. I wasn't curled up on his lap; I was *straddling* his lap. And we were still very much connected.

I squeezed my core, feeling his hard dick lodged deep. *Typhos.*

"Thousands of years, Cami," he replied, his use of my preferred name new.

Typhos had always called me Camillia, something that usually bothered me, as my parents had also constantly referred to me that way. However, I'd never minded hearing my full name on Typhos's tongue. He... he said it in a sexy way. One I rather enjoyed.

"I fully intend to live in your cunt until coronation.

Hell, maybe even then," he went on. "It would be a good way to inform the entire realm that you're mine."

Okay. Apparently, I needed to wake up.

I forced my eyes open, but I was staring at the side of the tub because my head had been resting on his muscular shoulder.

Clearing my throat, I gained my bearings and pulled back slightly to look at him. "If you try to put me in one of those metal dresses and fuck me on a stage, I'll kick you in the balls. Just like I did to that Hellhound."

Typhos's sapphire eyes glittered. "What if I just put you in the dress, then?"

I glared at him. "Your cock is inside me, *Your Majesty*. If you value keeping your dick in good working order, you'll reconsider the direction of this conversation." I clamped down around him, not that doing so really served as a threat, but it felt like the right reaction.

His nostrils flared, his jaw seeming to tighten. "I'll let you pick your coronation outfit, but I want you to wear something from me. A ring, perhaps."

My eyebrow lifted. "A ring?"

He stared at me. "If you won't let me mark you as mine with my chains, then yes, I want you to wear a ring."

"You mean I won't let you torture me again with your chains," I corrected him.

He frowned. "It wasn't meant to torture you, Camillia. It was meant to *tease* you, something I thought would be enjoyable. I've since learned that it was neither enjoyable nor welcome. And I've apologized."

"Yet you're suggesting I wear them again," I interjected.

"Because I realized that the sensual punishment was simply an excuse for my underlying need."

I stared at him. "What need?" I asked, confused now.

"My need to mark you," he replied. "I dressed you in those chains so everyone would know you were off-limits. At the time, I told myself it was for Azazel and Melek. But I now know that wasn't entirely true. Those chains were riddled in *my* power, therefore possessing *my* mark."

I… I didn't know how to reply to that. It wasn't at all what I'd expected him to say. And it changed how I viewed that whole experience. Because it added a level of possession to the incident that oddly made me feel better about it.

Which was a bit fucked up.

But that was my life here in the Hell Fae Realm.

Actually, it was my life… period. Nothing about my existence had ever been normal or smooth. I'd basically gone from one chaotic experience to the next.

"I was also punishing myself," Typhos went on. "Taunting myself with something—*someone*—I couldn't have." He cleared his throat. "Some might say I publicly claimed you that day. But I'm pretty sure you've been mine since the moment you arrived in my realm."

"*Ours*," Melek corrected as he entered the bathroom with a tray. "I brought *our* mate something to eat." He moved closer, his athletic torso on full display. I eyed his gray sweatpants with interest, the material seeming to fall at just the right place on his hips. "Or maybe she's hungry for something else?"

"The Source already reenergized her," Typhos replied. "She could absolutely fuck again."

My core squeezed as I curled into Typhos's massive chest. "Coffee first," I all but begged. Because I could smell the caffeine on Melek's tray and I very much wanted to dive into that scent.

Typhos chuckled, his fingers combing through my hair. "All right, little one. But my cock stays inside you."

My stomach warmed with his words, my insides clenching again. His demand should not be as hot as it was, but I appeared to be as insatiable as my mates.

Melek sat beside the tub, the tray on his lap, and handed me the steaming mug. The whipped cream on top had my lips curling. "Irish coffee?" I guessed.

"Courtesy of Ajax," he replied. "And this"—he slid his hand into his pocket to pull out a necklace—"is from me."

I eyed the bespelled jewelry, my mind instantly recalling the first one of these he'd given me. As well as the last necklace I'd worn—the one that had sent me to the Virtuous Fae Realm.

"You know, I haven't had good luck with necklaces since arriving here," I reminded him. "I'm not sure I want to accept that."

His lips curled. "This one is different." He unraveled the chain to show me the key-shaped pendant on the bottom. There were four gems decorating the length of the key, each one winking at me in the low bathroom lighting. "A diamond for me. Sapphire for Ty. Blue tiger's-eye for Ajax. And a black diamond for Az."

I stared at the glittering piece framed in yellow gold. "And the magic I sense?"

He shrugged. "It's covered in our essences. Protection. Love. A promise for the future. A necklace befitting a queen."

I narrowed my eyes. "That sounds very cryptic, Melek."

"He's marking you as ours," Typhos interjected, sounding amused. "The necklace will tell the realms who has mated you. It's a sweet but intentional gesture."

"You can't keep your cock inside her forever, my king. This seemed like a more practical alternative."

"I was actually thinking about making her wear that

chain dress for eternity instead," Typhos drawled. "But I suppose this is a kinder alternative. And it ensures no one sees our queen's finer assets."

He leaned forward to kiss my neck as I growled in response to his commentary on the chain dress again.

"Calm down, little queen," he murmured. "You're making me want to fuck you again."

"And you're making me want to kill you," I told him.

"Would you like me to wear a form of the chain dress to your coronation?" he asked, his mind telling me his question was actually genuine. "I'll let you make it for me."

I pulled back to look at him as images rolled through my mind. Sexy images of him in a kilt made of metal. All that sinewy strength on display. A carefully placed chain around his cock, one that tugged when he moved.

Warmth blossomed deep in my belly—a sensation Typhos might have even felt since he was still locked inside me.

But then I thought about how everyone else would see him in those chains, and I frowned. "No." He wasn't the only one with a possessive side. Because absolutely not. "You're not wearing that around other people."

However, in our suite... I mused, considering what I would do to him with those chains.

His eyebrow arched. "Topping from the bottom again?"

"You gave me the idea," I pointed out. "And it would be a fun way to punish you..."

Maybe he could rent out his club and let me have fun for a night.

"If that's the wish of my queen, then consider it done," he said softly, his fingers still combing my hair.

"Really?" I asked, surprised that he was not only agreeing but also sounding humble about it.

"Yes," he replied. "I'll do whatever you desire, Camillia."

I shivered, his return to my full name making my insides melt for him all over again. Then the glittering gems caught my attention once more, drawing my focus to the gift still lying in Melek's hand.

"In the Human Realm, mates wear rings," I told him.

"Would you prefer that?" he asked, his thoughts serious as he contemplated my desires.

I shook my head. "The necklace feels more symbolic." And the key charm was absolutely stunning. Not only because of the jewels, but because of the underlying meaning.

Melek had always seen me as the key to saving the Hell Fae Realm and his Hell Fae King.

Now he saw me as the key to their hearts. The being who had unlocked their souls and provided a renewed purpose in life.

"To think this all started because of those figments in the library," I mused as I reached for his gift. "They gave me Vita that day."

"I know," Melek replied. "I was watching."

Another shiver worked through me, his mind telling me I'd captured his interest from the very first moment he'd seen me. "Was it the number sixty-six?" I asked, referring to the candidate number from that stupid shirt I'd been forced to wear. "Or the insignificant stars?"

He frowned. "The stars weren't insignificant, Cami. They showed favor from the Source." He canted his head. "And no. I think it was the tight fabric stretched across your beautiful tits."

A laugh burst out of me.

"We should bring back the 'no undergarment' rule," he went on. "Make Cami wear only white in the bedroom."

"Or nothing at all," Typhos suggested.

I rolled my eyes. "I'm going to un-mate both of you."

Typhos caught my chin and pulled me in for a kiss. "Our Source won't allow that, Camillia."

"Doesn't mean I can't try," I returned.

He hummed, his eyes narrowing. "We'll just court you all over again."

"I don't think you ever courted me," I countered, teasing him. But a flicker of surprise met his features, his eyes widening.

"Would you like me to court you, my queen?"

My eyebrow lifted. "He asks while his dick is inside me."

His lips curled. "That's a different form of courting."

"How romantic," I drawled.

"Melek's the romantic one," he returned, again drawing my attention back to the gift. "I'm the one who makes you come so hard you pass out."

"Pretty sure we can all do that," Az said as he entered the bathroom with a coffee mug in his hand.

And no clothes.

I watched him approach, his impressive cock hard as he stepped up onto the platform and down into the oversized tub to sit behind me.

Ajax followed next, but unlike Az, he had on a pair of black track pants. A gold key hung from his neck, the glittering metal reminding me that Typhos had given it to him. *A symbol for the Warden.*

Or maybe it was a way for Typhos to mark Ajax as his, too.

These men were all very possessive.

Eyeing Melek's token, I said, "Okay, I'll wear it. But it'd better not be a conduit. And it'd better not cover me in glittery jizz."

Melek grinned. "My angel dust is just for sex, little angel. Promise."

I snorted. Because like I believed that. He'd covered me in his disco glitter several times before—no sex required.

Typhos gathered my hair away from my nape to allow Melek to affix the chain against my neck.

The key touched my skin, hanging just above my breasts. I stroked the chilled metal and the gems decorating the pendant. "It's very pretty, Melek. Thank you."

He brushed his knuckles along my cheek. "You've always been the key to our hearts, Cami. I knew it that day in the library. And I've known it every day since."

I leaned into his touch, hypnotized by his multicolored eyes. Az stroked his finger down my spine, and Typhos lowered his hands to my hips.

All while Ajax watched, his gaze thoughtful. "That's the day you found her reading Vita."

Melek glanced back at him. "Yes."

"Because the figments gave it to her," Ajax pressed.

Melek's brow furrowed a little. "What are you thinking about, Warden?"

But I already heard the words unfurling in Ajax's mind, his wondering if Vivaxia had somehow influenced the figments that day. However, he dismissed the idea in the next second, all too aware of their trickster ways.

They'd never allow someone to manipulate them, he thought. *Although, Vivaxia wasn't just anyone.* He frowned. *But let's say she did coerce them somehow. How could she have known what Cami would do with Vita?*

Now it was my turn to frown. Because he had a point. "She couldn't have known," I answered him out loud. "I didn't even know what I was going to do until I did it."

"Unless she compelled you somehow," he replied, his gaze meeting mine. "She had an anchor in Lucifer's mind, and we know she did something to you while you were in the Virtuous Fae Realm."

"She strengthened the funnel inside of Camillia," Typhos replied, obviously following our conversation, probably from both of our thoughts. *Since he's mated to Ajax now, too.*

But definitely not in the same way he'd mated me, as evidenced by his sensual claim beneath the water.

"It had already existed," he continued. "But she did something to deepen her hold."

"She said she *owned* me," I replied, frowning as I recalled everything she'd said and done in the Strigoi throne room. "She'd been able to force me to stop breathing."

Which meant it was entirely possible that she'd persuaded me to push all that power into Vita.

Hell, it was pretty clear that she'd been the reason the book had come to me in the first place. She'd planted it in the Hell Fae Realm, then activated me as her personal little siphon.

From what I'd gathered from Typhos's thoughts, Nos's contract with Vivaxia had been signed the day of my birth, thus making me the perfect age to qualify for the bride trials. And then she'd sent my father to make him the offer he couldn't refuse. Perhaps because of Vivaxia's own *persuasion* in Typhos's mind.

Fae, it had all been planned with such terrifying precision. If Vivaxia weren't such a bitch, I might have admired her for it.

"She couldn't have known you were going to train Cami," Melek pointed out. "Actually, I would bet she didn't anticipate that at all."

"True," Typhos agreed. "But this is Vivaxia we're discussing. Everything she does is in layers. Vita provided her with an entry point into our realm—via my mind and memories. Nos was her primary endgame. The portals were a distraction, one meant to capture my focus and keep me from sensing anything else. And Cami was a tool designed to steal my light."

"So you think it's a coincidence that Cami set off that trap in Vita," Ajax summarized.

"No, it was purposeful," I said, thinking through her whole strategy and everything I'd witnessed. "She couldn't have known that Typhos would overload me with power, but everything she was doing to me involved trying to make me lose control."

My mates fell silent while I continued puzzling out her intentions and desires.

"She wanted me to push power to the funnel inside me. But in case I didn't, she'd left me with another obvious option—Vita. A book *she* introduced me to. She might not have coaxed those figments, but she would have found a way to ensure that book ended up in my lap."

Which explained why it was always showing up in unexpected places.

"She told the book which images to show me. Though, I think Vita had been trying to communicate with me, too. But Vivaxia orchestrated it all."

Turning me into her own little puppet.

Her personal siphon.

"But I wasn't the heart of her plan," I went on. "I was simply one of her many layers."

Just like Typhos had said—Vivaxia favored *layers*, her strategy superior because of it.

"Pushing all that energy into Vita overpowered the funnel she'd left inside of it, which was just one of the many facets in her overall endgame," I concluded. "She played us all. But she lost because she lacked heart." And as I now knew, that was the key to maintaining the Source's light.

Caring for others was a pivotal part of ensuring that the power survived. Because souls and desires were what energized the core. One must love and be loved to manage such vitality.

That'd been Typhos's greatest weakness on the opposite end of the spectrum. He was so cherished and admired that he had too many souls to care for on his own, his Source growing wildly out of control as a result.

Bringing the brides tipped him over, his spirit taking on more burden and responsibility than one heart could manage.

But now he had a circle. He had *me*. And together, we would ensure his Source's vitality and strength.

There might be more power-hungry fae in the future, beings like Vivaxia who desired to take rather than give. However, they wouldn't stand a chance against us.

Because we ruled with love.

And love was the greatest power of all…

EPILOGUE
CAMI

One Month Later

I chose a dark red dress.

With no undergarments.

Because I knew exactly what Melek wanted to do when this coronation ceremony ended. I'd heard him planning it for weeks, his mind weaving knots and ribbon all around me.

He fully intended to present me as a gift to Typhos tonight. And I was very much going to let him.

The prince in question came up behind me and placed a kiss against my neck as his arms encircled my waist. "Have I told you how beautiful you are, little angel?" he asked, his voice soft against my ear.

I smiled. "A few times tonight," I replied. "But you can say it again."

"You're stunning," he whispered, kissing me once more. "And you're going to look even more stunning in about thirty minutes when I strip that dress off of you."

A shiver traversed my spine. "You say the sweetest things to me."

He chuckled, then moved to my side to survey the room with me. Ajax and Az were with Typhos, the three of them on a stage with several of Typhos's lieutenants and a handful of Hellhounds.

One of those Hellhounds was Payan. He looked particularly uncomfortable, mostly because he'd fallen victim to Vivaxia's control. And he'd nearly gotten Typhos killed as a result.

Fortunately for him, the Hell Fae King was understanding.

He didn't fault any of his fae for Vivaxia's trickery, knowing firsthand how manipulative and powerful she used to be. If anything, he blamed himself the most. Because he felt he should have known and stopped her sooner.

It was an unfair burden.

But I understood it.

Just as I understood what he was currently doing on that stage as he socialized with his lieutenants.

Well, I supposed they were *our* lieutenants now, as I'd been officially named the Hell Fae Queen earlier this evening.

The reception of the news had been one of great enthusiasm, the Hell Fae and Nightmare Fae cheering in approval.

Now, the energy had cooled a little, the fae all chatting amongst themselves about next steps for the realm.

Little did they realize that Typhos had another announcement coming. A big one.

But first, he was gathering all of his lieutenants in a show of solidarity. Because they already knew our intentions and had approved the plans a week ago. All that was left was sharing those plans with the Hell Fae Realm.

And the Hell Fae Bridal Candidates.

They were all in attendance. The unmated ones, anyway. Those who had been claimed during the initial trials were still in their respective Nightmare Fae Kingdoms.

Typhos had taken the time to talk me through everything he'd organized and had accounted for each of the six hundred sixty-six candidates.

Ajax had listened in, curious about the women who had joined willingly. He'd been under the same impression as I was—that most of the candidates weren't there voluntarily.

"I heard their screams and felt their fear," he'd said at one point in the conversation.

"Some didn't realize what exactly they'd agreed to" had been Typhos's response. "Others joined for the wrong reasons."

Which I later learned was why certain brides had been removed. If the Source discovered they were in the realm for the wrong reasons, they were sent home.

Or killed, I thought, shivering. Because the Source protected its own, something I very much understood now.

It wasn't the kind of power that gave second chances.

But it only hurt those who were a true threat.

And, unfortunately, some of those females had been sent to the trials for nefarious means.

"There will always be fae who wish to enter our kingdoms and cause problems," Typhos had said when addressing his lieutenants the other day. "I've tried to ensure they never cross my gates. But in doing so, I've neglected those with sincere desires to be here. Which is why we'll be changing to a new process in the Hell Fae Realm, a process that promotes free will."

The entire dynamic of our world was about to change. For better or for worse, we would move forward into a new era. One where the gates no longer existed and the Source accepted anyone who entered.

"The kingdoms will rule themselves," Typhos had declared. "With you as their true kings."

We'd support them with our power, bolster their territories as needed, but we wouldn't govern them. Unless, of course, fate required it.

Only the Hell Fae Kingdom would be ours to command. But even then, Typhos wanted to make it more open and welcoming to non–Hell Fae visitors.

It was a complete shift from his previous leadership, where he'd involved himself heavily in the affairs of his fae and barred many fae from entering.

But that had been the old Typhos, the one being manipulated by Vivaxia.

Now he was free.

And he wanted to share that gift with all of his fae.

Clearing his throat from the podium, he instantly captured the audience's attention. Though, a few glanced my way like they were surprised that I wasn't up there beside him.

But this was his final chapter to close.

I was part of the new book, one we would be writing together with our mate-circle. Maybe we'd find a way to re-create Vita. Or perhaps her memory would reside with his past in his mother's journal.

Regardless, we were moving into the future.

However, to do that, we needed to close the past.

I supposed Melek should be up there as his Hell Fae

Prince. He'd been part of the opening ceremonies for the Hell Fae Bride Trials, just like Az and Ajax.

I'm simply an ornament, little angel, he whispered into my mind. *The admirers can still see me. But I choose my own views. And right now, I rather like this one.*

I glanced at him to find him staring at me. *You're being cryptic again.*

Not really, he replied. *My riddle is fairly straightforward.*

"There's just one more announcement for this evening," Typhos said, his commanding tone drawing my focus away from Melek's playful commentary. Not that I knew how to respond to his newest riddle.

Or maybe he was just being straightforward, like he'd said.

With Melek, it was hard to know for sure. It was a trait that should annoy me, but I was beginning to love it. Because he kept everything fresh.

And he often served as my necessary escape from the intensity of Az and Typhos. Their dominant personas could be overwhelming at times, especially when they *shared* me.

My stomach clenched at the thought, my mind instantly recalling the other night when Az had held my arms at my sides while seated inside me. Then pulled me forward so Typhos could take my ass.

Our king is trying to make a speech, Cami, Melek whispered into my mind. *A speech that's about to end abruptly if you keep fantasizing about him and Azazel fucking you.*

I swallowed and met Typhos's blazing gaze from across the crowd. It reminded me of the time he'd focused on me in the arena. During the opening ceremonies.

How fitting, I thought.

Indeed, the Hell Fae King returned. *You're as enchanting as ever, Camillia. Now, unless you want me to fuck you in front of this crowd—which I will—I expect you to behave.*

My thighs clenched at the threat. *You wouldn't dare to share me in that manner.*

Even from across the room, I saw his eyebrow arch. *You're not wearing anything under that tight little dress, Miss De la Croix. It would be very easy to yank it up to your waist, bend you over, and fuck you while Ajax and Azazel stand guard. No one would see a thing. But they would absolutely hear you scream, my queen.*

Melek hummed beside me, no doubt sensing the heated conversation flowing between me and the Hell Fae King. While my mates couldn't hear specifics when I spoke directly to one of my men, they could pick up on moods.

And Typhos was absolutely giving off a punishing vibe right now.

I'll behave, my king, I told him softly. *For now.*

Though, if he wanted me to stop thinking about sex, he should probably stop threatening to fuck me.

Melek chuckled beside me. *Ty is giving me a list of items for this evening. It seems you've worked him up with your wicked thoughts, little angel.*

I rolled my eyes. *I was just thinking about the other day.*

"As I was saying," Typhos continued out loud, his tone commanding once more. "I have another announcement, and it's regarding the Hell Fae Bridal Candidates. First, I want to start by expressing my gratitude to you all for your patience while we've sorted through the recent events in the realm."

He surveyed the crowd, his charisma palpable throughout the ballroom. He truly was a magnificent leader. *Easy on the eyes, too,* I thought, admiring the cut of his flawless all-black suit.

Camillia.

Typhos, I returned. *You really should focus on your speech, my king.*

He mentally muttered something about having two brats in his head but continued out loud as though he hadn't been distracted at all.

"Second, I want to personally thank the bridal candidates for participating in the Hell Fae Bride Trials. When we began this journey, my goal was to diversify our realm by welcoming female fae mates. But given recent events, I've realized that the methodology was flawed."

Whispers erupted through the room, the fae surprised by Typhos's admission.

But that admission was what made him such a good leader. He wasn't afraid to own his faults. And more importantly, he wasn't afraid to correct them.

Which was what he proceeded to do now as he announced, "The Hell Fae Bride Trials have officially come to an end."

The whispers grew to louder chatter.

Chatter he halted with a raise of his hand.

"As you know, the gates are now open to our realm. That means the former candidates are free to leave. But I hope you'll choose to stay. To welcome in our new era of inclusivity. To be part of a progressive age of the Hell Fae Realm."

The energy from earlier returned, the fae buzzing with excitement over this proposed future.

That excitement only grew as Typhos announced that his council of kings—formerly known as his lieutenants—would reign in the truest sense of the word.

"I'll be there to provide guidance as requested, but your kings will be your leaders now. Work with them to establish your entry requirements. Manage your portals.

Do what you need to do to thrive. And know our Source will support you in whatever fashion you require."

There were caveats, of course, ones I already knew existed. Cruelty would not be accepted in our realm. Fae seeking to rule in a vein similar to the way Nos had would also not be tolerated.

But generally, we wanted the fae to choose their paths. Pick their mates. Find their purposes. And thrive.

That included the former brides, whom Typhos offered relocation services to. He also said they could remain in the bridal camp for as long as they needed. Then he announced that I would personally be available to provide guidance to any candidates with concerns or questions.

I'd anticipated that last part. And welcomed my first task as Hell Fae Queen.

Well, second.

Removing Vivaxia had technically served as my first task.

By the time Typhos finished his speech, the room was abuzz with enthusiastic support. "It's been a pleasure serving you all. Truly." He gave a bow, the gesture one of great respect. Then he raised his hand, flames dancing over his fingers. "To the next chapter!"

He sent the Hellfire flying through the room, causing all the candles to sizzle and burn as the flames changed from orange to a glowing red.

Then his wings burst from his back, and my mate vanished.

Only to reappear right behind me, his arms circling my waist. "Now, Melek" was all he said before teleporting us back to our suite.

Which really wasn't necessary. The coronation had been hosted in the ballroom of the palace. "We could have left like normal fae," I told him.

"There's nothing *normal* about us, Camillia," he returned, releasing me. "Now lose the dress and get on the bed."

Az ashed in with Ajax beside him, the two of them loosening their ties.

But Melek was nowhere to be seen.

I thought you were tying me up, I whispered to him.

His chuckle kissed my mind. *Eager for my ropes, little angel?*

Just wondering where you are, I admitted.

"Here," he replied against my ear as he switched positions with Typhos. "Now do what our king asked and get on the bed, love."

"I didn't *ask*," Typhos replied.

My lips curled, his impatience intensifying the moment.

The Hell Fae King was going to punish me for not immediately obeying him. And I very much welcomed whatever punishment he had in mind.

Because this was our dynamic.

I pushed him and he pushed me.

Melek indulged in riddles that always resulted in something informative. He also took care of me in his own way.

Ajax listened to me. Stood up for me. Would always have my back.

And Az was the mate that protected me without a shadow of a doubt. All while exploring my limits and introducing me to new horizons.

The five of us were our very own Source. A power unlike any other. A circle with more passion and energy than could be defined.

While they each meant something unique to me, they also had their own bonds. Some of them older than others. Some new. Some still growing.

But we had eternity to explore our inner connections.

To cherish one another. To *love*. To exist in our own beautiful utopia.

As the Hell Fae Warden, the Hell Fae Commander, the Hell Fae Prince, the Hell Fae King, and the *Hell Fae Queen*.

THE END

USA *Today* Bestselling Author Lexi C. Foss loves to play in dark worlds, especially the ones that bite. She lives in North Carolina with her husband and their furry children. When not writing, she's busy crossing items off her travel bucket list, or chasing eclipses around the globe. She's quirky, consumes way too much coffee, and loves to swim.

Want access to the most up-to-date information for all of Lexi's books? Sign-up for her newsletter here.

Lexi also likes to hang out with readers on Facebook in her exclusive readers group - Join Here.

Where To Find Lexi:
www.LexiCFoss.com

Reverse Harem Paranormal Romance - Never Choose.

J.R. Thorn is a Reverse Harem Paranormal Romance
Author who loves coffee, stormy weather, and heated
discussions with her inner muse. She can often be found
scribing her steamy stories in her writing cave far away
from the prying eyes of her toddler, husband, two vocal
cats, and canine pack.

www.AuthorJRThorn.com

facebook.com/BloodStoneSeries

amazon.com/stores/J.R.-Thorn/author/B01LYC5DM9

tiktok.com/@authorj.r.thorn